THE SPY '

A *Ben Sign* Crim(
Story
By

Matthew Dunn

FORMER *MI6 SPY* AND *BEST-SELLING* AUTHOR

CW00506652

ALSO BY MATTHEW DUNN
SPYCATCHER SERIES

BEN SIGN SERIES

PRAISE FOR MATTHEW DUNN

"Terse conversations infused with subtle power plays, brutal encounters among allies with competing agendas, and forays into hostile territory orchestrated for clockwork efficiency...." ---- *Washington Post*

"Great talent, great imagination, and real been-there-done-that authenticity.... Highly recommended." ----Lee Child, author of the *Jack Reacher* series

"Dunn's exuberant, bullet-drenched prose, with its descriptions of intelligence tradecraft and modern anti-terrorism campaigns, bristles with authenticity.... Save for the works of Alan Furst, good thrillers have been thin on the ground of late. Mr. Dunn has redressed this balance with an altogether gripping book." ----*The Economist*

"[Dunn] makes a strong argument that it takes a real spy to write a truly authentic espionage novel.... [The story] practically bursts at the seams with boots-on-the-ground insight and realism. But there's another key ingredient that likely will make the ruthless yet noble protagonist, Will Cochrane, a popular series character for many years to come. Dunn is a gifted storyteller." ----*Fort Worth Star-Telegram*

"Matthew Dunn is [a] very talented new author. I know of no other spy thriller that so successfully blends the fascinating nuances of the business of espionage and intelligence work with full-throttle suspense storytelling. ----Jeffery Deaver, author of *The Bone Collector*

"Just when you think you've got this maze of double-dealing figured out – surprise, it isn't what you think. All the elements of a classic espionage story are here. The novel moves with relentless momentum, scattering bodies in its wake." ----*Kirkus Reviews*

"[Dunn has] a superlative talent for three-dimensional characterisation, gripping dialogue, and plots that featured gasp-inducing twists and betrayals." ----*The Examiner*

"A real spy proves he is a real writer. This is a stunning debut." ----Ted Bell, author of *Patriot*

"Not since Fleming charged Bond with the safety of the world has the international secret agent mystique been so anchored with an insider's reality." ----Noah Boyd, author of *The Bricklayer*

"Once in a while an espionage novelist comes along who has the smack of utter authenticity. Few are as daring as Matthew Dunn, fewer still as up to date…. Is there anyone writing today who knows more about the day-to-day operations of intelligence agencies in the field than Matthew Dunn?" ----John Lawton, author of *Then We Take Berlin*

CHAPTER 1

Tonight a faceless robber was to be illegally executed for stealing secrets.

That's what senior diplomat Peter Raine of the British Foreign and Commonwealth Office hoped would happen.

He'd assembled a four-man lynch mob to do the dirty work. They were tough men, specialists, brutal, and exacting when given enough money to do a job that had no place in the eyes of the law. Tonight Raine was merely an observer. The fifty-three year old man was inside the back of a transit van. One of the team was with him. Empty cartons of takeout coffee, mugs of cigarette butts, bottles of urine, audio equipment, an assault rifle, spare ammunition and explosives, binoculars, audio equipment, thermal imagery probes, and a laptop, were crammed into the confined space. It was a far cry from the salubrious surroundings Raine typically inhabited. Still, he'd spent thirty one years in the diplomatic corps and had seen things and stayed in places that would have made a seasoned vagabond grimace in disgust. Though he looked out of place in his expensive suit and thick overcoat, this was work. He went where the tasks required him to be.

Five feet nine inches tall and with a slender yet athletic build, Raine had the looks and sartorial elegance of a matinee idol of days gone by; similar to the actor James Mason. He even sounded like Mason – steely, velvet, or, as *The New York Times* once described it, a voice that was an instrument comparable to a Stradivarius.

The man by his side was muscular, in his forties, wearing jeans and jumper and hiking boots, had a cigarette dangling from his lips, and a handgun strapped to his chest. He was staring at the computer screen. So was Raine. The screen was divided in two. On one side was a live video of the outside of a farmhouse that was twenty seven miles northeast of the city of Bergen, Norway. The property had been under surveillance by the diplomat's men for sixteen hours. The image was grey and grainy, because it was captured by night vision technology. The other side of the screen gave insight into real-time components of the farmhouse's interior; not most of it; just the parts that were needed. Short range audio and thermal technology enabled that to happen.

The residence had been violated to monitor a meeting between two people. One of them was in there right now. The other was not in the property or anywhere else that could be seen by the covert team. That was to be expected. The man by Raine's side and his three men close to the house were waiting for the second person to appear. He or she was the target. The green image of the man the diplomat could see on the thermal screen was inconsequential beyond his vital role in luring the target to the site. Raine didn't care if the lure lived or died in what would shortly happen. The target's death was the overriding priority.

The man by his side tensed as one of his men spoke in his earpiece. In English, but with a French accent, he replied into his throat piece. "Remember. Proof of exchange essential. Zero movement until my command." Without taking his eyes off the screen, the team leader muttered to Raine, "Person approaching house. On foot. Average walking pace. Approximately two hundred yards away on the track."

The track he was referring to was the only vehicular route in and out of the farmstead. There were no other buildings around the house, only undulating fields that occasionally would contain dairy cattle but were currently empty of livestock. Raine's van was nearly four hundred yards away from the building, parked off-road in a gully and not visible from the target location.

The team leader spat his cigarette on to the floor and crushed the stub with his boot. He positioned one hand to the side of the laptop and leaned closer, watching.

An amateur observer might have said something at this point.

Raine was no amateur. He waited in silence.

Time slowed down.

For the first time since he'd been in the van, the diplomat could now smell tobacco, stale coffee, piss, sweat, the musky smell of male testosterone, and gun oil and metal. Nothing alleviated the pungent blend of odours. Aftershave, eau de toilette, balms, gels, other lotions, and perfumed soaps of any kind had been banned from use before deployment. This was a grubby job. And though the ever-immaculate Raine had availed himself of neutral shower gel when washing before coming here, now he felt that a long bath was in order. That luxury had to wait. Like his colleague, he couldn't take his eyes off the computer screen.

In the last two weeks, so much had happened to enable this moment – surveillance of the man in the house, following him day and night including a trip to Russia, searching his home in central Bergen and the remote safe house they were now watching, installing eavesdropping equipment into both properties, and last night intercepting a coded SMS to the man's mobile. The message had been sent from a pay-as-you-go mobile phone purchased in Abuja, Nigeria. The message had read, *Safe place. 2300hrs tomorrow night.* Nothing else. All efforts to glean anything about the sender had drawn a blank. But, though it had been a devil of a job to do so, Raine had managed to crack the code. So, tonight was the night. Raine and his men were watching the safe place, hoping that at eleven PM the most dangerous person in the world would turn up.

The most dangerous person in the world? That's how Raine and others thought of the individual. There was no doubt that the person Raine sought was a British government official who had the highest level of security clearance in the United Kingdom. The official stole top secret British intelligence. The database containing the intelligence was impenetrable to external attack. It was an inside job carried out by a human being. But beyond the fact that the robber was a UK official nothing else was known about the individual. The perpetrator sold top secret documents to the highest bidder. The results of his or her actions were catastrophic to the national security of Britain, its allies, its sometime allies, and most of its stable enemies. The unstable enemies were the robber's clients. They were the problem. They liked the intelligence the individual stole.

So much time and human and technological resources had been devoted to identifying the traitor. Nothing had resulted from the biggest counter-intelligence operation ever conducted on either side of London, Washington DC, Moscow, or Beijing. And so Raine had been tasked to think about the problem from whatever other angle he saw fit. Rather, Raine had tasked himself on the matter and had been given the go-ahead by others who called themselves his superiors but in reality couldn't touch the untouchable diplomat and political high inquisitor. Raine had set to work and had engaged his four-man team of buccaneers. He'd used them before in the Ukraine, Sri Lanka, and Canada. They kept their mouths shut. And they had nothing to do with officialdom. Right now it was extremely difficult to ascertain which government agents were friends or foes.

His only lead was the man he referred to as the broker; the man who acted as the intermediary between the traitor and the clients; the man who was in the house. The traitor stole the secrets and brought them to the broker; the broker analysed the swag and made a decision on which country or outfit might pay the highest price for the intelligence; he then negotiated each deal. It seemed that the robber made no mistakes. So too the broker. But, when transactions are to be had there is always a weak link or an event that can scupper an otherwise perfect plan. Syria was one of the broker's clients. A Syrian intelligence officer was privy to the broker's deals and knew his identity. For a raft of reasons, the IO had been thinking about defecting for some time. He finally plucked up the courage to do so and handed himself in to the British embassy in Damascus. He was exfiltrated to Britain via Iraq. Ultimately, Raine had a one-to-one chat with him and ascertained the identity of the broker. Thankfully the defector hadn't mentioned the broker to any other British official who'd interviewed him. If he had done so, Raine would have been able to shut his colleagues up.

The team leader drummed his fingers adjacent to the laptop; then stopped. Both he and Raine had visual of a solitary person approaching the house. The team leader said quietly into his throat mic, "Not yet."

The person entered the house. He or she – it wasn't possible to tell gender from the visuals - moved through two rooms before entering the largest room in the house. It was the room containing the broker.

The room was so expertly and discretely bugged that one would be able to hear a whispered voice. But, though the two people were barely three feet apart, there was no audible sound whatsoever. No talking, thought Raine; no communication between the two people, the assumption that someone could be listening; clever. Something was handed to the broker by the person who'd entered the room. That person stepped back a couple of paces. The broker turned and appeared to lean over something; maybe a desk. Thirty nine seconds later the broker stood fully upright, turned towards the other person, and raised his arm to chest height. Raine's eyes narrowed. It was so difficult to see exactly what was going on. The thermal imagery was not precise. Raised his arm?

"That's it!" Raine exclaimed. "He's given the thumbs up!"

The team leader's tone was calm and matter-of-fact when he commanded, "Go, go, go."

On the left side of the screen and running to the house from different directions were the three operatives.

The team leader put their communications channel on to a speaker, so both men in the van could hear everything.

The men were breathing fast.

Raine kept watching the screen.

Two brilliant flashes of white light at either end of the building.

They belonged to the team's door charges.

The team were inside the building.

The broker and his visitor were moving.

They'd heard the explosions.

The visitor was one side of the room, stopped, moved back to the broker.

Raine frowned.

The broker appeared to drop to the ground just as one of the team entered the room.

Another flash of white light, obliterating everything on the thermal computer screen.

Gunfire.

Shouting.

More rapid breathing.

One of the team members. "Where the fuck is he?"

Another. "Room search!"

Thermal imagery was back.

The team leader said, "Shit!" and clamoured into the cab while shouting, "Keep watching the screen!" He turned on the ignition and drove over rough ground until he was on the road.

As he bounced up and down, Raine's heart was pounding. What the hell was going on?

"House clear. Tango not here, repeat not here." This from one of the team.

"We're coming from the east. Pursue your lines." The team leader was referring to the prearranged hunter-killer pattern his team would adopt if they needed to pursue the target outside of the property. One man would go south, one west, one north. They would shoot on sight.

Raine cursed while thinking fast. The white light in the room – it had to be a flash grenade. It had been enough to shield the target's escape. But, seconds before that why had the target turned and moved back to the broker before he fled?

The team leader stopped the vehicle. "Stay in the van!"

Raine ignored him. Now, there was nothing of value to be seen on the computer screen. And if the traitor was nearby, he hoped he would catch a glimpse of his face. If so, he'd wring his neck when back in London. He stood by the vehicle, looking at the house one hundred yards away and at the adjacent fields, hedges, and small copses. The air was icy and still; the Norwegian night was partly illuminated by a half-moon and a clear, star-filled sky. There were no tell-tale signs of any activity – no gunshots, shouting, rapid nearby movement, rustling, anything that might suggest that his quarry was close. The team leader had his gun raised at eye level. He was motionless.

Five minutes later he said, "Let's go in the house." He started walking, his gun still held high.

Raine followed him, feeling and looking like a football manager walking onto a pitch after the final whistle had been blown. They moved through a doorway that had been forced off its hinges, and along a corridor that led into one room and then another. The air was smoky and smelled of military-grade explosives. They reached the largest room. Like the contents of most safe houses, the room was functional and minimalistic. There were three armchairs, a small dining table and chairs, and flush against a wall was a desk; there were no pictures or anything else that could have softened the décor. But, what there was in the chamber looked like it had been hit by a hailstorm. Two dining chairs were upended and strewn haphazardly on the ground; strata of cordite were drifting between the ceiling and wooden floor, plaster on the walls was damaged by bullets, and wooden furnishings were splintered by projectiles. And on the floor was a body.

The broker.

Raine walked up to the man.

He was on his back, his hands frozen in a claw-like position above his chest, eyes wide, mouth open, expression one of utter terror.

There was a large pool of blood around him but no visible signs of an injury.

The team leader put his boot against the corpse's ribcage and pushed. Now on his front, it was easy to see where the broker's blood had come from. The team leader said, "Knife into the back of the neck. It's a difficult but very effective kill. Stab deep into the side of the larynx, yank knife sideways, sever carotid artery and jugular vein. There are easier ways to kill a man with a blade – the armpit for example – but a man dies almost instantly this way. It's that damn cartilage that's the problem. Very sharp knife, strength, and knowledge are required. The killer knows what he's doing. He's done this before."

Raine walked to the desk. On it was a single A4 sheet of paper that contained prose. It was an exact copy of a recent British intelligence report. The text was written on a cheap typewriter. "The killer's got a photographic memory," he said to himself. He read the words.

"Why did he kill his colleague?"

"Loose end? I don't know." The diplomat finished reading the report. "I realise there's only so much your team can achieve with the equipment and time you've got, but take what samples you can get. I'll need this report once you've tested it. Make sure this place is clean and presentable enough to be suitable for a holiday let in the morning."

"Of course."

"Drop me at a train station. I'll go to my hotel. Tomorrow morning, eight AM sharp, we'll meet for a debrief at our *pied-à-terre*."

The other men came into the room. Breathless, they all shook their heads.

The team leader said to them, "Forensics first; dolly domestic second. Get to it." He looked at Raine. "*Dolly Domestic*. That's the phrase, isn't it?"

Quietly Raine answered, "Yes, that'll do." He couldn't take his eyes off the report. "He or she was here. God damn it. The person was bloody here."

CHAPTER 2

At 0800hrs the next morning, Raine was in the lounge of the team's terraced safe house in Bergen. A match was struck, its burning sulphur briefly raging before calming. Cigarettes were lit. Four men sucked in tobacco, two of them emitting a sound akin to a distant wind as they drew their lips into small circles and shot streams of silver and blue-hue smoke towards the centre of the minimalist room. Raine was facing the four men who last night had stormed the farmhouse: Lucas, the only Frenchman in the room, former French Foreign Legionnaire, the boss of the other hired-help in the lounge, the man who'd been in the van with Raine; Aadesh, Nepalese, former Gurkha and highly decorated veteran of the Iraq and Afghanistan wars who'd fled his garrison in Aldershot after pistol whipping his English commanding officer to death; Parry, Russian, ex-airborne special forces in Spetsnaz Alpha, subsequently no-questions-asked gun-for-hire who'd done many interesting things in his life including immobilising a tanker so that it blocked the Panama Canal while he subsequently boarded a stationary cargo vessel and shot its captain twice in the head; Noah, Swedish, a special reconnaissance, counterterrorism and covert communications expert for the elite National Task Force of the Swedish police before he was asked to leave the force after he was suspected of stealing half a million dollars of drug money.

Lucas was in his mid-fifties, born and bred in Marseille's toughest streets, joined the French army as an officer cadet, excelled in the prestigious Saint-Cyr military academy, volunteered to join the Legion despite having the opportunity to join regiments more renowned for accelerating the careers of France's most gifted military talent, saw combat in many wars and other combat zones, and was happy to rise to the rank of commandant while knowing that he could have easily made the higher rank of colonel at the same age if he'd plumped for a cushier option in the army. But, Lucas liked to fight; he was exceptionally good at it; the Legion was the ideal home for his warrior spirit. Until he got dishonourably discharged for planning to lead his legionnaires into an assault on Paris and depose the president of France.

Everyone in the room was sitting where they could – Raine and Lucas were on the only chairs available; Parry and Noah were on the floor; Aadesh was on an upturned empty plastic bin.

Lucas said, "There's good news and there's bad news and then there's really bad news."

Raine said nothing.

The Frenchman continued, "The good news is we got a body. *Had* a body. It's now pig feed. Still, we had a body. The bad news is it's the wrong body. And then there's the really bad news. There is no trace whatsoever of the killer, the traitor, the robber, the… whatever name you want to give him."

"Or her."

Lucas momentarily shut his eyes. "It's a man."

"Maybe…"

"It's a man." Lucas didn't elaborate. "An exceptionally skilled man. No trace," he repeated. "By contrast, as you would expect, there are lots of traces of Lystad."

Torbjørn Lystad was the broker. During their surveillance of him Lucas's team had learned a lot about Lystad and had formed views about the man. Lystad was sixty four years old, Norwegian, a former private banker who'd spent most of his career working for a prestigious Swiss bank and its ultra-high-net-worth clients, had never married, and had no children. He'd retired from banking age fifty eight, but had squandered most of his sizeable savings in the casinos of Monte Carlo. He still had enough money to lead a comfortable life and for the most part portrayed himself as a contented man of simple and honest pleasures. Short and slender, a goatee beard, round glasses, and with a bohemian dress sense that included a corduroy brown jacket and matching sailor's cap, he looked like an aging artist who'd purchased his wardrobe in the heyday of the beatnik New York art, literature, and music scene. When in Bergen, he'd take a daily walk out of his metropolitan home, easel under his arm, leather satchel containing paint brushes and oils strung across his body, so that he could reach one of his favourite spots for capturing the fjords and mountains. He liked to stop for lunch at *Pygmalion* bistro on Nedre Korskirkeallmenningen where he'd usually order something from the adjacent fish market's catch of the day and ask the chef to cook it to his liking. In the evening he dined alone at his house, enjoyed listening to Dixieland jazz, spent time reading or adding extra touches to his paintings in his studio, went to bed at a reasonable hour and rose at a respectable time. All of this was irrelevant because his charmingly innocuous lifestyle masked the fact that he was an utter bastard. Also, he was now dead.

Raine addressed Lucas. "The intelligence report?"

The former legionnaire replied, "The white A4 paper is standard office print quality. Eighty grams. Cheap as chips, as you Brits say. Can be bought anywhere. The ink is okay, but it can be smudged if one applies enough pressure. The typewriter used has a standard font. Cheap paper, cheap ink, cheap typeset. It would be absurd to try to trace the manufacturers. Lystad's prints are on it; no other prints. There are a few microscope-evident indentations on the sheet, possibly from tweezers or similar tool. That'll be from your shy man. We've also run DNA tests. All we've got is Lystad."

"I see." Raine had expected as much. "You ran the tests more than once?"

Lucas raised an eyebrow.

"Of course you did." Raine looked at the others. "Did any of you catch sight of him?"

They shook their heads.

Aadesh said, "The grenade went off as we made room entry. Perfect timing."

"It was definitely a stun grenade?"

The former Gurkha nodded. "For sure. Flash. Bang. Wallop."

Parry said, "This guy plans. He'll have worn ear defenders for the grenade. Covered his eyes on detonation. He will still have been disorientated. He's got a hell of a lot of mental strength if he made that route while dizzy. The escape route was pre-determined." The Russian added, "But, one trip and we'd have shot him from three angles."

"How did he get out of the building?"

Aadesh replied, "We always knew there were multiple exits in the target site – other doors, windows. We couldn't booby trap them because we didn't know which entrance he'd use to get in the building. We couldn't scare him off. And we needed him on site because someone said we needed proof of exchange." He winked at Lucas.

The Frenchman waved his hand dismissively. "He wouldn't have escaped if I'd had more men. Never mind." He smiled at the Nepalese combatant. "An officer has to make do with whatever rabble one has at one's disposal." His expression turned serious as he looked at Raine. "Out of curiosity, I need to ask: how did you crack the SMS code in the message from the killer to Lystad? Among many other things, are you a mathematician?"

Raine had no time for this. "No. My degree's in history."

"And yet you cracked the code in one hour."

The diplomat checked his watch. "I didn't. Others did. I put the code out as a test to graduate applicants for GCHQ, NSA, and the FBI; serving officers who wanted to progress to counter-cyberterrorism in the Metropolitan Police and New York Police Department; students and teachers of cryptanalysis at MIT, Harvard, Oxford, and Cambridge; algorithms experts at Facebook and Twitter; and some software programmers at Nintendo, Sony, and Rockstar Games. I gave them sixty minutes. Rockstar Games came up trumps."

Lucas made no attempt to hide his incredulity. "How the hell did you do that? Don't answer. Your answer would probably scare me. What do you want us to do now?"

Raine breathed in deeply. "I've given you more than enough money for you and your men to lay low for the immediate future. Decline any other work. Keep your noses clean. Stay close to each other. Be prepared to deploy with all the kit you may need at very short notice." His voice deepened as he stared at Lucas. "Potentially *very* short notice."

"Deployed to do what?"

Raine shrugged and replied nonchalantly, "Deployed to do what you guys do: stalk and slit throats."

Lucas addressed his men. "You did a superb job on reconnaissance, surveillance, intelligence gathering. And the house entry was pitch-perfect. However, we failed."

Raine interjected. "I failed, although for understandable reasons." He looked at Aadesh, Parry, and Noah. "Your commanding officer's right. I should have employed more men for the takedown. But, I couldn't. A Norwegian tactical team, any tactical team for that matter, has a chain of command. Right now, chains of command worry me. So, it's us and only us. We've kicked the hornet's nest. I'll be interested to see what the killer does without his broker. That in itself is a result on your part. Get some rest, don't do anything silly, and be ready in case I need you to kidnap or murder our man."

They all stood, ready to depart and go their separate ways.

Noah hesitated and frowned. "I was the first into the room. Just before, I heard Lystad shouting. It was so brief. Then the grenade went off."

Raine was motionless. "Shouting?"

Noah nodded. "Just two sentences. He said, *Get out. I won't divulge a thing or implicate you.*"

"In English, presumably?"

The Swede shook his head. "It was in Norwegian."

Nobody else said anything.

Noah looked embarrassed. "It was definitely Norwegian. I speak Norwegian."

Raine pictured what he'd seen on the thermal imagery just before the grenade was detonated – the killer going to the far side of the room, stopping, going back to the broker, the broker falling to the ground. The diplomat's vast intellect connected the dots faster than it would have taken for Lystad to die and smack the ground. The broker had panicked and spoke aloud to his accomplice. Worse, he'd done so in a tongue that wasn't the killer's first language. In that split second, the killer realised he couldn't trust him to keep his mouth shut and not slip up. He silenced the man, withdrew the pin on the grenade, and vanished.

Raine thanked the men and watched them leave. Once alone, he stood in the centre of the room. He was oblivious to everything around him. If there were noises outside, he couldn't hear them. Nothing else mattered now except the one thought that was front and centre of his mind.

The killer was a British national who spoke Norwegian.

CHAPTER 3

NEXT DAY

"We have a visitor this evening, Mr. Knutsen." Ben Sign was in the kitchen of his two-bedroom flat in West Square, Southwark, London. The fifty year old former high ranking MI6 officer was preparing some home cooked snacks.

Tom Knutsen – thirty five years old and a very successful former Metropolitan Police undercover officer – was in the adjacent lounge. As well as being Sign's business partner, Knutsen lived in the flat, sleeping in the spare bedroom. It was a convenient arrangement, given that most of the initial consultations they had with new clients took place in the lounge.

Sign and Knutsen's business conducted highly sensitive investigations into matters that were too delicate to be taken on by the police or British Intelligence agencies. They'd been in business together for two years and during that time had cracked seemingly impossible cases.

Knutsen was stoking the fire. He sat in his armchair, next to the fire and opposite the armchair Sign always used, and took a sip of calvados from his tumbler. The air was rich with the aroma of Indian food. The smells seemed apt for the décor of the lounge. In the room were a raft of furnishings and items that had been sourced from various parts of the world – rugs from Mongolia, a sofa crafted by a Parisian artisan, paintings from China, Sri Lanka, Patagonia, Italy, and Britain, curtains that covered the only large window in the room and were sourced from a souk in Morocco, a wall-mounted glass cabinet containing a nineteenth century Arab dirk, also a wall-mounted musket from the American War of Independence, silks from Afghanistan, a chest that had been manufactured in Zambia by a man who'd stabbed to death a rival carpenter, an artificial Japanese tree, two plant pots that were growing a rare strain of chillies, gold and bronze tubs from Cambodia, mahogany drinks cabinet in one corner of the room, and lit candles purchased from a manufacturer in Hong Kong. Along one side of a wall was a library containing out of print leather-bound books and academic journals on eighteenth century explorations, philosophy, politics, poetry, mathematics, and anthropology. Above the fireplace was a shelf, resting on which were an array of items – a pistol revolver from the Boer War, figurine of the Hindu god Shiva, binoculars from Captain Scott's 1912 South Pole endeavour, a porcelain vase from Beijing, an old Cuban cigar box that was filled with bullets, an antique compass, eighteenth century rolled naval charts that were bound by red ribbon, and a photograph of Sign receiving Britain's highest award for gallantry from Her Majesty The Queen.

Sign had furnished the flat with items he'd collected during his extraordinary career. When Knutsen had moved into the flat he was initially unfazed by the exotic treasure trove. But soon he'd fallen in love with the adornments and ambience they created.

Knutsen – tall, blonde hair, athletic, first class degree from Exeter University, non-conformist, nothing like a cop, smart, agile brain that could enable him to switch personalities and accents depending on the circumstances he found himself in, not a Londoner but knew London beyond the precision of a metropolitan cabby, single, expert in shooting and unarmed combat, dry sense of humour, chucked out of the Met after he executed a scumbag who murdered a female police officer he was in love with, loyal to the death to Sign.

Sign – taller than Knutsen, short greying hair, thin but muscles as strong as tensile wire, widower, double first class degree from Oxford University, top of his class in MI6 selection, stellar career, tipped to be the next chief of MI6, unflappable, the most successful intelligence officer of his generation, incredibly brave, failed to reach the top job after he told MI6 to go fuck themselves.

Sign and Knutsen were misfits and probably too different on paper to have a work and friendship bond. Yet Sign had chosen Knutsen over a raft of other candidates to co-partner his business when he set it up. He'd rejected former special forces officers, intelligence operatives, and mainstream police officers. Knutsen had stood out. He was dislocated from the world. Just like Sign. And over time Sign's instincts had proven correct. He and Knutsen were so dissimilar yet so alike. It made for the perfect combination.

Knutsen placed his drink down and called out, "Who's the guest and what are you cooking?"

By comparison to the lounge, the kitchen was tiny. Yet that didn't faze Sign. He was an excellent cook and knew how to utilize minimum space to maximum effect. "Our guest is an old friend. He adores South Asian cuisine, as do I. I'm cooking him curry snacks to accompany a drink or two in the lounge. To be precise, chicken thighs with onions, saffron, cumin, garam masala, chilli, a dash of mixed herbs, finished off in a yoghurt and tomato sauce. Plus potato slices I've par-boiled and roasted with cardamom seeds and coated with fried turmeric and spinach. I've also prepared pickled okra, a blended mango and goat's milk dip, nan bread containing a hint of fennel flower, ginger and coriander, and I've made a chutney of finely diced shallots, mutton stock, vinegar, cracked black pepper, fennel bulbs, and star anise. It's not exactly my finest effort within this genre of cuisine but I was only given ninety minutes notice that our guest would be visiting this evening." He entered the lounge, laid an immaculate white cloth on a side table, plus cutlery and plates, three pint glasses, and three bottles of Cobra beer that had been in the freezer for half an hour, the exteriors of the glass dripping as the bottles confronted the change in temperature. He sat in his armchair.

Knutsen poured a calvados and handed it to him. "An old friend? I didn't think you had any friends."

Sign smiled. "I have you, don't I? That said, I suppose that's more akin to an unwanted arranged marriage." He checked his watch. "I should bring in the snacks. He won't be late. Listen out for the doorbell."

"It's not a *doorbell*. It's an intercom buzzer. How many times have I told you that? And how many times have I asked you what century you live in?"

Sign's eyes glistened as he replied, "It's important that I live in manifold centuries. To do so begets wisdom."

"Is he as dumb as you?"

"You decide. Man the gate. I will man the canteen." He re-entered the kitchen.

Five minutes later, at exactly seven PM, the intercom buzzer sounded. Knutsen pressed the button to allow the guest into the communal front hallway. He walked down four flights of stairs, past the three other flats in the building, one of them occupied by two female students who were being bankrolled by their wealthy Singaporean parents, the other two containing an investment banker and a ship broker.

The man at the entrance was middle aged and well dressed. He reminded Knutsen of an actor he'd seen in a black and white movie, but he couldn't recall which actor and movie. Maybe it was a film one of his many foster parents had watched.

The man said, "Ben Sign's expecting me."

Knutsen held out his hand. "Tom Knutsen. I'm Ben's associate."

As they shook hands the man said, "Peter Raine. Ben and I know each other. I arranged a consultation with him for this time. A *private* consultation."

The comment didn't faze Knutsen. "Come in. We're on the top floor. After I've shown you in, I'll make myself scarce if I need to."

Thirty seconds later they were in the flat.

Knutsen called out, "Our guest has arrived."

Sign came out of the kitchen, stood for a moment, then walked up to the guest and shook his hand. "How have you been, sir?"

"Gainfully employed." Raine smiled. "The last time I saw you was in that underground tunnel beneath the embassy in…" he briefly glanced at Knutsen. "At any rate, that must have been, what, five years ago? You look annoyingly well."

Sign nodded. "Mummified at birth."

"You should have been."

"Let me take your coat."

As he handed Sign the garment, Raine looked around. "I like what you've done to the lounge. The décor is appropriate."

"One must surround oneself with beauty and intrigue." Sign gestured towards his armchair. "Have a pew."

The comment shocked Knutsen. Ordinarily no one was permitted to sit in Sign's beloved armchair.

Sign was by the drinks cabinet. "You'll join us in a somewhat premature *le trou normand* no doubt." A 'Norman hole' was typically a glass of calvados, taken halfway through a meal in northern France in order to figuratively burn a hole in the stomach to make room for more food. Sign didn't wait for a response, pouring the drink. "It's not exactly *Lemorton Rarete Vieux XO*." He handed the glass to Raine. "I decanted it from a plastic bottle. It was a gift from a farmer near Gorron. He made it himself. Poor chap had fallen into some form of exhaustive fugue while attempting to deliver a calf. I helped him to his feet, tied a rope around the calf's ankles, we pulled, calf was delivered, mother and calf were healthy."

Raine raised his glass. "To mother and calf." He took a sip.

Sign grabbed a dining chair, swivelled it around, sat on it with the back facing forwards and towards the armchairs, and asked, "How was Washington?" He was referring to Raine's recent post as British ambassador to the United States of America. Alongside the ambassador posting to Paris, which Raine had also held, Washington was one of the most prestigious postings in the diplomatic corps. "You must be a cat's whisker away from being appointed head of the foreign office."

"Washington was playful. Being head of the corps holds no interest for me."

Sign smiled. "You prefer to be Sir Francis Walsingham's successor?"

"Walsingham was Queen Elizabeth's spy. I'm not a spy."

"Walsingham had no clearly-defined job, and yet there he was at the top, setting his traps, the true spider at the centre of the web. He was a schemer. Just like you."

Had anyone else made such a comparison and observation, Raine would have shredded the person's soul. But, Sign had spoken in jest. Plus, Raine had to be exceptionally careful around Sign. "I would prefer to speak to you alone."

Sign drummed fingers on the top of his chair. "Do you have a personal matter to discuss?"

"No."

"Do you know what Mr. Knutsen and I do for a living? We have no website, social media presence, online presence whatsoever, traditional media or other footprint, and our Company's House registration merely lists our activities under Human Resources Consultancy. We don't even have business cards."

Raine crossed his legs and intertwined his fingers. "You're a former spook. Mr. Knutsen is one of Churchill's men, late of the Metropolitan Police Service." He looked away. "Actually the quote is falsely attributed to Winston, and George Orwell for that matter. Still, I digress." He looked back at Sign.

Knutsen smiled. The quote Raine was citing was, "We sleep soundly in our beds because rough men stand ready in the night to visit violence on those who would do us harm". He laughed. "A rough man? I suppose that's one of my characters." His expression steeled. "How did you know I was in the Met?"

Sign replied before Raine could answer. "Mr. Raine makes it his business to know matters that one day may suit his cause." He kept his eyes on Raine. "And that includes the nature of the business that you and I run."

Raine nodded. "Ex spy and ex undercover detective join forces? It doesn't take a rocket scientist to make an informed guess as to what wares you ply."

In a forthright tone Sign said, "So, you are here to discuss a matter that pertains to your somewhat substantial sphere of operations. Mr. Knutsen stays for the consultation."

Quietly, Knutsen said, "It's alright, Ben. I can pop out. We're running low on washing up liquid and firelighters, so I've got a reason to head to a shop."

"You're staying. The bullet wound in your shoulder has been twinging of late. The cold weather won't do it any good." Sign was motionless as he kept his eyes on Raine.

Raine looked at Knutsen. He was silent for a moment. Then, "I hope you understand what just happened." He clicked his tongue and angled his head while looking curious. "Mr. Sign's stance is interesting." In a commanding tone he said, "The police service was never going to be your true *alma mater*, but it gave you the opportunity to refine your skills. Don't underestimate the hidden praise that your colleague," he gestured at Sign, "has just heaped on you." He rubbed his hands eagerly and his eyes twinkled with mischief. "Ben - I notice you've put on a fine spread. Gentlemen, shall we grab some grub and eat while I regale you with a somewhat diabolical mystery?" To Knutsen he said, "I believe you should stay to hear the story. It involves a component that is connected to the origins of your surname."

They served themselves some of Sign's excellent Indian food, and poured beer. Raine moved to the dining chair Sign had been sitting on, and used his foot to rotate it to face the fireplace. Sign sat in his armchair; Knutsen sat in his armchair. All three had their plates on their laps, knees clamped together, looking like naughty school kids who'd been expelled from the canteen and forced to eat in the corridor. As he looked at Raine and ate, Knutsen realised that Raine was the type of person who always did and said something for a reason. That included switching chairs.

Raine said, "Before I proceed with my tale, let's consider the vulgar issue of business terms and conditions. I'm here because I wish to very discretely engage your services. No one else knows I'm here. There is a problem that is lacerating British national security, as well as the security of other sovereign states. I want you to help me neutralise that problem. No one is to be trusted; not even me. Your potential assistance is unsanctioned. You have no safety net. If you die on the job, and I'm still alive, I'll toss you both into an unmarked pit." He wiped his fingers with a napkin. "I'll pay you fifty thousand pounds upfront if you take on the job and one hundred and fifty thousand pounds if you successfully complete the task."

Knutsen popped a potato wedge into his mouth. "Make it one hundred up front, another hundred if the job's complete but not to your satisfaction, or two hundred if we sort it out."

Sign said, "Three hundred thousand pounds if we solve the case. Does your slush fund have the stomach for that?"

Raine didn't need to delay responding, but he paused for effect. "Yes. I can stretch to that."

"Splendid, dear chap. Do tell us your story. We are all ears."

Raine asked, "Do you know what CHALICE is?" He looked at Sign.

The former MI6 officer gave the slightest of nods.

The diplomat looked at Knutsen.

"No."

"There's no reason why you should have heard of it." The senior diplomat took a swig of beer. "If word got out that I'd blabbed what I'm about to tell you, I'd be hanged in a gibbet and displayed above the battlements of The Tower of London as a warning to others." He spoke at length.

CHALICE was set up eighteen months ago and was the codename for the top secret, highly classified, database shared by select members of the FCO, Metropolitan Police Service, GCHQ, MI5, and MI6. It was a tool that was used extremely selectively. Only the most vital intelligence was posted on CHALICE and even then it was only intelligence that was deemed essential for the eyes of all five agencies. Without doubt, CHALICE was the most potent weapon in Britain's arsenal to combat threats to its national security.

But, during the last twelve months CHALICE had been compromised by someone who had security clearance to access the CHALICE files. That person was cherry picking intelligence and selling it to overseas buyers. Nobody knew who the person was and finding him or her was an ongoing devil of a job. There were currently nine hundred and eighty two people who were security cleared to access CHALICE, all from the five agencies. Each agency had conducted internal security investigations, but to no avail. That was no surprise. A GCHQ investigation of CHALICE-cleared GCHQ staff could not identify the culprit if the culprit worked for MI5, and vice versa. Nevertheless, it was hugely frustrating that the investigations, put together, had failed to identify one person who could be responsible for the catastrophe. The perpetrator was canny. He or she stole from CHALICE rather than solely from the organisation he worked for. He didn't want to be narrowed down to working for the Metropolitan Police, for example.

Knutsen said, "If you're going to shoplift, steal from a superstore, not a corner shop."

Raine nodded. "Precisely."

Knutsen asked, "Why don't you temporarily shut down CHALICE while making further investigations?"

It was Sign who answered. "That can't happen. The Joint Intelligence Committee knows it can't happen. So do the politicians. There are precedents. We can't shut down GCHQ because it once employed a traitor called Geoffrey Prime; disband the Metropolitan Police Service because of a few rotten eggs who like to steal money and kill black people; tell all members of UK Special Forces to pack their bags and take up jobs as landscape gardeners, because some of them have decided to write books about their time in the units; and there's the thorny issue of Donald Maclean, Guy Burgess, Kim Philby, Anthony Blunt and John Cairncross - if we'd cut off our nose to spite our face the Cambridge Five would have rendered most of us obsolete and we'd have been left with Dad's Army and Neighbourhood Watch to protect Britain. CHALICE stays because it is our best defence against hostile states, terrorism, cyberattack, and major organised crime. It would be a disaster if it went offline, even for just a few months."

Raine added, "It's a horrible conundrum. People like me have to gauge the number of causalities we're willing to accept to win the war. The casualties are caused by the leaks; but the war is still being won. Thus far, it's been unanimously agreed by policy-makers that CHALICE must remain open for business, at any cost. But, I don't discount the option of shutting down CHALICE. It would be a last resort and would come at an awful price."

Knutsen's mind was working fast. "The traitor is one of nearly one thousand security cleared CHALICE officials. Get rid of them all. Replace them with others from the five agencies. It won't help identify the traitor but at least it will take him or her out of the equation."

Raine sighed. "I wish it were that easy. To be considered for CHALICE clearance, all applicants must already be in possession of developed vetting status, the highest mainstream security clearance in the UK. On average, it takes between six to twelve months for a person to get DV approval. They're not allowed near their potential employer until that clearance comes through. To get access to CHALICE the DV-approved applicants must go through an entirely new security investigation. Like the DV process, it's long and much nearer on average to the twelve month mark. If we sacked all CHALICE staff and started interviewing new officers, we might as well turn off CHALICE for a year."

Knutsen frowned. "Why do you need a thousand CHALICE staff? Why not trim it down to say twenty or thirty members? Odds are you'd cut the traitor out by doing that. And if you didn't and he carried on pinching he'd be easier to identify."

Raine replied, "The answer to that is purely logistical. As things currently stand, we need a legion of fingers in a legion of pies. Though it's not officially recognised as such, CHALICE has de facto become an intelligence organisation in its own right. Twenty or thirty people would not be able to run CHALICE."

Sign said, "So we're left with the only option: identify the traitor."

"Yes. Which brings me to why I'm here." Raine watched them both, then proceeded. "I returned from Washington DC one month ago. While in the States, I knew about the attack on CHALICE. Obviously, I'm CHALICE-cleared. But, I was geographically removed. When I returned to London the full extent of what was going on hit me. The counter-intelligence operation to identify the traitor was massive, but it was failing. I felt it was like a vast army that had been deployed in the wrong direction. So, I kept myself to myself and decided to consider the problem. I also ensured that any leads relating to the traitor's identity crossed my desk. I gave myself considerable insight into the decision-making on counter-espionage efforts."

Sign smiled. "I told you. Walsingham."

Raine said, "Not quite Walsingham. He liked to play puppeteer, pulling strings. I prefer to leave the counter-intelligence effort alone. But, I feed off the information it gleans. And I run with that information as I see fit."

"Without telling others."

"Correct." The diplomat put his plate on the floor and picked up his beer glass. "Seventeen days ago I learnt that the traitor was using a broker to sell the stolen intelligence." He told them about the Syrian defector and Lystad. "The defector also told me that his source wanted to make one last grab of CHALICE intelligence and sell it to the highest bidder. He wondered if Syria wanted to make such a bid. Regrettably, the defector didn't know the outcome of the proposition. But, he thinks it unlikely that Syria will have the stomach for such a huge purchase. He surmised that conversation might be more palatable to the likes of China and Russia. I concur."

"As do I. Or the conversation might go the way of another intermediary who has deep pockets and the ability to sell the intel on piecemeal and at profit." Sign shrugged. "It should come as no surprise. The traitor can't sustain his current modus operandi forever. One day he'll be caught. Why not go for broke and sail off into the sunset."

"One last heist and vanish."

"The clock is against us."

"It is." Raine hesitated, and said, "I put four trusted associates on to Lystad."

"Trusted?" enquired Sign.

"Between them, they're wanted by the law enforcement agencies of twenty seven countries."

Sign nodded. "They can be trusted."

Raine breathed in deeply. "Matters were supposed to come to a head the evening before last." He told them what happened in Bergen. He looked at Knutsen. "And so hence the link to the origin of your surname, Mr. Knutsen. I'm looking for a CHALICE-cleared British officer who speaks Norwegian."

"*Fluent* Norwegian," Sign said. "Lystad shouted the words *divulge* and *implicate* in his panic-induced communication to the traitor. Understanding the two words suggests fluency."

"I agree." Raine sipped his beer. "Of course I did a background check on Lystad and in particular looked for any connection he may have to a British official. On the latter I found nothing." He shrugged. "That's all there is to tell. Lystad's dead; the traitor got away; and all I have to go on is that he or she - I'm told, most likely a *he* - speaks fluent Norwegian."

Sign said, "That's not all there is to tell, is there Peter?"

Raine looked at the fire. "No."

"During the hours between your return to London and sitting here quaffing pickled okra and Anglo-Indian beer, I suggest you've been doing a bit of snooping. I'd be so bold as to elaborate that you've been snooping on your colleagues; all nine hundred and eighty one of them. Who speaks Norwegian? That is the question."

Raine watched flames lick over a log. "Indeed." He looked at Sign. "I checked the personnel files of every CHALICE officer, looking at languages. When I was a youngster that would have been a mammoth job, going through hardcopy paper files. Now it's all click of a button territory. It took me seconds to ascertain that there are five CHALICE-cleared operatives who are fluent in Norwegian. One from each CHALICE agency. Chance is a curious thing."

"And chance or luck gave us the Norwegian-language lead." Sign clapped his hands, his expression utterly focused and intense. "It's what we do with a nugget of luck that defines our worth. Who are the five?"

"Gordon Faraday from GCHQ; Hamish Duggan, MI5; Rex Hare, Metropolitan Police; Edward Sassoon, MI6; and," he put his beer to one side, "me." He smiled, but looked sad and uncharacteristically confused. "There is a reason I told you to trust no one, myself included."

Sign stood up and used a poker to push burning wood into the centre of the fire.

Knutsen watched him.

Sign was silent for a moment. He placed the poker in the coal scuttle and spun around. "You're not the traitor, Peter. If you were and you came here to put me on the scent," he smiled, "you'd have been committing suicide, wouldn't you?"

"Yes."

"Why?"

"Because you'd have proven beyond doubt that I was the traitor. This lovely living room," Raine gestured towards their fascinating, homely, and idiosyncratic surroundings, "would have been my executioner's lounge."

"Quite so." Sign folded his arms and leaned with his back against the mantelpiece. "Or, if you had any absurd notions that in presenting yourself as a potential suspect it might cause me to trust you further and focus only on the other four, you'd have known that would have failed. If one percent of me thought you might be trying to trick me, I'd have stuck to your scent like a beagle on a hunt. Your misdirection would have failed. Correct me if I'm wrong."

Raine shook his head. "You're not wrong."

"But you could still be suicidal, the murderer who taunts the police because he wants them to stop him. That sort of melodrama. The problem with that hypothesis is I know you. You're many things, but you'd deem it ungentlemanly and crass to sell out your country for a few quid."

Raine wanted to make light of the compliment. "I've done a few questionable things in my time. I…"

"Have never sold out your country and never could unless we'd been taken over by a tyrannical regime. Even then you'd work for the benefit of the British populous, not against your fellow citizens." Sign held up a hand, in case Raine was going to say something.

But Raine said nothing.

Sign said, "So, the matter is satisfactorily addressed. We move on to the nitty gritty of finding out which rogue reptile is cavorting with the devil's harem." He glanced at Knutsen. "What do you think? Rogue reptile? Cavorting with the devil's harem? I just made up the descriptions. Rather good, I believe."

Knutsen sighed. "If it makes you happy, Ben."

"Splendid." He addressed Raine. "Do you have any insight as to why Duggan, Sassoon, Hare, and Faraday speak Norwegian?"

"No. The CHALICE records only state that they are 'native speakers'. It doesn't say if they were taught the language as part of their assignments, or whether they know the language for other reasons. That information will be on their agency personnel files, but I can't access them. Well, perhaps I could but I'm loathe to try as it may sound alarm bells."

"Don't bother trying. All that matters is that we know they speak Norwegian like a Norwegian. I presume you've checked to see if Faraday, Sassoon, Hare, or Duggan travelled to Norway during the last week?"

Raine nodded. "None of them travelled to Europe, travelled anywhere, in the last month. I've checked the travel records of all CHALICE staff. No one's gone anywhere near Norway in the last seven days. Least ways, not under their own name. But, I don't have access to internal databases of MI6, MI5, and GCHQ. If any CHALICE intelligence officer from that bunch travelled under an alias passport, I'm blind to that."

This didn't surprise Sign. "If I was the traitor, I wouldn't travel with any document that linked me to Her Majesty's Government. We should also consider the possibility that the officer entered Europe covertly and without the need for any passport, real or fake. Mr. Raine – we'll take your case. Do you remember that delightful Spanish restaurant in Pimlico? The one where you and I dined with a Russian scholar of oceanography and for five minutes and eighteen seconds changed the world?"

Raine nodded.

"We'll meet there at ten AM tomorrow. In the interim, I shall wrestle, break, tame, and order my notions."

"You have some preliminary thoughts?"

Sign waved his hand and replied dismissively, "My thoughts are multiplying exponentially, like bacteria on an incubated agar plate." He faced Raine and smiled. "No doubt my dear business partner wants to have strong words with me for saying something like that. Nevertheless, I have much to dwell on. Tomorrow at ten. No excuses." He held out his hand.

Raine stood and shook his hand. "Thank you, Ben."

"Don't thank me yet. If I proceed with one of the options I'm considering, I'll be putting your life in danger. Good evening sir."

After Raine had collected his coat and left, Sign said to Knutsen, "There goes the most powerful man in London. There are many times he wishes it were not thus."

After clearing up the food and kitchenware, Sign and Knutsen recharged their glasses of calvados and sat in their armchairs. Knutsen said nothing as he looked at his friend staring at the fire. Sign's expression was serious, his brain working at full capacity, all attempts at mischievous wordplay and distraction were gone. This was the true Sign; the one that Knutsen saw occasionally and trod carefully around. In these moments. Knutsen jettisoned his playful attempts at pointing out the eccentricities of Sign's masquerades.

But, the former cop also felt an overriding duty of care towards his colleague. He decided to break silence. "You alright, mate?"

Sign shook his head rapidly, as if he was trying to get rid of something, looked at Knutsen with a distant expression, breathed in deeply, appeared to be attempting to haul himself out of some faraway location, and half-smiled, "Dear fellow. Yes, I'm fine, Tom." He leaned forward, elbows on his thighs, fingers interlaced and cradling his chin. Quietly, he said, "But, we are entering the fray. This will be…" he paused and frowned. "Yes. This will be the hardest case we've worked." He took a sip of his spirit, leaned back in his chair, and said, "Matters may become unpleasant. We must be brave."

CHAPTER 4

The following morning, Sign entered the lounge looking every inch an impeccably-dressed Whitehall mandarin.

Knutsen was in the kitchen, but heard him. "Just made a pot of coffee, if you fancy a brew?"

Sign rubbed his hands. "A slurp or two wouldn't go amiss. Alas, I've no time for anything more substantial."

Knutsen brought him a mug and handed it to him. "Shame. I was in the mood for making some bacon butties."

"Next time, for sure." Sign remained standing while sipping his coffee. "I like what you're wearing."

"What?" He'd put on whatever he could grab when he'd swung out of bed an hour earlier.

"I have in mind a job for you this morning. You'll blend right in. You look like a…" he considered what he was about to say next, "painter and decorator. Or, maybe a road sweeper. Tagged criminal, perhaps."

"Shut up." Knutsen rubbed stubble on his face. "What have I got to do?"

Sign blew over the film of his steaming coffee. "I need you to study the immediate surroundings of Peter Raine when he leaves my meeting with him this morning. It's dry outside. Knowing him that means he'll probably walk if he's heading back to King Charles Street. But, if he's on the clock or needed elsewhere, be prepared that he may go mobile."

Slowly, Knutsen stated, "You want me to follow our client."

"Not him per se. Peter's got more coils than a python, but he wouldn't try any foolishness with me. However, I would be interested to know if anyone's following him."

"You suspect he might be in danger?"

"In due course he will be in extreme danger. Right now I don't know. Not knowing annoys me. I'll send you a message when he leaves the restaurant." He gave him the address of the eatery. "Make sure you're armed."

"Armed?! In central London?!"

Sign shrugged. "Bullets work in central London just as well as anywhere else."

"Yeah, they do. Particularly if they're fired from a police Heckler and Koch submachine gun at the head of some geezer who looks like a tagged criminal."

"You're a versatile chap. You'll be fine. The priority is escorting Mr. Raine back to the warm and cosy enclosure that is the Foreign and Commonwealth Office. However, if you do see anyone threatening, just, err, kill them."

Knutsen was about to say something.

But, Sign was quicker. "Now. Talking of versatility, when you're out and about could you get me a chess board?"

"A chess board?"

"After you've completed the health and safety thingy with Raine. A chess board, preferably antique. In return, I'll pick us up some lunch."

"Why oh why do you need a chess board?"

"I lost the last one I owned. It was beautiful; extremely rare. The figurines were probably Lewis Chessmen, dating back to the eleven hundreds. Manufactured in Scandinavia and strongly influenced by Norse culture. They're made from walrus ivory and wales' teeth. Still, the board and pieces fell off the back of my pony on the Khyber Pass. The ravine below was too deep. Lost into a black void." His lips vibrated as he exhaled. "Maybe one day I'll go back and have a look for it. I'm sure the pieces will have survived the winters. It is a shame though because there would have been a nice connection between my chessboard and the Norwegian angle in our case. Never mind. I need a new board. I can recommend some antique dealers if it helps?"

"You'll get what I can find. Why don't *you* get a board after your meeting?"

"Because I'm wayward and irresponsible. I once lost a week scouring London for a copy of the 1824 book *The Poyaisian Scheme*. It was about the fraud committed by the Scottish adventurer, mercenary, and general George MacGregor. There was a rumour the book had surfaced in London. I chased the rumour, with no care for time, sleep, food, or other duties. I never found the book." He smiled. "Wayward. Now is not the time for my flights of fancy. You, by contrast, can be trusted. It wouldn't surprise me if you picked up a board for a fiver from a charity shop."

"That's about right. Once again, why do you need a chessboard?"

Sign placed his mug down and checked the time. "To help me think. To arrange matters. To create symbolism. To summon logic amid chaos. To…"

"I'll get you a frickin' chessboard."

"Good man." He picked up his overcoat and walked to the door. "Time for us to earn the Queen's shilling."

The tapas restaurant in Pimlico was closed before lunch, but Sign knew the owner who occasionally afforded him use of the premises for private meetings. It was nine fifty five AM. Sign was sitting at a table within an alcove that had a scuffed wooden floor and white, rough-stone walls and ceiling. In times gone by it was a favourite part of the restaurant for Spanish insurgents, and their British friends, to meet and plot actions against the fascists in nineteen thirties Spain. After the civil war, many of the revolutionaries returned to London and continued to meet in the cave-like recess, smoking their cheroots and drinking tumblers of brandy while reminiscing about firefights in the mountains and the attributes of brave, fallen comrades. The revolutionaries had long ago passed away but Sign liked to imagine the proud warriors sitting beside him, their laughter, loud voices, belly-laughs, fists banging the table, trigger-fingers held high to summon more drinks and bread, and stained pieces of paper unfolded so that hand-written poems could be recited. Though Sign did not believe in an afterlife, he imagined the stubborn moustachioed Spaniards cocking a hoot at his non-belief and lingering amid the thick walls. This was their home and they weren't in a hurry to leave. Crucially, Sign imagined, they liked the fact that a member of the secret world kept their haunt abuzz with hushed and urgent words about matters of national and international intrigue.

Two cups and saucers and a pot of coffee were brought to the table by a chef who had a tea towel slung across his shoulder and a twelve inch knife tucked underneath apron strings. When the chef was gone, Sign poured coffee with no care that it would grow cold if Raine was late. He checked his watch – a timepiece he'd removed from the wrist of a Maltese man who'd tried to garrotte him in a chapel in Casa Millieri. He waited.

Raine entered the restaurant, removed his coat, and sat opposite Sign. He was in a suit and looked calm, if a little circumspect. Irrespective, he showed no indications of the strain that he carried on a daily basis, aside from the tell-tale lines either side of his eyes. He was, Sign had long ago decided, a man who hid the fact that he saw too much.

"Good morning. I trust you slept well." Sign slid a cup across the table to Raine.

"I dreamed of deliberately infesting the houses of parliament with vermin." The diplomat sipped his coffee.

"I do that sometimes. That and variations of the time I was chasing that godless fiend and his sack of heads in Bremen's Schnoor Quarter."

"We don't talk about that."

"No. I suppose we don't." Sign looked at the empty restaurant, beyond the alcove, and back at Raine. "But last night I spent most of the time thinking about CHALICE."

"I spent most of my night trying *not* to think about CHALICE."

"You failed."

"Of course." Raine dabbed his mouth with a napkin. "This morning the prime minister is chairing a meeting of COBRA; and the JIC is in session."

COBRA – Cabinet Office Briefing Rooms A. The emergency crisis council comprising different government departments.

JIC – Joint Intelligence Committee. The assembly of senior members of MI6, MI5, and GCHQ, together with members of the UK military and other relevant departments. The JIC presented its regular assessments to government.

Raine continued, "Both sessions are concerning the CHALICE breach."

"No doubt you had the choice of attending either meeting. Why didn't you go?"

"They clashed with our meeting."

Sign nodded. "Then we must do better than the others."

Raine laughed with a tone of cynicism. "There's only you and me."

Sign shook his head. "You have your four-man band of marauders, as we speak possibly holed-up in some rum-sodden Caribbean port." He smiled. "I have Tom. And we may get an extra one or two allies along the way. We have support."

"A rapier thrust rather than a broadsword swipe."

"Exactly." Sign added, "But yes – right here and right now it is you and me."

Raine said, "I have my own answer to what I'm about to ask, but looked at objectively why don't we just hand the four, well," he touched his chest, "five Norwegian-speakers over for investigation by CHALICE? There'd be no need for your involvement."

The former intelligence officer responded immediately. "I am one hundred percent convinced that fluency in Norwegian makes the traitor Hare, Faraday, Sassoon, or Duggan. One hundred percent convinced. However, and there is a big *however,* the slip of the tongue is in itself not enough evidence to put sufficient squeeze on the four suspects. Still, if we handed the names to the authorities, their dark-arts brigade would have a crack at them. But the lack of evidence would mean the investigators would not be able to use their most extreme methods. Instead, it would be hours and hours of interviews. I think the traitor would survive that. I suspect, though time will tell, that we're dealing with an exceptionally capable individual. Furthermore, even if the gloves were taken off, he may well be the type of character who'd see his way through torture. If so, he'd be released and either run or carry on. Making the Norwegian angle public, so to speak, could cause more harm than good. We've got to catch the traitor in the act. Subtlety is key. Your rapier analogy is perfect."

"Maybe the CHALICE counter-intelligence team could apply such subtlety, but with greater resources."

"If you believed that you wouldn't have come to me. And then there is the bigger reason why you sought my help; why you don't believe handing this matter over to CHALICE would be the correct course of action. You don't know who to trust."

Raine lowered his head, slowly nodded, momentarily closed his eyes, slightly smiled, and audibly blew out through his nose. "Thank you… yes… thank you."

Sign placed his hand over Raine's hand. "Dear fellow. Did you assume that I'd think the reason you didn't go public was because you wanted to save your skin? I know you. Always putting yourself last. You wouldn't have given a monkeys if you'd implicated yourself by making it known that the traitor speaks Norwegian. So, let's stop any silly-business thoughts. There's a good chap." He patted the diplomat's hand and picked up his coffee. In a colder and authoritative tone he said, "I have constructed a plan. It is dangerous."

Raine's demeanour also steeled. "Proceed."

Sign leaned forward, his mouth close to Raine's ear. Quietly, he said, "Imagine this. You, Faraday, Hare, Duggan, and Sassoon in a room. The five Norwegian speakers together. Five very senior and extremely adept members of respectively the Foreign and Commonwealth Office, Government Communications Headquarters, Metropolitan Police Service, Security Service otherwise known as MI5, and Secret Intelligence Service otherwise known as MI6. You exchange information and conspire. You become an exclusive and secret club. Your objective is to root out the traitor in CHALICE. And the curious thing is, only you know that one member of your secret club *is* the traitor." He leaned back.

Raine nodded and said, "Because of the language lead, I narrowed it down from a thousand to five. That was the easy bit. Peeling away a fruit's soft skin. You're now faced with a hammer-resistant nut."

"And inside the nut is the kernel."

"The traitor." Raine unnecessarily stirred his coffee. "How do we get the five together?"

"*You're* going to do it. You'll individually approach Sassoon, Duggan, Hare, and Faraday. You'll tell them the truth that you're working the shadows on the CHALICE problem. You'll bemoan lack of progress and creative thinking by the counter-intelligence task forces. You'll conclude that a radical new approach needs to be deployed. You need help from one very senior member from each CHALICE agency. The five of you will collaborate in secret. No one must know about the team's existence. You'll be working completely outside of the realms of officialdom."

"Doing what?"

"You have an idea. Each of you will recruit what you'll call a 'runner'. One runner from the FCO, one from MI5, et cetera. The runners will be very junior members of the agencies. They will be malleable, more likely to follow orders no matter how unusual. The runners will be picked and run by each member of your club. For example, you will pick your FCO runner based on his or her profile and you will be responsible for your runner. The others will have no input into how you manage your runner, although you will supply your team with the runner's details and progress." Sign paused in case Raine wanted to say anything. But, he was met by silence. He continued. "You will deploy your runners to nullify the worth of the traitor's stolen intelligence. That means they meet the end users; the likes of Russia, China, et al. Your runners will tell the traitor's clients that HMG is aware there is a traitor operating in its midst who is stealing some information that is fact but is also selling intelligence that is embellished or outright falsified by the traitor. Create uncertainty as to which is which. The runners will be conveying the message that the traitor is muddying the bigger picture of tried-and-tested bridge building discourse between Britain and its counterparts. The runners will say that HMG wants foreign countries to stop buying dodgy documents. Continuing to do so harms them and harms HMG. The objective of this tactic is to force the traitor's financial pipeline to dry up and the traitor to become desperate. That's when you identify the traitor. Least ways, that's your hope."

Raine frowned. "But, in telling my jolly band of Norwegian speakers all this, I'd be telling the traitor what we're doing."

"You have to. You have no other choice. You're inviting the traitor to the party and thus the traitor's going to know what the party looks and sounds like. But, agitation is at the heart of the matter. If you agitate something, it reacts. How it reacts is usually unpredictable. But, one thing is for sure: it *will* react if you agitate it. In laying out your tactic, you'll agitate the traitor and watch for a reaction."

"I've already agitated the traitor by killing the broker."

"I concur. Now let's really up the ante. Let's give him a loaded gun and tell him to point it at his head. After all, that's effectively what you'll be doing by presenting the tactic I've described."

Raine smiled. "And you think I'm the schemer and presser of buttons?" He chuckled then turned serious. "What if the traitor doesn't want to join the party? What if one or more of the others thinks the idea is absurd?"

"We have to hope. Alongside *agitation* and *reaction*, so much rests on the word *hope*. What if this and what if that? There are so many what ifs. So many imponderables. I've created a plan. But it's not a fool-proof plan." He raised a finger, pointing at Raine. "I am very reliant upon you. I need your powers of persuasion, your fleet-of-foot intellectual agility, and your ability to tear the rulebook up and improvise if confronted with a new threat. I don't say any of that to flatter you. Like all of us, you have flaws. But, I need to be objective about your strengths. In turn, you become an intrinsic and essential component of my plan. It stands no chance of success without your direct involvement and ability to fire on all cylinders."

At first, Raine didn't know what to say. "What about your involvement?"

Sign sighed. "I have to be careful. I will be the spymaster, or whatever label one wants to slap on me, but the game's over if I show my face anywhere near the four suspects. I'll be there at the end, for sure, and I'll be with you along the way, but for a chunk of the odyssey you'll have to make decisions on your own. I'll be reliant upon you."

Raine digested what Sign had just said. "You'll be my handler, in spy speak. The person directing me. I'll be your agent or asset."

"Agent. We're not American."

"Agent. But you're reliant upon me to make very high-level decisions at times when you can't be around."

"Correct. And those decisions will not always be your own. You'll be in a group of five. Each member is very different. You're all smart thinkers, and yet you deploy your intellects in contrasting ways. At times you'll feel like you're trying to herd cats. As a result, you'll need to be nimble. If a decision is made that is not yours, you'll somehow need to embrace that decision in a way that works to your advantage."

"I understand the sentiment, for sure." Raine narrowed his eyes. "You're running me; I'm running Hare, Sassoon, Faraday, and Duggan; but I'm running them without them knowing they're being run by me and without them knowing that I'm being run by you; and meanwhile my new pals and I are all running our runners. Oh, and by the by, you're now my boss but I'm still your client and I'm paying you three hundred thousand pounds so that you can tell me what to do."

"Yes. All of that while trying to catch a traitor who's sitting very close to you. Tis a bit of mental jiggery-pokery, I concede."

"*Jiggery-pokery*?!" The whimsical phrase's lack of enormity amused him. "I'd say. Has this ever been done before? In your world? This many layers of agent handling? This amount of human complexity?"

Sign looked Raine directly in the eyes. "No. To my knowledge, this has never been done before."

"How are you going to pull this off?"

"How are *we* going to pull this off? We must be courageous. It's the fact that the task may appear impossible that makes it possible."

Raine held his hands up in a surrender position. "You really should have been made the chief of your service."

Sign's eyes twinkled. "Ah, but then you and I wouldn't be sat here having all the fun."

Raine lowered his hands. "Amen to that I suppose." His mind was working through potential points of vulnerability in Sign's plan. "The traitor might do his homework and realise that every person in the room speaks Norwegian. It's possible he'd look for that given Lystad's slip up."

"It's possible. And if he makes the Norwegian connection, he makes you."

"And so we play the game." The diplomat rubbed his face.

"A game with dreadful potential consequences. You don't have to do this, Peter."

"Yes I do. I'm the most qualified fool for the job. There's no one else." He shrugged. "No one else, so it's me and that's the way the cookie crumbles. But, I'm confused. What will he do if he does make the Norwegian connection?"

"He'll react. Remember: *agitation, reaction,* and *hope.* If he makes the Norwegian angle, he'll be agitated and will react. Somehow he'll react, even if it's just resigning his membership to your club. We'll hope for that or some other tell. This is the only card game in existence where we can, if necessary, show our opponent our full hand at the commencement of the game and still win. I hope we don't have to do that, but if we're forced to do so then all is not lost."

Raine drummed his fingers and looked at nothing in particular while thinking. After drumming his fingers one final time, he looked at Sign. "There's no other way. Let's do it. When do I start chatting up the others?"

"No time like the present. Tick tock and all that."

Raine nodded. "For this to work, four people I barely know have to agree to my strategy. And it is *my strategy* now. I have to think that everything I do going forward comes from me, not you."

"You do. You're about to step on to the stage. The voice is yours, not the playwright's voice."

"While the playwright waits in the wings."

"With a gun in his hand, ready to pounce if the actor fluffs his lines. So, let's not over-wring the actor-playwright analogy!"

Raine laughed. "I agree."

Sign put a mobile phone in front of the diplomat. "That's how you get hold of me. I too have a deniable phone, solely for our communications. My number's stored in your phone's Contacts list under *Jeremy.*"

"Jeremy? That's your codename?"

"No, no. Well, perhaps. I don't know. It's just what Tom came up with. He sorted our phones. In any case, if you call or text Jeremy you'll be communicating with me." He exhaled sharply and tapped both hands once on the table. "Now. When we meet you must apply the most rigorous anti-surveillance tradecraft. Do you need me to refresh your memory on techniques?" He smiled. "You being a mere diplomat and all."

Raine put the phone in his inner jacket pocket. "I got through that rolling Moscow fiasco, didn't I?"

"With aplomb. I was merely checking to make sure you're not a tad rusty."

"It's hard to get rusty when one's memory is engraved with recollections of being followed by highly trained Americans, Mexicans, Swiss, French, Russians, Iranians, and Chinese."

"Don't forget the time you crossed the border between Ecuador and Columbia while in the undercarriage of an articulated lorry."

"It hadn't slipped my mind. I was hiding in a spare fuel tank that was bolted to the undercarriage. It's not an easy thing to forget. Don't worry, Ben. There's no chance of anything getting rusty."

"Good man. I'm going to secure a safe house for us to meet. We must assume that my West Square home is compromised. I'll text you with the address details."

Both men were quiet for a moment. They didn't need to say much more. It was as if a calm and complete understanding encased them both. In new-speak, they were in the zone. In their speak, they were two side-by-side fellows on horseback who had no further use for words as they stared down the valley of death before the call to charge.

Raine stood and held out his hand. "I'll try my damnedest to wrangle the mustangs. You'll hear from me in a day or two."

Sign stood and shook his hand. "We created this adventure from nothing. Isn't that something?" His voice deepened and his grip tightened as he said, "Up and at 'em, my friend."

Raine left the restaurant and walked. Knutsen followed him.

Two hours later, Sign entered his flat and placed bags on the dining table. "Mr. Knutsen. Are you home?" There was no answer. He hummed a tune as he laid the table for lunch. In his bedroom, he took off his suit and put on casual attire. Back in the lounge, in an attempt to eradicate the Spanish gypsy flamenco song that was in a loop in his head, he played a vinyl record of the London Symphony Orchestra performing Berlioz, assembled and lit the fire, and made a mug of tea. Outside, a fresh wind was bringing in rain; the sky was darkening. He turned on two dim-bulb hurricane lamps, adding a warm and gentle glow to the room, and sat at the table. He sipped his hot brew. For some reason, he suddenly felt very alone.

It was a relief to hear keys in the front door, and movement as the door opened and closed. Knutsen entered the lounge and placed a large carrier bag containing something on the floor.

Sign smiled. "Ah, marvellous. You're still alive."

Knutsen stood in front of the fire, warming his hands. "Me and Raine. He went straight back to King Charles. No hit squads on his arse; assassins in doorways; snipers on rooftops. No drama whatsoever. He wasn't followed by anyone but yours truly."

"Excellent."

"How was he?"

"I presented him with my plan. Mr. Raine is now officially activated." Sign told him what the plan was.

Knutsen sat at the table. "Does he know the risks?"

Sign nodded.

"It's a daring plan. What do we do now?"

"We wait. Everything now rests on whether Peter can assemble the team."

"Wait?" With sarcasm in his voice, he added, "Oh good. You don't do *wait*. You get… annoying."

"As do you. The last time we had a meaningful period of inactivity you enrolled in a four week Portuguese language course."

"I like Portugal."

"You liked the Portuguese teacher even more. I warned you she had a boyfriend."

"Yes, about that. How did you know she had a boyfriend?"

Sign shrugged. "A guess."

"Hmmm." Knutsen looked at the bags on the table. "What's this?"

"Sustenance!" He removed boxes from the bags. "After my meeting, I thought we might partake of Iranian food, so I ventured north to Edgware Road and picked up some bits and bobs." He opened food cartons. "*Kebab torsh.* It's traditional in the provinces of Gilan and Mazandaran. Sirloin beef marinated in a paste of crushed walnuts, pomegranate juice, chopped parsley, olive oil, and garlic." He opened another carton. "And here we have *Morasa polow*. Rice jewelled with barberries, pistachios, raisins, carrots, orange peel, and almonds. It's not a traditional rice accompaniment to kebabs, but I like it." He opened the third carton. "Finally we have some pickles - cucumber, tomatoes, cauliflower, chillies, and cabbage."

Knutsen said. "I'd have made do with a sarnie."

"Where's the joy in that?" As they ate, Sign said, "We believe we have explored and demystified every inch of Planet Earth. It is folly for humankind to believe we have captured all the secrets that exist in our environs."

Knutsen stuffed meat into his mouth and rolled his eyes. "Where's this going?"

Sign dabbed his mouth with a napkin. "A neurologist shares much in common with a sixteenth century seafaring adventurer. But, there are differences."

With derision in his tone, Knutsen muttered, "We're doing this, are we?"

Sign smiled and was unfazed. "Indeed we are, sir. The seafarer navigates his boat through unchartered waters. For all he knows, the sea around him is bottomless, stretches to the furnaces of hell, and is brimming with monsters. Courage and determination enable him to subjugate his fear of the unknown in favour of a thirst for truth and enlightenment. If he's fortunate, he finally reaches land. He is grateful to God, his compass, and the hull of his sturdy vessel, for enabling him to stand on terra firma. With the treacherous sea behind him, he whips out his sketchbook and diary and notes what he sees before him – strange animals, beautiful plants that cause vivid skin rashes when touched, a semi-naked tribe that believes it is in the presence of a creature that has washed up on the beach with drift wood, and a dense tropical rainforest that contains a cacophony of sounds. Everything is unusual and wondrous, but not difficult to decipher. After further exploration, he returns to his boat and rushes back to London where he reports his findings to the science communities. Knowledge is advanced. A neurologist shares the same spirit of adventure, but getting to new shores is easy by comparison to the ordeal faced by the ship's captain. All a student of the brain needs to access the tissue between our ears is the sturdy and precise hand of a surgeon, or the magnetic fields and radio waves of an MRI scan. The passage to the new frontier isn't perilous or difficult. But when the neurologist arrives on figurative terra firma he is confronted with matter than cannot be easily recorded on sketchpad and diary. Instead, he or she is confronted by something he has never seen before, cannot comprehend, yet must attempt to comprehend, even if the process of attempting that quest ruins his reputation."

Knutsen brushed crumbs from his fingers. "The mind is the last place on Earth to be fully explored."

"Yes. The exploration has begun and is ongoing. But our current understanding of the brain is not advanced. A seafarer does not just take one step into a tropical rainforest with the hope that solitary step will gift him absolute insight into the entire machinations of the wooded ecosystem. He must probe further. The neurologist must continue his adventure."

Knutsen often made light of Sign's profundities. In doing so, he kept both men grounded. But he was smart and on occasion gave Sign some slack. "You want to explore the traitor's brain."

"Bravo, Mr. Knutsen."

"You're not a neurologist."

"Maybe the seafarer sailed nothing more than dinghies in the Solent before embarking on his near impossible journey. Nobody told him he didn't have the expertise to confront huge waves and swells. So, off he went."

"Ignorance is bliss."

"When it confounds its critics."

Knutsen sighed. "Ben, the traitor is motivated by money. That's all there is to it."

"To what end?"

Knutsen frowned.

"If you were given ten million pounds tomorrow, what would you do?"

Knutsen shrugged. "Probably buy a nice house on the coast; hopefully meet a nice woman; get married; live the life."

"What life?"

"Err…"

"You'd have to consider the life. You enjoy intellectual curiosity. Endless walks along the clifftop with your belle won't be enough. The ten million pounds has to be a means to an end. But at this juncture, you can't say with certainty what that end would be. I wonder what motivates the traitor. Money is merely his tool to get what he wants. He must have a clearly defined set of aspirations for the remainder of his life. If I can understand his true motivation, I can understand the man."

"And if you can understand the man, you can narrow down four to one."

"In principal, yes. But in order to understand the man I need more data. To get more data, I need him to…"

"Fuck up."

"Err… words to that effect. Certainly, I need him to reveal his true character. The plan is designed to elicit that reveal."

"Right. That's that sorted then." Knutsen carried on tucking into the superb food. "What are you up to tonight?"

"I… Well, I was hoping to complete my monograph on why most psychologists are psychopaths. It interesting because…"

"The reason I ask is that I'm meeting Kristin in The Oddfellows Arms at eight. She's bringing along her friend Béatrice. Do you want to join us?"

Sign frowned. "Kristin and Béatrice? Ah yes, the French ladies. I seem to recall you introduced me at a book launch event in a ghastly warehouse in the docklands. Are you and Kristin in some form of courtship?"

Knutsen laughed. "Maybe. She likes rugby. England is playing France tonight. They're showing it live in the pub."

"Hardly grounds for *entente cordiale*, I would suggest."

"I'll take my chances. So, Béatrice is going to be there."

"Béatrice. Yes, Béatrice. She's…"

"Pretty and clever and your age. And she's a widower."

Sign threw his hands in the air. "We have dead loved ones in common. That's settled then. I must marry her with immediate effect." He smiled.

"Come along. It will do you some good."

"Ah, I'm not so sure, Tom."

"What are you going to do instead? Sit moping in here, writing about psychos getting online diplomas to they can weasel their way into the psychology so-called profession in order to make patients feel shit about themselves and at the same time not only deflect attention away from therapists but also fact-find about what makes a perfectly normal, compassionate human being tick and thus steal that persona and go out and do loopy stuff?"

Sign's eyes widened. "You have somewhat stolen the glory of my thesis's *denouement*." He grinned. "It appears my French words wish for an outing. This evening I shall therefore meet the beguiling Béatrice."

"Just don't be yourself."

"Roger that. Now, did you procure a chessboard?"

"I'm happy with what I bought. I'll show you after lunch."

"Jolly good. I've got a four PM this afternoon. Property rental viewing in Westminster. Potential safe house for meeting Peter. Our home is no longer secure. Why don't you tag along? In return, this evening I'll regale the French ladies with our audacious theft of the Parisian blackmailer's entire off-shore fortune. Kristin should be impressed when I tell her the part where you paddled across the Gulf of Saint-Tropez at night and boarded the blackmailer's yacht. It was a scene reminiscent of *The Cockleshell Heroes*."

"Westminster? Blimey, that's going to cost a packet. Still, makes sense. The whole Whitehall and Westminster area is Raine's patch. Nothing out of the ordinary for him to move around in that circle. Yeah, I'll come along. But, this evening *please* don't mention Saint-Tropez. Actually, don't mention anything about that case."

Twenty minutes later, Sign was sitting by the fire, eagerly awaiting the board being placed by Knutsen on the coffee table between the two armchairs. Knutsen pulled out a rectangular cardboard box from the bag he'd brought in earlier. He tore open the box, removed inner polystyrene casing and said, "Here we go."

Sign looked at the object his friend was holding. "What in God's name is that?"

Knutsen brought it over and laid it flat on the coffee table. "Touchscreen computer." He sat in his armchair and pointed at the electrical item that was nineteen inches wide and barely one inch thick. "Everything's in there. It's like a giant iPad. You just use your fingers to operate it as you see fit."

Sign stared at the object, as if he'd just been presented with something that had never been seen by the human eye before. "Where's my chessboard?"

"If you want a game of chess, there's one in there. Lots of games, actually. Loads of other apps. Plus you can do web browsing, emails, social media, videos, photos, everything." He leaned forward and turned it on.

When the home screen loaded, Sign gave an involuntary huff. "It's just like a computer."

"It *is* a computer, you numpty. You can personalise it. Look, I'll show you. The home screen design can be changed." He started using his forefinger to adjust settings. "Green home screen. Orange. Yellow. Black. No, I don't think you should have black. One with bubbles. One with a lake. Another with a tall ship stuck in ice. You might like that one."

"No, no," Sign said hurriedly swiping his hand in front of him. "I like the first one. The blue one."

"The blue one. Okay." Knutsen put the computer back onto factory settings. The background of the screen was now electric blue.

"Much better. Suits the ambience of the lounge. Good juxtaposition. Old and new. Makes perfect sense."

Knutsen breathed deeply in and out. "Alright. Let me show you what's on here." Four minutes later, he asked, "So, you want this one?"

Irritably, Sign replied quickly, "Yes, yes. Nothing else. Just the whiteboard app."

"You don't want to upload the chess app?"

"No. No more chess. The Khyber Pass has the chess. It can stay there. The whiteboard's better."

"There are other things on here that you might…"

"Not interested. Just the whiteboard app."

Knutsen felt that he was in the presence of an entranced caveman. He sighed. "The whiteboard it is. Do you want to give the file a name?"

Sign's face was close to the screen. "Name? Yes. CHALICE."

With resignation, Knutsen said, "Of course. CHALICE." He created the file name and stood. "You're good to go. There's enough juice in there for now. While you're having a play with CHALICE, I'll set up the extension lead power cable. I'll make sure the cable is discretely hidden so we don't trip over it. Don't forget to press 'save' when you've finished and want to exit."

"Yes, yes, carry on, I'm fine." Sign was completely oblivious to anything else other than the white electronic board that filled the screen. He spoke aloud to himself as he used his finger to write and draw on the screen. "Okey-dokey. Peter Raine." He wrote the diplomat's name. "Square around the name. Good. The rest of you blighters. Edward Sassoon. Gordon Faraday. Hamish Duggan. Rex Hare. Squares around each of you. Move squares with two fingers into centre of screen. Arrange squares in a sort of circular shape. Lines connecting all of them. In the centre of the gang-of-five put a new square. What to go in most central square?" He wrote the word 'Traitor'. "Super-duper. Me on the far left of the screen. Waiting out of sight in the wings indeed, Mr. Raine. Tom nearby. Squares around each of us. Line connecting me and Raine. Somewhere out here on the top right – far flung corner of the world - put one square for Raine's cutthroats. Splendid. What's missing?" He leaned back. "Ah, yes." He leaned forward. "Big square in top left corner. Title: 'DEAD'. Lystad brackets 'Broker' goes in there. File save." He reclined in his chair, clasped his hands in front of his chest as if he was praying, and stared at the whiteboard app.

Knutsen stood by his side and looked at the screen. In particular he looked at the box in the top left corner. "That's a big square for the 'Dead' category."

Sign glanced at him and smiled, but his expression suggested his thoughts were elsewhere. "You did well getting me this, Tom. Clever thinking. Alas," he looked at the screen, "it is anything but a game."

CHAPTER 5

Twenty five hours later, Sign was in his newly acquired safe house, on the banks of the River Thames and close to the houses of parliament. It was a one bedroom apartment within a purpose built block that was primarily used by members of parliament and other government officials during working weekdays. Because of the vocation of the residents, the building was fortified so that it was partly resistant to bombs. When flats became vacant, they were not advertised openly. He'd secured the flat via his connections.

It was tastefully furnished, but contained the bare minimum. After taking short-let possession of the property, Sign had purchased tea, coffee, milk, and whiskey. Nothing else was needed. The building had state-of-the-art locks on the door, video surveillance cameras at the ground floor entrance to the block and in the corridors and lift, and a twenty four seven manned reception area that all residents and guests had to report to when entering and leaving the building. It wasn't completely secure – he'd already identified four ways to reach his apartment door without being detected – but the existing security features were enough to deter a moderately capable potential intruder.

The safe house was on the top floor of the nine-story building. It was blessed with a small balcony containing a table and two chairs that was accessed by sliding glass doors in the tiny lounge. The balcony allowed stunning views of the mighty river below. Of course, he had no idea how long he'd need the flat. He'd paid for one month's rent, with the option to extend, though he hoped he didn't need to extend given the cost of the place. Still, if the weather allowed, he looked forward to sitting on the balcony and admiring the activities on the waterway. He knew Raine would enjoy that, too. In matters of culture, manners, finery, and historical interests, the diplomat was like him; a man who was at least one hundred years out of time, according to less urbane mouths. And like Sign, Raine was a thoroughbred adventurer. Together, they'd sit on the balcony, with a mug of coffee or something stronger, watching day turn to night. They wouldn't need to make small talk. Their respective imaginations would be crammed with images and sounds of nineteenth century tea clippers, coal-fired tugboats, schooners, the occasional Royal Navy cruiser, watchful and motionless black cormorants atop water-based pylons, loud sailors' voices being carried over the river surface, vessels' horns and bells, the light from embankment lamps creating a blue and white shimmer over ripples, lingering mists and fogs, and overall an evocative sense of industrious traveller activity along the slithering, moody, and intrigue-laden river.

In many other ways, Sign was nothing like Raine.

The doorbell rang three times. The number of rings meant nothing because Raine and Sign had no use for an attempt at codifying the rings. All codes are useless if the sender or recipient is captured and made to reveal the code. So, right now someone was at the entrance. That was all there was to the sound. Sign looked through the spyhole, saw Raine, and opened the door. Raine entered.

After closing the door, Sign asked, "Is that for me? Housewarming gift, or similar?"

Raine was holding a pot plant. "It took me nine minutes and sixteen seconds to get here from my office on foot. And that included stopping off at a vendor on Parliament Street to buy this." He slightly raised the plant. "It's a loganberry plant. Mrs. Raine likes horticulture." He looked at the plant, its pot held in the palm of one hand. "Is horticulture the right description? Botany maybe?" He looked back at Sign. "She likes plants. Spends more time in the greenhouse than in our kitchen."

"Saves you having to buy a shed to hide in. Come through. I'd show you around but you'll have seen everything there is to see the moment I let you in."

Raine put the plant on a side table and walked to the sliding glass doors. "Ah, but I hadn't seen this. What a view."

Sign went to his side and followed his gaze. "What do you see?"

"Beauty, barbarism, wonder, skulduggery, heroism, mystery, laughter, sorrow, power, crime, and murder." Raine glanced at him. "That lot to be getting on with, at least." He smiled.

"It'll do for starters." He turned toward the diplomat but said nothing else.

Raine faced him. "I have them. All four. I bloody well have 'em."

Sign made no attempt to hide his enthusiasm and delight. He shook Raine's hand. "Well played, sir! Superb effort!"

Raine told him about his approaches to Duggan, Hare, Sassoon, and Faraday; how each person responded to his pitch; details about their demeanour; the observations they made and questions asked; concerns; and ultimately how each one had concluded that Raine's initiative was a damn sight better than anything else being done to counter the CHALICE breach. "I'm giving you the headlines, of course. The process was… exhausting, to say the least. It wasn't easy."

"I'm sure it wasn't. Your initial thoughts on each man?"

"I warned you before you sent me on my way that I didn't really know them. Actually, I didn't know them at all. Previously I met Duggan and Sassoon once, in a meeting containing others. Faraday I'd only spoken to on the phone. Hare I'd had no contact with although a couple of his reports crossed my desk."

"Lack of prior knowledge can be an advantage."

Raine nodded. "Duration of time with each man ranged between two to three hours. Locations varied. One pub, one park, a restaurant, and a museum. I saw policeman Hare first. He wanted to know that, even though my idea was off the record, we had clearance to do this. I lied and said we did. But actually I don't think he cared. I suspect he projects a rulebook persona but underneath is anything but. GCHQ Faraday? What to say about him. The bloke's one can short of a six pack. He thinks in numbers. I could feel him crunching numbers as I spoke. Maybe there's more to him though. I have a feeling there might be. And he's exceptionally clever. He's hiding something. But that something could be any number of things. MI5 Duggan?" The diplomat laughed. "Imagine moulding a high court judge's brain with that of a champion gladiator. The result is Duggan. I've got to be careful with him. Like Hare, he projects an image that he feels others find understandable. In Duggan's case, it's bloodthirsty insightfulness. You know the type – can summarise a term of lectures into one sentence. The problem is, what lurks beneath? Finally your former colleague Sassoon. The trickiest of the lot, by a thousand leagues. I can't get a handle on him."

"You won't."

"Did you work together?"

Sign shook his head. "We were deliberately kept apart throughout our careers."

Raine frowned.

Sign said, "It happens. Particularly in MI6. Not often, but it can happen. There's probably a scientific comparison one could make. Two organisms that shouldn't be in the same host. Some such comparison. Regardless, I'm glad you're wise to the trappings that other people might succumb to. It would be easy to slap labels on each character. Hare the *Lawless Detective*. Faraday the *Secretive Boffin*. Duggan the *Warrior Tactician*. Sassoon the *Maestro Conductor*. Or other shorthand descriptions. Characterisations are useful because they jog the memory and typically contain elements of truth. I agree with you, however. Each person you met has depth. It was to be expected. What of the runners?"

"It's been collectively agreed that I make the first move with a runner of my choosing. He doesn't know it yet, but I've selected my runner." He gave Sign details. "His boss doesn't know why I need him but she's let me have him. I've worked fast. So have others. My runner's got a meeting this Saturday." He told him what had been set up. "Duggan, Sassoon, Hare, Faraday and I are meeting at nine PM tomorrow evening." He told him the address for the meeting.

"Impressive and very swift. I commend you. What will you do if the runner refuses to play ball?"

"Oh, you know." Raine pretended to look menacing. "I'll tell him that I'll not only destroy his career, I'll publicly humiliate him and anyone who cares to associate with him. I'll add that failure to do one's duty when presented with an issue of national security is regarded as cowardice and punished as such. Death by firing squad is still, I will advise him, an option when confronted with such treachery." He smiled. "I wouldn't say any of that. Leadership carries many burdens. Getting the job done is one of them. So too duty of care for your men and women. I've picked my runner for many reasons, including my belief that he has excitement-driven gumption and would be mightily enthused by a quest. I will direct those laudable traits. I will also worry about him. He's so very young." He added quietly, "In the unlikely event that he gets the jitters and can't go over the top, I'll tell him there's no shame in that and will ensure he returns to regular diplomatic duties without a smear on his name. I'll keep an eye on him to make sure he's okay. And meanwhile I'll find another runner. The show must go on."

"Spoken as a true officer. You've set everything up perfectly. Now the job gets harder. In your meeting tomorrow evening, keep an ear out if someone mentions the possibility that the traitor might have a broker."

"You think that if one of them mentions the broker it could say something about that person?"

"Maybe, positively or negatively. But at this stage it would be impossible to deduce what it might say about the person. That said, it could be relevant in due course."

"I understand. Presumably you don't want me to tell them the broker's dead?"

Sign shook his head. "Let the traitor sweat. He has no way of being certain that you know Lystad's dead, or that you had anything to do with his demise. There's any number of possibilities why the broker's safe house was attacked that night. For example, Lystad came to the attention of the Norwegian authorities due to something he did that made them suspect he was a dodgy financier; they tried to arrest him; it went wrong."

"I agree." He exhaled. "Good."

Sign gestured towards the door.

Raine grabbed the plant pot and walked to the exit.

Sign watched him. "Peter. How are you feeling?"

Raine stopped, hesitated, and turned. He bowed his head and considered Sign's question. He raised his head. "I have a strong sense that this case will test our characters. You were right yesterday to observe that I have flaws. We all do. Within reason, it's the nature of things. Perfection, or some arbitrary person's notion of what constitutes perfection, is such a dull man's vision. But, when push comes to shove, we want to do the right thing. A problem arises when we are forced to do the wrong thing and have absolutely no tools at our disposal to avoid that eventuality. More accurately, are we *forced* to do things that are seemingly out of character? Or do we *allow* external events to reveal our true character?" He angled his head, still deep in thought. "Yes. That's how I feel." He smiled but looked reflective. He pointed at the window-door and the river beyond. "Joseph Conrad's story was narrated on that river. Conrad was right to pose the question: are we civilised people or savages? Good afternoon, Mr. Sign." He left.

Sign was still. Raine had referred to Conrad's 1899 novella *Heart of Darkness*. The narrator, Charles Marlow, told his story to others aboard an anchored boat on the Thames. His tale recounted his obsession with finding the ivory trader Kurtz. He'd journeyed along a vast snake-like river into central Africa. Conrad drew parallels between London, *the greatest town on earth*, and Africa as places of darkness. Few other stories have been analysed as much as Conrad's. The heralded narrative has also garnered misunderstanding, confusion, and unfounded criticism. Sign and Raine understood that the book was about people. The clue was in the title. But the way the story unfolded deliberately or accidentally misdirected some readers to clamour about geographical references. Maybe Conrad was partly to blame for that misunderstanding. Perhaps it wasn't thoughtful writing. Regardless, the central message should have been clear: within all of us a war is taking place for ownership of our souls.

Sign stared at the door. Raine believed he was Marlow, questioning his moral compass while in search of a traitor whose soul had been consumed by darkness. The traitor was Kurtz. Sign didn't like the comparison. It was too linear; too populist. But, he was concerned that Raine had made the reference. He needed the diplomat to manage the journey from a position of certainty and strength, not encroaching self-doubt. He decided he would need to give Raine some of his mental fortitude.

He grabbed his coat and left the flat and building. As he walked towards home he thought about dinner and wondered if Knutsen fancied a slow braised oxtail stew with mashed potato and green beans. Or maybe the former cop would prefer takeaway pizza? Halfway along Westminster Bridge, he stopped and looked at the river. He didn't know why. Rain was falling and he shouldn't be loitering. But he stayed for a moment anyway, watching the Thames. A thought occurred to him. Mental fortitude? Was he kidding himself? The river below was strong and had withstood so much. Men and women came and went. He was staring at fortitude; he was a mere human. No, he reminded himself. The Thames had been dammed by people. The right person could outwit and tame a river as powerful as the one he was looking at right now. In the context of a seemingly unstoppable secret force, he was strong enough to stand firm. Therefore, he had strength and ingenuity aplenty to spare some fortitude for Raine.

He continued his short walk back to West Square. He knew Knutsen wouldn't be in when he got home. He was taking Kristin to a matinee movie. It was good that his flat mate was dating again. The process would be tentative, no doubt. The murder of his loved one a year ago had poleaxed Knutsen. Sign wondered if his flatmate had told Kristin what had happened. He also thought about Béatrice. It had been lovely to get reacquainted with her. And it would have been lovely to have taken her to watch a film together. Alas, she was returning to France to get married.

He entered his flat, dumped his coat, and sat in his armchair. He turned on the touchscreen computer and loaded 'CHALICE'. Sometimes he wondered if all he had left was what was in his head. And right now nothing symbolised that notion better than an electric board. He looked at the names. Next to the four suspects he put a line each and a nickname.

Rex Hare - *Lawless Detective.*

Gordon Faraday - *Secretive Boffin.*

Hamish Duggan - *Warrior Tactician.*

Edward Sassoon - *Maestro Conductor.*

There were no boxes around the nicknames. They were just notes. He looked at the fifth box in the circle of Norwegian speakers. He drew a line from Raine's box and wrote *Charles Marlow.* He muttered, "Hold fast, Peter. Don't become that man." From Raine's box he drew another line and created a new box. In it he wrote five words in uppercase.

RAINE'S FCO RUNNER. ALEX WICK.

CHAPTER 6

Alex Wick was a junior diplomat in Her Majesty's Foreign & Commonwealth Office. He was twenty-three years old; a fast track graduate entrant with only one year under his belt in public service, and was late of Magdalen College, Oxford, where he majored in English and minored in pranking his tutors. He had a super sharp brain, was single, mischievous, and always saw the funny side of life. People liked Wick. He lit up rooms with his energy and boyish grin. And he'd go far in his job, providing he realised when to put on a straight face and not do something silly.

He was a good-looking young man – brown hair that was just about short enough to pass muster in the corridors of power yet hinted at a desire to grow out to a full-blown foppish Oscar Wilde-look if left to its own devices, physique that was no good for Westminster School's rugby team but was perfect for its cadre of fast bowlers, dashing aristocratic devil-may-care features that were yet to succumb to the ingrained weariness associated with worrying about repairs to hundreds of windows in the crumbling ancestral country estate that one day he'd inherit, and a snappy dresser who wore tailored Saville Row suits with the classiness of a nineteen thirties prince yet couldn't resist rebelling against the look by wearing retro nineteen sixties ties that were handmade by a hippy chick in Notting Hill.

It was nearly ten AM. Wick was in an open-plan office in the regal FCO headquarters in Whitehall, London. He shared the room with two other young diplomats and two administrative staff. They were busy tapping on their computer keyboards while staring at screens. By contrast, Wick was reclining in his chair with his legs resting on his desk, while folding sheets of today's *Daily Telegraph* newspaper into aeroplanes and tossing the makeshift gliders at his colleagues. He was bored. Such moments brought out the worst in him.

A young female diplomat from two doors' down entered the room and addressed Wick while glancing at a note she'd scrawled a moment earlier. "Peter Raine wants to see you. Room 79b. He said, and I quote, *"No fannying about. Eleven this morning at the latest. It would serve him well to get here earlier"*." She folded the note and shoved it into one of her trouser pockets. "He rang my secretary by mistake."

One of the administrative employees – a middle age woman who'd spent nearly thirty years having to put up with the annoying enthusiasm of over-privileged golden boys and girls who entered the corps at twice her paygrade – scowled, looked over her glasses, and said in her best school-mam voice, "They stopped calling us *secretaries* around the time when your mother and father's groins accidentally touched and got you on the go."

The woman looked at her, a grin fixed on her face. "Yes. Of course." She looked back at Wick. "Raine."

"Never heard of him." Wick put his feet on the floor and examined his *Church's* brogues. "Does he have homosexual tendencies?"

The woman was unfazed. "If he does he's barking up the wrong tree."

"Have I dishonoured him and he wishes to challenge me to a duel at dawn on Hampstead Heath?"

"It's possible. However, his message was brief."

"Maybe," Wick angled his head and adopted a faux inquisitive tone, "Peter Raine esquire loathes the very ground that I walk on and wishes to put me on a punishment posting to Papua New Guinea."

"I hope not. The last guy we sent there went crazy and kept telling us that the Aussies wanted to grab the country off *Queen Liz* and put it back into Australian administration. He tried to sail his tiny yacht to Sydney Harbour so that he could stomp over to Canberra and give the prime minister a stern talking to. He never made the crossing. They found him and his yacht upside down, both half-eaten by sharks."

Wick was about to say something.

But the woman leaned against the door frame and said, "Honestly, I could do this all day. Really. It would be better than finishing my cluster-of-boiled-bollocks report on trade tariffs between Mongolia and Iceland."

Wick stood and sighed. "Who is Mr. Raine of Room 79b?"

"Man without portfolio, as far as I can tell. Bigwig though. Ex Paris and Washington. S2." S2 being a grade that put him only two notches below the head of the entire Diplomatic Corps. "Let's hope he's not an Arabist." To herself she muttered, "God, I hate Arabists." Her smile returned as she said with jollity, "Ta ra. I must attend to the lesser-known Ulaanbaatar-Reykjavik silk route." She went back to her office.

Wick left the room.

The woman who didn't like being called a secretary said to the other administrative officer, "*Silk route*, my backside. She works on the Brussels desk. I bet she dreams of sitting in a tent with nomads and the like."

It took Wick precisely eleven minutes and thirty eight seconds to find room 79b. He'd have been a minute or two quicker had he not stopped to ask *Lovely Lucy* if she'd care to join him for a drink one evening. After Lucy had rejected his advances by telling him she had a boyfriend, he'd carried on his meanderings. And here he was. As per protocol, he knocked on the door once and entered without waiting to be summoned.

A man was sitting behind a desk in a room that seemed too big, given it had nothing in it save the most bland and functional of furniture and basic office equipment. The man was wearing a shirt, tie, and suit trousers.

Wick beamed. "Are you Raine?"

"Who else would be incarcerated in this bloody mausoleum? Sit down."

Wick did as he was told, his smile refusing to budge from his face.

Raine swept a hand in the air. "Two weeks I have to sit in this depressing room, before they find me somewhere better. What would you do to cheer the place up?"

Wick looked around. "Only two weeks? You could have some fun. Maybe go for a first-year-at-uni-1980s-dorm-look. My Mum was at St. Andrews back then. She's still got *Athena* posters she put up on day one at university. My Dad hates it. He won't let her get them out."

"That's a bit *gaslight* of him."

"He's ex-army."

"Ah."

"Anyway, Mum's secretly shown them to me. They're pretty good. And they should piss off the cleaners when they come to do this place. Plus, your bosses will think you've lost your marbles if they visit you here. It might spur them on to find you a better room."

Raine nodded as he stared at one of the bare walls. "I don't really have bosses. Still, it's a good thought. What do these posters look like?"

"Tennis girl scratching her bum. She's got no knickers on. I like that one. Photo of Bob Marley smoking a joint. It's been given an Andy Warhol makeover. I think it's Warhol. Oh yes! CND logo. You know – the back-in-the-day emblem. My Dad *really* hates that one."

"I bet he does."

"Others." Wick was trying to remember. "Mostly pop bands and singers. Duran Duran, Rick Astley, Kajagoogoo. Many more that I can't remember. I could find out."

Raine looked around. "*Kajagoogoo*," he said to himself. Looking straight at Wick he said in an authoritative voice. "Good thoughts, but I was thinking more along the lines of some oil paintings, Turner could work, lots of books, and Oriental artefacts."

"You're not an Arabist, are you?"

Raine frowned. "No I'm not. Why do you ask?"

Wick shrugged. "No reason."

"One must always have a reason for saying something; otherwise one is just a blathering idiot."

"I agree, sir."

"Don't call me *sir*. We're not in your father's army. Peter will do just fine."

"Right you are Peter. Sir. Peter."

Raine sighed and said with rapid words that carried a tinge of chastisement, even though he couldn't care two hoots about the subject matter or what Wick called him. "In civilian circles *sir* is the address used when a spotty American adolescent boy introduces himself to the father of a girl he wants to escort to prom night and get sticky with on the back seat of a vehicle. Are you calling me *sir* because you want to get intimate with my daughter?"

Wick shook his head. "Certainly not. How would I know if I want to get intimate with your daughter? I've never met her."

"Fair point." Raine picked up a thin file. "What are you doing this Saturday?"

Today was Thursday.

"Jog in Hyde Park, breakfast, bit of cricket with the lads, pub lunch in Fulham, back home, shower, change, dentist for check-up, pick up a suit that's had alterations done, some other shopping if I've got time, back home again, then dinner with my parents at my father's club in St. James's. But, I'm not doing any of that, am I?"

No." He tossed the file to Wick. "Read that. Won't take long."

It didn't take long. There were only two pages in the file, one of which was a photograph. Wick closed the file. "A male Chinese diplomat…"

"More likely an intelligence officer. Still, he wants to playact being a diplomat so we'll take him at face value. You're meeting him on Saturday. In Munich."

"Sir…sorry, Peter, I know nothing about the Chinese."

"Doesn't matter. All I need you to do is deliver a message. He's a fluent English speaker so you'll have no problems with communication."

"What message?"

"Tell him it's a delicate matter; that relations between the UK and China are strained at the best of times but we've uncovered a problem that may or may not worsen relations between Britain and China."

Wick wondered how he felt about being a mere messenger boy. He decided the status of the job was irrelevant compared to the fact that he'd never been to Munich and had heard good things about the city, plus he'd not been looking forward to dinner with his parents. "What's the problem we need to share with the Chinese?"

Raine drummed his fingers and momentarily averted his gaze. He locked his vision on Wick. "Someone around here has got a loose tongue. Tell the Chinaman that we've got a twisted British soldier-of-fortune who likes to steal British secrets and sell them to overseas swamps of shit."

"A Brit?"

"Yes. Someone in our government service."

Wick rubbed his hands. This was getting extremely interesting, he decided. "It might be best if I don't tell the Chinaman that Her Majesty's Government refers to the Chinese government as a *swamp of shit*."

"It doesn't. I do. So…"

"And it's probably an idea to keep descriptions a tad more brief. Perhaps I should refer to the hawker of secrets as a *mole*."

"He's not a *mole*. Mole suggests someone who works on instruction for a foreign agency. Our chap doesn't seem to care who he flogs his swag to." Raine exhaled slowly. "Alright, *mole* it is. Meet the Chinaman. Tell him we've got a mole who's not overly concerned about the accuracy of the intelligence he's selling to foreign parties. Add that we're all grown-ups – we know China spies on us and China knows we spy on them. We take informed actions as a result. That's one thing. But if our mole approaches China with a load of codswallop, we'd be saddened if China saw fit to do something rash based upon the mole's fake intelligence. The mole is making fools of the foreign countries he or she is selling to. We'd hate China to be one of those duped countries. And the UK has self-interest. We want to catch the blighter in his tracks and prevent him from scuppering our attempts to cautiously build relations with the likes of China. Conclude by saying that while we respect that China will do what it likes with any intelligence gleaned on us, we would be extremely grateful if it would be very circumspect if it was presented with any UK-centric intelligence that seemed too good to be true." Raine leaned back on his chair. "Got it?"

Wick nodded, his heart racing fast, all desires to make quips eradicated from his rapid thoughts. "Does the diplomat know why he's meeting me?"

"He knows the headlines, but needs to hear it again from," he smiled, "a *London apostle*." He looked serious. "He knows there's a Brit selling our secrets. Our man in Berlin has teed up the meeting with that nugget of information. You're meeting the diplomat to reassure him that we're putting a positive spin on our breach when it comes to our view of China."

"I see. What time am I off? Other details?"

Raine handed him a plastic folder containing flight e-ticket printouts and other information. "It's all in there. The Chinaman's expecting you. Only you. You'll also need this." He gave him a black leather zip document holder. "In there is twenty thousand pounds in cash and a mobile phone. The phone is not to be used on anything Wick-related. There's only one number stored in the Contacts lists. It's mine, although it's not my day-to-day number. Still, you'll get me on it, day or night. Don't take the cash and mobile to Munich. You're Alex Wick for the duration of your Germany trip. The money and phone are for when you're back, and solely for use in the UK."

Wick weighed the leather document holder in one hand. "What's going on?"

Raine placed his ankle on the thigh of his other leg and put the tips of his fingers together. "When you get back from Germany I want you to lay low for a while. Don't come back to work; have zero contact with anyone you know; don't tell a soul where you are; not even me. Go somewhere small enough and big enough to fade in to the background. A town makes most sense. You could be on holiday, although it might be an idea to have a general reason as to why you've chosen to stay in the town. Perhaps you're a freelance travel journalist, or similar, and want to soak up the ambience. Something like that. Wherever you go and whoever you are, make sure you stay in the UK and for the time being forget the name Alex Wick. Remember your FCO training. I don't know what they call it now but in my day the instructors used to nickname it *The Going Dark Bit*. I know that segment of the course is aimed at what to do if you need to leg it from an overseas UK consulate or embassy and vanish. Still, the same training principles apply, whether you're in Luanda or Liverpool. The moment you get back onto British terra firma, go off the grid and stay that way until you hear from me."

Wick was uneasy. "Does the Munich trip put me in danger?"

"No, no, no." Raine smiled. "But it does make you an unnecessary potential complication. I want you to do your job and then stay out of the way until we catch the mole. It's for the best. Spend the money on accommodation, grub, other essentials, and anything else that takes your fancy. You don't need to account for a penny. And you'll still be receiving your FCO wage. Just make sure you don't take your wallet, personal phone, or anything else associated with you that can be used to track you down. Remember your training," he repeated.

"My boss..."

"Is taken care of. As far as she's concerned I've taken a layabout off her hands. She was trying to work out what to do with you until you get your first overseas posting. I've solved the problem for her, in the immediate term at least."

"Well, er..." He felt like adrenalin might be kicking in. He composed himself. "Well, this wasn't quite what I expected." He fixed a grin back on his face. It took an effort to do so but at least it tricked part of his brain into thinking everything was normal. "Right you are, sir. Peter, I mean. I won't let you down."

"Good." Raine looked at some other papers on his desk and waved his hand in a gesture that meant he wanted Wick to get out of his room. As Wick walked to the exit, Raine kept his eyes on the documents in front of him and said in a loud voice, "Wick. Don't fuck it up!"

Wick hesitated, opened the door, and left.

Knutsen was in the lounge of the West Square flat, examining his long-range digital camera. It was on a tripod and was a Nikon P1000. Its optical zoom was so immensely powerful that it was able to photograph objects on the surface of the moon. For what it did, the camera was regarded by experts as the best on the market. But it had drawbacks – it was very big, had a slow maximum aperture, and required careful ownership. The ex-cop was giving it the once over.

Sign brought him a coffee. "What do you think?"

Knutsen looked at the camera. "It's good to go."

Sign wanted photographs of Sassoon, Faraday, Duggan, Hare, and Raine. He'd told Knutsen about their nine PM meeting this evening. Given Knutsen only knew what Raine looked like, this evening's meeting was the perfect opportunity for him to put faces to the names of the other Norwegian-speakers. From distance, Knutsen was going to capture their images as they arrived at the meeting location. Sign was going to join his colleague for the jaunt. At eight PM, they'd set up the camera on the south embankment of the River Thames, and ensure its lens was pointing across the river and into the heart of the metropolis.

CHAPTER 7

In a narrow cobbled side street, between The Strand thoroughfare and the north bank of the River Thames, is a bookshop within a short row of buildings that was constructed over two hundred years ago on land that had seen settlements in the Middle Ages and considerably earlier. During the last two centuries, there'd been minimal change to the facades of the side street and other objects within the passageway. The buildings were occasionally scrubbed clean of black car exhaust and brought back to their pristine white regency prime. The four lamps that were erected in 1821 were respectfully maintained to create the impression that they still provided illumination from gas or candle. Save those of an emergency or commercial supplier nature, vehicles were not permitted down the street. There was no pavement, possibly a deliberate omission to deter pedestrian tourists from straying into the hidden gem by accident while escaping the hustle and bustle of The Strand and its noise, theatres, restaurants, and pubs, and Covent Garden's eateries, market stalls, street performers and throngs of idlers carrying cameras and snacks. Whether by design or luck, the side street was a quiet oasis, incongruous amid the vibrancy and urgency of its neighbouring arteries and districts. This came at a cost. As well as the bookshop, there were two other businesses on the seventy yard stretch of old London – a vintners and a timepiece manufacturer. The other buildings were residential. Two of them were owned by former newspaper editors who back in the day enjoyed the walk along The Strand to the part where it became Fleet Street. Three belonged to elderly lords who could reach Westminster on foot if they could be bothered and their aching limbs allowed. One was the hangout of a French painter who'd one-time sold a work of art for a ridiculous sum of money and was therefore able to buy his two million pound London house, even though he subsequently had barely enough money to buy food. Three were the weekday bolt holes for property developers of dubious heritage. And one was owned by a Royal Shakespeare Company actor who'd been the darling of theatre land in the '50s and '60s and had made a fortune in the '70s in British and Hollywood movies before the industry turned its back on his charming hellraising ways and matinee looks when it realised that he was no longer drinking from the bottle but rather the bottle was drinking from him. The vintners, timepiece manufacturer, and bookstore didn't get custom from casual passers-by because there were no passers-by. They struggled. Then again, they'd struggled for two hundred years and they'd probably struggle for another two centuries. They survived, somehow.

It was nine PM. Raine was standing outside the front door of the bookstore. Light from a street lamp illuminated him and the shop's display window. The light was sufficient for Raine to note that the shop's proprietor had recently changed the interior's display to showcase antique books that shared a theme of flora and fauna. Even though Raine privately thought there was little point in changing the store's client-facing displays every week or so, he liked the fact that the shop's owner stubbornly carried on as if business was booming and people cared about the place. The shop had been shut since six PM but Raine knew its owner was in – dim lights were still on within parts of the shop and the residential area above the venue was lit up. He pressed the door's bell.

A woman answered – in her seventies, average height, slightly plump, silver hair that had been immaculately sprayed in place, a pearl necklace resting over a starched high-collar white blouse and cardigan with leather elbow patches, pleated knee-length charcoal grey skirt that had been robust-enough to survive repeated wear since she first wore it at her girls' school in the 1950s, and black shoes that her parents had bought for her for one pound and six shillings but over the subsequent years had cost her nearly one thousand pounds in repairs just to make them look as new as they were when she'd first tried them on and wondered if they matched her new skirt. She deliberately adopted the look, in part because it was practical – she was a widower and had no one to help out in the store and all its associated activities including lugging boxes of dusty books, and delicate restorations requiring a steady hand, razor-sharp blade, and the precision and courage of a surgeon. But equally, like all good spies, she was a master at misdirection. Technically she wasn't a spook anymore, although she was still on the payroll of MI6, listed under *Housekeeping*. Now, she maintained the backroom of her shop as a discrete and unlikely meeting place for members of the secret world. It was her only connection to days gone by. There were so many stories she could have told, were she not modest and cast-iron silent on matters of British national security. Those who'd served with her would sometimes talk about her wayward escapades. There was the time she'd parachuted into the Andes during treacherous wintry weather to locate and assassinate a devil. On another occasion she'd held her nerve while playacting being a billionaire's advisor who was negotiating the release of his kidnapped daughter. That had been as hairy as pulling her parachute's chord while being hammered by two hundred miles per hour ice-laden cross winds. Sitting in a basement in St. Petersburg, across the table from her was the boss of the kidnappers. On her knees in the corner was the billionaire's daughter, bound and gagged and wearing a negligée, a length of razor wire wrapped around her throat and held in position by a very cruel-looking man. The bookstore owner was playing poker with the boss while she had a gun held to her head. The deal was simple – if she won the game of cards, the kidnappers would accept her terms and would release her and the girl. If she lost, she'd get a bullet in her brain and the daughter would lose her head. There were so many other stories. But they were different days. Now they were kept locked up in her memory palace, and were only briefly allowed out to stretch their legs while she warmed her feet by the heater after a long working day and while partaking of a nightcap of single malt.

Raine smiled. "Mrs. Carmichael. It's been too long. I've not been followed."

Mrs. Carmichael stood to one side to let him in and said in a well-spoken, no-nonsense accent and tone, "Bloody diplomats. You really are so terribly amateurish at important matters. Of course you haven't been followed. If you had been tailed you wouldn't be here. Least ways, you *shouldn't* be here." She took his coat and hung it on a stand.

Raine touched her arm, the gesture one of tenderness. "I'm glad to see that nothing's changed."

She reciprocated. "My Peter – always willing to pretend to old ladies that he doesn't know his arse from his elbow." There was a twinkle in her eyes as she smiled.

"You wouldn't want me any other way." He looked at the back of the shop and breathed in deeply. "Are they here?"

"There's four of them. I've never met them before. Was four the number you expected?"

"No more, no less."

"Right you are." Mrs. Carmichael closed the door. "I'll be making a pot of tea, poured onto rum in mugs."

Raine shook his hands as they ached from getting warm. "If you were born a decade or so earlier, you'd have been marshalling French resistance types in the Ardennes forest. Rum-laced tea would have been their tipple on a cold, wet night, methinks. And a damn fine drink it is." He walked through the shop and entered the rear room.

It was the shop's reading room. Though it bore little in common with London's well-known, salubrious, and history-laden reading rooms, the tiny annex was in many ways infinitely more interesting and quirky compared to the likes of the famous rooms in the British Museum and British Library. Barely big enough to hold six people – five was a squeeze – the room was a place for discerning customers to read rare works within an atmosphere of tranquillity and visual stimulation. It contained numerous hard cover leather-bound books on mahogany shelves, a large coffee table, handcrafted by Mr. Carmichael from a Smithfield butcher's block, a gilt-framed painting by Mrs. Carmichael that depicted a studious and bespectacled Victorian gentleman peering at a big open book on a plinth within a library or book-strewn store not unlike the one in the adjacent room, three other similarly-themed paintings, artefacts, a leather sofa and four mismatching leather armchairs, and framed black and white photographs, including one of a young and handsome Mr. Carmichael - before he knew of the existence of Mrs. Carmichael *née Banbury* – standing in an open-air book market in Khartoum.

Raine stood for a moment before sitting in the only vacant chair. "Good evening." He looked at the four people who were sitting in the room.

Detective Chief Superintendent Rex Hare. A high flyer in the Metropolitan Police Service. Head of SO15 – Counter Terrorist Command. The youngest chief superintendent in the Met. A career spent combating the darkest and grimiest depths of crime. Of medium height and average build, the black-haired and green eyed detective looked and sounded nothing like a cop. It took criminals by surprise. That included the man who cut out the eyes, tongues and hearts of three schoolgirls in Blackheath. When Hare caught him on his own, the murderer whimpered and shivered as rain lashed his face and trussed body while Hare smoked a cigarette and ignored his pleas for him to call his colleagues so they could deal with him humanely under the due process of law.

Gordon Faraday. GCHQ. Head of Signals Intelligence Missions, utilising cryptanalysis and mathematics, IT systems, linguistics and translation, and the intelligence analysis unit. The flaxen-haired wizened man had a second string to his bow – that of being part time professor of applied mathematics at the prestigious Massachusetts Institute of Technology, more accurately referred to as MIT. It was a position that had the backing of GCHQ's closest ally, the NSA. And it was one that allowed him to use his academic status to receive The Fields Medal, often referred to as the Nobel Prize of Mathematics.

Hamish Duggan. MI5. Director of counter-espionage, counter-proliferation and protective security. He had unruly brown hair and was built like a prop forward, a frame that was utilised in his younger days as captain of the University of Edinburgh's rugby team, a sport he engaged in with ferocity when not studying law. He still carried on playing until he graduated with a first class degree, despite having his spine reconstructed with steel. Over the years he'd tried to soften his appearance and persona – dapper suits, a leading role in the Civil Service Men's Choir, and at times of need a near-feline character. But, no amount of makeovers and raised vocal octaves could hide his true self: that of a growling, axe-wielding, Highlands clansman.

Edward Sassoon. MI6. Head of all matters Russia and Eastern Europe. Tall, slender, immaculate blonde hair that was cut in the style of an Edwardian aristocrat. He was a chameleon who'd lived so many different lives that it was hard to know if *he* knew who he really was. He did, but even he conceded that his true self was a complex patch-quilt of different influences and experiences. The son of an English Reuters journalist and a French-Russian aid worker, he spent the first seven years of his life in Vientiane, Laos, until his parents put him on a canoe on the Mekong River and pushed him away while they ran in the opposite direction in an attempt to draw the attention of rabid, gun-wielding soldiers. He never saw his mum and dad again. Monks cared for him for years, until he was a young man. He studied medicine at Sorbonne University and was talent spotted by MI6. His career in the service soared to giddy heights. To him the secret world was an intriguing family of sorts, to be manipulated, toyed with, but always ultimately pacified if things got out of hand. He became whoever he wanted to be. But, he always remembered where he came from. In a tiny locked chest in the bottom of his wardrobe in his Chelsea pad was something no one else knew about – the pyjamas he'd worn, age seven, as he'd drifted down the mighty Asian river while staring at the sun by day and the stars by night as tears ran down his face.

Raine, Hare, Faraday, Duggan, and Sassoon.

Raine supposed he was the group's chairman of sorts. He took on the role, not knowing if the others wanted him to have that title. "Thank you all for coming. You know me. I hope you know each other. If not, get introductions out of the way." Nobody said a word. "Good. That saves a bit of time. So, we're live. Today I activated my runner. His name's Alex Wick." He gave them further details about Wick. "At two PM this Saturday he's meeting the Chinese diplomat. His brief is as we agreed."

No one spoke for a few seconds.

Faraday asked in a Mid-Atlantic accent, "You're sure he's up for the job?"

Raine nodded. "I assess him to be unreliable when disinterested, and wholly focused when excited."

Duggan slapped one of his big hands on his thigh, as if he was slamming a try-scoring rugby ball onto turf. When he spoke, it was in the accent of his native Scottish Highlands. "You've lit a fire under the young lad's bum. Good job." The MI5 officer pointed at the others and this time said in a tone and delivery that made him sound like a posh English army officer, "Four more runners waiting in the wings. One belongs to Faraday, one to Sassoon, one to Hare, and one to me. The question is, when do we unleash them?"

Like Wick, the other runners were young and inexperienced. And it was important that together the runners represented the five agencies present in the room. Faraday's runner was a GCHQ officer; Hare's runner was a Met officer; Duggan's was MI5; and Sassoon's was MI6.

Raine answered, "Let's see how my lad Wick gets on. But, success on Saturday only means we've nipped the Chinese in the bud. And whether he is or isn't successful, you'll need to activate your runners quickly. That said, I think we should wait until Wick's back before we make a decision on whether the remaining runners should be deployed incrementally or en masse."

Police officer Hare asked, "What happens if the Chinese tell our other targets that they've been approached by us? What would they say to the other targets?"

It was Sassoon who answered, not looking at him or anyone else in the room, his precise tone of voice carrying an almost ethereal quality. "There is no answer to that. The Chinese *could* tell the Russians that HMG is in panic mode. They *could* ask the Russians whether they too have been approached by us. *If* they do so and *if* the Russians oblige them by saying yay or nay, then the Chinese will have to establish not only whether our agenda is pure, but they'll also have to second guess the Russians. It becomes a quagmire. The truth is in there somewhere but can we be bothered to wade through muck to get to it, et cetera et cetera? Thus, on our part it becomes not an *answer* to your question, detective, but rather a matter of *judgement* in response to your question."

Duggan sighed and addressed Hare. "Put more simply, superintendent…"

Hare raised an eyebrow. "Detective *chief* superintendent."

"Okay. That." Duggan didn't care one iota what ranks cops called each other. "Put more simply, *Mr* Hare, we don't know so we've just got to roll the dice and hope for the best." He looked at Raine. "Anyway, we're speculating. I agree with you. We wait until Wick gets back, and then reconvene."

"Good." Raine looked at the others.

They nodded.

Mrs. Carmichael brought in a tray of drinks and biscuits.

Raine thanked her. When she'd closed the door behind her, he continued after taking a sip from his mug, adopting the same timbre he used when he was an ambassador in Washington and Paris, addressing members of his embassy. "I have spoken to you individually, but not as a group. Nothing I'm about to say to you is new. But, I will repeat myself so that all of us are in absolutely no doubt that this group is armed with the same data and is singing from the same hymn sheet." He paused, watching them, before proceeding. "Our overriding priority is to protect CHALICE. The breaches that we know about are as follows: first, MI5 identifies a Syrian spy in London – the spy is urgently rescued by the Syrians; second, a Russian diplomat walk-in offers his service to an FCO diplomat in Hong Kong – the Russian diplomat is assassinated by the Russians; third, a Mexican drug cartel plans to flood the streets of British cities with a new drug – the cartel turns its boats around before reaching the UK; fourth, a terrorist cell plans to blow up a shopping mall in Edinburgh – instead it hits summer festivities in a touristy Cotswold village, killing nineteen; fifth, MI6 plans to capture a war criminal aboard his yacht in the Caribbean – the war criminal isn't on the yacht on the day of the assault, sets a trap, his team kills the MI6 team; and sixth, GCHQ is gaining gold intel from an intercept operation against a major arms dealer – the dealer and his team conduct a campaign of misinformation." The senior FCO official's voice grew sombre. "All this mayhem and we can't stop the blighter. The traitor is winning his or her skirmishes, and by God they're nasty skirmishes. But CHALICE is winning the war against terrorism, rogue nations, nuclear and chemical proliferation, major organised international crime, hostile espionage, and cyberattacks. It's down to us to get this bit of grit out of CHALICE's workings."

"Bit of grit?" Duggan laughed. "That's a bloody understatement."

"Enough, Hamish." Raine leaned forward. "For the record and so we're clear - no one, repeat no one, else knows the five of us are collaborating. No politicians, no agency colleagues, no spouses, lovers, anyone."

Hare said, "Mrs. Carmichael knows we're here."

Raine said quickly and with irritation, "She only knows me and she'd rather hurl herself from a thousand feet onto The Shard's spike than disclose what goes on in her shop. She doesn't know what we're discussing and nor would she ever want to know. The secret is in this room." Raine wanted to take the tension out of the meeting. "So far we've lost the fights against the mole's skirmishes. So, we must be unconventional. I've mustered a band of irregulars." He swept his hand in front of him. "Us lot. The generals and their soldiers don't know we exist. We pick up arms, get the problem resolved, and when it's done we disband and go back to our day jobs."

Hare said, "You told me we had clearance to assemble and consider this tactic, even though it's all off the record."

Raine stared at him. "I lied. You knew I lied and you don't give a damn that we don't have a safety net. We proceed. Problem?"

Hare was surprised by the diplomat's forthright and rifle-shot accurate assessment of his state of mind. He shrugged. "No problem."

Sassoon wasn't listening to any of this. Instead he was staring at the ceiling. "I find it most instructive that the traitor only steals intelligence that doesn't contain the identity of the source."

"Oh here we go." Duggan shook his head. "Bloody poncy MI6 riddles. Or more likely Edward Sassoon poncy riddles." The seasoned MI5 operative asked with resignation, "What are you wittering on about, comrade? All CHALICE reports omit source ID. You know that."

Sassoon angled his head and nodded, eyebrows raised. "For sure, dear fellow. I do however find it rather… interesting that our naughty boy pinches reports whose value is unaltered by the omission of its author's name."

Faraday pointed. "The Zulus are just about to come over the horizon and attack Rorke's Drift. Who cares who the author of that intel is? Stack up the sandbags and make ready the infantry."

"Yes. But what if the Zulus are fifty miles away and are *thinking* about whether they should attack. The Rorke's Drift commander would need to know more about the Zulu intel and would need to know its author so he could make an assessment about the author's credibility, before the commander cancelled all sleep and put his garrison on high alert." Sassoon briefly glanced at Faraday. "Our naughty boy only steals intelligence where the author's identity is irrelevant. He nicks the juicy, immediate-action, stuff. He can't flog the *getting into the mind of a Russian spymaster* long-game stuff. I find it all very instructive."

This time it was Raine who couldn't hold back. "You're talking in circles, or riddles, or whatever you're bloody well saying! The traitor steals immediate-action intel because it sells without the sources ID. He can't sell long-game intelligence without a source name. It's as simple as that. There's nothing *instructive* to be had. And, for the last time, *all* CHALICE intel – regardless as to whether it's immediate-action or long-game – has no source ID."

Sassoon shrugged. "I concede it says little that we don't know already about the traitor's modus operandi. Therefore, on that level, it most certainly is *not* instructive. But I wasn't referring to our ne'er-do-well. I was referring to *our* efforts."

"Jesus Christ…" Faraday was about to add more.

But Sassoon held up his hand. "I am merely reflecting. Think nothing of my meanderings." He looked straight at Raine. Lesser men would have been completely unsettled by his gaze. "Continue."

Raine held Sassoon's gaze for a moment, then looked around. "I suggest we meet back here at the same time Monday evening. By then I'll have spoken to my runner. Agreed?"

They nodded.

Raine was relieved the meeting was over. Sitting in the room with three spooks and one detective was not his idea of fun. "Same time Monday, then." He stood.

"Hang on." Duggan held up his hand and quickly regretted doing so. "We need code words for us and the person we're trying to catch. Code words that only we use."

Raine smiled. "You lot love your code words. But yes, why not. Any thoughts?"

Sassoon spoke first. "We meet here." He swept his hand in the air. "It is quiet. I like the ambience. And the books are an engaging touch. Maybe we should call ourselves *The Library*."

Duggan nodded slowly, as he digested the phrase. "Yeah. The Library. I like it."

Raine looked around. Hare and Faraday nodded. "So, we are The Library. Now, what shall we call our..." he looked at Sassoon, "ne'er-do-well?"

Hare said, "Maybe something cryptic. No, not cryptic. Something nonsensical, something..."

Faraday was dismissive when he muttered, "Bloody cops don't know a thing about intelligence work."

Before Hare could speak Sassoon interjected. While looking at his watch he said, "In less than sixty seconds, forty seconds I'll wager, Detective Chief Superintendent Hare will give us the perfect codename for our quarry." He looked straight at the detective and said, "Don't think of this as an intelligence operation. We're not looking for a traitor, or a mole, or any variations therein. We're seeking a highly intelligent person who steals our crown jewels. For certain he's going to need a fence, I believe you call them." He glanced at the others. "Our ne'er-do-well won't have the overseas connections to sell his jewels, or if he does he will want a cut out to broker deals. There's another code name to throw into the pot – *The Fence*, whoever that may be."

Raine was silent. The dead broker Torbjørn Lystad had now become The Fence. And it was Sassoon who'd mentioned a broker.

Sassoon returned his attention to Hare. "Think. What are we doing here? What is the nature of the problem we're facing?"

The detective was deep in thought. "It's... it's like. No, it *is* a police operation. He steals things. People like me try to identify him and arrest him."

"Bravo, detective." Sassoon kept watching him. "Nearly there." He looked at his watch. "I've got a wager, remember."

Hare smiled. "The person we're after is a thief. Yes! He's *The Thief*."

"Excellent!" Sassoon looked at Raine and said in a quiet voice. "That's a bottle of Old Tawny port you owe me. The forty year tipple, I might add. But I'll tell you what, dear fellow, I'll bequeath it to our chief police officer here. He deserves the reward."

Raine chuckled. "Whatever you say, Edward. Right. *The Thief* it is. Nine PM sharp on Monday. I'm optimistic I'll be the bearer of good news."

Thirty minutes later Raine was walking towards London Liverpool Street station to get a train home. Before entering the station, he called Sign and gave him a summary of the meeting. Sign listened carefully, bade him a good evening, and ended the call.

The former MI6 officer was by the fire in his lounge. He opened up the computer's 'CHALICE' file. He erased the word 'Traitor' in the central square and replaced it with *The Thief*. He drew a complete circle around the outside of the five Norwegian-speaker boxes and put a note next to it – *The Library*. In the 'Dead' box containing Lystad he added *The Fence* next to the man's name. Thanks to Knutsen's IT literacy, the five Norwegian-speaker boxes now had one photo each in them. Knutsen's shots had been perfect. There was no mistaking the images of Faraday, Hare, Duggan, Sassoon, and Raine.

Knutsen entered the lounge, having just had a post-run shower. He poured two drinks of cognac, handed one of the glasses to Sign, and sat in his chair.

Sign pressed a button to swivel the whiteboard around so that his colleague could read the updates on what was on there.

Knutsen studied it for a minute. "Looking at this, the solution seems so obvious. Kill everyone in The Library." He smiled and took a sip of his drink. "I'm joking."

"I've considered it as an option." Sign's expression was deadpan. "Seriously. It *is* an option. Four innocents would die, but in the grand scheme of things their sacrifice is a drop in the ocean compared to the damage caused by The Thief."

Knutsen pressed the button so that the whiteboard swivelled back to Sign. "We're not going to murder The Library."

"No, we're not." Sign saved the document and shutdown the computer. He leaned back in his armchair and swirled the cognac in his brandy glass. "We're not assassins."

"Apart from that time in Dubrovnik."

"More akin to euthanasia."

"Pretoria."

"A regrettable mix up."

"Addis Ababa."

"We were suffering from altitude sickness and weren't ourselves." He arched his back. "We're not going to kill The Library because that would mean killing Peter. I quite like Peter. Also, he's rather good at preventing wars. Best we let him be."

"That's agreed then. What's happening next?"

Sign told him about Wick's trip to Munich the day after tomorrow.

"Do you want me to go to Germany and keep an eye on him?"

Sign shook his head. "The thought had occurred to me. We must let this play out. There can be no interference, even if interventions are well intentioned."

"Are you sure?"

"No."

CHAPTER 8

It was Friday lunchtime.

Gordon Faraday was in GCHQ's headquarters in the outskirts of west England's market town of Cheltenham. Technically, his office was in an open-plan segment of the huge, circular, main building, but he preferred to work in one of the many smaller buildings that surrounded the primary building. He liked to think his de facto office was in a World War Two Nissen hut - the type they had in the grounds of Bletchley Park, the English country-manor codebreaking facility that was the precursor to GCHQ. His office wasn't in a steel prefabricated Ministry of Defence construction, but rather was in a nondescript bricks and mortar tiny structure that could seat eight analysts but in reality and on his insistence only seated him. Faraday liked the peace and quiet to concentrate. What mattered to him were numbers. People were a distraction. And yet that wasn't strictly true. The other reason he liked to keep his pretend Nissen hut empty of others was because he liked to populate the work space with real people who were now dead – the brilliant Bletchley minds of numismatist Joan Clarke, chess champions Hugh Alexander and Stuart Milner-Barry, mathematician Bill Tutte, historian Harry Hinsley, and logician Alan Turing. He imagined them working in near silence, only occasionally looking up to express progress or lack of progress on cracking the likes of the Enigma machine, and so many other problems, or pacing back and forth while frustratingly articulating a self-loathing annoyance with a mental roadblock.

As Faraday ate his homemade lunch of a corned beef and mustard sandwich, he imagined one of his pretend colleagues asking him if he'd care to join the rest of the hut for a spot of cricket on the green. Not today, he'd tell them. In just two hours this morning he'd single-handedly completed a job that would have taken most of his peers weeks if not months to solve – cracking the interception of a one-time-code burst transmission from a Russian spy in Lisbon to her handler in Sevastopol. But the imaginary game of cricket would have to wait because he was currently grappling with a different subject-matter that was way beyond the purview of numbers and his brain – that of morality. A young officer, a runner as The Library called him, had been sent in to the field, unarmed with the full facts and think-on-your-feet experience to deal with unpredictable variables. And yet it was essential for the runner to be an uninformed pawn in a game of such high stakes. But what happened if something went wrong? Maybe Alex Wick would fluff his lines, the Chinaman could laugh at him, mock his ineptitude, instruct him to tell the British government to go fuck themselves because they'd sent a child to do a man's job, and Wick could return to England a shattered reflection of his former self. These things happened. If, for whatever reason, Wick's mission failed, Wick's career could be destroyed. The Library would be to blame. Faraday sighed. His numbers knew the answer to this conundrum – runners needed to be put at risk for the sake of the bigger picture. But numbers didn't look at a shell-shocked fellow whose hand was shaking so much he could barely lift a cup of tea. Faraday pushed the remnants of his lunch away and wondered if he was doing the right thing.

Detective chief superintendent Rex Hare had increasingly wondered about the differences between intelligence officers and cops. It was a complex question because, as far as he could ascertain, defining the makeup of an intelligence officer was in itself nuanced and variable. In large part this was because each organisation within the intelligence community was very different, and thus the types of people each agency recruited were different In the UK, GCHQ recruited personnel who were wholly unsuitable for the work of MI6 and vice versa. MI6 officers were a different breed of animal compared to those in MI5 and Cheltenham. And, since Hare had been CHALICE-cleared and granted access to the secret world, he'd had contact with other agencies and units. In Britain that had included Special Forces, Defence Intelligence, and the Joint Terrorism Analysis Centre. Exposure to overseas organisations included contact with operatives from the United States' Central Intelligence Agency, Federal Bureau of Investigation, and Drug Enforcement Administration, France's Direction Générale de la Sécurité Extérieure, Germany's Bundesnachrichtendienst, Italy's Agenzia Informazioni e Sicurezza Esterna, and even Russia's Sluzhba Vneshney Razvedki Rossiyskoy Federatsii. Each agency was different. The people inside each organisation were different. And then there was the problem of trying to discern common personality traits of cops. My goodness, in his experience that task was a fool's errand. Though they'd all started out in uniform and with a desire to punish lawbreakers, thereafter commonalities between cops ended. There were those suited to street work, pedestrian policing, mobile policing, detective work, community liaison, rural or urban beats, firearms, non-firearms, quasi-intelligence work, leadership roles, team or loner or two-man partner roles, deskbound analysis and administration, those who liked to work with dogs, others who like to police while on horseback, tactical squads, and the list went on. He was a mishmash of some of those things, but that was to be expected given his rank. Most cops beneath his grade chose their individual path and stuck to it throughout their career. Trying to identify the makeup of an intelligence officer was as hard as trying to do the same with cops. It was a minefield before one even attempted to compare cops to intelligence officers. And yet there was one thing he knew for sure: put a police officer and an intelligence officer in the same room and one could tell within seconds who was who.

They did have one thing in common. Police officers and Intelligence Officers dealt with matters that other members of societies never saw or should never see. He reflected on this as he stood in one of Paddington Green police station's sixteen high-security subterranean cells. He was there because there had been a problem. A suspect terrorist had been arrested. At some point during his arrest, transportation to London's highest security police station, or preliminary interview, he'd been brutally assaulted by one or more officers. Hare needed to get to the truth. Other officers were in the room. The suspect was sitting behind a desk, his wrists and ankles in cuffs. His head was face down on the table, but he looked up when Hare took a step towards him. He was young, maybe early twenties, Anglo-Pakistani, face puffy and bloody, eyes scared. He was here because he had masters who'd told him to plan something that others didn't like. Hare thought he was a piece of scum. Then again, no doubt the young man thought the same about him. He wondered how he'd feel if his young runner was caught, doing his bidding, and beaten to a pulp by people who despised him. He would, he decided, go somewhere private, smoke too many cigarettes and drink more than one glass of beer, and then next day brush himself off and carry on while knowing that his life had yet again been shortened by at least one year.

The last time Hamish Duggan could remember feeling this tetchy was in southern Ireland back in '91. Then, he'd been a young MI5 officer who'd been deliberately withheld from operational duties, in what should have been his burgeoning formative years, in favour of priming him for a strike against the Irish Republican Army. HMG wanted to know who in the IRA was managing the arrivals of armaments from Libya into the Irish southern coastline near Cork. And it wanted to know the human chain of IRA operatives who were involved in getting the guns and other weapons from Cork to Belfast. Britain's plan was direct and ruthless: identify the smuggling chain, and deploy an SF unit from the 'Det' to one-by-one kill them all. Duggan's role was the starting point. To attempt the momentously risky task, Duggan had to pose as a Scottish mercenary who'd returned from Africa and was considering using his ill-gotten gains to purchase a farm near the town of Kinsale, approximately twenty miles south west of Cork. The farm was chosen for a reason – it was owned by a young Irish woman called Cara who'd been a widow for fourteen months after her husband had been killed by a Royal Anglian Regiment bullet. She'd distracted her grief by making bombs for the IRA. It was assessed Cara must know the gun smuggler. Duggan had to get close to her, charm her, do whatever was necessary to gain her trust, maintain the fiction of wanting to buy her property and thereby solve her financial woes, and ultimately get the name of the man the Brits wanted to eliminate. It was all going so well until Irish men had barged in to Cara's kitchen and caught her and Duggan in a somewhat delicate embrace on Cara's kitchen table. There was no embarrassment to be had by Cara. She'd laughed and spoke to the gun-brandishing men like they were her brothers. She'd wised up to Duggan and sold him out to the IRA. That realisation had made him tetchy.

Now, he was sitting in his office in MI5's headquarters in Thames House on the north bank of The River Thames. The interior of Thames House was different from that of MI6. It was tasteful, beautifully and creatively lit, contained marbled floors, oak-panelled walls, paintings, sculptures amid dramatic atriums that stretched from ground floor to roof and were illuminated by searchlights, and was delicately fragranced with electrically-charged air fresheners that alternated emissions of pine and cinnamon and flowers depending on the season. By contrast, the interior of MI6 was functional and stripped to the bones, reflective of the transient nature of its occupants, and had about as much appeal as the décor of temporary office floor space rented by fly-by-night, cold-calling, chop stock brokerage firms who needed to pick up their computer terminals and run if government regulators and cops knocked on their door. And the exteriors and locations of MI5 and MI6 were deliberately different. MI5's Thames House smacked of pride and stoicism, the 1930s building being only a stone's throw from the Houses of Parliament. MI5 was the government's Pretorian Guard. It was trusted and kept very close to the seat of power. MI6 was on the south bank of the river, in the rather down-at-the-heel Vauxhall Cross. Kept well away from the pomp and ceremony of London's elite epicentre, MI6 was a bastard rogue warrior; a necessary evil that was allowed to rampage on behalf of HMG but could never be trusted to enter its castle fortifications. Thus, its building was a fortress in itself, projecting an image that was wholly suited to the nature of its role and the tasks it gave its operatives. The MI6 building was suggestive of a lone operative who'd been dropped deep behind enemy lines. It was isolated, armed to the teeth, and had an expression that said *leave me alone and fuck off or accept the consequences of ignoring what I just said.*

Duggan paid no heed to his surroundings. He was staring at an A4 piece of paper, on which he'd written notes. It had taken him over twelve months to orchestrate the operation that was supposed to have come to fruition today. Twelve months of piecing together mountains of intel, running and tasking sources to bolster the intel, creating strands of misdirection to befuddle and trick his quarry, numerous complex surveillance details, collaboration with agencies he didn't particularly like or respect, deployment of officers under deep cover, and so many exhausting long days and nights. All that to catch an Irish man giving ten million dollars to a Lebanese woman in a PIRA safe house in Battersea. This morning he'd sent in the heavy mob to nab the terrorist couple *in flagrante delicto*. They'd been there, sitting together, drinking coffee, making small talk. But, there was no ten million dollars. Without the dollars, there was no successful sting operation. The couple had laughed at the paramilitary MI5 officers, standing there in their fire-retardant tactical attire and pointing their M3 Super 90 shotguns and G36 Carbines at them. The couple had been cuffed and searched, the room searched, the couple questioned. There was nothing to be had. With smirks on their faces, the couple had threatened legal action. The MI5 officers removed the cuffs and vanished. Twelve months for nothing.

Duggan continued scrutinising his notes. He'd written down every possible angle in the operation, every human input, anything that could have caused a leak that had tipped off the couple. He rubbed his face and punched his index finger against one word. It was the only word on the paper that could explain the origin of the security breach. Just one word.

CHALICE.

The Thief had dealt his latest card.

In the neighbourhood of Goutte D'Or in Paris, the district - commonly known as Little Africa - was abuzz with locals heralding from North African and Sub-Saharan former French colonies. Senegalese, Tunisian, Algerians and many others who'd adopted Paris were shopping in the bustling street-market for food, clothes, and other items. The skin colours of people in the street varied, from the black pearl sheen of those who were from the equator to the polished bronze tone of people closer to the Mediterranean to the snowy pigmentation of locals and tourists of northern hemisphere genus. Languages were manifold, some correct to their native land, others a mongrel bastardisation of two or more tongues injected with street slang and colloquialisms. Pedestrians' expressions were focused, jovial, uncertain, nonchalant, or impatient. Everyone was loud, trying to shout over each other and the pervasive and discordant blend of music from systems up and down the street playing pop and rock.

The nuanced environment suited Sassoon. He was here to buy ingredients for the Provençal fish stew bouillabaisse, which he would make this evening once he'd taken the Eurostar train back to London. He was also here to meet a spy.

Today he looked nothing like an aristocrat. He was wearing desert boots, blue jeans, and a quarter-zip, heavyweight cream-wool, submariner's jumper. He had no hat to cover his blonde hair that today was deliberately tousled, though he was wearing wrap-around mountaineering sunglasses to counter the day's bright light. On one shoulder was slung a hiking daysack, containing his alias passport, today's edition of *Libération*, and two cooler blocks.

He stopped by a large stall selling fresh and dried fish. The venue's aroma of the sea was intermingled with the scents of Moroccan oils and soaps from an adjacent stall and with the beguiling fragrances of sumac, saffron, cumin, forest dried nettles, berbere, harrisa, wild za'atar, and other vibrantly coloured herbs and spices atop a nearby cart that was designed to be pulled by a wooden pony but these days was dragged in to position by a shopkeeper of Spanish and Mauritanian origin. Sassoon examined the fish stall's catches of the day. In fluent French he asked the vendor to bag-up half a kilo each of red rascasse, sea robin, and European conger.

A man stood by his side. He was twenty years old, French of Algerian descent, and was wearing clothes that suggested he could be an underground DJ, street poet, or gang member. "Good fish, mister," he said in heavily accented English.

"Yes," Sassoon replied. He took possession of his purchase, put the bag of fish in the main body of his rucksack, and peered at the other produce on the stall's bed of ice. "Was your bus late?"

The twenty year old shook his head. "Ma brother big problem. His girl cause trouble. Brother need me to speak to her. Calm her down, you know?"

"I see." Sassoon addressed the vendor and asked for a medley of gilt-head bream, mullet, turbot, hake, and monkfish as well as a separate bag of octopus, sea urchins, mussels, and velvet crabs. After putting the produce in his bag and paying the shopkeeper, he sauntered through the market. The twenty year old stayed by his side. "I'm less interested in your brother's lady problems. I'm rather more intrigued as to when he's likely to press the button."

"I… I no…"

Sassoon switched to French, repeating his statement.

The man looked around, petrified that someone might hear their conversation.

Sassoon had chosen to meet in the crowded venue for a reason. "You belong here." He gestured to the market stalls and throngs of people buzzing around them. "It's a place of beauty. If circumstances were different, you should come here more often and talk to people. They're like you. They want to create passion amid the everyday ritual of purchasing food for the table and clothes for their families' backs."

"I know some people here."

"That's a shame because one day – poof! All this may be gone. Displays will be spoiled. People will be spoiled. No more music. Banter is replaced by moans of agony. Cigarette and weed smoke is replaced by cordite. Places like this are turned into carnage by hooligans who want to be brainwashed by religion so they can have their figurative Friday-night-on-the-lash fisticuffs."

The man didn't have a clue what Sassoon was talking about.

Sassoon knew that. "What time is your brother planting the bomb in Marché aux Puces de St-Ouen?" He was referring to the biggest 'flea market' in Paris, possibly the largest in the world.

The man bowed his head. "Eleven in the morning, tomorrow."

"Will you be there when it happens?"

"I drop him there in his car. I wait. He comes back when he's done. We leave."

They reached the end of the market. Sassoon stopped and looked back along the bustling street. "I'm going to tweak the plan. You'll drop your brother off, wait until he's out of sight in the market, and then you'll get out of the car and walk. Keep walking until you're tired. Then get a train or bus or taxi, I don't care which, out of Paris. You won't be touched. Never come back to Paris. Never speak to anyone you know here. Start a new life far away from here."

"My home…"

"Will not be your home if you're dead!" Sassoon looked at him. "You've done very well. The French wanted to string you up. You understand? I made sure that wasn't going to happen. But, I can't guarantee they won't change their mind at some point in the future. I've bought you some time to escape." He withdrew the newspaper and handed it to the man. "Taped inside there are the means to give you breathing space and to start afresh. After that, you're on your own. Get a job. Start selling your paintings. Be your own man."

The spy looked at the newspaper. "Why you do this for me?"

Sassoon shrugged. "You seem like a decent chap."

"What… what will happen to my brother?"

"He will be executed on site by expert marksmen from France's GIGN. They won't miss."

The man was silent.

Sassoon put his hand on the man's shoulder. "You knew from the outset this was going to happen. Your brother is going to die. If you tell him what's going to happen tomorrow, he'll be killed on another day and in another location. GIGN's in death-squad mode. They won't stop until what's left of your brother's body is in the morgue. And if you don't stick to my plan, almost certainly you'll be caught up in all this. If that happens, I won't be able to protect you." He tightened his grip and asked commandingly, "Have you got this, soldier?"

The young man nodded.

"Your courage is commendable." He stepped back and smiled. "One day I hope to walk into a small gallery on the Mediterranean shores of Montpellier and buy a painting from a man who looks just like you." He saluted. "Bonne chance, mon ami."

He turned and walked off, meandering between market stragglers, sometimes visible to the young man, sometimes not, until he vanished.

Pater Raine was in a place that right now he didn't want to be – the Foreign and Commonwealth Office; more specifically one of the grandiose meeting rooms reserved for the most senior members of the diplomatic corps, government ministers, and visiting dignitaries.

He was sitting at a twenty-seater oak table, a handcrafted piece of furniture that had been hewn from an aged tree by British cavalrymen in the Crimean War after an allied Sardinian musket sharpshooter had got badly injured and tangled in the oak's highest branches and could only be lowered to the ground by felling the tree. Around the table were other senior diplomats, the FCO permanent undersecretary, and the secretary of state. The wags in the corps dubbed these weekly encounters *Around The World In Eighty Minutes*. In reality the meetings usually took closer to three hours. They were time-consuming but necessary board-level updates on the good, bad, and stagnant issues that were affecting the existence of over seven and a half billion people living on a ball that rotated at one thousand miles per hour. One by one, the senior mandarins gave updates from their plots of land. There was talk of Irish fishermen boarding French vessels in the North Sea and viciously assaulting the Frenchmen with cod; informed speculation that a prominent Asian premier would step down due to complaints that he'd chastised his female members of staff for talking too much; latest news on the Finnish figure-skater who'd been incarcerated in North Korea on charges of espionage; an update on the Kivu conflict in the eastern Congo and corroborated reports that one of its key Hutu warlords had been eaten by a lion; disagreement over whether the Australian prime minister should sit on the same table as his New Zealand counterpart, at the forthcoming Buckingham Palace Commonwealth Gala dinner, after the Australian's unfortunate description of the Auckland accent; a new farcical turf war between chilli growers and coca plant farmers in the Peruvian mountains; a blow-by-blow update on every military and humanitarian engagement involving Great Britain and its closest allies; and unanimous consent that a blanket media ban must be maintained on the terrible scandal surrounding the Welsh women's book club in Winnipeg.

CHALICE wasn't mentioned. That subject was reserved for other forums.

Raine's brain tuned in and out as others spoke, but for the most part he just plainly and simply wanted to be any place but here. He wasn't in the mood. The huge room didn't help his temperament – red carpet, gold this, gold that, gold more or less everything apart from the carpet and blue chairs. Even the huge paintings were done with gold oils, or bronze, or tawny, or any other variation that blended with a colour scheme that would make Fort Knox blush with envy. Opulence and superiority didn't even begin to describe the décor of parts of the FCO headquarters. And the paintings didn't help – Union Jack flags planted on South Sea beaches by eighteenth century Royal Navy captains; kings and queens sitting on their thrones; sea battles; dukes in hunting gear and on horseback; and various scoundrels on one knee with a sword on their shoulder as they received knighthoods. Though he could, at times and only if he wished, deploy the statesmanship and manners of the finest British leaders, Raine had gone to a rough school and grew up in a loft in Kent where he read adventure books and dreamed of seeing the world. All of this regal showmanship was not for him. Still, outwardly he played the game. Inwardly, right now he was looking at the paintings and couldn't prevent a trace of a smile appearing on his face. He imagined sneaking in to the room late at night and swapping the paintings with his own. *Athena posters - tennis girl scratching her bum; Bob Marley smoking a joint; CND logo; Duran Duran; Rick Astley; Kajagoogoo*. Well, they were Wick's choice but given Raine's current location he couldn't help but agree with the young diplomat's suggestion. Wick had more verve in his heart than the entire collective of designers and architects who'd put this vainglorious place together. Raine liked Wick. So, why had he got the lad involved in Library business?

"Peter? Peter? Peter?!"

Raine snapped out of his reverie and looked at the head of state for foreign affairs. "Yes?"

"Your update – if it's not too much to ask?"

Raine composed himself. "My update. Yes." He looked around the table. "The world's still a pile of dog poo and..."

"Peter!" The permanent undersecretary was not pleased.

Raine smiled. "Alright, alright." He sighed. "Updates on negotiations with Washington. We're heading towards a deal on the Dolby extradition issue." He carried on talking, providing a superbly constructed verbal summary of the salient points, the nuances of the legal case, and his jaw-dropping, clever solution. But, he wasn't really listening to a word he was speaking, and his brain might as well have been in neutral on the matter at hand. Instead, he was thinking about Wick. The Munich job was such a simple task, he told himself. His runner only had a minor part to play in the identification and capture of The Thief. It was the job of The Library to confront any danger. The Library had the brains, capabilities, and experience to do that. And what of Wick when he was allowed back to regular work? Due to the structure of the young man's career path, he would be sent on his first overseas posting once he'd done his compulsory three years in London. But that was twenty four months away. In the interim it appeared that London didn't know what to do with him. At best he'd be fed scraps of work, here and there; nothing important; nothing as seemingly innocuous yet vital like the German job. Wick's enthusiasm and enquiring mind could become nullified by inactivity. That would be a great shame. Perhaps that could be addressed. Raine was in need of an *aide-de-camp*. Having a dynamic and intelligent assistant would be of tremendous value to the senior diplomat. But the role would also be a superb opportunity for Wick. Raine couldn't think of any other junior diplomats who'd been given such an opportunity. Wick would travel, be involved in meetings of the highest priority, watch Raine, learn from Raine, and ultimately have two years of a rollercoaster ride of dizzying proportions. Raine's wife was an excellent judge of character. When he'd tell her what he was planning, she'd insist on meeting the young man, probably give him dinner because she'd want to feed him up, and after dinner and in private she'd say to Raine that Wick was a perfect choice and that her husband was being a lovely softy because the real reason he'd given Wick the job was because he viewed him as the son her never had. He'd have her backing. Thus, it was a superb idea, That was settled. Wick would be his aide-de-camp upon his return. No more cloak and dagger stuff. Time for the young man to focus on principled matters of arch diplomacy.

He finished talking and looked around. Others were jabbering away ten to the dozen. He didn't listen to them. A question kept buzzing around in his brain.

Why, of why, couldn't Wick have been someone he didn't particularly like?

CHAPTER 9

SATURDAY

Wick was in a taxi and only ten minutes out of Munich Airport, his Lufthansa flight from Heathrow having landed in Germany at close to noon. The taxi was taking him to the Hotel Opéra, a boutique luxury hotel located in the heart of the city. That's where he was going to meet the Chinese diplomat in under two hours' time.

In broken German he asked the taxi driver to stop approximately three hundred yards from the hotel, repeated the instruction in English when it was clear the driver didn't understand Wick's dire attempt at the local language, got out and slowly walked. Three hundred yards – that's all he had to soak up the city, before reaching his accommodation and making preparations for his meeting. Still, it was better than nothing and in any case was par for the course unless one was on a posting overseas. He'd heard older, more experienced, diplomats talking about the numerous trips they'd made to places where they'd seen nothing of the country they'd landed in – fly in at night, taxi to hotel, hotel is like any other five star hotel elsewhere in the world, meet someone important in the hotel's fine dining restaurant, eat something that could be served by a fine dining restaurant one thousand miles away, grab a few hours' sleep, check out first thing, taxi back to the airport before the sun rises, fly home to London. At least in Munich Wick had his three hundred yards, in daylight. Had he more time, he would have liked to have seen the baroque architecture and grandeur of Bernheimer-Haus, the Bavarian beer gardens and halls, take a ride on a tram, eat fresh fish from the Danube in Viktualienmarkt, go to the enchanting The Rose Island to stand in the place where King Maximillian II, Ludwig II, Tsarina Maria Alexandrowna and Richard Wagner looked over the waters of Lake Starnberg towards the Alps, maybe catch an evening show at the lively and fun Drehleier Theater, and do so many other things. To do the things he'd read about, Wick needed time. But, he'd be returning to London immediately after conveying his message. His first trip to Germany was nothing more than a scant foray. Still, he absorbed what he could hear and see – police cars whose sirens sounded nothing like those in the UK; German tongues of perambulating tourists and locals whose intonation suggested they belonged to people who were articulating an orderly and business-like running checklist of the city's inventory; independent shops selling art, antiques, tea, and huge slices of eye-catchingly indulgent cakes; and flecks of snow that were buffeted in the air by swirls of light wind and didn't look threatening enough to cause problems for the airport's runways.

He reached the Hotel Opéra. It was adjacent to the charming Anna Square, and its restaurants and stores, and a stone's throw from the Pinakothek museums, Lenbachhaus, Bavarian State Opera and Munich Residenz. The small hotel's exterior was elegant and smacked of monied refinement, but was near identical to the neighbouring, attached nineteenth-century converted houses. However, inside was a pristine cavern of Romanesque meets German Renaissance and Romanticism splendour, with marbled floors, thick stone columns that went from base to high ceilings, long and heavy sashes of rich coloured velvet and linen, an eclectic mix of reproduction masterpiece paintings by Albrecht Dürer, Caspar Friedrich, Michelangelo da Caravaggio, Johann Bockhorst, and Raphael, small tea-time tables and chairs inside a conservatory and garden that resembled an opulent Roman spa, and wall mirrors that played tricks on the eyes and suggested to guests' reflections that hidden in corners behind them were blue, gold, white, and red jewels and metals.

After checking in, Wick went to his room. He'd been advised by the receptionist that all of the other bedrooms were occupied and were different in style. He now wondered if Peter Raine had carefully chosen the style of room he wanted Wick to be in. The place was stylish, whimsical, yet also made complete sense. As well as the bedroom and bathroom, there was an adjoining meeting room containing rich cream carpet, large sapphire ceiling light, weighty satin curtains that were held open by silver-platted clasps, Biedermeier south German walnut coffee table, and two matching golden chairs and a sofa. Wick imagined the room was of the standard and design required by a Bavarian premier to host a visiting Manchurian high emissary of the Qing Dynasty.

He entered the bedroom, parked his small trolley bag and briefcase, and placed his suit holder on the bed. After hanging his winter coat, he stripped out of his smart-casual attire until he was naked, and carefully removed all items from his suit holder – a bespoke royal navy suit by Savile Row's esteemed Henry Poole & Co, from the same couturier a white double-cuff and cutaway-collar shirt, plain square platinum cufflinks, his trusted highly polished *Church's* black shoes, M&S socks, *Tom Ford* boxer briefs that his mum had bought for him in Harrods and said while handing the purchase to him, "No man-made fibres, so you won't get a rash down there", and a Claret Stag Head silk tie from *Huntsman*. Aside from the *Marks & Sparks* socks, he wouldn't have been able to afford any of this on his salary. He'd not asked them to buy the finery, but he had his wealthy parents to thank for the wardrobe. His parents had ulterior motives. His mother thought her son looked like a young Hugh Grant who needed the telephone number of Colin Firth's tailor. As if it wasn't bad enough trying to get his head around that, his father once told him man-to-man that the only time a gentleman should not be impeccably dressed is when he has a buxom beauty's thighs wrapped around his waist.

After he'd removed all apparel from its plastic, cloth, or paper protection, he laid out each item on top of the duvet, aligned with the same precision a young Household Cavalry officer cadet might deploy before awaiting a room inspection by his commanding officer. With his toiletry bag in hand, he entered the bathroom, shaved, showered, applied lotions and a dash of Penhaligon's *Blenheim* eau de toilette, and attended to his hair. Back in the bedroom, he dressed, examined himself in a full-length mirror, entered the meeting room, and sat in the centre of the sofa, facing the door at the other end of the room.

He felt calm and in control, his inexperience offset by a self-belief that had been buoyed by his achievements in his youth and his success in gaining entry into the Diplomatic Corps – one of the hardest jobs in the world to obtain. He was young, wet-behind-the-ears, at times a benign miscreant, but by God right now he looked and felt like a Commander of the British Empire. As he sat, stock still, an air of watchfulness, poised, waiting to issue his orders, he amused himself with a somewhat absurd notion – that of feeling like Ian Fleming's James Bond, sartorially elegant, sat here, waiting for a deadly foe or a stunning femme fatale, tapping an unlit three-gold-band Morland Balkan-Turkish cigarette on his gun-metal cigarette case. He knew that the reality of his encounter with the Chinese diplomat was not going to be an edge-of-your-cinema-seat bombastic experience. But, it was nevertheless cloak and dagger high-intrigue. After all, he'd been handpicked to catch a mole. *This* would be some tale to tell *Lovely Lucy*, if ever she succumbed to his advances.

He had nearly forty minutes to wait until it was two PM.

Inside his rooms one could hear a pin drop. In the corridor outside, he heard a German man and woman talking as they walked past his room and opened and closed their bedroom. For some reason it made him feel good that all the other rooms on his floor were occupied; almost certainly the feeling was there because it heightened the fact that he was on top secret business that was *none* of the business of those in close proximity to him.

He waited.

Raine was in the London Fencing Club, watching his eighteen year old daughter lunge at her opponent with her épée, her preferred weapon. She was practising for a forthcoming national competition. Raine was here because he not only wanted to see how she'd progressed, but he was also under strict instructions from his wife to take her shopping for certain pre-university attendance essentials, prior to ensuring he bought her home safely to their large residence in Hertford. He was proud of his daughter and watched her every move on the piste.

But he was also very conscious of time.

Specifically, the current time in Germany.

He checked his watch.

It was one fifty-nine PM in the Hotel Opéra. Wick was steady, focused, waiting for one thing, and one thing only – a knock on the door. Nothing else mattered. He'd already decided what to do if the Chinese diplomat was late – nothing. The diplomat was no doubt smart. He'd correctly judge it churlish if Wick deigned to mention he was late. So, Wick would ignore what could have been an excusable *faux pas* or more likely a deliberate attempt by the Chinaman to control the ground. And if the latter, Wick wouldn't give him the satisfaction of knowing that his late arrival had irritated the young Brit. So, they'd set to business. That was fine. But what was not fine was how Wick would feel if the diplomat failed to turn up. It wouldn't be Wick's fault if that happened. He'd done everything right and was primed. It could be the fault of the Chinaman, the FCO Berlin-based diplomat who'd set up the meeting, or even Raine. Then again, it could be the fault of heavy traffic or cancelled flights. But, the whys and the wherefores of a no-show would still feel like a kick to Wick's stomach. Raine would be furious, to say the least, but not with him. However, not being at fault would in no way soften the blow of being a pivotal component of a meeting that never happened. Wick would return to London with his figurative tail between his legs.

He waited, forcing himself to breathe correctly, staring at the door.

Come on, come on, he thought.

He imagined a clock ticking.

There was no audible clock in the suite of rooms.

Just silence.

Until there were three knocks on the door.

CHAPTER 10

Wick opened his hotel room door.

A middle age man was standing there – very well dressed in dark suit, crisp white shirt, no tie, and dark shoes. The man was Caucasian and when he spoke his accent was British. "Are you Alex Wick?"

"Yes, but…"

"Good. You're expecting Mr. Zhao Haisheng?"

"Er… yes, I was. Who are…?"

"I'm Mr. Haisheng's assistant." The man smiled. "He's waiting in the lobby. First, I just need to check your rooms are okay. It's just standard security. It'll only take me a moment; then I'll call Mr. Haisheng and he'll come up. May I?" He looked over Wick's shoulder.

Wick wondered if he should ask for proof of identification. Raine hadn't mentioned that the Chinese diplomat may have a bodyguard. Presumably that meant he didn't foresee this happening. Asking for ID could, he decided, unnecessarily antagonise the situation. He stepped to one side. "Come in. I'm the only person here. There's nothing for Mr. Haisheng to worry about."

The man stepped in to the room. "It's audio equipment and bloody drill-hole cameras that piss me off. The technology's so good these days that even pros can miss a trick. Still, keeps men like me on our toes." He shut the door and walked quickly in to the bedroom, spent ninety two seconds in there, went in to the bathroom and opened and shut cabinets and shower and bath soap bottles, entered the meeting room and examined the sofa and two chairs, and returned to where Wick was standing. "I can hand on heart say there's no one else in these rooms. As to whether there's any naughty kit in here, that would take me at least an hour to find out. So, I'll conclude that these rooms don't pose a physical threat, but that there is the possibility that they've been bugged to kingdom come."

This was all out of Wick's area of expertise. "I can assure you that the British government hasn't…"

The man grinned. "Don't worry. If your lot had put kit in the rooms, there is a strong possibility they wouldn't have told you. It doesn't matter. I'll fetch my man. You sit tight." He was about to leave, but paused and frowned, looking at the far end of the meeting room. "Those curtains. What do you think? Open or closed? Maybe I'm getting paranoid in my old age. But, there are lines of sight from across the street into this room. Easy pickings for a sniper."

Wick turned to look at the windows. "I'll close the curtains."

"Good idea."

The blow to the back of Wick's head gave him a nanosecond of pain. Then everything was black. No thought. No feeling. Nothing.

The Thief stepped over Wick's slumped body, grabbed his arms and dragged his limp body in to the bedroom, pulled him partially on to the bed, walked quickly to the suite's door, leaned out into the hallway, picked up a bag that he'd deposited adjacent to the exterior of the room, re-entered, placed a 'Do Not Disturb' sign on the door handle, and shut the door. He walked in to the bedroom, withdrew a length of rope from the sack, positioned Wick's body so it was central on the bed, and checked Wick's pulse. The diplomat was alive. Good. The Thief set to work.

The sensation of regaining consciousness was awful; as if he'd been drowning in a vat of tar and someone was slowly pulling him out. His head thumped, breathing was laboured, disorientation abounded, every muscle ached, and then his heart started thumping fast as abject fear kicked in.

Wick was tied to the bed with thin rope that had been wrapped around his body and the underside of the bed so many times that the result made him looked like a heavy item that had been lashed to a ship's deck during a hurricane. Only his untethered head and feet had mobility. The rest of him was in a vice-like grip.

He tried to speak. What came out of his mouth was a wretched sound. No words. He was looking at the ceiling. So bland; austere; white. He tried to speak again. "Whatever... whatever you're thinking..."

"You don't want to know my thought processes." The man's voice belonged to the person who'd come to the door. He was somewhere in the room. "They are a bit complicated."

Wick moved his head to one side. He could see him now. The man. Sitting in a chair in the corner of the room, a bag on his lap. "Who... who are you? What do you want?"

The man's voice was icy as he replied, "In your heart of hearts, you know who I am." He stood, placed the bag on the chair, and walked to the side of the bed. "I want a slither of information. You probably don't want to help me out. I hope you don't. Do you want to know why?"

Wick tried to move his body. It was pointless. He'd been expertly trussed. "Whatever you're thinking, I... I... I don't have anything you'd want. I'm just a... just a... "

"Messenger?" The man laughed. "Maybe. But even messenger boys know information that can be of value to the right pair of hands. But there's something far more important that you have than titbits." He leaned in close to Wick's face. "How old are you?" he said to himself. "Maybe twenty five? About that, I suggest. Maybe a year or two younger. So, let's err on the side of caution and go for twenty three. That's a chunk of life, isn't it? Twenty three years. That's eight thousand three hundred and ninety five days. Or, if you're counting, over two hundred thousand hours. I can't be bothered to work out seconds. Still, you get the point. Your skinny little behind has been on this planet for quite some time. That has to mean something. One can't really put a price on it, can one?" He stood and asked in a louder voice, "Who sent you?"

"I'm..." He tried to muster any ounce of courage he might have. This was so awful. Too much to bear. No, no, no, he told himself. Have to fight. Have to get a grip. "I'm an authorised representative of Her Majesty's Government. I work for the Foreign and Commonwealth Office. I'm a diplomat. I have diplomatic immunity and protection under international law as per the Vienna Convention. By assaulting me and tying me up you are..."

"Breaking the law? Do you honestly think that hadn't crossed my mind?" The man unzipped his bag and started placing items on a side table.

Wick's eyes widened when he saw what the items were. He fruitlessly struggled again. But the ropes were so tight they made his arms and thighs bleed underneath his clothes. Sweat was running in to his eyes. His heart felt like it was going to explode. His mouth tasted metallic.

Once again and in a calm voice the man repeated, "Who sent you?"

"F… FCO. I came to see Haisheng."

"He's not here. I am." He placed the last of the items on the table. "Give me a name."

Wick couldn't take his eyes off the table. Why didn't the foreign office train diplomats for situations like this? Surely, resistance to interrogation exercises shouldn't be solely reserved for spooks and soldiers? He had to think. Think his way out of this. No training. So, problem solve. Think. He breathed heavily and fast. He wasn't faking it, but nevertheless his respiratory irregularities helped reinforce his desperate situation. "Foreign office… sent me. A man. Don't know his name."

"Yes. About that. It's not true." The Thief picked up a bottle of sparkling mineral water and unscrewed its cap. "People who've drowned and have been resuscitated say that drowning is the worst form of death. I've often wondered about that. How would they know there aren't worse deaths than drowning? Have they died in other ways as well and have the benefit of comparison? Anyway, I assume they're not lying about drowning being horrendous. Let's find out." He grabbed Wick's hair, yanked his head back, put his knee on his forehead to hold the head in its tilted position, slapped a hand on his mouth, and poured fizzy water down his nostrils.

Total pain.

Pandemonium.

Instinct to breathe.

Instinct to live.

Futile.

Death very close.

The Thief lifted his hand and removed the bottle from his nose. "I'm sure that wasn't pleasant."

Wick thrashed his head, coughing, wishing he didn't cough because it made his lungs and all airways burn, back wanting to arch but held firmly in place, head reverberating louder than a bass drum, eyes feeling like they'd been skewered by kebab sticks. "Help!" His voice was too weak. He sucked in air, even though it was agony to do so. In a stronger voice he again said, "Help! Help!"

The man was upright. He took a swig of water and pulled out a mobile phone. "Do you think your neighbours in this corridor might come knocking or phone someone?" He made a call and said, "You can all leave now." He ended the call and looked at Wick, who was watching him. "That's the corridor cleared of all paying guests. *My* paying guests. We're completely alone."

Wick thought he might be in a macabre dream. His captor had paid for every room on this floor and filled each room with his cronies. Their role had simply been to make the level look busy and innocent. And now, with just one phone call, they were gone.

"It seems to me you've got your breath back. Let's have another crack at this." He grabbed Wick's head and repeated the water torture. Only it wasn't torture; it was death by water.

Wick's brain and body wouldn't let him blackout. It wanted him to fight. To swim. To do something. Anything to get air. The bubbles made everything a thousand times worse. It was like swallowing the foam of a terrifying and speeding fifty foot wave. Oh, how he wanted to die.

But The Thief stopped again. "Are you getting the gist of this yet?"

As he thought he might be vomiting – he didn't know; his bodily functions and reactions right now made no sense – he couldn't help picturing the young woman who'd delivered the message that he was to see Peter Raine. What she'd said kept going over and over in his head.

Honestly, I could do this all day.

"Please… please… please…"

"Stop? You want me to stop?"

Wick nodded, his teeth feeling like they were being wrenched out, or falling out, or both. Get the woman out of your head, he kept telling himself. Get the name *Peter Raine* out of your head.

"Who sent you?"

Wick thought he might be crying. He didn't know. He was shaking, for sure, Utterly miserable. Desperate. Scared beyond belief. But, he was a Westminster boy, goddamn it. What did that mean? He didn't know. Didn't care. It was all he could come up with. "John… John Potts. He sent me."

"Did he?" The Thief was motionless, his eyes locked on Wick. Slowly he said, "John Potts of the Foreign and Commonwealth Office. I suppose he must be senior, given this Chinese job of yours isn't exactly run of the mill stuff. But here's the thing. You don't know anyone called John Potts. Or, if you do, he's probably a former science teacher of yours, or family vicar, or anything from your not-so-distant past. But, I'll bet my bottom dollar that there's no bigwig in the diplomatic corps called John Potts." He looked at the water bottle and sighed.

More water was poured down Wick's nose.

Whatever was left of it, Wick felt that he was losing his mind.

Random images entered his thoughts.

Swimming with a giant turtle off one of the Maldives islands.

Challenging his first girlfriend to swim the width of a pool underwater.

Grimacing as he eased himself into a bath in an attempt to ease a cricket injury.

Jumping off rocks into the sea in north Devon.

All water. Bloody water.

Please. Die now.

The Thief lifted the bottle. "You're hanging on in there. Impressive. I've known lads and lasses with much more experience than you call it a day after two tipples from the bottle. It's all about mental fortitude, isn't it? You're a tough 'un on that level, for sure. I tell you what – let's play a game. This fictitious John Potts of yours – let's flesh out what he looks like. You give me a bit of a description; I quench your thirst; you carry on; I carry on; and at the end of it we have ourselves a lovely mental picture of the chap who doesn't exist. Sound good to you?"

Wick shook his head. "No!" No!"

"In that case, who really gave you your packed lunch and sent you on your merry way?"

Wick imagined his father watching him and saying *well done for being so brave*. Not now, Dad. With all due respect, fuck off. "John... John Potts. Maybe... maybe his full name's Jonathan. Don't know. Called himself John."

The Thief raised his eyebrows. "Gilding an artificial lily, are we? Good try."

More water.

More unadulterated hell.

When it stopped the young diplomat had nothing left. Nothing.

The Thief crouched and moved the bottle back and forth between his hands. Quietly he said, "In a perfect world I'd somehow get a missive to your superiors stating how remarkable you were under intolerable duress. I would cite your unwavering bravery and commitment to duty. I'd conclude that you should be given a medal of the highest order. But," he stood up, "we don't live in a perfect world. Tis a pity."

Wick looked him in the eyes. "Please. Just get it over with."

The Thief moved to the table. With his back to Wick he said, "You've already achieved the near-impossible. I commend you for that. However, you have no fuel left in your tank. Give me the name. I will leave. On my way out I'll ensure the hotel gets you medical attention. You'll live. But, I need the name for that to happen. Otherwise matters will get worse."

Wick looked away. His torturer was the last person he wanted to remember. At this moment he wanted a good memory. But all was lost. He couldn't help it. Hated himself for it. Hoped the man didn't arrange emergency care and instead let him die. Was that true? He didn't know. All he knew was he couldn't do the water again. No more water. "Peter Raine. Peter Raine." His head lolloped sideways on to the pillow; his feeling one of utter self-loathing.

The Thief turned and leaned against the table, his hands clasped behind his back. "That's more like it. Peter Raine, late of Paris and Washington. One of the untouchables. Well, well, well. You must have done something right for someone like him to put someone like you on this job. The thing is though, I knew Raine sent you. All this water malarkey wasn't about identifying Raine. It was about sending dear Peter a message." He walked up to Wick while keeping his hands behind his back. "I told you I hoped you wouldn't help me. I asked you if you wanted to know why. You didn't ask me, but then again we did get busy on other matters." He moved his hands to his front.

In one hand he was holding two towels.

In the other he was gripping a hammer and a fourteen inch knitting needle.

He placed one towel under Wick's head.

Wick screwed his eyes shut.

The Thief thrust four inches of the needle into Wick's mouth and the entrance to his oesophagus. "Why didn't I want you to help?" He put the other towel over his head. "Because your life was all that mattered to me. All those years, days, hours, and seconds. All that time and effort to make you who you are right now. Ending your life was what mattered to me."

He pulled back the hammer and used all of his strength to strike it against the head of the needle.

Two hours' later, The Thief left the Hotel Opéra. He did so using unconventional means and via an employee exit, without being seen by anyone. Outside, he pulled up the collar of his haute couture gentleman's suit jacket, walked for half a mile in increasingly bad weather, and located a payphone that he'd previously identified. He entered the booth and dialled an international number. A woman on the switchboard of the Foreign and Commonwealth Office in London answered. The Thief withdrew his mobile phone and brought up various pre-recorded audio files that he had stored in the device. He pressed play on the first file and held the phone against the payphone mouthpiece. The prerecording was of a woman's voice. The woman was an algorithm character, courtesy of Apple. She said, "I'm calling from Munich. I need to get an urgent message to Mr. Peter Raine." He stopped the playback.

The switchboard woman asked, "Who's calling please?"

The Thief activated another file. "I can't give you my name. I'm affiliated to the Chinese man Mr. Alex Wick was supposed to meet. Mr. Raine knows who Mr. Wick is. Please tell him the meeting didn't happen."

"Let me transfer you to the duty officer."

He pressed another file. "I don't have time to speak to the duty officer. Just pass the message on." He played another file. "Mr. Wick is ill and is sleeping in his hotel room. You can call the hotel to check he's okay. In fact it would be a good idea for you to liaise with the hotel. I'm not sure when Mr. Wick will be returning to London. When he does return he'll be in a bit of a state. Please pass my message in entirety to Mr. Raine. It's urgent. Goodbye."

The Thief left the phone booth and walked.

Peter Raine was in his garden, using secateurs to deadhead multi-coloured roses that had dropped their petals in autumn. He didn't really know what he was doing, but had watched various videos on YouTube to find out how to attend to aspects of the garden. His family had only been here for one month, having been repatriated after their Washington DC three-year posting. The house and grounds didn't belong to Raine. His family home was in Normandy, France. But for now he needed to be close to London and was generously compensated by the FCO for renting the property.

His wife opened the sun-room door and shouted, "Darling. Work's on the phone. Says it's important."

He muttered, "Alright," and walked to the house.

Inside, his wife was pouring a fruit smoothie drink for her two daughters. As he walked through the kitchen towards the hallway, she said, "You really must get on to your IT department and get us a mobile phone signal booster. It will save us having to take work calls on the landline."

He picked up the handset. "Raine." He listened to the FCO duty officer. "That's it? Nothing else?" He listened some more. "Alright." Half-heartedly he added, "Leave it with me. No further action from your side." He ended the call and looked at the kitchen and his family. They weren't paying him any attention. Bloody Wick had fallen ill. Useless idiot, he thought. Then blood drained from his face. Involuntarily he exclaimed, "Fuck!"

His wife looked up from the breakfast table. "Darling..?"

Raine was jogging up to a bedroom, while calling out, "I need to go. Now! Overnight bag. Suit. Passport. Shit!"

CHAPTER 11

It was ten twelve PM in Munich. Raine had arrived in Germany one hour ago. Now he was standing outside the Hotel Opéra.

Snow was heavier than it had been earlier in the day. And the scene outside the hotel was in sharp contrast to that which had greeted Wick when he'd arrived here nine hours' ago. There were four stationary police cars parked directly outside the hotel entrance, their emergency lights on, no sirens. Two police officers, armed with Heckler & Koch submachine guns, were standing guard at the hotel entrance. A police truck used by forensics experts was adjacent to the squad cars. An inner police tape cordon surrounded the law enforcement vehicles and uniformed and plain-clothed officers who were stationary on foot, or in their cars, or coming and going from the hotel. An outer taped cordon protected the inner cordon. More armed cops were there; and beyond the tape was a small crowd of inquisitive pedestrians, routed hotel employees, and two news networks with cameramen. Manned barricades were further away, blocking off the entrances and exits of the side street. Despite what was happening and the location being in the centre of the city, the area was quiet. Civilian onlookers rarely spoke, but when they did it was in near-whispers; the film crews had done their first reports upon arrival at the scene, and for now were drinking coffee and waiting for further developments; the cops were watchful and silent; forensics officers wearing all-in-one white disposable overalls were not making a sound as they moved back and forth between their van and the hotel; the only notable noise came from occasional bursts on police radios.

Raine waited close to the onlookers. He was wearing a suit and beige overcoat, next to him was his tiny trolley bag. He was feeling utterly devastated. He knew Alex Wick had been murdered in his hotel room. How had he been killed? He didn't know. Why? He'd been speculating on that throughout his rushed journey to Germany. A man exited the hotel, ducked under the two cordons of tape and approached Raine.

He was Mark Hogarth, 1st secretary political and economic, Foreign and Commonwealth Office British Embassy, Berlin. Hogarth – a tall, red-haired, middle aged career diplomat – was wearing a suit and holding a rain mac over his head. He was the man who'd arranged the meeting between Alex Wick and Zhao Haisheng, although he'd had no involvement in the initiative. He'd simply been the right man, in the right place, to make things happen. "Peter. I'm so sorry about all of this. Thanks for coming at such short notice."

Raine shook his hand. "I'm here because I need to be here."

"Quite. Let's get you inside. Blasted weather's in for the night."

Raine followed him in to the hotel, the cops letting them pass after Hogarth flashed his embassy ID.

In the lobby Hogarth removed his mac from his head, shook it, and said, "All guests have been checked and rehoused to other nearby hotels. Witness statements have been taken. Trouble is, there are no witnesses to speak of."

Bavarian State Police officers from the Polizeipräsidium München were moving around the lobby and ignored the two diplomats. A plain-clothed woman in her late forties was speaking to the concierge, the only hotel staff member still permitted in the building. She glanced at the two Brits, finished her chat with the concierge, and walked over.

"Hello Mark," she said in English.

Hogarth pointed at his colleague. "Peter Raine. Peter, this is detective *polizeirat* Karin Lebrun."

Raine knew that polizeirat was the equivalent of superintendent. He shook her hand.

Hogarth added, "She works for the *Kriminalfachdezernate*, the Investigations Bureau."

"Yes, I know what it means." Raine asked her, "You're in charge?"

The detective nodded.

Raine didn't need it spelling out to him that the reason why someone of Lebrun's rank and specialism was here was because the murder of a British diplomat on Bavarian soil made the matter one of German national security. "Thank you for allowing me to come here."

Lebrun waved a hand dismissively. "Pleasantries over. The hotel got a call from you at sixteen fifty-eight hours. I need to know what prompted you to make that call." She pointed at the man behind the hotel desk. "The concierge went to Alex Wick's room in person. He knocked several times and got no response. He let himself in to the room. He saw what he saw. He came back to the lobby and called us. Then as per your request, he called Mr. Hogarth in Berlin. Another question I have – why did you want him to call Hogarth? I understand that Mr. Hogarth then called you before you boarded your flight. You did well to get here so quickly. I'm guessing your driver broke multiple laws to get you to Heathrow and I'm further guessing that a Munich flight was delayed take-off until you arrived at the airport." She smiled. "The privileges of being a senior diplomat." Her smile vanished. "A first responder unit was here in two minutes and twelve seconds after the concierge's call. An ambulance was here in three minutes and one second. The rest of the task force you now see, including forensics, were here within thirty minutes of the call. I wasn't so prompt. I've only been here for two hours. And as you can probably tell from what I'm wearing, I wasn't expecting to work today." The bob-haired brunette was in jeans, a windcheater, and hiking boots. "I was half way across the country when I got the call."

Hogarth quipped, "Without your sidearm."

"I could have procured one when I got here. I didn't need to."

Raine said, "By all accounts I wasn't the only one to break laws to get here. So, polizeirat…"

"Unless you're on the payroll of the Polizeipräsidium München, Bayerische Staatliche Polizei, Bundespolizei, or any other unit or agency that requires German nationals to carry a law enforcement badge, you can call me Karin."

"Karin it is. Would you be so kind as to give me an update on your investigation, as embryonic as it is?"

She looked at the concierge and nodded towards him. Quietly she said, "He's going to need counselling. It'll take time. Maybe he'll never recover." She looked at Raine. "That much I can be certain about. The rest is…" she frowned as she searched for the right word, "odd. When it's complete, I'll give you the full forensics report, but so far we've got nothing. No finger, palm or foot prints, no shoe prints, no saliva, third party blood, or any other third party secretions, no DNA from anywhere, no fibres, no sightings of a potential killer, no video or audio, no mislaid items, no traces whatsoever." She shrugged. "No trace."

"Surely there must have been traces of other people in the room? Even if they're innocents. Cleaners, previous guests, other hotel staff…"

Lebrun was unfazed. "You'd have thought so. But, the rooms have been wiped clean. Look. I could give you an ongoing blow by blow update on every single thing we've done and will do. You can have it all if you want. The amount of detail will spin you out, but it's up to you. Or, you can accept that I recognise you're busy people who need to cut to the chase and just need my headlines."

Raine said rapidly, "It's a murder investigation. The headlines are all we need and want. You know what you're doing."

"I don't know what I'm doing when it comes to why Wick was here. Are you going to tell me? And do you have a suspicion as to who the killer might be?"

Raine replied, "I don't think the killing was politically motivated. If you can identify who the killer is, please tell me."

"Hmm. Your response can be interpreted in different ways. Still, headline number one. We're dealing with someone who's really thought this through. A professional, for sure. But it goes way beyond that. I've never seen this type of detail."

"In terms of sanitising the crime scene and its surroundings?"

"That in itself is remarkable. Plus, how he got in and out unnoticed."

"It could be a she."

Lebrun nodded. "Could be."

Raine said, "Maybe there are two or more killers involved."

"Maybe. The reason I say the murder is remarkable is because this type of killing is difficult to pigeonhole." She briefly looked away. "It's unlike any murder I've worked on or heard about. It's clinical but also… artistic. Yes. Clinical *and* artistic."

Hogarth frowned. "What do you mean?"

Lebrun replied, "Put Prokofiev in a test tube and you might get the idea." She was hesitant as she looked at both men. "I'll show you Wick if you want. Or I can show you the photos. I wouldn't blame you if you went for the photos."

Raine addressed Hogarth. "Have you sorted me out a room for the night?"

"You're in the Mandarin Oriental. Booking's in your name."

"Thank you. I want you to head back to Berlin now. I need you there on standby to firefight any political flak if it happens." He gestured to the detective. "Karin needs to do her job without any crap from London or Berlin."

Hogarth said, "Peter. I can see this through. I've seen dead bodies before. Blimey. Rwanda, Bosnia, Syria…"

"I know." Gently Raine added, "You'd be doing me a favour. In case of need, you'll be able to tap more contacts in Germany than I can."

Hogarth knew that Raine was sparing him from seeing Wick. He looked at Lebrun. She said nothing. He looked back at Raine. Reluctantly and with an attempt at solidarity he said, "Berlin it is. Take care old boy."

They shook hands.

Hogarth left.

Raine looked at the detective. "It's all on me. Hogarth had nothing to do with this. Let's get it over with."

He followed her up one flight of stairs, past forensics officers, armed cops manning key sections of the hotel, and down the corridor containing Wick's room. There were two police officers standing either side of the open door.

Lebrun stopped. "You don't have to do this."

Raine's voice was commanding when he replied, "Lead on."

They entered the suite of rooms.

The first room was normal, save for the fact there was a forensics officer in its centre, writing something on a clipboard. Lebrun spoke briefly in German to the officer and then walked to the entrance to the bedroom. The door was shut. She glanced at Raine. Didn't say anything. She opened the door. They walked in.

Raine stopped and was motionless, staring at the wall above the bed head.

On it was Wick.

Naked and in the foetal position.

His head had been shaved.

The body was somehow attached to the wall. Its bottom was two feet above pillows.

Around the entire body was a clear plastic bag.

Inside the bag was blood; streaks and smudges of it in the lining of the bag; more on parts of Wick's body.

The opening of the sack was above Wick's head, wrapped tight with elastic bands.

Through the bag's entrance and into Wick's mouth was a knitting needle.

There was nothing else out of the ordinary. The bed was clean and tidy. The rest of the room was as it should be.

Raine was momentarily speechless.

Lebrun said, "Clinical and artistic."

"Prokofiev in a test tube," Raine's voice sounded distant.

The detective took a step closer to the bed. "What do you see?"

Raine didn't want to answer her. He felt that he was looking at something that he couldn't understand. And yet he knew exactly what he was looking at. He didn't want to be looking at it. He didn't want any of this. "It's… it's an unborn baby. A foetus."

"The plastic sack?"

God, this wasn't happening. Shouldn't be happening. "The… it's the amniotic sac."

"And the needle?"

Raine moved to her side. "Who could have done this? Jesus!"

"The knitting needle. Focus!"

"The needle is what killed him."

"Correct. It was long enough to puncture the heart. It would have been hit with something heavy. Most likely a hammer." She looked at Raine. "I… I've seen things. I don't like this. Not one bit."

Raine nodded slowly. "How is he fixed to the wall?"

"Glue. Deno Monopox."

Raine stared at the display. "Alex Wick," he said quietly. "I'm so very sorry. Alex Wick…"

Lebrun turned to him and said quietly, "You're finished here. Understand? You're finished here."

"Finished," Raine echoed.

"Tomorrow morning at ten I'll meet you for coffee at your hotel. I'll give you an update. Plus, maybe you'll tell me what the hell's going on here."

"Okay. Yes. Okay." He pointed at the wall. "You know what this is?"

Lebrun didn't answer. She didn't need to.

Raine shook his head in disbelief as he looked at the young, bright, talented man who he'd unwittingly sent to his death. "His life was ahead of him." He turned to Lebrun. "This is… What you and I are seeing is..." He looked at Wick one last time and said between gritted teeth, "It's a backstreet abortion."

CHAPTER 12

It was nearly ten AM. Raine was in the lobby area of the Mandarin Oriental hotel, sitting at a table and drinking coffee. He was wearing smart slacks and shirt, looked well-turned-out, fit and well, but inside felt awful. Though his room was of the luxurious high standard one would expect from one of Munich's finest hotels, he'd slept badly. He'd been relieved when the sun had come up so that he could start the day. But he'd felt disconnected with his surroundings as he'd shaved, showered, dressed and descended for a breakfast that he barely touched. When he was a smoker, he'd probably have gotten through at least half a pack by now. These days he indulged in a vaporiser. Now, he occasionally took puffs on the device; discretely though – he didn't know if vaping was permitted in the establishment. In part feeling like a furtive schoolboy having a crafty fag behind the bike shed and in part feeling like a repulsive specimen of mankind, he sipped his drink.

Karin Lebrun walked in to the hotel, looked around, spotted Raine, and sat opposite him. She was wearing the same clothes he'd seen her in last night. She looked exhausted but focused. "Good morning, Mr. Raine."

"Good morning. I'll get you something." He signalled to a waiter.

When the man came over Raine ordered more coffee. Lebrun ordered tea and a bowl of mixed berries.

"I take it you worked through the night?"

Lebrun nodded. "I've just finished work. Well, this might still be considered work. After, I'll go home and sleep. I've asked my husband to take our kids out for a few hours. Hopefully that will buy me a bit of time to rest."

"You live in Munich?"

"Sure. Why not?"

Raine smiled. "Why not, indeed."

She looked around. "Your Foreign Office must have deep pockets. When I travel with work they tend to put me in somewhere considerably cheaper."

"I wouldn't complain. A bed's a bed. They have silly policies relating to grade in my organisation. One of the best night's sleeps I've had was on a mud floor in Guinea."

"You've been around."

"I have."

"And what do you do now? What's your… *patch*, I believe you call it."

"I don't have a patch. I'm brought in for here-and-there stuff."

Lebrun rubbed her fatigued face. "A big gun for hire?"

"Something like that."

Their drinks and Lebrun's fruit were brought to their table. The German detective had a swig of tea and started tucking into her berries. She spoke with her mouth full. "Why did Alex Wick come to Germany? Why did you ask the Hotel Opéra's concierge to check on Wick and call Mark Hogarth? Why was Wick murdered? Why are you here?"

Under other circumstances Raine would have laughed by way of response to her machinegun rate-of-fire questions. Right now laughter was impossible. "I sent Alex here. He had a mundane task – meet another diplomat and relay a message from the British government."

Lebrun kept eating. "Who was the diplomat and what was the message?"

Raine watched her carefully. "Nil response on both counts."

"Nil response?" Lebrun smiled but looked cynical. "Matters beyond my paygrade?"

"Yes and no. The 'no' bit is that this is a murder investigation. The German police have supremacy. The 'yes' bit is you'll be crushed by my German equivalents in Berlin, if you try to pull the *cop-needing-answers-to-everything* card."

"Crushed by them or by you?"

Raine didn't reply.

"So, I must stay in my channels?"

"I didn't say that."

"What are you saying?"

Raine breathed in deeply and lowered his voice when he said, "Wick was a junior diplomat. I tasked him on a menial task within a matter that is anything but menial. I want you to catch his killer or killers. I won't get in the way of that. But, I'm not going to answer questions that I don't want to answer. With the killer apprehended, at that stage it might get a bit political. But even then, justice will be served, whether in your country or mine."

"I thought you said this wasn't a political killing."

"I don't think it is."

"What is it then?"

Raine pondered the question. "I'm not sure. And that's not a nil response. Or smoke and mirrors. Or a fudge. I genuinely don't know what this is."

"*Genuinely...*"

He leaned forward. "Look. This isn't random, or bad luck, or personal. I'm sure of that. Someone killed Wick for a reason that has to be to do with his presence here. But I can't think why it would benefit anyone to kill him." What Raine wasn't saying was that the FCO had received a call from a woman who'd said that Wick was ill. He suspected her voice was computer-generated. He'd find out when his IT specialists analysed the recording of the call when back at work tomorrow.

"Why did you call the concierge?" she repeated.

He lied. "Protocol. Wick was supposed to have reported in at a set time. He missed that deadline. I called the hotel. Simple as that."

"Hogarth?"

"I was en route to the airport. My phone signal was intermittent. I knew Hogarth could take action, if there was a problem." This much was true. "As to your last question, I'm here because I thought it was strange that Wick hadn't called me at the prearranged time. I headed to the airport. I was fully anticipating getting a call from Wick or Hogarth and aborting my trip. Hogarth called. He told me what had happened. I got on an aeroplane. Here I am."

"Here you are." Lebrun finished her fruit and pushed her bowl away. "Maybe a bit of what you just said is correct. One thing's for sure – nothing you've said helps me find the murderer."

Raine kept his eyes on her. His tone of voice was measured and precise when he asked, "Who do you work for?"

The question seemed strange. She replied, "I answer to the Bavarian Landespolizeipräsident, the supreme head of all police in the state."

"I see. I answer to no one."

Lebrun frowned. "You must answer to the head of the diplomatic corps, your head of state for foreign affairs," she smiled, "and the queen."

"In theory, yes. In practice, no." He chose his words carefully. "One gets to a certain level of seniority where one is no longer an employee but rather an ally. The concept of unwavering obedience is replaced by a reciprocal arrangement that shifts according to self-interest. Thus, the contract between us is at best united and at worst downright precarious. If the Foreign Office wants me to do something I don't want to do, I won't do it. Sometimes there are things I want the office to do that they won't do. We're like siblings. We live together, sometimes we play together, but we do have a tendency to squabble."

Lebrun's eyes narrowed. "What is your self-interest?"

Raine smiled. "Ensuring that my country doesn't do anything to push the world into the mire."

"How very noble. To further your analogy, you are the older and wiser brother who ensures your impetuous younger brother – your country – doesn't do anything stupid?"

"Something like that."

"You'll break rules if necessary?"

"You're missing the point. In my head there are only my rules. Providing my moral compass is pointing in the right direction, I'm prepared to follow my own path. I'll ask you again – who do you work for?" Raine waited. So much depended on what she said next.

She lowered her head and stared at the empty fruit bowl. It took her nearly thirty seconds before she lifted her head and asked, "Do you have memories? Or is it all just a blur of five star hotels and glorious boardrooms in London?"

His response was quiet and exact. "I've seen things you wouldn't believe. They are my memories. No one else owns them. No one else *can* own them"

She nodded and looked away. "Yes. I have memories too. I live with them. My Landespolizeipräsident doesn't own them."

"So, like me, you fashion your own path."

She nodded. "Where is this leading?"

"Where do you want it to lead?"

"To the truth."

"You'll get some of that from me."

"And the rest of what you tell me?"

"Some of it will be the truth, but you won't know if it's the truth. Other things I say will be lies."

Lebrun shook her head.

Raine's eyes glistened, his thoughts rapid. "We share common ground. We both want the killer captured or killed."

"I never mentioned killing the murderer."

"You didn't. But I don't think you care whether you put cuffs on him or a bullet in his head. Either way you want the investigation solved. That means our stars are momentarily aligned."

"Yes, but…"

"But what?" He drank more coffee and delicately replaced the cup onto its saucer. "I transition with impunity through circles of power. I wonder if you could do similar."

"To what end?"

"To avoid bullshit and bureaucracy. To get the job done. Here's a scenario. Peter Raine. He's a Machiavellian Brit. He turns up in Germany. Knows more than he's letting on but is probably telling the truth when he says he doesn't know the identity of Alex Wick's killer. He has a coffee with a very high ranking German detective called Karin Lebrun. Her position in the Bavarian State Police suggests she's a creative thinker and smart. It also suggests she's a foot soldier, loyal to the cause. Lebrun's nose gets put out of joint by the fact she's not getting full cooperation from the British Foreign Office. She escalates matters to her police chief and the minister of interior, maybe further. Then she's forced to stand aside as a pissing contest ensues. This is no longer a murder investigation. It's become a political spat. But, those in the know in Germany realise this has to be resolved. They know they can't win. They capitulate. That decision filters down. Lebrun is told to wrap up the case as best she can. She hates that. Justice hasn't been served. Her pride and professionalism is affronted. She's never been told to back down from a job before. She has two choices: see out the rest of her service, knowing she's a shadow of her former go-get-'em self; or, resign. I think she'll resign. Meanwhile, the killer's still out there."

"You go too far!"

Raine smiled. "I could have painted a fanciful picture of your post-police wilderness years – maybe marital problems, issues with drink, financial difficulties et cetera." He waved his hand. "I jest. You don't strike me as that type. Or, maybe all of us can be that type if pushed over the brink. Irrespective, the scenario I've illustrated is possible and can come to fruition. It all depends on you."

Lebrun stared at him, silent for a while. "What do you want?"

Raine held her gaze and deliberately didn't reply straight away. "I want you to work with me."

"*Transition with impunity through circles of power*?"

"You can't do that. You're not powerful enough to have impunity. But you can move through those circles covertly."

"Skulking in the shadows?" She drummed her fingers on the table, deep in thought. "You want me to break rules." It was a statement.

"Remember – I want you to stick by *your* rules. I want you to answer to no one…"

"Except you."

"We would be momentary collaborators."

She picked up a tea spoon and stirred her tea, while watching the liquid swirl and form a dip in its centre. "You're trying to recruit me. Use me because of my expertise, location, and access to state and national police."

"Recruit is an indelicate word. It doesn't capture the essence of what I'm trying to achieve."

"Which is?"

"Hoping to God that I'm not sat opposite someone who has no imagination, does everything by the book, and can't be trusted to receive off the record intelligence. If you're not that person, I'll break British laws and protocols to help your investigation, with certain limits attached. I'm willing to do that. But if I can't trust you because you're some knuckle-dragging cop, then I'll walk away."

"After you've crushed me?"

"After I've crushed you."

Lebrun smiled. "I don't know whether you're jesting again, or being exact." She clasped her hands together. "How do you feel?"

"Right now?"

"Yes."

Raine looked at her for a while, trying to assess what she meant. He decided. "Thank you for asking. I'm not squeamish. I've seen men and women strung up in the jungle; horrific gang retaliation killings in Mexico City; the ins and outs of the bloodbath that was Former Yugoslavia; beheadings; you name it. But, this is the first time…"

"You've lost someone on your watch."

"How very observant of you." Raine made no effort to hide his sadness and frustration. "Has it happened to you?"

"It has."

"Tough old gig, isn't it?" God, he wanted to pull out his vape and have a long draw on the device.

"Yes." She hesitated, then said, "The preliminary examination of Mr. Wick's body suggests he was tortured before... it happened. We're certain he was repeatedly water boarded."

Raine shook his head and muttered, "Bastard!"

Lebrun kept watching him. "If Wick knew your name, so does the killer."

"Yes."

Lebrun could see he was in pain. She made a decision. Quietly, she said, "I'll be your eyes and ears. Off the record. Munich's a city of over one and a half million people. Not one cop here would challenge me. The same applies across the state and the entire country. But, you do realise there is a strong possibility the killer isn't German and isn't in Germany now?"

"I realise that. However, you're an investigator, first and foremost. Borders won't worry you. Plus, I'm asking for your help because I judge you have the right skills and mind set. Your nationality is irrelevant." From his pocket, he pulled out a sheet of paper and handed it to her. "The man in the photo is Zhao Haisheng. He's a senior diplomat in the Chinese embassy in Berlin. Wick was supposed to meet him in his room at the Opéra. He either turned up for the prearranged meeting at two PM yesterday and killed Wick. Or, he didn't turn up and someone else killed my lad."

"Or he turned up with someone who killed Wick in front of Haisheng. The murder was carried out on Haisheng's order."

"I think it's unlikely that Haisheng was present at the time of the killing. I don't think the Chinese are involved, not directly anyway."

"Why not?"

"Because if someone like me or someone like you could prove that China killed a British diplomat on German soil it would be an act of war."

Lebrun was temporarily stunned.

Raine's voice was sombre when he said, "Welcome to my world, detective."

Lebrun composed herself. It took a while. She frowned. "If that's the case, why are my local officers and I investigating the murder? I was brought in because matters were delicate enough, given the vocation and nationality of the victim. But, an act by China that could lead to war? Right now, I should be a bystander in an investigation that was swamped by spooks, Berlin detectives, and tactical teams. My phone should be constantly buzzing with calls from senior ministers. And your lot would have deployed an armada of its own to join the show here. With all due respect, they wouldn't have just sent you."

"It wouldn't be the first time that I've been sent solo to stop a war. But, I take your point."

Lebrun was still frowning. "It doesn't make sense unless… unless…" Her eyes widened.

"Unless no one in British and German high command knows about the Chinese angle."

She couldn't believe what she was hearing. "No one but you."

"And now you."

"You… you sent Wick to meet the Chinese diplomat without anyone knowing?"

"Correct. Now Wick's dead. I'm here. You're here. There's no one else."

"Shit!" Her eyes were venomous as she said, "You have to level with me, Raine."

"I don't. My rules. I repeat, there are things I will never tell you. But, I'll tell you something. Are you paying attention?"

She nodded fast.

Raine imagined every British head of this and that agency and organisation screaming at him if they could hear what he was about to say next. The thought was a temporary amusing alleviation from the sorrow and self-loathing he felt. "There is a traitor in British government service. He or she has been stealing top secret intelligence from a database that is shared by my organisation, The Metropolitan Police Service, and our secret agents. The traitor's selling the secrets to our enemies. Multiple countries. I decided on a tactic to muddy the waters – approach the end users, in this case China, and tell them they were receiving dodgy goods. I sent Wick to Munich to convey a message to Haisheng and by extension the Chinese government. It was a tweaked form of backchannel diplomacy – ignore the crap you're buying and continue efforts to build trust between our countries. My objective was to use the same tactic with other countries. Munich was the test case. I thought the worst possible outcome was Haisheng laughing in Wick's face. I most certainly didn't expect this. So…"

"You've failed."

"Yes, superintendent. I've failed."

"Will you try your tactic on other countries?"

"I don't know."

"Maybe there's another tactic you could use?"

"Possibly." He sighed. "The issue is the traitor. We've done so much to try to identify the individual. We've turned the," he smiled, "empire inside out trying to get to him or her. Nothing."

Slowly and with stern deliberation, Lebrun said, "You think the traitor killed Wick."

Raine nodded.

"If so, we're dealing with a British government official."

"Yes."

"Why would the traitor kill Wick?"

"It's possible the Chinese warned the traitor that we wanted to meet them to discuss our traitor. Maybe they told the traitor to sort out his mess. Haisheng didn't turn up here. The traitor did. Maybe I'm wrong. Regardless, it gets worse. The nature of the killing is a message. I've no doubt about that. It's what's kept me up most of the night."

Lebrun said to herself as much as to Raine, "An aborted foetus."

Raine thought about the other members of The Library and their runners. He didn't yet know who those runners were. No doubt they were of a similar age to Wick. "The Chinese didn't kill Wick. Nor do I believe they had the knowledge that he might be killed. Thus, I don't care about the Chinese. At this stage, all I'm asking is that you keep me posted if you get any whiff of my traitor."

"Okay. But if the traitor is the killer, that's still my," she cocked her head mischievously, "jurisdiction."

"Indeed. And what a strange jurisdiction it may turn out to be." He stood. "I'm returning to London today." He handed her his business card. "Don't trust anyone else in Germany or Britain, unless I tell you otherwise." His voice became uncertain as he asked, "What will happen to Wick?"

"His body's at the pathology lab. After he's been processed, he'll be flown back to England. I'll leave it to you to explain to UK authorities why he might have been here."

"I'll come up with an excuse." His voice was once again commanding as he said, "This may be a cross-border issue. Keep your passport and gun close to hand at all times."

"Sure. The message? An aborted foetus. What does it mean?"

The glisten in Raine's eyes was completely gone as he replied, "Wick has been made to look like an unborn child. Untested. Innocent. Cocooned. Wick becomes my son. I think he's safe. He feels he's safe. Neither of us anticipates a knitting needle and a hammer. The unborn child is aborted. I grieve. My instincts kick in. Maybe I should have more children, knowing that one day they will have to face the world. The killer is telling me that if I do that there'll be more abortions."

He left the hotel and called Sign.

At five PM Sign and Knutsen were in the Westminster safe house. Both of them were wearing smart clothes – sports jackets, open collar shirts, slacks, and brogues. They'd adorned the clothes because they knew Raine would be wearing similar in his journey back from Germany. Also, they wanted to look respectable for what they knew would be a sombre meeting. This was not a moment to turn up in typical Sunday casual attire.

Raine had just arrived. He'd told them that he'd come to the flat direct from the airport. He was sitting on the tiny sofa, his trolley bag by his feet. Knutsen was perched on one of the two dining chairs. Sign was making tea.

The former senior MI6 officer brought the drinks to the men and remained standing as he sipped his drink. "Not an ideal weekend."

"It most certainly is not." Raine held his mug with both hands, and was leaning forward, his mind racing. He was glad Sign and Knutsen were with him. They were the only people on Earth he trusted.

Over the telephone to Sign, and in person upon arrival at the flat, he'd told them everything – the way matters had unfolded to prompt Raine to travel to Munich, Wick's death, the crime scene, German police investigation, his secret agreement with Lebrun, scheduled meeting with The Library at nine PM tomorrow, and the fact that no members of The Library yet knew about Wick's death. Later, Sign would update the touchscreen 'CHALICE' file to include a new square containing detective superintendent Karin Lebrun, with a line connecting her and Raine. Regrettably, he'd need to draw a cross over Alex Wick's square, and he'd need to write Wick's name in the 'Dead' box.

Raine said, "The Thief killed Wick."

"Yes, he did." Sign watched the diplomat, careful with his use of language. Raine was grieving. Sign was very sensitive to that. He also needed to be a rock for the man while at the same time ensuring that Raine knew Wick was gone.

"He?" Raine sipped his tea and withdrew his e-cigarette vaporiser and a small bottle of liquid. "Lucas was convinced it was a man."

"The person who killed Alex Wick was The Thief. Lucas is right. The Thief is a man."

"I see." The diplomat slid open the tank-fill component of his *Vaporesso* device, squirted menthol liquid into it, slid the lid shut, and put his liquid bottle in his jacket pocket. After adjusting the wattage on the device's electronic screen, he activated the fire button and vaped. "How do you know it's a man?"

"Now's not the time for me to give you my analysis. I predict Sassoon will deconstruct matters and rebuild them in tomorrow's Library meeting. Listen to him. He'll be right. For now, and to quote the, by all accounts, excellent and unusual Detective Superintendent Karin Lebrun, you need headlines; definitive answers that cut through detailed examinations."

Raine nodded and blew out a plume of steam. "I should have done something…better."

Knutsen looked at Sign. Since the former MI6 officer had told him about the junior diplomat's murder, his overriding thought today had been about Sign's state of mind. Sign had decided not to send him to Germany to keep an eye on Wick. And now here they were, in London, wondering what to think. If Sign had made a different decision, it wouldn't have changed the outcome. Wick was murdered behind closed doors. Almost certainly The Thief had entered the hotel via an unconventional route. All Knutsen could have done is loiter in the Hotel Opéra lobby and wait while, unbeknownst to him, upstairs an abominable act was being committed. There'd have been no suspicious activity before that moment – no tailing of Wick, or anything else that might have indicated that the diplomat was in danger. The scene of Wick's transformation into an aborted foetus had been predesigned. Nevertheless, Knutsen knew Sign. His colleague and friend would be feeling awful. Credit to him, Sign wasn't showing that emotion. Knutsen expected nothing less.

Sign sat next to Raine, and leaned forward, elbows on knees, hands clasped. "Before this is over, there will be more death."

"I believe that to be the case." Raine looked at him. "Don't worry, Ben. I'm okay. I haven't put my soul on the rack. No matter what you may think, I'm not Marlow. I'm just so very, very, disappointed with myself."

Sign placed his hand on the diplomat's forearm. "When a gun jams, we clean the gun. I should know."

Raine looked at the glass doors leading to the balcony. He uttered a barely audible exclamation of understanding and said, "Onwards."

"Onwards."

Raine stood and walked to the balcony. "Why did The Thief tell me he knew I sent Wick?"

Knutsen replied, "You know why. He was trying to scare you off."

"Yes, but in doing so he risks me finding out his identity."

Sign said, "No, he doesn't. Look at it from his perspective. He doesn't know that you know The Thief is one of four suspects. As far as he's concerned, he's one of a thousand suspects. He tortured Wick and got your name that way. But, even if torture hadn't been used, there is a strong possibility he linked Wick to you. After all, you summoned Wick to your office; other people in the FCO would have heard your name being used in the context of that summons; and we cannot discount the possibility that wet-behind-the-ears Wick was indiscrete and mentioned to others that he was doing a job for you. Also, there could have been a reference to you by your colleague Mark Hogarth. In turn, the Chinese could have passed your name to The Thief. The Thief's identity is safe. He knows that, or rather he believes that."

"And so he's free to taunt you." Knutsen raised his eyebrows. "And that means you're well and truly shafted, Mr. Raine. He's on to you."

Raine was well aware of that. "Mr. Knutsen, I have a job for you."

Sign was about to say something.

But, Raine swivelled around and addressed the former MI6 officer. "Did you expect this to be a traditional case officer-agent arrangement? You telling me what to do? I've never been very good at doing what others instruct me to do." He smiled. "I told Lebrun that the relationship I had with her was based upon collaboration. You'd do well to ponder on the word *collaboration*. I'll listen to you, Ben, because by God you make sense. And you've got the experience to back up your insights. But a man like me doesn't get to where I am without having his own bag of tricks. You're not my boss; I'm not your boss. Understanding that will grease the wheels. I do hope you concur."

Sign shrugged. "I understand, dear fellow. And now that it appears that your grieving process is at an end, it's perhaps appropriate for me to state that the last time I told a person *not* to do something, it resulted in a man-boy having a knitting needle hammered down his gullet and into his heart." He smiled but the look was cold and challenging.

Knutsen had seen that expression before. Whatever came out of Raine's mouth next, the former undercover operative dearly hoped it wasn't something that would fuel Sign's temper. In nature, Sign was a kind man. But, in his arsenal he did have a ferocious intellect that if deployed could melt flesh off bone. Raine could do similar to the most accomplished actors in his political arena. He was no match for Sign.

Raine said, "I will take that barb, but I should clarify that my posturing should in no way mislead you into thinking that I no longer feel like an organ has been ripped out of my gut."

Gently, Sign replied, "Quite so, Peter. Quite so." He breathed in deeply. "Please give Mr. Knutsen your order."

Since when do I follow orders, thought Knutsen. Still, he was happy that the atmosphere hadn't plummeted into the bowels of Hades. Sarcastically he said, "Yeah, go on then. Private Tom Knutsen reporting for duty, sir."

Raine smiled. "Hardly a private. I have you pinned at the rank of major. Possibly colonel." He looked at Sign. "What do you think, Ben? Major or colonel?"

Sign raised his eyebrows. "Definitely major. They wouldn't promote him to colonel after that incident with the baron's daughter, her gossiping maid, the stolen barrels of brandy, and the missing church."

Raine laughed. "Major it is." He looked at Knutsen. "As things stand, Lebrun is merely on hand to provide me with any relevant tittle-tattle she gleans from her division's investigation. Her detectives won't uncover anything of use. And she's far too talented to be underutilised. So, I've changed my mind about her role. You will go to Germany. You'll carry my handwritten letter to her. The letter will tell her that the bearer of the message is to be completely trusted. She is to travel with you to England." He swept his hand in the air. "Bring her to this residence. It will be her temporary home while we try to catch The Thief. She will become a member of our team."

Knutsen frowned. "What's her function? You're our *maître d'*, Ben's our *grand chef de cuisine*, and I'm more like a soddin' *plongeur*. I don't mind though. Being the kitchen porter means I get free grub and all that."

Raine considered the analogy to a restaurant's *brigade de cuisine*. "With the greatest of respect to you Tom, though you were a cop I suspect if left to your own devices you'd have ended up having a magnificent career as an armed bank robber. It will be good for us to have a real cop's nose in the team. Therefore, Lebrun becomes our restaurant's *sommelier*. In a fine dining restaurant, a sommelier pairs wine with food. Lebrun can pair our brains and unusual skills with good old fashioned police work."

"Okay. Fine by me."

Raine asked, "By the way, why do I have to be the maître d'?"

Knutsen smiled. "Mate - in our adventure, you're front of house. Plus, you're a diplomat. That means you've got the slime to charm the pants and purses off punters."

The alliterative phrase made Raine and Sign laugh.

Raine looked at Sign while pointing at Knutsen. "You certainly dug up a chest of gold." He turned serious as he addressed Knutsen. "Bring Lebrun here. Don't take no for an answer. Leave today. Return tomorrow or the day after at the latest. *With* detective superintendent Karin Lebrun." From his jacket he withdrew an envelope and handed it to him. "That's the letter."

"You'd already decided to get Lebrun on board? Good job me and Ben are the accommodating types." Knutsen looked at the letter, weighed it in his hand, rotated it, and raised it to his eyes as if he was short-sighted. He secreted the letter in his inner jacket pocket. "You didn't come straight here from the airport. You went to your home in Hertfordshire. That's alright. But, you made a mistake."

"How..?"

Knutsen said in a matter-of-fact tone, "The envelope's from *Smythson of Bond Street*. It's their Imperial brand. It'll have a watermark on the flap, but I can't see it because there's one sheet of nine by seven inches paper inside that's preventing translucency. The letter itself will also be *Imperial*. One doesn't mix and match stationary when a clutch of this brand will set you back over two hundred quid. You met Lebrun this morning. You didn't have time to go back to your Mandarin hotel room and write a letter. In any case, why would you feel the need to pack expensive stationary, purchased in London, when you were in a dash to catch a flight out of the UK to find out what had happened to your boy? And, if the thought to bring her here had occurred to you in Munich, you'd have mentioned it to her face-to-face before you left. The stationary was in your study at home. Given there's no writing on the envelope, I can't tell you about the ink and pen you used. I'm guessing it was a good quality fountain pen. Possibly bought in Smythson, or maybe purchased from somewhere like *Antica Cartoleria Novecento* in Milan. Who knows? Anyway, you wrote this at home, *after* you knew that Lebrun was on board with your little secret. The mistake you made is you're sending Mrs. Lebrun a message that could be wholly misconstrued." He clicked his tongue. "As the second *messenger boy* who you've sent out in just four days, I feel it only right to point out that you might be in danger of fucking up again. When you wrote the letter you had eau de toilette on your wrists. It was the *Intense* scent by *Issey Miyake*. As the name suggests, it's designed to attract; only to be worn if you're on the pull. I reckon you've never worn it before. Your brand is the rather pricy *Enigma Parfum Pour Homme* by *Roja Parfums*. You're wearing it now and you wore it when I first met you. I'm betting you weren't wearing the *Issey Miyake* number when you had coffee with Lebrun this morning. More likely, you gave yourself a little spray of it while you were on your way home and killing time in a shop at the Munich airport. Thought you'd see what it smelled like; plus, you were probably feeling a bit psychologically grubby. You got home, maybe gave your wife a kiss, held up your wrist to her nose, and asked her what she thought. Perhaps she told you to stick to your normal brand. Doesn't matter because the important thing was, you brought the new scent to her attention, just in case she jumped to the wrong conclusion as to why you smelled different. You thought nothing more about it, went to your study, wrote the letter, sealed it, jumped in the shower, got dressed, put on your *Enigma Parfum,* caught the fifteen thirty nine from Hertford East, and came here." He shrugged. "You should have thought about scents."

Sign clapped his hands. "That, Mr. Raine, is a *real cop's* nose! Put that in your vaporiser contraption and smoke it!" Even he was impressed by Knutsen's knowledge and deduction. His colleague continued to surprise him. He chuckled. "Oh dear, Peter. Superintendent Lebrun is going to think you have intentions towards her. A *come-at-once* missive; scented paper; a discreet pad on the Thames. The evidence, *M'lud,* is somewhat damning."

Raine didn't see the funny side of this. His tone was huffy when he said, "Unlike you two, maybe she's not weird."

Sign couldn't contain his laughter. "Dear chap – she's a detective. Ye gods, man."

Still, Raine wasn't willing to lighten up. He said to Knutsen, "Just tell her you spilled some perfume on it in Duty Free. Tell her whatever you like. Or don't say anything. I don't care. Just bring her here."

Sign calmed himself. It was time to get back to business. "In tomorrow's meeting there is a strong probability that a new tactic may be suggested. I have an idea what that may be, though I could be wrong. Alternatively, if put to the vote, it's possible The Library may wish to shut itself down. Either way, I doubt anyone will wish to continue with the first tactic. Whatever happens, we must hope The Library remains extant. Peter – that is your priority."

"It most certainly is." The diplomat checked his watch. "I've got to go home. My wife's expecting me for dinner. She's had a lifetime of seeing me toing and froing, but she'll be unsettled and confused by the last twenty four hours. Apparently, at this stage in my career I'm supposed to be slowing down."

Sign stood. "Go home to your family. Nothing more can be done until The Library meeting tomorrow night. We'll meet immediately after. Mr. Knutsen may or may not be with us for that meeting, depending on his progress or otherwise with the German object of your affections." He made ready to leave, but hesitated. "Peter, I realise that right now you'll be searching for order amidst chaos. The death of Alex Wick is extremely unsettling. I am fully sympathetic to how you must be feeling. And because of that, now more than ever you deserve my leadership. I am your handler; and you are my agent. That pecking order is cast in stone. Are you clear on that, or do I have to whittle you down until every ounce of your body understands your place in this investigation?"

Raine stared at him. He'd known Sign for long enough to see what he was capable of. But, this was the first time he was at the receiving end of a presence and direction of words that made him feel miniscule. "Yes... yes, I understand. It is as it should be."

Sign smiled and changed the tone of his voice. "Splendid! Come Mr. Knutsen! You have a bag to pack, a flight to catch, and a love letter to deliver."

CHAPTER 13

MONDAY

It was mid-evening. Raine was walking along the Strand, London. He was wearing a suit and overcoat; his umbrella was open above his head. The road was thick with slow-moving cars, their headlights on full and capturing sight of constant precipitation. A dim, neon glow was emitted from pubs, hotels, theatres, eateries, and some late-night shops. For Raine, the ambience of this part of London seemed to match his mood – morose, grubby, not for cheerful public consumption, in need of a deep cleanse. Despite the rain and the chill in the air, he was walking unhurriedly. He had ample time to reach his destination. He needed time to think.

He'd had a busy day at the Foreign Office, with little opportunity to focus on more pressing matters. Now was different. All of his thoughts were about Wick and his killer.

He turned into the side street containing Mrs. Carmichael's bookstore. Normally, Raine would have thought the ambience and current conditions made the route look evocative. Now, the street seemed eerie, gothic, and haunted. So much depended upon what happened in the dark, old street.

He continued walking, the only person in the street, not knowing if being here made him feel like a saint or a sinner or one of a multitude of other personas within the spectrum. He pressed the buzzer on the bookshop's front door.

Mrs. Carmichael opened the door and raised an eyebrow. "You're a bit early for your nine o'clock appointment."

Sight of Mrs. Carmichael made him feel that the world still contained the magical adventures he'd so dearly sought when he was a child. "I finished work early. I had an early supper of steak and ale pie at the Holborn Dining Room. I finished eating early. I walked here, knowing I might be early." He smiled. "I arrived early."

"Well, I can't have you loitering outside, putting off all my customers. In you come, *Sonny Jim*. Give me your coat and I'll put the kettle on."

He followed her through the shop and stopped as she entered a cupboard that contained brooms, a kettle, wooden Dutch Indies cigar box of tea bags, salt cellar filled with sugar, mini fridge, mugs, and a bottle each of whisky and rum.

As she made tea she talked about Mr. Carmichael getting soaked by a monsoon during an archaeological dig in Tibet in '72, handed him a mug when the drink was made, and said, "You're not getting any younger. Weight of the world on your shoulders, and all that. You'll be feeling it more and more these days. Here," she opened a vintage BBC film reel canister, "have a biscuit. I didn't make them. Rubbish at baking. I bought them from Mr. and Mrs. Fingerhut's place. A biscuit won't solve whatever's bothering you." She adopted a knowing school mam expression as she looked over her reading glasses. "Yes. For someone like me you're an open page. But have a biscuit anyway. More biscuits equals fewer hijinks. That's what they should be teaching you diplomat types." She ushered him backwards. "Take your tea into the reading room and grab a pew. I'll play sentinel on the watchtower and will let your *Boys Club* come through when they arrive." She walked closer to the shop front door.

"Thank you, Mrs. Carmichael."

With her back to him she waved her hand dismissively.

Raine entered the reading room and sat down.

Between ten and fifteen minutes later, one by one Faraday, Hare, Sassoon, and Duggan arrived. They sat in silence – no pleasantries, small-talk, or banter. All eyes were on Raine.

The diplomat looked at each of them. "I regret to inform you that Alex Wick is dead."

"What?!" Hare glanced at the others before returning his gaze to Raine. "How?!"

Calmly, Raine answered, "He was killed sometime on Saturday afternoon, in his hotel room in Munich. A knitting needle ended his life." He gave them full details about the crime scene and how he was initially alerted to a problem in Germany. "I'm convinced the killer is The Thief."

"As am I." Sassoon put his fingertips together and against his lower lip. "The nature of the death is instructive."

"*Instructive*!" Duggan looked like he wanted to punch Sassoon. "It's a bloody horror show!"

Sassoon nodded. "Yes, it is."

Faraday pointed a finger at Raine. "The Thief knows you're on to him. We know that from the telephone call to the FCO switchboard. On that – have you checked out the call?"

Raine answered, "It was made from a payphone in Munich. The voice was female and computer-generated." He shook his head and stared at the floor. "I know he's on to me." He lied. "Almost certainly the Chinese tipped him off." What he said next wasn't a lie. "The call. The… way Wick was displayed. The Thief sent me a message. It was a warning."

Hare could tell Raine was uncharacteristically perturbed. "There's no way you could have known something like this could have happened. The risk to Wick was failure, not death. And not a death like this. I've never heard anything like it before. And that's saying something."

Sassoon wasn't looking at anyone; instead was deep in thought. "Murder of youth, including unborn children, has been done before. It's still being done in the darker corners of our planet. But, in modern times it is usually limited to tribal fighting. So too in history it's been tribal or military-motivated, with the exception of pernicious acts by rivals against royal families."

Duggan snapped, "Thanks for the history lesson. For God's sake, Edward. Time and place."

Raine held up a hand. "It's okay, Hamish." He bent close to his knees and asked earnestly, "Edward – what are your thoughts about The Thief?"

Sassoon looked at him. "I have many theories. But, without more data my theories become baseless speculation. Grains of sand in a torrid desert wind. However I can, if you wish, present some preliminary suspicions?" He waited.

Raine nodded.

Sassoon partly swivelled on his chair and quickly leaned forward so that he was closer to Raine. Right now he didn't care about the others in the room. "Just some initial thoughts. The killer's a man; acted alone; isn't suffering a mental illness; has killed before; likes playing God but doesn't believe in God; has the precision of a strontium atomic clock; is strong, fit, and healthy with good heartrate and cardiovascular function; highly intelligent; usually impeccably dressed and cares for his hygiene and appearance; understands fear; is a still life artist and showman; creative and a lateral thinker; objective-driven; in common with magicians and painters he hates and loves an audience; is disdainful of mundanity; mischievous in nature; has a strong emotional intelligence; and can be utterly ruthless if he deigns it necessary to be so." He leaned back. "In Biblical times, one could be forgiven for thinking the person I've just described is an angel."

No, thought Raine. The person you've just described is you, Sassoon. "How…"

"…many hours do you have for me to give you a blow-by-blow in-depth explanation of my hypotheses?" Sassoon looked at the others.

Duggan said, "Alright. Well, give us an example. The no mental illnesses bit. Sounds to me like the guy's a psychopath!"

Sassoon tutted. "The Thief does not have antisocial personality disorder. Psychopaths cannot distinguish between right and wrong. Our killer is highly attuned to that differential. Hence the disturbing nature of his masterpiece. He is showing us *wrong* and using it against us. As for any other signs of mental illness, The Thief was in control throughout the process of creating the image. Balance and symmetry are two words that spring to mind when considering the result of his efforts. There is nothing out of kilter in his brain." He looked at Raine. "Did the German police take measurements from the body to the edges of the wall?"

Raine frowned. "I don't know. Maybe."

Sassoon rolled his eyes. "I suspect the body was positioned dead centre in the wall. That will have been important to The Thief. The wall was his blank canvas. The edges of the wall were his frame. I once again commend you to consider symmetry."

Hare wanted less esoteric dialogue. "What about some of the other stuff? How can you be sure?"

"I can't be sure. Each observation is merely a starting point, to be proved or disproved if further data is obtained. Thus, at this juncture we are mixing ourselves a heady cocktail of scant information blended with some facts and a good glug of imagination. Take my analogy of a magician. The magician needs strength and dexterity. Lifting a body requires such athleticism. Magicians like working alone or with an audience-distracting accomplice. The Thief does not require a distraction. Nor, I suspect, does he want someone else to help him and take some of the credit. So, he works alone. Like most magicians, The Thief is a man. We can sit here and cite so many examples of certain women who are stronger than an average man, but let's play the statistical instrument on that matter and say that probability tells us it's a man. He has a flair for creating redolent yet distressing imagery. Hence artistry, creativity, and a contempt for banality. But he is also mischievous. After all, he could have shot Wick. The message, though less impactive, would have been the same. I suspect it amused him to rub our noses in the killing. His entry in to the hotel, the killing, and his exit have clockwork precision. And that precision applies to the way he cleansed the crime scene and its environs. He is a precise man. My imagination tells me he dresses accordingly, is clean shaven and ensures his body is always immaculate."

Faraday asked, "What about fear? You said he was scared."

"No, Gordon. I said he understands fear. To use fear effectively, one must understand fear. I suspect The Thief is a scholar on the matter."

"God complex? Not believing in God?"

Sassoon shrugged. "Our magicians and painters have god complexes. They create in their vision. If they are successful, they enrapture their audience. If the audience antagonises them, they burn the painting or let the chained pretty assistant drown in the water tank. Though The Thief is an artist, he is also methodical and analytical; a man of science and reason, yet one who can also create wonder. His left side of the brain is as advanced as the right side of the brain. He is God. He doesn't need another idol. So, he doesn't feel the need to believe in one."

Raine was thinking fast. "A non-believer who…"

"He believes in himself."

"Yes. Alright. Nevertheless, someone who doesn't believe in God and yet can create imagery that has connotations of deference to a god - the creation and nurture of life; God's ability to destroy life, if He so wishes; God's absolute power over life and death. Religious imagery created by a non-believer."

Sassoon nodded. "Michelangelo rejected faith. And yet he painted the ceiling of the Sistine Chapel, Throughout his career he produced numerous religious works of art – paintings, sculptures, architecture. In some ways Michelangelo is very different from The Thief, notably his personal habits which left much to be desired. But there are interesting parallels. Did you know that Michelangelo was referred to as *Il Divino*, the divine one? His contemporaries revered his *terribilità*, his ability to instil a sense of awe."

Faraday narrowed his eyes. "The Thief is a logician who's in love with magic. That doesn't help us narrow down his vocation within the CHALICE world. His discipline could be any number of things."

Sassoon agreed and held the GCHQ officer's gaze. "He could be a mathematician." He looked at Duggan. "A combatant." At Hare. "Referee." At Raine. "Philosopher." He touched his chest. "A…"

"… freak of nature." Duggan laughed. He turned serious. "I think we're all convinced Wick was killed by The Thief. We could be wrong. What if the Chinese executed him?"

Raine said, "The Chinese had nothing to do with Wick's death. I'm certain of that. For them to kill a British diplomat on German soil would be an act of war. I think they know that if they pursued such a reckless path, we'd ultimately prove their involvement, no matter how many deniable cut-outs and foreign nationals they used to plan and execute the job. But there's no doubt they pulled out of the meeting. At best they got cold feet. At worst they spoke to The Thief and warned him about our intentions. If the latter I suspect he told them he'd handle it. But, it wouldn't have served him well to tell them what he was really planning to do to Wick."

The others agreed.

Faraday asked, "What do the Germans think?"

Raine wasn't going to tell the others about his special arrangement with Lebrun and that he'd told her about the existence of a traitor within British ranks. "The Germans don't know Wick was meeting a Chinese diplomat. Channels of communication between the Germans and me remain open. Thus far, they've made no progress trying to identify the killer. I've projected a role of trying to act as a pacifier to ensure the matter doesn't become political. My credentials and motivation have not been questioned. I have Germany under control."

"About time." Duggan used his big hands to delicately tighten the knot on his tie. "What about flight rosters? Any data on human movement in and out of Germany last weekend? Needle in a haystack territory?"

Raine sighed. "Alas, yes to your last question. Sea ports, air ports, cross-border checks, unchecked free movement within the European Union – it's all against us."

Sassoon added, "In any case I suspect he didn't take a conventional route in and out of the country. If it was me, I'd have gone to Portugal, bought a local car for cash, and driven up to Germany on EU plates."

Duggan muttered, "It's a minor miracle you know where you are at any given moment, let alone *others* knowing where you are." He addressed Raine with a measured and formal tone. "Peter. I'm very sorry for your loss. I can only speak for myself when I say that I know what it's like to lose one of your own. But, I suspect there are others in this room who also know that feeling. Please forgive us if we speak as if this is a tactical setback, rather than the barbaric loss of your colleague. We do not mean any offense by that. We…"

"…have a job to do." Raine smiled. "Thank you Hamish. I appreciate your kind words. But," he clapped his hands and said commandingly, "a job is to be done. Now, more than ever, I want The Thief identified and nailed to a cross." He looked at Sassoon and winked, "Let's get Michelangelo to capture that scene."

They were all silent for a moment.

Hare said, "We must consider whether we continue to proceed with the current tactic. There's a good chance the Chinese tipped off The Thief. What's to stop our other priority targets – Russia, Iran, Syria, North Korea, and organised crime and terrorist cartels – doing the same? We've got four more runners. Wick's death was a shot across the bows. Correction – more likely a ninety eight-gun man-of-war broadside. Our remaining runners could die if we ignore The Thief's threat. I don't want us to sit here four more times and on every such occasion have a conversation that's near identical to this one. But, at the same time we're not going to let the bastard get away with this. We're not going to stop."

The others agreed.

Raine spoke to Sassoon. "In our last meeting you said you found it instructive that the traitor only steals intelligence that doesn't contain the identity of the source. When pressed, you elaborated that you were referring to our efforts. What did you mean?"

Sassoon replied. "It's most likely one of my flights of fancy. I am prone to them, dear chap."

Raine wasn't going to give Sassoon the satisfaction of a reply stating that Sassoon's so-called flights of fancy often resulted in tectonic plate-shifting results. "Get on with it."

Sassoon was quiet for a moment. Then he asked, "What would happen if the only way The Thief could make more money is if he can sell intelligence that contains the author's name?"

Faraday audibly blew out air. "Nothing would happen. CHALICE reports don't contain source ID. The Thief would pack up his bags. We'd never know who he was."

Sassoon wagged his index finger. "Let's put ourselves in The Thief's shoes and work back from the problem. The Thief is motivated by money. Least ways, that objective is in play, though I wonder." He looked away, then back at the others. "I digress. His endgame is to make a pile of cash and ride off in to the sunset. But, I think he's got a broker on his back – The Fence – and no doubt The Fence takes a healthy percentage cut of every brokered deal. Thirty percent has a certain ring to it. The Thief and The Fence don't yet have enough money in the retirement fund." He glanced at Hare. "Much like your bank heist experts, they need one last big job. So says The Fence to The Thief. Thus, they remain focused and desperate. They will take calculated risks, though will not make mistakes through complacency or cutting corners. They'll remain professional to the end. However, they need the money."

Raine agreed. "Go on."

Sassoon angled his head. "My flight of fancy. We create an irresistible lobster pot. The lobster has to go in; but once there he cannot get out."

"A trap," said Duggan.

"A funnel trap," said the senior MI6 officer. Sassoon looked at the others, knowing how angry they were at Wick's death and how much they relied upon his leftfield thinking. "What if we take away all immediate action CHALICE intelligence – the stuff that sells without a source ID - and only allow The Thief to feed on long game intelligence?"

"Oh, this is ridiculous," said Hare.

"He won't feed on stuff he can't digest!" said Faraday.

"Put more bluntly," snapped Duggan, "you'd be closing down our operation."

But, Raine said nothing. He kept looking at Sassoon.

That didn't go unnoticed by the MI6 officer. "We could make him believe the remaining intelligence was digestible."

Hare had lost all semblance of patience. "We can't get rid of all immediate action intelligence from CHALICE. Even if we could, the remaining intelligence would have no value to The Thief, for reasons we've banged on about time and time again!"

Sassoon shook his head. "It would have tremendous value if it was gold dust and if The Thief felt he could identify the source."

Duggan and Hare started shouting.

Faraday tried to speak over the noise.

More shouting.

Another effort to speak by the GCHQ officer.

"Shut up, everyone!" Raine looked at Faraday and asked quietly, "What did you want to say?"

The room was silent.

Faraday looked anxious. "Actually, we can strip CHALICE. Or rather, I can. I can get rid of all immediate action intelligence from the database. Temporarily, of course. I'd probably get away with a one week period of no new immediate action intel on CHALICE. After that, questions would be asked if I didn't re-upload the intel. Even then, seven days would be pushing it."

Hare looked quizzical. "How would you be able to do that?"

Faraday shrugged. "I'm a CHALICE gatekeeper. A nightclub doorman. I let in who I like; I kick out who I don't like."

Duggan said, "There's a handful of other CHALICE gatekeepers."

Faraday nodded. "Your woman from MI5, Hare's guy from the Met, Raine's woman from the FCO, Sassoon's man from six. Those gatekeepers don't have my technical skills. For a limited time, I can make them see double. I can…"

"… corrupt CHALICE without anyone noticing."

"Not without the other gatekeepers noticing; but, certainly without them thinking something's awry." Faraday nodded. "Seven dayss only. Maximum, even for me."

Raine looked quickly at Sassoon. "We leave only long-game intelligence on CHALICE for that timeframe. What next?"

Sassoon flicked his right arm through air. "We cast the perfect fly; the one that the largest trout in the vast lake will go for, over and above any other fly."

Raine's eyes were intense. "Edward – I've cut you a lot of slack with your cryptic analogies, because of the way you think and because of what you achieve. I'm asking you to speak plainly at this precise point in time."

Sassoon said, "Once all immediate action intelligence is removed from CHALICE we create a subsection file on CHALICE. One of my favourite fishing flies is the mayfly. Though we are not in the correct season for its use, the mayfly seems apt. Trout relish it when it hatches on the surface and feeding can be frenetic. If the fly survives the fish it dies a natural death a short time after it is born. The subsection file is codename MAYFLY. In it we upload grade-one intelligence. It is infinitely superior to all other intelligence on CHALICE. The Thief cannot resist the file. But, he must identify the source of each report in MAYFLY. That's how we get him – the process of him trying to identify the source. He will do things he's not done before. We hope for a mistake. We grab him and make him pay for what he did to Wick."

Duggan grinned. "Now you're talking, comrade."

Raine didn't smile. "The mayfly we cast; the one that catches the huge fish; the fly that is irresistible - there are four of them, all identical. They are the attractors. The bait."

"The runners." Hare lowered his head.

Raine said with deliberation, "The Thief can only access the identity of each report's source via the source's agent handler. We will be asking each of our runners to pose as an agent handler and to post completely fictitious intelligence. Each report will, as per standard protocol, state the code ID of the agent handler. For example, Wick would be WE17C, denoting which department he works for in the FCO, which team, and his role within that team. Were Wick alive and operating in our new scenario, The Thief would try to identify who was WE17C, get to him, make him talk, and get the name of WE17C's source. At that point The Thief can sell WE17C's report with a source name attached." He looked at Sassoon. "Even if The Thief works for, say, the Metropolitan Police it wouldn't be difficult for him to identify WE17C. You're suggesting we put our runners in the most severe danger. They could end up like my lad."

Sassoon replied, "I'm not arguing for anything. I'm presenting an option. The decision on whether we proceed or not is open to joint consideration."

Raine didn't know what to say. Nor did Duggan, Faraday, and Hare.

Quietly, Sassoon said, "We don't have to go down this path. If we get caught corrupting CHALICE the four of you would be sent to prison for life, no parole. It would be solitary confinement on a disused air force base somewhere in Britain or our colonies. My fate would be different. I'd be put in a small wooden box with lead weights and sunk over the Mariana Trench. If we get away with moulding CHALICE to our liking, then we must send out our runners. There is no point attacking CHALICE if we have no intention of following through with the tactic. Thus, the decision we have to make in this room tonight is do we proceed or not? There can be no half measures."

Raine looked around the room, conscious that his shirt was starting to cling to his back. He locked eyes on Duggan - the counter-intelligence and security expert in the room; the operative who knew how to analyse risk better than the rest of The Library. "Hamish - how do we minimise risk to our runners?"

Duggan considered the question. "Wick was going to lay low after a job that we stupidly thought was routine. If only the poor bloke had made it back to Britain. He'd still be alive. We don't need to send our runners overseas. Uploading our fake intel can be done from the safety of each runner's office. Immediately after upload onto MAYFLY, the runners vanish. But, they stay in Britain. If there's any doubt that they don't know the full meaning of going dark then we must remind them how to conduct themselves. Once off the grid, they stay in hiding. We must not know where they are. After all, The Thief is on to Peter. Therefore Peter is a chink in our armour. Get to Peter, get to the rest of us. So, let's assume The Thief can identify all members of The Library. No matter what he does to us, we can't blurt something we don't know. The runners are kept safe. In summation, if we are willing to die we can do so knowing we've protected the youngsters. There is no risk to the operation aside from The Library being slaughtered."

Hare rubbed his face. "And The Thief getting away with murder and no one to pick up where our dead bodies left off."

Duggan nodded. "Yes. This operation would begin and end with us." He tried to smile. "At least one of us old bastards has to stay alive so we can nab the blighter."

Raine asked Sassoon, "What's The Thief going to do wrong to enable us to identify and grab him via this ruse?"

Sassoon held his palms up and outwards towards his colleagues. "We're casting blind. I can't say for certain what he'll do. I think he'll be desperate and aggressive." He looked at Raine. "Sorry, Peter. Even *more* aggressive. But, beyond that I don't know. We would now be in the realms of hope. *Hope* that he makes a mistake. *Hope* that he somehow reveals his identity. *Hope* that we get lucky. That's it. I wish I could say something more insightful."

"Hope," said Raine in a near-whisper, recalling that Sign had used the exact same word. Sassoon and Sign were so alike. He could see now why they were kept apart in MI6. Allowing them to join forces would have been disastrous, for others but also possibly for themselves. He looked at the team and asked in a stronger yet genteel voice, "So, my band of irregulars, what say you?"

There was silence for ten seconds.

Duggan spoke. "I say we go for it. I'm in."

Raine looked at Sassoon.

The MI6 officer said, "If the paupers from Thames House want a tipple from the top table, then the top table had better join the party. Publish and be damned, say I. Can't have MI5 getting all the glory. I'm in."

Raine looked at Faraday.

The GCHQ mathematician imagined putting the decision to his pretend colleagues in his make-believe Nissen hut. In his mind their vote was unanimous. "Yes. I'm in."

He looked at Hare.

The Metropolitan Police detective chief superintendent had a bittersweet smile. "I thought I'd go out in a riot, or gun battle with drug smugglers, or something like that. Never imagined it could be something like this. A story for my grandchildren to talk about, I suppose. Not that I've got grandchildren." He nodded. "I'm shoulder-to-shoulder with Hamish, Edward, and Gordon."

Raine breathed out slowly, while closing his eyes. "Dereliction of duty was no longer an option for me when I saw Alex Wick's body glued to a wall. I'm fully committed, no matter what." He opened his eyes and sat upright. "We proceed with the new tactic. Morally, what we're doing is highly questionable. Legally, our actions will destroy us if we're caught. Technically, it's possible one or all of us will die. But, we're adventurers. We proceed." He looked at Faraday. "How long will it take you to corrupt CHALICE?"

"I can get it done by tomorrow."

"Good." Raine addressed everyone. "From tomorrow, we have a seven day window to make MAYFLY work and catch THE THIEF. All of you must meet your runners tomorrow and instruct them that they go live at ten AM the day after. They must go to ground that day. Any questions?"

Nobody said a word.

Raine said, "Right. Let's discuss the fake intelligence our runners are going to post on the CHALICE subsection MAYFLY. Also, I want each of you right now to declare the identities of your runners. If anything happens to one or more of us, the survivors in The Library must be armed with all the facts needed to continue the operation."

After forty minutes, they'd covered all outstanding matters.

Hare, Faraday, Duggan, and Sassoon were making ready to leave.

Raine watched them and said, "Before you go, there is one other thing we should be aware about. If we fail with our new tactic, immediately after the seven day MAYFLY window I shall hold an emergency meeting with our prime minister. I will tell him that we must shut down CHALICE and rebuild a new system, with new personnel, to share our agency intelligence. I'm confident he will reluctantly agree with me. Our failure would mean that in one weeks' time CHALICE will be dead."

The others were stunned.

The Thief particularly so. This was not expected and changed everything. He had to think fast.

Faraday said, "You'd me making a catastrophic mistake."

"State suicide," added Duggan.

"Cowardly capitulation," said Hare with anger.

Sassoon's tone was cold when he said, "You'd blunt our sword."

Hare pointed at Raine. "Who are you to make this decision? I doubt you have the power to make such an extraordinary order."

It was Sassoon who answered. "Oh, Peter Raine has power. Be in no doubt about that."

Raine picked up his coat. "We have to make the MAYFLY tactic work within seven days. That seven day window starts tomorrow. After that, I have to enact the last resort. Good evening, gentlemen."

It was close to midnight when Raine and Sign convened in the safe house. Knutsen couldn't join them as he was still in Munich. Fourteen hours ago, Knutsen had messaged Sign saying that Lebrun had laughed when she read the letter. Thirteen hours ago Lebrun had messaged Raine, asking if the letter was for real.

The senior diplomat and the former MI6 officer were sitting, facing each other. Raine gave Sign a blow-by-blow account of The Library meeting. He concluded by saying, "So, the *Big Push* is the day after tomorrow. Then, we're in *No Man's Land*."

"Casting blind, as Sassoon put it." His head was bowed, index fingers against the crown of his head. "Fourteen days until you pull the plug on CHALICE? I didn't see that coming from you. A very strong move. Time will tell if it's the correct move."

"It puts The Thief further on the back foot. His panic is our hope." Raine frowned. "In our last meeting you thought you knew what the new tactic would be, the one that Sassoon proposed this evening, the one we're going for. Were you right?"

Sign had been right. But he merely waved his hand in a dismissive gesture. Out of frustration, he asked, "Do you suspect anyone?"

Raine exhaled loudly. "It's just so difficult. I'm used to the complexities of dealing with people, but this is off the chart. Any one of them could be The Thief. In the meeting I just had, I actually found myself imagining it, pictured each of them murdering Wick and displaying him in that awful way. Every imaginary scene worked. In my head, all four of them were born to play the role of The Thief."

Sign completely agreed. "I'm in danger of overthinking things. At this stage, instead of trying to establish who *is* The Thief, maybe we should try to work out who *can't* be The Thief. A process of elimination."

Raine replied, "In principal I agree. But, I tried that with travel on the weekend Wick was murdered, hoping to find something revealing in the movements of Hare, Faraday, Sassoon, and Duggan. That drew a blank. And not just with the four suspects. I couldn't ascertain whether anyone from CHALICE had been to Europe last weekend. Apart from me, of course. I was yards from the scene of the murder. That aside, it was impossible for me to know for certain whether any of my Library colleagues were in Britain on the day of the Germany killing."

Sign removed his fingers and raised his head. "Who doesn't have the strength to lift a man and stick him to a wall?"

Raine had previously pondered the question. There was no doubt Sign had too. They were clutching at straws. "Duggan's part-human, part-steel. And he looks like a contender for the Scottish Highland Games. He's got the strength. Faraday surprised me. I did some digging on him. He's not much to look at but in his spare time he trains for triathlons. Also, last year he ran from John O'Groats to Land's End in a thirty pound badger costume. It was for charity. Still, crazy man. Hare looks... *unusual*. The black hair and green eyes don't help, but it's more than that. In size he looks average. But, the way he deports himself suggests a significant amount of hidden strength. Proof is in the pudding. Amongst many commendations, he got one for carrying an unconscious seventeen stone colleague down four flights of a burning building. He got him out of the inferno, put him in an ambulance, then went back into the building to rescue more trapped people. Sassoon?" He waved his hand. "I don't know. He's slender and looks fit. But, that means nothing. He's a closed book. There's no digging to be had."

Sign said, "Sassoon can climb sheer mountain rock faces, without ropes. For kicks, he completed the MI6 special operations paramilitary course. People die on that course. Age is against him, and the others, but I'll wager he's still fitter and stronger than most athletes half his age. State of mind is key. Sassoon would have easily been able to lift Wick and hold him mid-air while he calculated the exact position he needed to be mounted on the wall. Is there something in their private lives? Who doesn't need money?"

Raine answered, "I checked their CHALICE vetting records. Their finances were analysed with a fine toothcomb. There's nothing untoward there."

Sign shook his head. "I was referring to *contentment* or otherwise. Who's happy with their lot?"

Raine shrugged. "It's impossible for me to know. I'm trying to get inside their heads, but it's early days. I wonder if I'll ever get the answer to your question."

Sign recalled his description to Knutsen of the seafarer's journey and the neurologist's journey. "In different ways, they're all clever. We know that. There isn't one of them who doesn't have the brain to not only pull off this heist but also put their head in the lion's mouth. From the way you've described The Library meetings, they're all speaking as if they're not The Thief. Whoever is The Thief has an intellect that motors like billy-o. He's pretending to be someone he's not. Actually, it's almost like he's pretending to himself that he's not The Thief." He asked in a louder voice, "No sign of nerves? Twitches? Anxiety? Apprehension?"

"Yes and no. Yes on the death of Wick and the debate about the new tactic."

Sign was dismissive. "The Thief is playing a natural part within that discourse. The 'no'?"

"In all other respects, The Library members are exactly what you would expect from such senior members of the intelligence and security apparatus: thoughtful, professional, brave, and cool-as-cucumber. If one of them was nervous, I'd have spotted it. And I *would* have spotted it."

"You would." Sign breathed in deeply. "As things stand, no member of The Library is presenting themselves as an innocent party. Nor are they making gaffs that could suggest they're guilty. The Thief is playing a straight bat. The moment Faraday, Sassoon, Duggan, and Hare enter Mrs. Carmichael's establishment they are Faraday, Sassoon, Duggan, and Hare. No one is The Thief. That is somewhat annoying. *Under thinking* doesn't work. I must return to *overthinking*."

Raine smiled. "I'm not sure who's spinning more plates – you or The Thief."

"We're all spinning plates."

Raine frowned, took out his vaporiser, inhaled on the device, and blew out steam. "Everything Sassoon said grabbed my attention. But he said one thing in particular that I found particularly intriguing. He said The Thief is showing us *wrong* and using it against us. What did he mean by that?"

Sign was silent for sixty seconds, his thoughts racing through his vast memory, recalling books, lectures, articles, school room classes, and other academic forums and publications. But he also kept a warehouse full of other non-academic-related information in his head, including scenes from movies and TV shows, real overheard conversations, observations that may one day come in useful, sounds, smells, usual and unusual emotions and actions, and so many other things that contributed to the beating heart of Planet Earth. Collectively, he had a database in his head that was so big, nuanced, and ultimately human that no computer could or ever would be able to compete with its capabilities. But that was only one small part of his brain. It was the changing room as he sometimes liked to think of it. The majority of his brain was the playing field; the place where his intellect was unleashed. Right now he was cherry-picking his kit from the locker room, taking it onto the field, and crafting a win. He said, "It appears that science has a study to conduct and a new theory to present."

Raine said nothing.

"The study will be entitled 'Aposematism in Humans'.

"Two things, Ben. First: what the hell is aposematism? Second: what has it got to do with Wick's death?"

"Aposematism refers to the deliberate ways animals warn predators not to attack them or eat them. There are many ways this is done – toxicity, smell, colour, sharp spines, foul smell or taste, et cetera. Aposematism has been well documented in insects, reptiles, birds, and non-human mammals, but research into identifying aposematic behaviour in humans has, with the exception of embryonic studies of suicide, not been conducted. Sassoon said The Thief is showing us wrong and using it against us. He's referring to fear."

No stranger to academic rigour and problem-solving, Raine was fully engaged. "The problem is that it's hard to identify human behaviour that's universally accepted as a means to repel all other humans. What human actions *repulse* or *repel* other humans? What is *fear?*"

Sign nodded. "There are many subjective examples we could come up with. You may be repelled by a maggot infested body. Another human may be intrigued by it. Hutus in Rwanda have used machetes to lop off the limbs of their enemy tribe the Tutsis. This worked to some extent, but the Tutsis decided to retaliate by committing even greater atrocities. History is littered with such tribal techniques to ward off or subjugate foe. But fear is in the eye of the beholder and is usually specific to the circumstances of the beholder. Such circumstances can include society, tribal affiliation, education, religion and other beliefs and influences. People in Haiti are terrified of magic. They're not in Hampshire."

Raine said, "But, fear *is* repulsive and *does* repel humans. Identifying a universal fear is the problem."

Sign clasped his hands. "*Universality* is the operable word. And it is the word that takes us up a blind alley. Some scientists would have us believe that aposematism is a universal contract between two or more non-human species. A certain type of frog is toxic to a certain type of snake, and it has colourings to ward off the snake. The assumption is that the contract between frog and snake applies to all in both species. But what if the snake is blind? Or it wants to die? Other variables?"

"Universality doesn't exist in the animal kingdom full stop, and that includes us."

"Correct. So we drop 'universality' and we move to 'contract'. In humans, aposematic behaviour can only exist as a contract. Fear, repulsion, and deterrence only work if all three *matter* to a human predator. Does it matter to the likes of Britain and France that North Korea has nuclear weapons? Not really. Both predators could obliterate the country if they wished to. And they'd do so without receiving so much as a scratch in return. By contrast, does it matter that Russia has such a capability? Yes. Russia is also an apex predator. Best the big cats maintain a respectful distance from each other."

Raine considered this. "The Thief is using fear, repulsion, and deterrence by killing Wick. My employee's death matters to me and others. We fear that if we continue, others will meet a similar fate. Therefore we are pushed away – repulsed – and we are deterred."

"Exactly. Sassoon is right. The Thief has shown us what will happen if we try to attack him and eat him. We are therefore scared of him. The Thief is our fear." Sign's eyes were unblinking as he stared at Raine. "Which is why Sassoon's tactic is perfect. Other things considered, The Thief shouldn't touch MAYFLY. He knows it's a trap. The obvious thing to do, therefore, is nothing. But, he knows The Library is considerably more potent than conventional UK counterintelligence operations. The Thief wants The Library to close down. More than that, he wants to destroy the confidence of each Library member. If The Library calls it a day, its members will return to their day jobs. But they will be broken men. And the reason they will be broken is because The Thief will have shown them absolute fear. They will be in awe of that fear."

Raine nodded. "The MAYFLY tactic becomes the perfect conduit for him to enact the type of fear that we currently dread the most – the death of another runner, and in a certain manner, together with the possibility of our own deaths."

"We set the MAYFLY trap, and we do so knowing it may spring against us." Sign shrugged. "The Thief will saunter up to MAYFLY, examine it, and turn it around so that it's pointing at us." He wondered how Raine was going to react to his next request. "I want your buccaneers here."

Raine frowned. "Lucas, Aadesh, Parry, and Noah? Why?"

"Guns and glory."

"If it's come to this, then yes, I'll get them here."

"They must leave wherever they are with immediate effect. When they arrive, I must meet them without you being present. I will advise them that they are to have no contact with you and must not tell you what instructions I've given them."

Raine was taken aback. "You want my team and you want me to relinquish my command of them?"

"They are not *your* team and you have no *command* over them. They're mercenaries. If anyone can lay claim to being their commander it's Lucas. I could easily get my own team of similar calibre. However, Lucas' team have a unique selling point. They've never let you down and are one hundred percent discreet. Your connection to them and attestation of their qualities is priceless. I want Lucas' team and I want to direct their talents. Please do not object."

"Whatever you're planning for them, why do you want to cut me out?"

"For the same reason The Library cannot know the location of the runners when they go in to hiding. Knowledge can be a fickle slut."

Raine smiled, nodded his head, and said quietly, "Or a powerful gun that's dropped on the battlefield and picked up by an enemy combatant." He was silent for a while. "I'll get it done and will text you when they're here. Anything else?"

"Not for now."

Raine stood, conscious that his head was starting to thump and fatigue was encroaching fast. "Too late for me to get a train back home, so I've got my driver waiting for me at the office. A few minutes of air between here and there will do me some good. The other members of The Library are going to call me once their runners have done their job and vanished. I'll let you know one way or the other how things go. And if Lebrun does decide to grace us with her presence tomorrow," he looked at his watch, "correction, today, I'll need you to be on hand for introductions. Sleep well my friend."

After he was gone, Sign remained in the flat for a while, deep in thought. When home he'd need to update the 'CHALICE' file with the runners' names and the inclusion of a square for the MAYFLY file. In the square, he'd put one-liner notes on the fake intelligence each runner was going to post.

GCHQ – Proposed Anglo-New Zealand attack on North Korean military comms.

MI5 – Delay exfiltration to UK from Russia of codename Promise for 8 months.

Met Police – Irish police handover to Met running of 2 senior PIRA sources.

MI6 – Israel at stage 3 for nuclear strike against Iran.

He'd add a note next to Sassoon's box.

Tactic 2 his idea.

He thought about his discussion with Raine about aposematism and his conclusion -for aposematism to work, the contract between two or more humans must have a mutually agreed understanding of fear, repulsion, and deterrence. Something was nagging him. He rubbed his face. Raine wasn't the only one who felt tired. Think, think, think; drive on fumes if need be, he told himself. What was nagging him? He stood up, walked to the balcony door, and pulled it open, uncaring that in doing so a blast of cold hit him and the flat. He stood there, breathing in the night air. Think. He looked at the river below. There was nothing on it. But the embankment lights cast glimpses of the waterway. At times like these the Thames most certainly resembled Conrad's evocation of a giant serpent. Despite its foreboding presence, the serpent still attracted insects to busy themselves on its skin. That was it. That's what was nagging him about his explanation of aposematism.

What if The Thief didn't want to repel and deter The Library by doing something it feared?

What if instead The Thief wanted to *attract* The Library?

Aloud, Sign said, "Oh dear God. Ben - please be wrong."

It was 0242hrs on the island of Zanzibar. Lucas received a call on his mobile phone from Raine. The former French Foreign Legion officer swung out of bed and listened to the diplomat. After ending the call, he put on jeans, boots, and a jacket, shoved a cigarette in his mouth and lit it with a Zippo lighter, grabbed a holdall bag, looked at the sleeping black woman in the bed, and left the shack. He tossed the bag on to the rear of an old open-top jeep, got in the vehicle, and drove along a deserted dirt track. To his left were palm trees and a continuous stretch of sandy beach, beyond which were the warm waters of the Indian Ocean and Tanzania. He reached an isolated shack, near identical to the one he'd just left. He stopped the jeep, entered the building without knocking first, and poured a half-drunk lukewarm bottle of beer over the head of his sleeping Swedish colleague, Noah. Five minutes later, both men continued driving further north, keeping the sea by their side. It took them forty minutes to arrive at a wooden hut that was on top of a jetty over the beach. Lucas entered the hut, looking for Parry, his Russian associate. The hut was empty. He called Parry's mobile. The phone by the single bed rang. He cursed, walked out of the hut and looked along the jetty. Two hundred yards out at sea was a small light. He knew it was on a tiny boat that the Russian used to catch fish. He cupped his hands and shouted several times. No answer. Probably Parry had headphones in his ears, listening to dreadful nihilistic Russian death metal music. He re-entered the hut, pulled out a box from under the bed, grabbed what he needed, and walked to the end of the jetty. He raised the flare gun, took aim, and fired. The red flare arched through the air and landed on the bow of the boat, illuminating the craft and a rather angry Parry. After the boat was berthed, the Russian hung his fish in the kitchen, wrote and left a note for the woman who rented him the property, and stowed his kit in the vehicle. The three men drove to the northern-most point of the island. Aadesh had water up to his waist as he was standing in the sea, making adjustments to a small wind turbine that he'd made out of scrap metal, wood, and bits of wiring and mechanics from cannibalised transistor radios and clocks. The turbine had malfunctioned half an hour ago, causing the lighting in the nearby shack to go out. He could have turned on the conventional electrical power, but that wasn't the point. The owners of the shack had scant cash and had moved in with relatives in the island's Stone Town so that they could benefit from the former Gurkha's rental payments.

The turbine was his gift to them. It would save them a few Tanzanian shillings. He saw the jeep getting close to the shack, but continued using a wrench to tighten a clasp on one of the machine's cables. The lights in the shack came on. The Nepalese man smiled and waded ashore. Ten minutes later the four men were driving to the port, where a local man called Freddie had been put on standby to drive his boat to the Dar es Salaam mainland, if they needed to leave the island at night and when the regular ferries weren't running. In just over four hours' time, they'd be on a Turkish Airlines flight to London.

CHAPTER 14

It was Tuesday, ten days after Raine's men had tried to capture or kill The Thief in Norway, three days after Wick's murder, and the first day of the seven day MAYFLY window.

Rex Hare was wearing casual winter civilian clothes. He entered the Artful Dodger Café on Old Kent Road, south London. The place was small, had eight four-seater tables, and only two other customers were in the venue. This was normal, even for breakfast. The place did a roaring trade but most of its custom was takeaways for nearby market tradesmen, road workers, couriers, shopkeepers, bookies, cab drivers, and employees of pubs that only sold booze. He stopped halfway along the tables, glanced at a young woman who was hunched over a mug of black coffee, saw she was shivering even though she was wearing a hoodie and other layers, and walked to the counter.

"Rex. You alright, mate?" The café owner was a wiry, middle-aged man of Italian descent. He was arranging sausage rolls in the display. He knew Hare was a cop but it didn't bother him. He had other things to worry about, such as his business being potentially firebombed by a nasty north London family. "What can I get you?"

Hare didn't bother looking at the chalkboard menu. "Plate of your finest, please, Terry. Extra sausages and toast. Two mugs of black would go down a treat as well."

"Got it. Take a pew. I'll give you a shout when it's ready. No table service at the mo'. Tough times we live in."

The senior police officer sat opposite the young woman and said quietly, "It's all over now. You don't have to be scared anymore."

The woman scoffed and looked away. She had her shoulder-length brown hair tied back in a ponytail, was thin at the best of times but now looked emaciated, five foot nothing, and was twenty years old but on good days looked sixteen when she didn't apply makeup and on bad days looked like a street urchin whose age was indefinable. Today was a bad day. Her name was Molly Crease. She was a cop who could easily have been mistaken for a crack addict. The look was deliberate. She'd spent the last six months loitering in East End bedsits, dosshouses, and lockups, hanging out with drug dealers and other criminals, trying to work out the name of the person in continental Europe who supplied the kingpin in charge of the fuckwits she was surrounded by. It was her first undercover job and would probably be her last. Like many Metropolitan Police undercover operatives, she'd been grabbed for the role while still in uniform and only just out of her two-year probation period. She was fresh meat. Now the assignment was completed, she could try to get her nerves back in order, sit her detective exams, and move on to pastures new. But first she had to decompress. And that, as Hare knew from his own experience, was one hell of a gig. It was also probable that Crease had a drug problem. She wouldn't declare it to her employer; her employer wouldn't ask. It came with the territory, but technically was verboten. So, she'd have to handle drug withdrawal herself. Cold turkey was probably her most discreet option. Some people died from choosing that route.

"Have you been home?" Hare's words were soft, sympathetic, yet authoritative.

She nodded and swigged her coffee.

"Has your handler been to see you yet?"

"Yeah maan." She shook her head in disbelief and said in her own accent, "Yes. She's been over to my place." She smiled. "She bought me clean knickers and bras. They're the wrong size. Dappy cow."

"She means well."

"Maybe. But meaning well doesn't *cut the mustard*. Does it?"

"No it doesn't." He knew exactly what she meant. In Crease's line of work the more she was surrounded by chaos the more she needed to control her life with millimetre precision. Even if the millimetres had to playact being a drug-addled waster. He asked, "What does your handler want you to do now?"

Crease shrugged. "Nothing surprising. Check in, debriefs, statements, didn't-you-do-well chats from the inspector and super, probably tea and sympathy from welfare. They'll give me a couple of weeks off, I reckon."

"Do you have friends or family you could see?"

"I thought you'd read my file."

Hare had. Molly Crease: No known father; mother diseased from an alcohol-related disease; a brother whose coffin was loaded with bricks because his body was nowhere to be seen thanks to an IED that had struck his army personnel carrier in Mosul; few friends; GCSEs and A levels from a London comprehensive school that might as well have been a 'feeder' for Her Majesty's Prisons; joined the Met age eighteen; top of her class at Hendon Police College; single; very smart; loner; unsuited for senior positions; question mark over whether she was an adrenalin junkie or more likely had a death wish.

"Grub's up, Rex!" Terry was standing at one end of the counter, in front of him a plate that was piled high with an all-day breakfast, two steaming mugs of black coffee next to the food.

Hare collected the food and drinks and put the plate in front of Crease. "Eat."

"Jesus." Crease looked at the food. "Really?"

"Yes, really." He sat down and watched her put salt and vinegar on chips and squeeze tomato ketchup on the side. "I've only got thirty minutes. But I'm not leaving until you eat."

Mockingly, she replied, "Yes *dad*." She picked up a knife and fork and began eating. "What else? Want to check that I've washed behind my ears? Can still remember the oath of allegiance? Know that it's wrong to mug grannies?"

He ignored her and withdrew from his pocket a clear plastic envelope containing vitamins, herbs, and a drug, all in cardboard packets and labelled. He handed the envelope to her. "You'll be run down. These will help."

She took the envelope and barely glanced at the contents. She looked at Hare while swishing the package from side to side, mid-air. "Multivitamins, passionflower, vitamin C, ginseng, acetyl-L-carnitine, and clonidine. Nice little blend. I wonder why you think I might need it. Clonidine? For fuck's sake."

"You're run down," he repeated. "That's all there is to it."

"Yeah, right." She stuffed the package in her pocket and started at him in silence for a few moments, her gaze penetrating and defiant. "We do what we have to do."

"We do. I'm not here to judge. How could I? When I was your age it took me months to recover from a badly loaded hypodermic. I kept getting involuntary shakes. When I was back in uniform my custody sergeant thought I had a drink problem. I let him believe that. He helped me out for an addiction that I didn't have. Still, an addiction's an addiction I guess, so my sergeant kind of did the right thing. *Discretely* did the right thing. He didn't understand undercover work. I suppose he didn't need to. A parent doesn't need to have visited Shit Street to know what it's like for his son to live in that street."

"Or daughter."

"Or daughter." Hare nodded at her food, a silent instruction for her to continue getting solids down her neck. "No one from our lot knows I'm talking to you."

"Yeah, this is off the record, blah blah."

"There's no *blah blah* about it. The thing we spoke about last time we met – I'm going to need you to get it done tomorrow at ten AM while you're knocking around the Yard." Scotland Yard, the headquarters of the Met. "This is what I want you to do." He spoke to her for fifteen minutes.

When he finished, Crease said, "CHALICE? I've heard of it, but I thought it was only used by our Special Branch lot."

"It has considerably broader reach and usage than that."

She was making good progress on the food, even though it was making her feel sick. "Maybe. But I won't be cleared to do anything with CHALICE."

He shook his head. "You and every other member of the Met is cleared to access the database. But you're not cleared to access it in entirety. You can only post reports on there, and even then they're held in limbo, pending assessment and clearance. After that, you lose control of what you've posted. The database is moderated by gatekeepers. An assessment is made on whether your intel is worthy of CHALICE. If it's not, it's binned. If it is A-grade, it goes through the gate. At that point it can only be read by those with the highest security clearance. In the Met, that includes me. You can't read *any* of the approved CHALICE reports. I can read them all."

"People like me can feed CHALICE, but we can't take it for a walk."

"That analogy will do." He smiled. "I didn't have you down as a dog-lover."

Crease shrugged. "I don't mind. Don't like pit bulls though. The twats had them. Chained up most of the time. Until they weren't. Fuckers." She sighed while patting the pocket containing the medication. "Thank you. This'll help. I've... I've got to somehow get through the next couple of days."

"I know. And that's going to be tough. Very tough. So, let's buy you some time."

"Time?"

"To not look like a strung-out junkie tomorrow in front of your colleagues; to avoid being forced in front of a disciplinary board. And," he leaned forward, "to do the job I've asked you to do without blacking out because you're suffering the DTs."

She watched him and said slowly and with deliberation, "You want me to keep using."

"Just for tomorrow and while you find yourself somewhere to lay low. After that, you'll have to batten down the hatches and get the monkey off your back."

She tried to smile. "*Monkey off your back*? Alright grandad. You might need to hit the streets again. Terminology's changed since your 1960s *The Cross and the Switchblade* days."

"I'm not *that* old."

Her smile faded. She looked at the blank adjacent wall. Her voice was barely audible when she said, "Keep using?"

"Just until you've persuaded the Yard that you're okay and you've uploaded our report on to CHALICE. After that you vanish with the money and phone I told you about. You'll use that time to detox. It's perfect." He withdrew an empty shotgun cartridge that was wrapped in cling-film and foil. He kept his hand on top of it as he slid it across the table and placed her hand on top of his. He removed his hand, knowing she could now feel the hidden cartridge. "I can't risk you scoring on the street, or getting gear through other means." He nodded. "The batch I took it from has been tested. It's the perfect ratio. You won't OD if you take it correctly. It will last you three days. When it's gone, get that fucking monkey - or whatever it's called these days - off your back."

"Is that an order, chief superintendent?"

He placed his hand back on hers. "Molly – it's a request. *Please*."

She withdrew her hand and the cartridge and placed the crack cocaine in her trouser pocket. "Three days," she said to herself. She stood and stepped into the aisle. Her voice strengthened when she said, "I'm not going to ask why I need to do what you want me to do to CHALICE. You'd probably lie. Maybe you wouldn't. Who knows? It doesn't matter because all I need to know is one thing – is it worth it?"

Hare looked at his runner. "Yes. It's worth it."

She walked out of the café.

Edward Sassoon walked along a manicured path in Greenwich Park. Either side of him were trimmed frost-covered grasslands and trees that in season would contain coral blossom. Now the trees were bare, their dark trunks and branches appearing all the more stark due to the white backdrop. The park contained the National Maritime Museum, The Old Royal Observatory, The Royal Naval College, and The Queen's House. It was a place of serene civility. Sassoon came here to discretely meet opponents, turncoats, executioners, confidence tricksters, and on more than one occasion a poisoner who was adept at using his potions to render his victims alive but completely immobile. Today was different. He was meeting a young MI6 officer called Toby Bancroft. To Sassoon's knowledge, the youngster had never deliberately hurt anyone let alone severed arteries or injected a precisely diluted curare into someone's arm. Bancroft was unsullied.

He was Sassoon's runner.

The senior MI6 veteran sat on a wrought iron and wooden bench, crossed his legs, removed his leather gloves, and opened the morning edition of *The Times* newspaper. He wasn't interested in the media journal, aside from seeing whether his planted article had been positioned on the correct page and had been perfectly typeset. He read the article, was satisfied it would prompt a rather repugnant Croatian ambassador to flee for his life, turned to another page, and pretended to read. He was wearing a suit and woollen overcoat, his hair immaculate, his shoes pristine. To a casual onlooker he could easily have been mistaken for an out-of-uniform admiral who was getting some lunchtime air in-between his addresses to senior and junior officers in the naval college. There was no doubt he looked distinguished; but, also someone who no longer needed to be a rigid conformist. He'd transcended rank and grade and had reached the place where he could be himself and not give a damn about protocol and orders. Like all senior leaders, he was comfortable in his skin. However, it would be impossible for a casual observer to discern that the extremely rare gentleman on the bench had manifold layers of different skins.

Bancroft walked past him, a slow pace, no eye contact.

Sassoon folded his newspaper, tucked it in his overcoat pocket, put his gloves back on, got up, and walked alongside his runner. "All well, young man?"

"All well." Bancroft was wearing similar attire to Sassoon. He was slightly plump, had a cherubic face, dark hair, and a physique that suggested his nickname of 'runner' was not wholly apt. "We could have met somewhere nearer. It's bloody freezing out."

Sassoon adopted his cold, precise tone as he replied, "And what happens if one day soon you're packed off for a stint in Eastern Europe? Will you be conducting your work solely in the summer months?"

Bancroft felt awkward and didn't reply.

This was the second time the two men had met. Bancroft had been nervous in the first encounter. He was no different now. It wasn't just Sassoon's reputation that unsettled him; it was his aura. But Bancroft had hidden his nerves as best as he could and had accepted Sassoon's tasking – wait until told; then make ready to toss a nugget of misinformation into a whirlpool. It had been an odd request, but MI6 was full of odd requests, plus one didn't question the likes of Sassoon. Bancroft didn't know what misinformation he had to impart, how he had to do it, and why the job was important. He wondered if he'd find out today.

"At exactly ten AM tomorrow I want you to carry out the little job we spoke about." Sassoon looked along the arrow-straight path. At its end, three hundred yards away, was the Old Royal Observatory. He handed Bancroft a piece of paper. "They're my notes. Just bullet points. You can create the fat as you see fit. The result will be a report. You'll post the report on CHALICE and attribute it to yourself as case officer of the unnamed source. Memorise the detail in front of you. I want the note back before you leave."

The young MI6 officer read as he kept pace with Sassoon. He gave him the paper. "That's... erm... some report. But, CHALICE? My God. Why?"

"I need to see if your report will flush someone out; someone I will dismantle cell by cell."

Bancroft felt sick from what he was about to ask next. "I'm... err... cleared to do this? This comes from *on high*?"

"*On high*?" Sassoon pondered the phrase. "Who do you think you're walking alongside at this precise moment?"

"I'm sorry. Of course. I..."

Sassoon smiled. "No fuss to be had, young man. Yes, you're cleared. This is all above board."

As *above board* as anything else in this job, thought Bancroft. "Having read your notes, I now realise why you chose me, or at least someone from my team." MI6's Iran Team, headquartered in London. "Still, there are others with far more experience."

Sassoon waved his hand dismissively. "When I was your age I recruited a Soviet general and got him to spill the beans on what was going to happen to the union's nuclear arsenal when the federation inevitably went in to meltdown. Was I too young or inexperienced?"

"I take your point."

"I'm glad you do." Sassoon kept his eyes on the observatory.

Bancroft was about to say something but had to stop walking when Sassoon stopped.

The senior officer stared above the observatory rooftop. "When you get home tonight you'll find a parcel in your hallway. Inside it is a good-sized sum of pounds sterling and a mobile phone. Keep the package safe. Tonight I want you to write the intelligence report. In your head. Keep every word there until tomorrow morning." He looked at Bancroft out of the corner of his eyes. "You read classics at Balliol College, Oxford." It wasn't a question.

"Err, yes. Why do you ask?"

"I didn't ask. For a reason that will become apparent, I wanted the comment to awaken the slumbering literary part of your brain."

Bancroft couldn't be bothered to ask Sassoon what the hell he was talking about. "Cash. Mobile."

"After you post the report you're going to disappear for a while. The cash and mobile will help. And when I say *disappear* I mean really disappear. The mobile is for emergency contact with me, if ever needed. Other than that you can use it as you see fit, providing there is no link to your name. Do I need to spell out what I mean by that?"

Bancroft shook his head.

"Disappear, but stay in the UK. It's vital you don't leave Britain. Lay low until I instruct you to return to your life."

"Why?"

"I don't want you to be hounded by paparazzi."

Bancroft asked, "What about my boss? Does he know about this?"

"Nope."

"He has to know!"

Sassoon shrugged. "I do things that our chief isn't cleared to know about. Nobody *has* to know anything. Absolute knowledge is not a birth right. Your boss is being kept out of the loop on this matter. I'll deal with your boss. Focus on your task."

Bancroft was conflicted. On the one hand he felt this might be unconventional; on the other he'd signed up to be unconventional. "My boss will think I've done something crazy. I'm not senior enough to go off the grid without questions being asked."

In a stern and measured voice, Sassoon repeated, "I will deal with your boss and any chaff surrounding him."

Bancroft breathed in deeply. It was pointless pressing Sassoon further on this matter. Sassoon would either clam up or use word and analogical trickery to run rings around him. "It's just that… Forgive me. I thought we never lied to our colleagues."

"You have much to learn." Sassoon looked him straight in the eye. He was silent for a few seconds, studying the young man. Gently, he said, "A career spent in MI6 is a career spent writhing on the floor while grappling with one's integrity. It is a battle for the rights over one's soul. Few survive that battle."

Bancroft was breathing fast. "You've survived."

"At what cost? I am the doyen of all that I purvey. And yet I dine alone." He partially smiled, his expression sympathetic. "Some people sell their soul to the cause. They die when the job is done and the sun sets. Not me. I've cheated the devil."

For some reason, Bancroft's nerves had evaporated. "Do you speak to everyone under your control like this?"

"The range of notes on a piano is staggering. By contrast, the human condition is epic. Words must reflect the human condition." Sassoon turned and pointed. "I'm going the way I'm facing; you're going the way you're facing." He walked off.

Bancroft looked over his shoulder and watched him. He didn't quite know what to think. He was about to head towards North Greenwich tube station.

But Sassoon briefly spun around and called out, "I knew a simple soldier boy." He nodded quickly and only once, turned, and walked away.

Bancroft was motionless. *I knew a simple soldier boy*. It was a line from Siegfried Sassoon's *Suicide In The Trenches*. Was Edward Sassoon referring to him? If so, what did he mean? Sassoon never said anything unless it had purpose, even if that purpose was only recognisable to him. As he watched the senior MI6 officer walk down the centre of the path, he now knew why Sassoon had made reference to Bancroft's English degree. He quietly uttered the last lines of the poem. "You smug-faced crowds with kindling eye, Who cheer when soldier lads march by, Sneak home and pray you'll never know, The hell where youth and laughter go."

It was the week of the world-famous Cheltenham Festival horseracing event, held in the huge outdoor complex in a natural amphitheatre, in England's county of Gloucestershire. The jewel in the crown of the 'old' and 'new' tracks' many annual events, the festival attracted over a quarter of a million race-goers, with daily ticket sales exceeding sixty thousand. Hundreds of millions of pounds were spent during the festival, not just on bets but also the lavish and not so lavish facilities that were on hand to VIPs, ordinary folk who brought their families here, and those who loved the buzz and craved a party. Some people watched races and ate in the auditoria. Most milled around the various enclosures adjacent to the tracks, burgers and drinks in hand, shouting to be heard amid the noise of the crowds, tannoy systems, and the thunder of hooves as horses passed spectators. Bookmakers were on pedestals using tic-tac sign language to communicate odds. Touts were on the ground or in *The Centaur* building, providing racing tips to film or radio stations. The sheer energy and cacophony of activity made it an excellent venue to remain anonymous and not be casually overheard by others. The number of spectators made the festival a surveillance team's nightmare. Gordon Faraday loved numbers.

He was standing close to the pre-parade paddock, where horses were brought by their trainers from their nearby stables. The pre-parade was the most useful means to check a horse's form before it was taken off to have its saddle and other gear fitted before a race. Faraday had never bet on a horse before, let alone been to a track, but today he was tempted to put a tenner on *Pinkerton*, a five year old bay gelding who had interesting odds and good promise if he stopped falling over fences. *Pinkerton* was slowly walked around the paddock with eleven other horses who'd soon be participating in a two mile race. The GCHQ mathematician analysed his horse's physique, gait, and temperament and recalled and enumerated from his photographic memory every single statistic and other pertinent data he'd read about the horse. In another life, Faraday would have been a superb professional gambler.

Rishi Prasad moved next to him and leaned against the paddock's rail. He was in the exact spot he was supposed to be in and at the correct time. Faraday had been precise on both matters when giving Prasad his instructions. Prasad was twenty two years old, born and raised in the county of Berkshire and schooled at the prestigious Sherborne independent boarding school for boys. His father had started his career in Wall Street as a forex trader with J.P. Morgan investment bank before being headhunted to be managing director of equity sales with Merrill Lynch in London. His mother was a renowned doctor and subsequently professor of biochemistry at Stanford and latterly Cambridge universities. Both were Punjabi-Hindus, had married in America, and conceived Rishi during their honeymoon in the Indian state of Tripura during Holi, otherwise known as the festival of love. Prasad gained a double first in mathematics from the University of Oxford. His parents wanted him to become a diplomat or a politician. Instead, eight months ago he joined the invisible ranks of GCHQ and moved to its headquarters, four miles away from the racecourse. He didn't care a hoot that his parents couldn't boast to their friends and extended family about his vocation. He was stable and happy. Unlike his flighty sister who'd gotten herself in all sorts of bother after she'd hooked up with a Bollywood lothario.

"That's my horse," said Faraday, pointing at *Pinkerton*. "He may come fourth today. He's never good on the third fence. It will lose him two places. Thereafter, he will be distracted, his confidence will have taken a knock, and he'll only perform at seventy percent of his capability. Fourth place means I won't get a return on my wager. But, I'm still going to bet on him."

"Why?"

"Because freewill has a habit of sticking two fingers up at science. Even if he's injured and trailing by half a furlong, the horse might think 'fuck it' and decide to come first."

"You're betting on possibility, not probability."

"Yes."

Prasad's accent varied between east coast American, melodic Indian, and posh English. Frequently, one tone dominated the other two, depending on the reason for him to speak. Now he was in posh English mode. "Why are we here? I thought it was unusual when you told me to meet away from the doughnut." The 'doughnut' being the nickname for the main building in GCHQ's headquarters, so-called because of its shape.

"Unusual meaning unsafe? Do you think it's *safe* to meet in the epicentre of the world's most sophisticated eavesdropping organisation?"

"There is that." Prasad looked at the horses. "When I was doing my A levels at Sherborne, some of my pals and I went to the greyhound races at Wembley. That's the nearest I've ever come to anything like this."

"Fascinating." Faraday looked at his runner. "Why are you wearing a suit?"

"You didn't tell me not to."

"Alright. If anyone asks you if you work here, tell them no and that you are the go-getter for a wealthy Emirati sheikh who owns some stables in England."

"Really?"

"No, not really. Tell them you're a supervisor at the nearby Tesco's supermarket, you're on your lunchbreak, and you're here because you've heard there's some hot totty in town."

Prasad was about to question that suggestion as well.

But Faraday said, "Use whatever cover you like. If there is a next time requiring you to mosey away from your computer terminal, think carefully about your attire."

"Right you are, Mister…"

"Steady," interjected Faraday in a deep drawl. He sighed. "There is a reason why they didn't let you near the *other lot*." Meaning MI6 and MI5. "Best we keep you indoors, eh?"

"Doesn't need sunlight but does require warmth and hydroponics." He grinned.

Faraday didn't smile. "Thankfully, I have a job for you that, in part, *is* indoors. Tomorrow morning at ten AM I want you to write a little note." He withdrew his phone, loaded a file, and showed Prasad what was on the screen. "The note will look just like that. *Exactly* like that. Remember every word you're looking at right now. All bets are off if you forget anything."

Prasad stared at the screen. The 'note' was a draft of the CHALICE report he was to post about a twelve-month joint project that could, if it was successful, enable two Royal New Zealand Navy Anzac-class frigates to intercept communications between mainland North Korea and the country's coastal fleet. After one minute he said, "Got it."

Faraday believed him. He put the phone away. "I've already told you why our little arrangement is so important. And now you know how you're going to contribute to the war effort."

"Is it true? The… note?"

"Do you want me to answer that?"

"Not really, no."

"I thought not." He examined Prasad. "You're untested. That may or may not be an issue. The question I have is will you say 'fuck it' to yourself?"

Prasad glanced quickly at *Pinkerton* and back at the senior GCHQ officer. His smile returned. "Free will, and all that."

"Or blinkered equidae stupidity." He pointed at the paddock and its ensemble of horses. "Now, you're not alone. There are others involved. But, once the whip is cracked you'll become very alone. Tell me about your life outside of work - free time, weekends, holidays."

Prasad pulled an expression that suggested he was daunted by the question. "Chilling out in my house-share on Courtenay Street. Sometimes football on Pittville Park with my house mates – they're all from the doughnut. Other times we play Xbox together. Friday nights we might hook up with others from work. Go somewhere like the *Cosy Club* in the *Old Brewery* district. Try to chat up girls. I'm single and heterosexual, in case you wondered. No holidays since I've lived in Cheltenham. Weekends vary. At least once a month I have to see my relatives. My parents live in Sonning. Grandparents on both sides live near Reading. All Berkshire. I get over there when I can. Until recently, it's not been easy. A bit *stressy*. My younger sister's been in trouble. Met the wrong man. She was in India; wouldn't or more likely couldn't leave. My mum was beside herself with worry. My dad took matters in to his own hands. He hired one of those private specialists, the type that extracts and deprograms people who've been brainwashed by cults or other shitheads. Please excuse my language. The specialist went out to Mumbai to bring her home, willingly or unwillingly. It was successful. My sister's at home with my parents. Huge relief. The detective that got her home has to see her every day, for however long it takes, to get her right in the head. My Dad's got deep pockets, so that's not an issue. Big coincidence really because the agency the detective works for is the Pinkerton National Detective Agency. And here you are betting on a horse that's called…" He bowed his head and said quietly. "It's not a coincidence, is it?"

Faraday didn't answer. He'd come up with the plan to extract Prasad's sister, and had sourced and contracted America's best specialist in this field; Prasad's father had provided the cash. It was a private matter between the two men and the female Pinkerton expert. "I'm glad your sister is safe. But, after tomorrow's job you'll have no contact with her or anyone else you know. For the immediate future, that is. After that, everything will go back to normal." He pushed himself away from the railing. "I'm not worried about the component of your job that requires you to be inside. I am, however, rather more concerned about what comes after that. Walk with me. I'm going to teach you a marvellous trick. It's called *The Vanishing Act*. You're my apprentice. And you're going to listen very carefully to what I'm about to say.

The sun was setting as Hamish Duggan walked onto the Millennium Bridge on the River Thames. The pedestrian crossing connected Bankside and the City of London, with picturesque views of St. Paul's Cathedral in one direction and the Tate Modern museum in the other. Duggan was walking towards the imposing cathedral that was bathed in external artificial light, as if it was a permanent night-time *son et lumière* performance. The four meter wide steel suspension bridge was a sprung structure that had been constructed low so that it was as unobtrusive as possible amid the idiosyncratic and eclectic assembly of buildings either side of the river, all of which seemed to be vying for attention and had been designed with no care to assimilate with adjacent architecture. And yet the futuristic bridge had a performance of its own, particularly at night when its aluminium flooring emitted fine blue fibre-optic light-beams. The MI5 officer stopped midway along the walkway, leaned against the stainless steel handrails, and stared at the slow moving river that right now seemed black and gave the impression of being an organism that was hatching tiny neon fireflies. He looked at the north side of the Thames. London was such a contradictory mishmash of styles, he thought, and yet the mighty city was ever thus a continuum of sin, glory, and blood.

His breath steamed in the cold, still air. Daylight was almost gone. The bridge, at full capacity able to hold the weight of five thousand people, contained only a handful of late commuters spread along its length of over three hundred yards.

A woman stood next to him and followed his gaze. "New meets old."

"Are you referring to this bridge versus the rest of London? Or you meeting me?"

"Take your pick."

"No."

The woman turned to face Duggan, while resting one arm on the railings. She was Kazia Baltzar, twenty three years old, and a Romani-British national. The Roma's grandparents were nomadic itinerants from Turkey and Macedonia; her mother was Finnish, her father British. She was born in the Netherlands and raised by her parents in several camps in England. Some people referred to her and her folk as gypsies. When she was old enough to understand the words, if confronted with the word 'gypsy' she'd typically say to the person that the use of the exonym was pejorative due to its connotations of illegality and irregularity, and she'd say that while holding a knife over their genitals and waiting for their response. She was five feet seven inches tall in her black block-heel biker boots, had a swarthy complexion that could have derived from Turkey, elsewhere, or the north India origins of the Roma, a featherweight boxer physique that she usually chose to adorn with expensive designer clothes such as the tan *Ralph Lauren* chord jodhpurs and *Harvey Nichols* racing green box jacket she was wearing today, and long, straight dark hair. Now, her hair was plaited and resting over one shoulder. Jauntily set at an angle, she was also wearing a black Greek fisherman's hat. She was fiercely intelligent, gregarious when she wanted to be, solitary when the mood or circumstances dictated such, had a wicked sense of humour, and was contrarian in outlook and behaviour. Her multi-layered attributes and personality were married with a command of languages – fluency in Para-Romani, the traditional vernacular combined with varieties of the Romani language, English, Finnish, Turkish, and Romanian; and a moderate speaker in three other European languages.

Duggan had found her in a camp near Birmingham, when she was sixteen. The MI5 officer had three reasons for approaching her. First, she had no family - her parents were dead, father from a punch that had sent his weak heart into shock, mother from suicide. Second, because he wanted to train her to one day infiltrate organised criminal gangs in Europe that had links to the UK. And third, because she was very unusual. He'd mentored Baltzar, cared for her, ensured she attended her new school, was proud of her when she gained superb final school grades, and was even more proud of her when she achieved a distinction in her degree of Sanskrit Language and Indian Old Civilisation and Culture from the University of Bucharest. At that point, Duggan began to have reservations about the MI5 plan. As tough and brash as he could be, Duggan was a principled man who'd grown very fond of his spirited care. He wouldn't have minded if she hadn't stuck to her side of the bargain and not attempted to join MI5. But, relinquishing on a deal was never going to happen. Baltzar was wired to honour an agreement, no matter what. Her application had required some favours pulled by Duggan, given Baltzar didn't have three generations of British nationality behind her. But aside from that, she'd been on her own when applying. Out of the thousands of applicants per job in the Security Service, she was successful and joined MI5 as a fast stream intelligence officer. It was at this stage that Duggan fully turned his back on the original reason he'd approached the somewhat feral sixteen year-old. Instead of directing her against criminal elements within the Roma, he decided her talents lay elsewhere. And he thought it was immoral to use her against her proud heritage. Though he wasn't her boss in MI5, he ensured she worked on his old stomping ground – Ireland.

"I've never asked you if you liked London." Her accent was well-spoken.

"I'm Scottish."

Baltzar smiled. "So what? You fled the penal colony and headed south."

"I naturally gravitated to London, that great cesspool into which all the loungers and idlers of the Empire are irresistibly drained."

"Somebody important once wrote that line."

"A fellow Scot." Duggan looked at her. "I'm glad you plaited your hair today."

"Why?"

"Because, when you leave it untethered it tends to act as a warning to others that you're feeling somewhat psychotic."

She prodded her finger against his ribcage and joked, "You taught me well."

He looked back at the river. "Had no bloody choice, did I?"

She asked, "Did you get my delivery?"

"I did. It was good, thanks. I hadn't had Vietnamese food for a while." He remembered walking along the embankment with his beautiful, cheeky, adorable girlfriend cum fiancée cum wife; his *Love-Of-My-Life London Lady*, as he called her. "That said, just because I'm divorced doesn't mean I've forgotten how to cook. But, thank you anyway. Given it was from you, the gesture was just the ticket. Are you still knocking around with that Michael bloke?"

She shook her head. "Miguel. No. I came to realise it was just all sex and him doing his shirtless flamenco shit in Sadler's Wells Theatre."

"He did seem to be in love with himself."

"Yep. Mind you, he is a good dancer. And the ladies in the audience loved him. I bet he got them all bubbly in the gusset."

Duggan sighed. "Kazia, Kazia, Must you have such a provocative vocabulary?"

She laughed. "Of course. It winds you up."

"No. It wears me down," he said with resignation. He smiled. "Still, I wouldn't wish you to be any other way. So, no flamenco dancer. Anyone else significant?"

"Only you."

"Don't go for the sympathy vote." His tone of voice changed to reflect the reason they were here. "But, only me is good. Tomorrow at ten o'clock we go live." He gave her specifics. And because of his extraordinary relationship with her, he told her more than his colleagues told their runners, though he didn't give her names.

Baltzar nodded while digesting what he just said. "I know you. This isn't cleared, is it?"

"Since when do you and I care about pettiness like that?"

"Damn right. What are the other runners like?"

Duggan shrugged. "I don't know much. Only identities and brief bios. Never met them. Doesn't matter. What does, is that they're young and stupid. Just like you."

She smiled. "Things change. One day I'll be old and have pretentions of wisdom. Just like you."

"Can't say I can argue with that."

Her expression turned serious. "You're sending us out as bait. The Thief is a tiger. He'll come for us."

"We're giving him your scent. But, the scent's coming from all directions. He can't find you. While he's pacing back and forth, we'll bag him with a big-game double-barrelled rifle."

"You'd better have a steady hand and a good aim."

"We better had."

"Do you trust the others you're working with?"

"To a point." He pointed at the Thames. "Upriver there's a unit of duplicitous, over-educated, preening, adroit, hellraising officers that even famished rats and cannibals assess to be unpalatable. My colleagues are members of that unit." He glanced at her. "Does that answer your question?"

"It does." Gently, she placed a finger over his. "What happens if the tiger gets your scent?"

He looked fully at her and smiled with an expression of sad resignation. He didn't say anything.

She rubbed her finger quickly against his. When she spoke her voice carried uncharacteristic emotion, even though she attempted to make her words jocular. "Mr. Duggan. You're not getting all chivalrous on me, are you? Wanting the carnivore to come after you instead of me?"

He turned to her. "Best we don't talk about that, eh young lady?" He hugged her and patted her back as he softly repeated, "Best we don't talk about that."

Sign was on foot in Tottenham, within an area that was previously known as 'Little Russia' after Russians had fled there during the 1917 revolution. Though the area had been redeveloped in the 1970s and immigrants had for the most part dissipated from the once toughest neighbourhood in North London, it wasn't difficult to imagine how the place used to be – terraced streets, barrow boys with horses and carts delivering and selling fruit and vegetables, bobbies walking the patch in pairs because it was too dangerous to police the area solo, and overall an atmosphere of crammed poverty, desperation, and brawling survival amidst a populous of scared foreigners trying to make their way in the brutal backstreets of Greater London.

He entered a building that was once a pub where horses were led through the establishment and allowed to rest and feed in the rear courtyard. Now it was a small restaurant that specialised in Russian and Eastern European cuisine, catering for a lingering minority of descendants of émigrés, as well as intrepid and curious foodies. He was greeted by a young woman of sallow complexion who was wearing a *Wolf Alice* T-shirt and had nothing to identify her as being an employee of the eatery. But, she said she worked in the place when Sign said he was looking for a man called Parry. She told him to go through the kitchen and into the back room. She didn't go with him as he walked through the kitchen, past simmering pots of stocks and vegetables and herbs, pans frying poultry, beef, and offal, and two chefs who were sticking wafer-thin knives into a cooked pig to see if the flesh bled as they withdrew the blades. He entered the back room.

Lucas, Aadesh, Noah, and Parry were sitting around a kitchen table, mugs of coffee in front of them, cigarettes in fingers or mouths. All of them were tanned, and in jeans, boots, and T-shirts. None of them got up or looked surprised by his arrival.

Lucas squinted as smoke wafted over his face. "You'll be Sign."

"Call me Ben." He held out his hand.

The Frenchman gripped his hand. "Yeah alright, Ben." He waved at the table. "If you want coffee there's some in the pot."

Sign sat. "Is it good?"

"It's made by Russians."

"In that case I'll pass."

Lucas smiled and pointed at Parry. "The guy that looks like Nosferatu is Parry. Russian. Some of his relatives own this place. He was a Cossack. Or Waffen-SS. Something like that."

"Fuck you." Parry addressed Sign when he said, "Ex Spetsnaz Alpha. Russian Special Forces."

"Yes, yes, he knows what Spetsnaz means." Lucas pointed at the man next to Parry. "*Life of Pi* over there is Aadesh. Likes killing English Gurkha officers. Not much else to him. Makes good goat curry, though. And the man next to me who looks like a 1970s porn star is Noah. Swedish. A repentant bent cop who's gained salvation by doing things that no cop, bent or otherwise, would do."

Noah muttered, "Stop calling me *bent*." He said to Sign, "Cop only in name. I never did any police work. I was counterterrorism special operations."

Sign nodded. "I know your backstories." He looked at Lucas. "And what of you? A French revolutionary who has escaped Madame Guillotine?"

Lucas shrugged. "The revolutionaries operated the guillotine."

"True, but then there was all that petty infighting. Some of the revolutionaries didn't fare so well. Turns out you were one of them. Next time, perhaps you'll be smarter?"

Lucas' grin vanished, replaced by a steely look. "Peter Raine informed me that you told MI6 to go fuck itself."

Sign smiled.

Lucas blew out smoke. "So, perhaps we are all ousted revolutionaries, with no causes and only old stories to tell. Or maybe not. We're here. You're here. Speak."

Sign immediately took to Lucas and his men. There were aspects of them that were to be expected of such seasoned warriors – a toughness that was evident from fifty paces; thousand yard stares; gallows humour; plethora of scars; athletic, muscular physiques; and overall a poised demeanour that suggested all the fun and frolics of downtime were merely stop gaps between the sole reason they were put on Earth – to cause absolute mayhem and carnage in war. Men like this were rare, even within the best forces of battle-hardened warrior nations that had hewn their combatants via circumstance and history. But that's not what interested Sign. Rather, he liked the fact that they were not bothered one iota by meeting him in the back room of an odd restaurant in North London, having just flown from Tanzania to London via Istanbul. They were unconventional.

He chose his words carefully when he said, "Your objective is to kill a senior British official. He carries the codename The Thief. He is the man you tried to kill in Bergen. His identity is unknown, although we have four suspects. An equally important objective is to protect two male and two female junior British officers. Tomorrow at ten AM they will be conducting a manoeuvre which I hope will prompt The Thief to take action; namely kill one or more of the four. But, I've taken precautions. The four, collectively known as 'runners', will go into hiding tomorrow, somewhere in Britain. They don't know each other. They will be operating alone. For a reason I will come onto, Raine isn't to know where they'll go to ground. Your job is to covertly follow them, ascertain the location of where they hole up, watch them without them knowing, and kill anyone who seeks to cause them harm."

Lucas asked, "Anyone?"

Sign nodded. "I don't care if they're wearing civilian clothes or uniforms, If one person or multiple persons poses a threat to the runner you're watching, kill that person or persons."

Lucas shrugged. "Okay."

Sign shifted his gaze between each member of the team. "There was a fifth runner; a young man, selected by Raine. The Thief killed him. I should have anticipated what happened. The other runners must be kept safe. But, Britain is a hostile territory. Trust is a major issue. You answer to me and Peter. No one else. But, I've told Raine that he's not to know your orders. The Thief is onto Raine. The only reason Peter's still alive is because it suits The Thief to keep him alive."

"Why?"

"I can't go into specifics, but suffice it to say sometimes it pays to keep one enemy alive so that he can run back and tell his comrades what happened."

Lucas stubbed out his cigarette. "But, that could change. The Thief may become desperate and go after Raine and put the squeeze on him. You're keeping Raine in the dark on some issues so that he can't spew what he hasn't eaten."

"Yes." He opened a briefcase and handed Lucas four dossiers. "Each runner. Detail is scant, but you've got in there names, mugshots, London home addresses, and a brief synopsis of their current jobs and what's known about their families." It had been tricky, but Sign had obtained the information earlier in the day without consulting a soul or anything linked to the agencies the runners worked for. "They're under instructions to go completely off the radar, but they're youngsters and may break rules or mess up. That said, my feeling is they'll stick to the script and go somewhere neutral in Britain."

"What if one or more of them tries to leave the UK?"

Sign sighed. "God, I hope they don't. But, if that happens you're going to have to take extraordinary action. Whoever's watching the runner is going to have to do a hard intervention. Go up to them, speak to them, and tell them to about-face and get away from the ferry port or airport or wherever they are. Make sure that they're under no illusion that leaving the UK is a catastrophic mistake that won't be tolerated. Once they've complied, follow them from distance and resume UK-centric duties."

"Sure." Lucas didn't bother opening the dossiers. Instead he flicked one each to his team members and said to them, "Examine your runner. I want codenames for use in comms." He opened his file and looked at the contents while saying, "Mr. Sign – I hope my allocation of resources is self-evident." He scrutinised the only photo, closed his file, and looked at the others. "I have MI6 officer Toby Bancroft aka *Baby Face Nelson*."

Noah frowned. "Who's Baby Face Nelson?"

"American gangster in the twenties and thirties. Hung around with Dillinger." He prodded the photo in his dossier. "MI6 are a bunch of extortionists and racketeers. Bancroft works for MI6 and has got a youthful, slightly chubby face. So, Baby Face Nelson."

"Makes sense." Noah peered at his photo. "I've got GCHQ guy Rishi Prasad. I can't think of any gangster shit for him, so I'm going to go for *Ravi Shankar*."

Sign smiled. The others looked nonplussed.

Noah elaborated. "You know – the famous Indian sitar player. He was really good. I like the correlation between Shankar's command of notes and Prasad's command of numbers."

With solemnity, Parry said, "You've chosen the name because he's Indian. Have you considered that in doing so you are being racist?"

"That's a bit rich coming from you, Mr. Aryan-Race." Noah smiled.

"I'm Slavic, you fuckwit."

Noah raised his eyebrows. "Whatever. Back in the day, you'd have been there, collaborating, sorting out the extermination camps. That has you written all over it."

"I..!"

Aadesh said, "Look - Ravi Shankar's Indian; Prasad's not exactly a surname that came from the Anglo-Saxons. Just fucking get on with it."

Parry shrugged. "Just so long as my objection is noted by the committee." He smiled. "I've got Metropolitan Police officer Molly Crease. Now, she reminds me of this goth chick who loved me many times when I was once on leave in the Russian army. You wouldn't believe what she…"

Aadesh grabbed his file and gave him his. "On the basis that you can't be trusted with her, I'll have goth chick." He looked at Lucas and waved his newly acquired file. "*Goth Chick*. Cool with that?"

Lucas nodded.

Parry opened his file and rolled his eyes. "Oh good, a gypsy. Outstanding." He tossed the file onto the table. "Alright. MI5 officer Kazia Baltzar aka *Screaming Harridan*."

"I beg your pardon?" Lucas leaned forward, grabbed Parry's file, and looked at Baltzar's photo. "She's young and beautiful." He slid the file back to the Russian.

Parry nodded. "She reminds me of the lead singer of a Moscow death metal band called *Screaming Harridans*."

The former legionnaire said, "Please tell me you didn't touch the lead singer when you were on leave."

"Not to my knowledge, no."

"Alright." Lucas sipped his coffee and said, "That's settled then. I've got MI6 officer *Baby Face Nelson*; Noah's got GCHQ officer *Ravi Shankar*; Aadesh's got Met Police officer *Goth Chick*; and Parry's got MI5 officer *Screaming Harridan*. Any questions?"

The others shook their heads.

Lucas looked at Sign. "We'll get onto this straightaway. Communications equipment, weapons, and other kit, we've got covered. We'll need a link to you. Let's go over communications and other protocols."

Sign and the team spoke for ten minutes. After they were content with logistical arrangements, Sign stood and said, "I remind you that you are behind enemy lines. Trust no one but each other and me. If Raine contacts you, always assume that he's doing so with a gun being held to his head. Good hunting, gentlemen."

At nearly ten PM, Knutsen and Lebrun entered the Westminster safe house. Lebrun was pulling a medium-sized trolley bag; Knutsen had a mountaineering rucksack slung over one shoulder. Raine was sitting at the small dining table, a large plastic carrier bag, plates, cutlery, glasses, and a jug of water in front of him. Lebrun pulled her bag along the tiny hallway and stopped.

Raine said, "Good evening, Mrs. Lebrun. Welcome to London."

The German detective looked around and said, "Yeah, great."

Raine smiled. "The River Thames is behind me, your bedroom is to your left, so too the bathroom, and the lounge and kitchen are where you're standing. There's nothing more to your immediate surroundings, so please sit down and eat."

Lebrun sat at the table.

Knutsen said to Raine, "That's me done. I've got to see if I've still got a girlfriend." He left.

Raine addressed Lebrun. "How do you feel?"

"In need of answers. Aside from that, I'm used to the unusual."

"No doubt." Raine started withdrawing cartons of food from the bag. "I thought you might fancy a takeaway. It's from a place not far from here. Should still be warm. But, I didn't order it. Let's see what they supplied us with." He opened the cartons. "Lamb; chicken; rice; potato dish; yoghurt; fresh salad." He nodded approvingly. "It seems we are in for a Levantine treat. Tuck in."

Nothing fazed Lebrun. But she was alert and on her guard. She helped herself to food and poured water. "When eating one-to-one in Mediterranean countries it's traditional for the woman at the table to serve the man. We tend not to do that in Germany. Still, we're eating Mediterranean food and we're in an anything-goes situation." She served him food. "Tom was nice. He likes you, though thinks you need to improve your cloak-and-dagger skills. Something about perfume." She smiled. "Whoops."

Raine ignored the comment. "How did you manage to extricate yourself from your German police duties?"

"I told my boss I was pursuing a lead related to the Wick case. He asked for more details. I told him I wasn't prepared at this stage to divulge information. He started talking in a raised tone. I walked out. Here I am." She ate. "It's okay. My boss is hot air. He trusts me."

"Your husband? Children?"

"My husband's an inventor and spends most of his time working from home. He'll look after the kids. My family's used to me packing my bags and heading off on a case. They're fine." She nodded approvingly. "I wasn't hungry but this is amazing. You should let the takeaway restaurant know."

The diplomat wasn't going to tell her that Sign had cooked the food when he heard Lebrun had landed. "After dinner you're going to find out everything. With you here, there are four of us involved, though we do have support in the guise of four other paid individuals. And we're up against four. There will be no more secrets. If you let me down, the end of your career will be the least of your problems. Are you happy with that arrangement?"

"Four of us? You, Knutsen, me, and one other?"

"One other."

"Up against four?"

"One of whom killed Alex Wick."

"Murdered by your British traitor?"

"Correct." Raine ate. "In Munich, I told you to trust no one in Germany and Britain unless I say otherwise. I'm now saying otherwise. The two men in our team, one of whom you've met, are to be wholly trusted."

"If you say so." She made no attempt to hide the sarcasm in her voice.

"I say so. This is no time for antagonism within. You'll agree with me after you've heard all the detail about what's happening." He smiled and said gently and honestly, "Superintendent Lebrun – we wanted you here for a reason. More specifically, I suggested to the others that you should join our team. I don't make such decisions every day or lightly."

She raised her eyebrows and nodded. "Okay."

It was time to change the subject. While they ate their meal, Raine enquired about her knowledge of London. Though she was well travelled, both through work and pleasure, she'd only fleetingly been to London a couple of times. He told her about the nearby layout of central London, where he worked, transportation systems, a potted and selective history of the capital, and that in the bottom drawer to the left of the cooker was a manual containing a list of instructions and emergency telephone numbers in case of need by the occupants of the flat. "Think of this place as an Airbnb. Imagine you're on holiday. Except you're not on holiday. At all." He smiled.

"Airbnb?"

"When someone rents out their home. Actually, maybe Airbnb's the wrong description. The last person to stay here was a member of parliament who blew his brains out to avoid standing trial for corruption. Holiday let will do."

She momentarily closed her eyes and smiled. "Brilliant. Sleeping in a bed that was previously the place where someone painted the bedroom with brain matter."

"No. That took place in here. In the exact spot you're sitting in, as it happens." He stood. "I'll clear up while you unpack. Then, you're going to take a walk across the river. For security reasons I can't come with you, but I'll give you directions." He started placing empty cartons in the bag, and then paused. "The person you're going to meet tonight, the fourth member of the team, is… different. He's a former MI6 officer."

"What's MI6?"

It wasn't surprising she didn't know. There was no reason for a German detective's path to have strayed so fully into the secret world to know what MI6 was. Raine told her and concluded, "Forget what you think you know from books or the movies. When you meet him, imagine that you're in the presence of an alien of contrarian intelligence who's taken human form. Or imagine him sitting on the toilet. I find the latter imagery works for me. Either way, keep telling yourself you're a good person who knows her own mind." He breathed in deeply, looked away, and said to himself. "Yes. That should work." He walked to the kitchen and commenced his chores.

One hour later, Lebrun was in the lounge of Sign's West Square flat. Knutsen wasn't here. Sign was.

Sign shook her hand and said, "Let me take your coat. It seems you've suffered our British weather."

She handed him her sodden garment while looking around. "We get rain in Germany. What is this place?"

"Ha!" He hung her coat on a stand. "I am a magpie that drifts on the Earth's thermals. I descend when something takes my fancy."

"A very discerning magpie." She walked to the mantelpiece and touched a skull. "You have an interest in anthropology?"

Sign came to her side. "I have very precise channels of enquiry into history. The rest is tedium and therefore irrelevant to me. But this fellow is somewhat more current. He was a brute of a man with a brain to match his sizeable skull. He still interests me. Alas, my hand was forced to end matters. Were circumstances different, it would have been good to keep him under lock and key so that I could examine him." He gestured to the armchairs. "Where are my manners? Please take a seat." He stood in front of his chair, forcing her to choose Knutsen's chair.

She sat next to the crackling fire; close to her knees was the coffee table containing the horizontal touchscreen computer.

Sign didn't ask her if she wanted a drink or, if so, what kind. He went to the drinks cabinet, poured two glasses of *Bunnahabhain* single malt whiskey, brought the drinks over, handed her a glass, and sat down. He studied her. "Welcome to the front line." He sipped his drink while keeping his eyes on her. "What news from Germany?"

For some reason Lebrun felt like laughing but couldn't. She wanted Sign to stop looking at her. "Local elections are imminent; protests in Düsseldorf against the proposed banning of the burqa; protests against the protests; the free-movement spat with Poland continues; violent crime in Frankfurt has increased by twenty two percent last year; there is intelligence that this year's Oktoberfest will be infiltrated by expert pickpockets from Czechia; and the frontrunner for the Chancellor election is…"

"Going to withdraw from the race in precisely fifty eight days' time or my patience with him will wear thin. Good. That's Germany sorted, then. And meanwhile here you are, in the eye of the storm."

Lebrun took a sip of her single malt. "Who are we up against?"

"A brilliant anarchist who wishes to shortly retire with a whopping pension." Sign's next words were cold and slow. "He is also the most dangerous man in the world."

Lebrun frowned and her tone was dubious when she said, "That's some assessment."

"It may sound grandiose, but I'm not prone to exaggeration."

"What are you prone to?"

He waved a hand. "If any label can stick, it's one that accuses me of being a scholar of the human condition."

"You find people interesting?"

"I find most of them insufferably dull. But then," he smiled and his tone changed as his words sped up with enthusiasm, "there is the good stuff."

"Your laboratory."

"My playground."

"I doubt that's the right description for your activities." She cleared her throat while feeling unsettled for some reason. "Why is he the most dangerous man in the world?"

His expression reverted to one of seriousness. "He is like me but no longer cares about suffering."

She replied in a stern tone, "Let's hope you keep caring otherwise we'd have *two* most dangerous *men* in the world."

"Yes." Sign glanced at the fire and looked back at her. "He doesn't care about wars – local, regional, international, or global. Pain, suffering, and death are irrelevant. Honour, integrity, friendship, and love are of no consequence beyond the purpose they serve. He has given up on fellow man and woman."

"Sounds like he has no conscience."

Sign shook his head. "Once he did, as well as having heart. I suspect that to be the case, at least."

She thought about some of the murderers she'd arrested. "Do you think something snapped in him?"

"No. I believe that one day everything made sense to him."

Lebrun's mind raced. "He's playing God."

"Not *playing* God. But, you're not the first to make such an astute connection." He turned on the computer. "Peter trusts you. His instincts are always right. Therefore the assumption is that I should trust you. Do you believe I'd be right to do so?"

The question was so calmly delivered that at first she didn't know how to answer. "Yes. Well... I suppose it depends on your relationship with Raine. But, I don't see why not."

Sign's gaze was penetrating. "Do I trust you? Yes or no?"

Her heart started beating faster. She hated that. "Yes."

Sign kept looking at her for a few seconds, then looked at the computer, brought up his 'CHALICE' picture file, and pressed the rotate button so that it was facing the detective. "This outlines what is happening. Look at it as I speak." He told her about the setup of CHALICE and the number of people cleared to access its files, The Thief's theft of CHALICE reporting, The Thief's clients, Raine's return from Washington DC and self-instructed tasking to identify The Thief, how a Syrian defector had given Raine the lead of Torbjørn Lystad aka the broker aka The Fence, the assault on Lystad's safe house by Raine's team, Lystad's death, The Thief's escape, the Norwegian language angle and how that had whittled down nearly one thousand suspects to five, his role in creating a plan to identify and neutralise The Thief, bios of The Library members, their runners, deployment of runner Alex Wick to try to dry up Chinese payments to The Thief, Wick's murder, and the new tactic to lure The Thief towards intelligence requiring him to identify the sources in order for the intelligence to have saleable value. "Today, the four remaining runners have been fully activated. Also, Faraday successfully removed from CHALICE all immediate action intelligence. The Thief is left with very interesting intelligence that won't be of use to him; but he's also left with our newly created MAYFLY file. Tomorrow that file will be filled with four runner reports. The runners will then immediately go to ground in Britain." He partially lied. "None of us know where they'll go into hiding. Superficially, it is our dear hope that MAYFLY will be irresistible to The Thief and that he will make every effort to identify and track down each runner. Providing each runner maintains impeccable tradecraft, The Thief won't find them. In reality, The Thief knows that MAYFLY is a work of fiction and is The Library's tactic to get him to make a mistake. So, The Thief is left with two choices: do nothing; or, play along as if he's trying to steal MAYFLY intelligence that in due course he can fully source."

"Why would he play along?"

In a measured tone, Sign replied, "He wants to instil fear in us. We've gifted him the ideal means to do that. He knows we're dangling the runners as bait. He also knows The Library's dangling itself as bait. And he knows we think we'll nab him that way. So, he'll play along and go after the runners, or us, and he'll do so in a way that puts the fear of God in us. He hopes we'll implode. He carries on. No one is closer to identifying him." He shrugged. "Or, he may do nothing. I find myself in the horrible position of hoping he does something."

"Such as going for Raine."

"And anyone associated with Peter."

She looked up. "*Anyone* means The Library…"

"One of whom is The Thief."

"And you, Knutsen, and me if The Thief finds out what I'm doing here."

Sign nodded. "If he gets you on your own, he'll savage you and kill you once he's got what he wants. There'll be no other outcome."

She shook her head and muttered, "Just one man."

"Hold on to that thought. Just one man who'll die if any of us put a bullet in his brain. We need to be in a position to take that shot."

She stared at The Library entry on the whiteboard. "So much depends upon whether The Thief knows about the Norwegian language angle."

"Incorrect. I'm sure he knows each member of The Library speaks Norwegian. Thus, he knows that Peter knows that one of four members of the assembly is The Thief. But, that leaves three innocent officers who may or may not know they all speak Norwegian."

"If they find out, they'll turn on each other."

"Maybe."

Lebrun looked at him. "Maybe? What do you mean?"

Sign shrugged. "I mean that I don't know."

At that moment she decided she trusted Sign considerably less than Raine, who she'd already pegged as a slippery character. She posed many of the options and questions that had been raised at Library meetings and by Knutsen, including rounding up the suspects and interrogating them.

Sign answered each point and concluded, "The route we are taking is the only route available to us."

"Your route."

"My route, yes."

She was silent for a while. "It's very clear to me what your role and Peter's role is in the operation. But, what about Tom and I? What do we do?"

Sign breathed out deeply. "With Peter's help, I've set everything up. We are about to enter unchartered waters. As of tomorrow we are deploying a significant tactic of agitation. It will be a game-changer. But, we cannot predict how events will now unfold. My suspicion is that everything is about to go to…" he considered the next word, "shit. Yes. It's all about to go to shit. That's my cerebral conclusion." He smiled.

"*Deliberately* go to shit. This is what you want. Give the anarchist your anarchy and see who wins."

"I'd thought about it in more scientific terms but yes, that is what I wish for. As a result, you and Tom will be needed. I very much doubt this will end with Wick being the only casualty. Early tomorrow morning, Tom will come to your flat and tell you what I have in mind for you both."

"I see." She gestured towards the computer screen. "I hadn't realised it was as complex and serious as this."

"Now you know."

"Now I know." She finished her drink and looked at the fire. "The Thief is… rare."

"He is."

While watching the flames she said, "I believe there is another reason why you think The Thief may play along with the MAYFLY tactic."

Sign was motionless. "Clever, detective."

She looked at him. "Not that clever, because I can't work out what the reason could be. Why won't you tell me?"

"Because I've only just met you." His smile returned. "We are still in the courting phase."

She stood and extended her hand. "If you have your gun trained on The Thief, don't hesitate. You are not looking at you. Goodnight Mr. Sign."

He shook her hand, helped her with her coat, walked her to the downstairs communal door and wished her goodnight. Back in the flat, he sat by the fire while deep in thought.

Knutsen arrived thirty minutes later. He made a couple of mugs of tea, brought the drinks over to the fireplace, and sat down. "What did you think of her?"

Sign was dwelling on other matters. He forced himself to fleetingly consider his friend's question. "Intelligent; circumspect; unsure about me; likes you; perceptive; good reader of people; feels out of her depth; brave but not to the extent of foolhardiness; and currently feels like she's the outsider in our team. She's an unconventional individual by nature but has never had the opportunity to be unconventional in work. This is all new to her. She will treat you as a stalwart brother, Raine as a firm-but-fair father, and me as a curiosity. Probably there'll be necessary tweaks to that assessment."

Knutsen sipped his drink. "What next?"

"I want you and Lebrun to keep a weather eye on Peter. Two of you can't do round-the-clock surveillance, but choose peak times to be close to him – when he moves, is out of the FCO building, and moments of your choosing when he's at home."

"You want us to protect Raine?"

"I prefer the word 'watch', but protect, yes." Sign's mind was working at a rate of knots. "Make sure you know where he is at ten AM tomorrow. That will be the commencement of your detail. It will continue thereafter until further notice. Go to Lebrun no later than seven AM. Bring her a coffee, pastry, and a sidearm. On the breakfast table, lay out a map of London and a map of Britain. Make sure she's geographically orientated. Sort communications between the two of you." He stretched but refused to give in to fatigue. "In fact do what you do and sort everything."

"Sure." Knutsen could tell that his colleague was unsettled. "Big day tomorrow."

"Indeed it is."

"Are you worried about the runners?"

"Alongside identifying The Thief, their safety is my overriding priority." Sign breathed deeply to get oxygen into his brain. The action helped. "I've assigned four devils to protect the runners. They're Raine's men, though he has no control over them and nor does he know my instructions to them. Peter must not know the location of each runner and ergo he must not know what orders I've given the devils. Nor must Lebrun. That information is for your ears only, my friend."

Knutsen nodded. "Understood."

Sign looked at him. "You've kept your trusty SIG Sauer clean?" He was referring to Knutsen's P226 handgun, a devastatingly effective model that was the preferred pistol of many Special Forces units.

The former undercover operative smiled. "Stop fussing. I'm good to go."

"Yes, of course." His voice trailed as he said, "Forgive me." He looked at the flames. "If things go bad for you, remember every single component of our *Crozier* plan."

The plan was named after Francis Crozier, the Irish Royal Navy captain of HMS Terror who'd disappeared in 1848 while exploring the Artic Ocean's unnavigated North West Passage. *Crozier* was a last resort. It involved a series of steps that needed to be taken if one or both of them had done something that meant they had to vanish from the face of the planet. In understated terms, Sign referred to the escape plan as needed *if the wheel comes off.* By contrast, Knutsen used the somewhat more robust description of Crozier as a means to *get out of Dodge if everything turns into a goddamn motherfucking heap of shit.*

Knutsen said, "I'll be alright, mate."

Sign nodded slowly. He leaned closer to his friend, bowed his head, and asked quietly and earnestly, "Do you judge me to be an intelligent man?"

Knutsen laughed. "For fuck's sake."

"It's a serious question and one that is not posed to elicit a flattering or otherwise response. I trust your judgement. Your answer may be wholly pertinent to the likelihood of me succeeding or failing."

"Oh come on Ben. Do I really need to spell it out for you?"

Sign's thought process was in another zone. "I must gauge my intelligence comparative to The Thief's intelligence. If we are of equal, above average intelligence, then I stand a chance of succeeding. If one of us is out of kilter with the other, then my wholly misleading allusion to Lebrun of resultant anarchy may turn out to be prophetic."

"Why did you tell Karin we were heading into anarchy?"

"To keep her on her toes and to ensure that she's armed with the concept that I can get things wrong. It's my hope that what's about to happen will be anything but anarchy and instead will play out with clockwork precision. But, if The Thief and I are mismatched then anarchy may well prevail."

Knutsen was quiet for a moment, deep in thought. "A grand chess master fears a novice far more than another grand chess master because a novice is unpredictable. A novice can induce anarchy. Strategy goes out of the window. You hope you're facing a chess master, so that you can strategize. If you're facing an amateur, you can't predict what might happen next."

"Quite so."

"Everything suggests you're facing a grand chess master. The question is, have you got a plan to beat him?"

Sign scoffed. "I have a plan to see if he makes a mistake so that I can topple him. Aside from that, my plan is to see if his plan is precisely the plan that I predict he'll conduct. That's it, dear fellow. Right now I'm in a flight holding pattern, circling close to a runway that I hope has been configured by another and in exactly the way I predicted. If the runway is higgledy-piggledy I might as well jump out of the cockpit."

"Yeah but you're missing an obvious problem."

"Which is?"

"What happens if The Thief's smarter than you?"

The comment lifted Sign's spirits. "He may well be because I hadn't considered that possibility."

Knutsen chuckled then turned serious. "Either way you're about to play each other, without meeting and without knowing who you are. What are you not telling me?"

"Lebrun asked me the same thing." He stood. "I haven't told you what I would do now if I was The Thief."

"Which becomes irrelevant if, one way or the other, The Thief isn't your equal."

"Correct." Sign walked to a sideboard, opened a drawer, and withdrew his L131A1 Glock 17 pistol, checked the double-stack 9mm Parabellum seventeen round magazine, stood in the centre of the room, expertly held the gun in two hands, adopted the correct stance, and aimed at the skull Lebrun had prodded. He imagined the slight recoil he'd receive if he put three perfect shots into the side of the head, nodded, placed the gun on top of the touchscreen computer, and sat back down.

Knutsen said, "Let's assume you're right and you get The Thief in your sights. *How* are you right? What the fuck ain't you telling the bloke who's saved your arse quite a few times?"

"Four times, to be precise. And one of those times was a fluke." Sign finished his tea. He was conflicted. Should he tell Knutsen everything? He trusted his colleague implicitly and had never withheld information from him before. But, he could be wrong about what might happen next and he didn't want Knutsen to second guess something that could turn out to be patently inaccurate. That said, for all of his occasionally dumbed-down, guttural utterances, Knutsen was razor-sharp, could out-think most people Sign knew, and had the ability to remain calm, focused, and juggle multiple scenarios in even the most exacting of situations.

What to do?

He made a decision and told him everything.

CHAPTER 15

Today was the day.

The pieces were about to be placed on the board.

The players were ready to assemble on the pitch.

The soldiers were combat-ready to step onto the battlefield.

Whatever analogy one wanted to use, today was the day when anarchy could commence, everything might turn to shit, or dark events would begin with note-perfect orchestration.

At 0645hrs Knutsen arrived at the Westminster safe house, carrying breakfast, communications equipment, a change of clothes, cash, the maps Sign had spoken about, ammunition, his SIG Sauer handgun, and a Smith and Wesson M&P Shield compact .45 ACP pistol which he gave to Karin Lebrun. She expertly checked the weapon's workings and asked whether he'd selected her gun because she was expected to shoot The Thief through several building walls. While munching pastries and swigging coffee they set to work.

Lucas, Noah, Aadesh, and Parry were exactly where they wanted to be – outside the homes of each runner.

At 0701hrs, Peter Raine boarded the train from Hertford North to London King's Cross. He'd be in the Foreign & Commonwealth Office in King Charles Street, Whitehall, by no later than eight thirty. He'd kept his diary clear of FCO meetings today. But, he would be noticed by colleagues who no doubt would assume he was spending the day at work doing admin tasks.

Edward Sassoon, Gordon Faraday, Rex Hare, and Hamish Duggan, left their homes at slightly different times but they'd all be in their headquarters at no later than nine. Like Raine, they'd ensured that there would be no internal or external distractions to divert their attention away from what was about to happen.

Rishi Prasad exited his house-share on Courtenay Street, walked to Cheltenham's High Street, caught a bus from outside *Poundland*, arrived at GCHQ headquarters, went direct to his desk in an open plan office within the doughnut, spent an hour drafting his fake report, checked his watch, and waited for ten o'clock to happen.

Toby Bancroft was unaware that he was being followed as he walked from his apartment in South London's Kennington to the local tube station. Spies tend to only deploy anti-surveillance drills when they're working. For the rest of the time, including commuting to work in the spy's home country, they're like everyone else. Ordinarily the junior officer might be thinking about something trivial such as what to have for lunch. Today was very different, but nevertheless his head was figuratively in the clouds and he was oblivious to the make-up of the pedestrians close to him. He took a train to Vauxhall, the nearest stop to the main MI6 building, went to the floor containing the Iran Team, and began writing his MAYFLY report.

After six months of the helter-skelter of undercover work, Molly Crease felt weird going to Scotland Yard at a time when most office workers were heading to central London. As she walked from her pad on Old Kent Road to her nearest bus stop, she had the strangest sensation that she was betraying the night-time and early-hours workers that she passed – taxi drivers, café employees, road workers, and others who kept odd hours and had never experienced the humdrum of nine to five Monday to Friday routine. The unusual sensation was compounded by her inhalation of crack cocaine smoke before leaving her home. Still, the drug stopped her body going into meltdown. She caught the bus, entered the Yard, said a few hellos to colleagues she hadn't seen for a while, explained that she had to dive straight into a mountain of post-undercover paperwork, logged-in on a spare computer terminal, and wrote a work of fiction.

Kazia Baltzar did what she usually did when she travelled from her flat in Highgate, North London, to MI5's Thames House building – she ran with a backpack containing work clothes and toiletries. Only, today her pack contained extra clothes and other items. She reached the headquarters, used her swipe-card to pass through a security pod, went to the gym, and showered and changed. From the cafeteria she bought coffee and two slices of toast and marmite, went to her office, put in earphones so she could listen to her music and not be disturbed by others, and began tapping on her computer keyboard.

At ten o'clock the runners were poised.

For the final time, Prasad read his report on the proposed Anglo-New Zealand attack on North Korean military communications between the Korean mainland and its coastal fleet. He was satisfied it was a perfect replication of the script Faraday had shown him. Part of him felt pride that he'd not only been entrusted to perform this duty but had also done everything correctly to get to this point. However, he was also fully aware that this wasn't a case of getting a pat on the back for excellent grades at Sherborne independent boarding school for boys; or for producing a superb paper on combinatorial number theory at the University of Oxford. This was something else. And so much depended on what position he held in Faraday's no doubt complex equation. Faraday was hard to fathom. In part the man seemed like many of the eccentric boffins who populated GCHQ. But, was it playacting? Prasad had seen glimpses, just the slightest of glimpses, of another man altogether – someone who had steel and knew so much more about the world than he was letting on. And one didn't get the extremely rare and prestigious The Fields Medal for mathematics by simply being superb with numbers. One had to be a game-changer, a tactician, and ultimately a leader and shepherd of numbers. So, Prasad decided he was in the hands of a genius. What nagged him was whether Faraday had a heart. Never mind. This could be fun. He accessed CHALICE and the subsection MAYFLY file, pressed 'Upload File', selected his report, positioned his cursor over the 'Submit' icon, hesitated, felt exhilarated, smiled, and clicked his mouse button.

Bancroft's report was ready. According to him, Israel had elevated its state of security preparedness to Stage 3 in order to ready itself for a potential nuclear strike against Iran. As Sassoon had instructed, he'd omitted details of whether the Israeli assault would actually happen and if so when. The strike was possible, not certain. That ambiguity was crucial. After all, this was long-game intelligence, not immediate-action. He was in no doubt that he'd go through with the task, but felt uncertain. He knew the job was needed to catch a traitor. But he was also cognisant that he was operating in the dark on most matters. He wasn't naïve to Sassoon's predilection to be a manipulator, a liar, and a man who takes the truth and carves it into a shape of his liking. But, though he couldn't be sure, he also suspected that Sassoon cared about his welfare. His reference to the *Suicide In The Trenches* poem he'd cryptically cited in Greenwich Park had been telling. That said, did he trust Sassoon to look after him? Or did he trust the senior commander to ensure Bancroft was fully fit before Sassoon sent him to his death? God knows. He uploaded the file and sent it into MAYFLY.

Crease had to slowly read her draft MAYFLY report ten times to ensure she'd hadn't been clumsy in her writing. She felt she was thinking clearly, but was aware that the drug in her system was making her *think* she was thinking clearly. She didn't trust her judgement and therefore approached the task like an inebriated person who has to grapple with his or her drunken state when confronted by a very serious and unexpected situation. After her painstaking and torturous last read, she was satisfied the report looked like it had been written by a sober officer. The content was really going to cause a shit-storm, she concluded. If the report got into the wrong hands, the Provisional Irish Republican Army would tear itself apart trying to find two non-existent senior PIRA officers who had been spying for the national police service of the Republic of Ireland and handed over by the Garda to the Metropolitan Police Service which was continuing to run them. She didn't know if she was doing the right thing, but was so exhausted and run-down from her previous assignment that she didn't really care. All that mattered is that Hare thought it was important. What she did care about was spending time away from duties so that she could get her health and life back. Even though she thought Hare was secretive, overly quiet and watchful, and an incredibly intelligent individual whose reason for being in the police was inexplicable to other cops, he always had purpose and his track-record of success was outstanding. Crucially, he'd gifted her a window of opportunity to get her shit together. She clicked 'Submit'.

Baltzar placed one booted-foot on her opposite leg, leaned back in her chair, put her fingertips together in front of her chin, and looked at the report she'd written. It was good to submit, but she waited for a moment. The report was sensational and could cause Russia pain if it learned of its contents. It suggested that the UK secret agencies were running a Russian agent, codename *Promise*, who was potentially in danger of being discovered by his or her Russian masters. Promise wanted out. But, a decision had been made by MI5 to keep Promise in play for another eight months before arranging the agent's exfiltration to the UK. Eight months was a long time. During that period, the Russian intelligence services would be on high alert to identify and neutralise Promise. As with many witch hunts, there could be problems along the way including false allegations against colleagues, resignations, job losses, unjust imprisonments, maybe worse. The irony of dangling a fictitious traitor to catch a real traitor was not lost on Baltzar. Just one document on a computer screen in London could cause untold damage so far away. During the brief time she'd been in MI5 she'd done a few crazy things; some quite dangerous. And she'd had a baptism of fire of learning how to make snap decisions on her own in pressurised and time-sensitive situations. This felt different and she knew why. This was the first time she was doing something with the full knowledge it would put her and Duggan in danger. She didn't know who Duggan's colleagues were in his venture; nor did she know who the other runners were. As a result, she couldn't worry about them. Duggan was different. It seemed like yesterday that the burly Scotsman had swaggered into the tough Roma camp near Birmingham, without a care in the world that men with muscles on their spit were looking at the intruder. Her sixteen year old self was sitting on grass next to her caravan. He'd squatted before her. She remembered that the move had made her think he looked like an Olympic power lifter. When he spoke to her he had such conviction, clarity in his eyes, certainty, and compassion. Her Dad had been dead for a year and to be honest in his last couple of years he'd preferred gambling and brawling to fatherhood. By comparison, Duggan was, she'd thought back then, the real deal. She'd thought the same ever since. They had a strange, intertwined relationship – him helping her become a woman, her helping him through his unwanted divorce, and together both of them confronting the world in a way that was no doubt akin to a loving, at times edgy, father-daughter unbreakable unit. And here she was, about to press 'Submit' and in doing so maybe jeopardising everything. She reminded herself that Duggan was made of metal. Yeah, but metal gets worn and rusts, she countered. Still, aching limbs or otherwise, the MI5 man still had the mental and physical fortitude to crush men half his age. Keep telling yourself that, she thought as she pressed the button and uploaded her file onto MAYFLY.

Three runners waited for trains out of London; Prasad was on a train platform in Cheltenham. Lucas and his men expected that. Staying in London and Cheltenham would have been stupid, so travel was required. Car hire and flying were ruled out because both options would have required identification documents. The runners were only permitted to use cash. Long distance taxi journeys were deemed too personal – the driver was likely to remember the passenger and obviously would know pick-up and drop-off points. Getting a coach was possible but unlikely given a pre-booking would probably be needed. If the runners were professional and had been mentored correctly, they'd have avoided pre-bookings of any sort. Plus, coaches were visible, vulnerable, held passengers captive while mobile, and afforded people little flexibility to change direction and coach, save in major coach hubs. Trains were much better – quick, busy, multiple stations allowing flexibility when adjustments to travel were needed, and if boarded by hostiles trains had enough exits and other options to enable potential escape. Plus, train tickets could be paid for in cash.

Crease was on the 1104hrs train from London Paddington to Barnstaple, Devon. Aadesh was in the same carriage. Rain was beginning to fall but visibility out of the carriage was still good – so unlike the old slam-door trains that the former Gurkha used when he was a young soldier doing his training in Shorncliffe, Kent. Back then, when the newly-arrived Nepalese man was sitting on a crammed British train during inclement weather, he felt like he was in third class on the Kathmandu to New Delhi train in the monsoon season. Times had changed. The carriage he was now in was clean, well-ventilated, high-tech, and spacious. Crease appeared to be taking advantage of the comfort by trying to get some sleep before they had to change trains at Exeter St. David's station. When he'd caught glimpses of her during his surveillance in the last sixteen hours, she'd seemed tired and weak. Sleep would do her good. And if she didn't wake up as they approached Exeter or Barnstaple, he'd rouse her by accidentally spilling coffee on her.

At 1115hrs Prasad was on the train departing Cheltenham Spa to Darlington. The three hour and forty five minute journey would cover two hundred and twenty three miles to reach the north-eastern market town that was just over twenty miles south of the city of Durham. He had no luggage, meaning he intended to buy all required items when he reached his destination. though had made time to pick up a takeout cup of tea and a packet of biscuits from a coffee shop at the station. He was also carrying a small booklet of Sudoku and a pencil, both of which he placed on his lap as he stared out of the window while sitting in seat 12a. Behind him, Noah was in seat 18b. Because there was currently nothing particularly captivating to look at outside, just flat uninspiring countryside, the Swede wondered if this was the first time the GCHQ officer had travelled north in England.

Lucas was standing behind Bancroft as the MI6 officer approached the counter of the ticket office in Marylebone Station. He bought a single off-peak ticket to Stratford Upon Avon, citing the 1137hrs train that he was going to catch. When the ticket was procured and he moved out of the way, Lucas bought a ticket for the same journey and time. He moved onto the small concourse, withdrew a flask from his rucksack, and poured a coffee. Bancroft was approximately twenty yards away, standing, reading a book while occasionally glancing at the electronic departures board. Like Prasad, he had no bag. At 1130hrs, it was announced that the 1137hrs was ready for boarding on platform 3. Bancroft inserted his ticket through one of the barriers, entered the platform, and boarded the train. Lucas followed.

At 1200hrs, Baltzar walked along the train platform in Euston, while carrying her rucksack. She was wearing a jacket that's hem rested above her hips, slender trousers that flared at the ankles, her black square-heel biker boots, and her long dark hair was pinned off her face and produced three haphazard yet stylish swathes that resembled rotary blades. Not that he cared, but Parry assessed she was beautiful and had a fashion sense that suggested an idiosyncratic and independent nature. When he'd watched her during the last few hours and she'd had space to move, he'd noted that she deported herself with the elegance, strength, and bewitchment of a matador. Now was different. The platform was crowded and she was hurriedly walking in a manner akin to a hunter following the zigzag route of her hound as it excitedly picked up the scent of its quarry. She boarded the train. Four hours later, she and Parry were in Glasgow Central. She bought a ticket for the train from Glasgow Queen Street to Mallaig, the village and port on the west coast of the Highlands of Scotland. Parry bought a ticket for the same five hour journey and maintained suitable distances away from her as she went to a nearby shop, onwards to the other station, bought and ate a burger, and waited. She caught the train,

That evening, The Library convened in Mrs. Carmichael's shop. The mood was sombre and devoid of levity or banter of any description. Members were uncharacteristically quiet and reflective.

Raine looked at the others. He kept asking himself, which one of you is The Thief? "There's nothing we can do now except wait." Each of them had already told him that their runners had successfully posted their reports and had vanished. Earlier, he'd checked CHALICE and saw that the four reports were in MAYFLY.

"What's The Thief going to do?" Faraday was rubbing his temples. It wasn't clear whether his question was to his colleagues or to himself.

Hare said, "We haven't really discussed how much we think The Thief is selling his CHALICE reports for." He looked at Duggan. "How much would MI5 pay if a Russian version of The Thief approached the UK with stolen Russian intelligence?"

Duggan shrugged. "Depends on so many things. Among them would be the credibility of the source and the significance of the intelligence; the potential to run the source against the target for future intelligence; the circumstances of their domestic and professional setup; other variables."

"Alright, but how much would you pay The Thief?"

The MI5 officer didn't reply straight away. "We would consider him to be A-Grade. He'd be a very wealthy man."

"Per report, five figures, six, seven?"

"Minimum six."

"Meaning seven is very possible." Hare looked at the others. "Our reports have value to multiple potential clients. Take my report. Of course it has significant value to the PIRA. But it also has value to the PIRA's friends and enemies - arms suppliers would want to know if the PIRA can be trusted or whether senior management's a leaky ship; big wallets like America would want to know if we now know about America's support for Irish terrorism against America's closest ally; and so on. As a result, The Thief can produce a bidding war. Loyalist paramilitaries like the Ulster Volunteer Force might offer fifty thousand for the intel; the PIRA a hundred and fifty; the Yanks a million; and then there are the your-enemy-is-my-enemy brigades including Russia. They might outbid America two to five-fold, just so they can get the PIRA back on its feet to keep having a pop at Britain and take our eye off the northern flank. And that's just my report."

Sassoon said, "Presumably you mention this to address Mr. Faraday's question. You surmise that the prospect of such significant financial gain means The Thief will do everything in his power to identify the sources of the MAYFLY reports."

Raine asked him, "Do you disagree?"

Sassoon's expression was cold when he replied, "No. I most certainly do not disagree. Our detective is right to remind us of the large quantity of loot at the end of the rainbow. The Thief will want to have a tête-à-tête with our runners."

Duggan leaned forward, held his head in his hands, and quietly sighed as he looked towards the floor. "Gordon – you'd better be all over who's accessing the MAYFLY file."

Faraday replied, "I am. So far, two hundred and sixteen CHALICE officers have opened the file. By tomorrow I think everyone will have accessed MAYFLY; all nine hundred and eighty two of us."

"So, that's no fucking good then." Duggan raised his head, looked away, gently hammered a fist against his thigh, and looked at Raine. "He's got to identify the names of our runners. That's easy to do but will require a bit of snooping. He'll have to speak to people on the inside of the agencies he doesn't work for. That's one point of vulnerability, *if* we can capture those conversations. Because we don't exist, no one's going to come to us. But, people know you're looking for The Thief, Peter." He looked at Raine. "Officers carrying suspicions about a *Snooping Tom* might come to you."

Raine agreed. "They might. Which is why I've already set in place a mechanism whereby official or casual enquiries about the identities of the MAYFLY authors must come to my attention."

Duggan smiled. "Good man."

"*If* people adhere to your instructions, Peter." Sassoon asked, "And what happens if The Thief doesn't have to snoop? What if he can find out the runners' names through other means? Or, what if The Thief already knows their names?"

Raine didn't answer, but watched the others.

Faraday said, "There are no other means. Official requests for the data or unofficial internal enquiries are the only means open to him. Unless... unless he matches the designations of our officers to names via intel from foreign agencies."

"Yes." Sassoon angled his head and raised his eyebrows. "My designation is CCEE1. I'd bet my bottom dollar that Russia, among others, can match that designation to Edward Sassoon. Still, I'm senior. My Toby Bancroft is a whipper snapper. Would a hostile agency hold the name and designation of a junior officer? Maybe."

Raine thought something wasn't quite right with what Sassoon had just said. But, he wasn't going to challenge him.

Faraday said, "I'm in complete control of CHALICE and MAYFLY. Peter's set his traps to see if he can catch a whisper of someone enquiring about our runners. Rex, Edward – there's nothing you can do except keep your runner phones close to hand. Peter's right. We wait. And we hope The Thief fucks up."

As per protocol, they left one-by-one, allowing each other enough space so that they didn't reconnect by chance outside the bookstore. After Raine, Sassoon, and Hare had left to head home, Faraday wished Duggan goodnight and departed. Duggan waited five minutes and left. He walked along the side street and entered the Strand. Traffic was lighter than usual for this time of evening. He caught sight of Faraday, standing with his back to him while looking for a cab to hail so that he could be taken to Paddington station and get a train back to Cheltenham. Duggan stopped, thinking he should wait until the GCHQ officer was on his way. He decided to break Library protocol. He stood next to Faraday.

"Times like this I bet you wish you lived in London and didn't need to leg it halfway across the country."

Faraday kept his eyes on the road. "You can keep London. In the end it will drive you insane."

The MI5 officer nodded. "Everyone under the age of forty should live in London at least once. Everyone over the age of forty should move out."

Faraday smiled. "Yes." He kept his eyes fixed on oncoming traffic. "What are you doing?"

"Standing next to a fish out of water in theatre land. You're not the only one who needs a taxi."

"I'm not sharing a taxi with you."

"Because of who I am or because of who I work for?"

"Probably both."

"Fair enough." Duggan looked at the night sky. Rain had been on and off throughout the day. He sensed more was on its way. "Have you ever wondered why Raine chose us to join his little gathering?"

Faraday saw a taxi, but its roof light was off meaning it was occupied. He cursed and said with impatient irritation, "Because we're all senior, successful, and have broken rules at various stages of our careers. I'd have chosen us."

"True. But, there are other high-ranking, effective, mavericks he could have chosen. With the exception of Sassoon, that is. No one else is like that aberration."

"We all have our eccentricities. But, you do make a good point. I can't see Raine using 'weirdness' as a criteria for selection."

"It's something Sassoon said to me the other day. He wondered why us. It's been nagging me ever since. Still, we've got far stranger things to worry about, I suppose." He spotted a taxi with its light on. "That'll be you. Have a good one." He walked away in search of a better place to get his own ride to a station.

Faraday entered his cab. As it pulled away he reflected on what Sassoon had said to Duggan. He decided he had a job to do.

Knutsen was relieved to get off the train after it pulled in to the small Hertford East station. His legs were stiff from earlier spending hours standing around in Whitehall, watching the FCO building, and only gaining some respite from inactivity when Raine went to the Strand for The Library meeting. Now, he could exercise. Only two other passengers got off at the market town. One of the passengers was Raine, wearing a suit and overcoat and carrying a briefcase. Knutsen was grateful for the tranquillity and lack of bustle as he walked alone along a mile-long route. The air was windless, sky black, air filled with a fog so thick that it would have been impossible to see anything beyond one's outstretched hand were it not for occasional ornate and antique-style street lamps that acted as minimal ruby-orange dim-glowing beacons for the way ahead. He wandered along a thin old road that took him onto a bridge over the river, carried onwards past a large wild area of parkland that within its centre contained a tiny church with external white lights illuminating its lonely façade and three red deer, saw no houses or any other buildings until he reached the high street, traversed the near-empty market town, and walked into an area of countryside that only contained occasional and standalone large residential properties. He imagined this must be where the wealthy commuters to London resided – people who were investment bankers, lawyers, property developers, or senior Whitehall mandarins like Raine. He couldn't be sure because he didn't know Hertford beyond what he'd researched about the place and specifically what he'd discerned when analysing a map of the area. Knutsen was an expert in many things. Map reading was one of them. Maps allowed him to understand an area better than locals who'd lived there all their lives. And on this occasion, a map had told him the precise route to take from the train station to Raine's home.

Raine was ahead of him, appearing and disappearing in the mist, oblivious to the fact that he was being followed. The diplomat walked into a driveway that led to a large detached property with a substantial front and rear garden. The house had internal lights on. There were glimpses of the diplomat's wife and two daughters. Raine entered the house.

Knutsen stood still on the other side of the lane, close to trees and other foliage. There was no traffic. All was silent. The mist remained thick. Light was minimal. Lebrun came to his side. She'd been here for nearly two hours, watching the house and awaiting the arrival of Raine and Knutsen. Knutsen nodded at her, didn't say anything, and walked off. For the most part he did the reverse of the route he'd just made, but stopped in town and went to the Hertford House Hotel where he and Lebrun had a superior twin bedroom. It was the only room available at short notice in the town's sole central hotel. The room was a stage-post, not necessarily a place to sleep, and in any case Knutsen and Lebrun were professionals and weren't embarrassed to be sharing a bedroom. He ordered coffee to be delivered to the room, went there, sat on a bed, took his boots off, placed his pistol next to him, and waited for Lebrun. She'd be here sometime in the next few hours, after the Raines had gone to bed and she was satisfied the house was secure and that no one was anywhere near the property. Tomorrow morning they'd both follow him to work and toss a coin to ascertain who was on day or night surveillance duty.

Baltzar arrived in Mallaig and checked into a hotel. Parry accessed the WhatsApp group chat that Lucas had set up for the team and Sign. Each member of the group had nicknames. Parry was *Nosferatu*. He wrote, *Screaming Harridan's in The Steam Inn, Mallaig. Suspect she's going to get a ferry to one of the islands. Next crossing's tomorrow.*

The others had already written their entries the day before.

Lucas, aka *Cyrano de Bergerac*, had written, *Baby Face Nelson's in the Crowne Plaza, Stratford Upon Avon.*

Noah, aka *Max von Sydow*, had written, *Ravi Shankar's in the Mercure King's Hotel, Darlington.*

Aadesh, aka *Life Of Pi*, had written, *Goth Chick's holed up in The Park Hotel, Barnstaple.*

Given Parry's latest entry, Sign – aka *The Day Of The Jackal*, so named by Lucas – wrote, *Well played. Agree, Screaming Harridan likely to move on. Also, Goth Chick. Others not sure.*

Lucas wrote, *Noted. No news is good news.* He meant, don't bother with chat-chat and only impart logistical or vital updates.

Armed and alert, Lucas and his team continued their vigils.

Upon arrival in Cheltenham, Faraday didn't go straight home. Instead, he went to his office in GCHQ. Some people were working late in the main building, but it was quiet in the area containing his office and other outbuildings. He turned on his computer terminal and sat alone in his pretend Nissen hut, his desk-lamp the only source of illumination in the unit. Once he'd logged in it didn't take him long to find what he was looking for – the personnel records of Raine, Hare, Sassoon, Duggan, and himself. Others in the UK intelligence services would have had difficulty accessing the files from five different agencies. But, Faraday was a CHALICE gatekeeper. He had access to almost anything and everything. It took him six minutes and twenty two seconds to find a unique commonality between each member of The Library. But, he persevered for a further forty three minutes, looking for other potential areas of overlap – postings overseas and in the UK, joint agency operations involving two or more of The Library members, dates of recruitment into each organisation and activities thereafter, British or foreign persons in common and of interest, hobbies and other leisure pursuits, family and friends, salaries, political leanings, and the security vetting assessments of each person. There was nothing unusual to link them all, save for what he'd spotted from the outset.

Everyone in The Library spoke fluent Norwegian.

He turned off his computer and stared at nothing while deep in thought.

He decided the Norwegian angle could be a major problem.

It was nearly midnight as Sign headed home on foot along the embankment of the Thames. He'd been walking for an hour, with no direction in mind, to get some air, exercise, and to think. Right now, the people that mattered to him were where he wanted them to be – Knutsen and Lebrun were monitoring Raine, the runners were spread across the UK, the cutthroats were guarding them, and the other members of The Library were in or close to London and Cheltenham as per normal. But, one of them was The Thief. He couldn't control that person. All he could do was second-guess him. Pretend he was him. Imagine he was him. Be him.

He walked into West Square. Tonight the place was quiet and the other houses surrounding the square were in darkness. He stopped, looked around, and not for the first time wondered why he liked being encased by what some may perceive to be a cliché of English civility. He supposed that, for all of his worldly and otherworldly attributes, he was deep-down a dyed-in-the-wool Englishman. Back in the day, seafaring adventurers came back from exotic climes to places like the one he was now standing in. It's what they dreamed of when navigating unchartered waters or stepping onto hitherto undiscovered lands. England was a home that had been polished and refined over centuries. For them it was their refined base of operations; the place they could take a breather; a safe haven. But, nowhere – England included - was safe for Sign. So, he created his own home; the one he was standing in front of. And he very deliberately allowed himself to be suckered-in by the Georgian, Victorian, and Edwardian architecture that pervaded metropolitan and rural England. It was all a fantasy, conveniently forgetting that behind the walls of those eras there were atrocious crimes, injustices, abuse, and horrors. But, it was a good fantasy. He had to grapple with true horror. If one knowingly bought-in to the superficial politeness of times gone by, one could take a break from treating smashed body-parts like jigsaw pieces to reconstruct a human being. Combat-hardened cops and soldiers watch comedies, not war movies and police dramas. He didn't watch comedies but he did like strolling through St. James's Park and having a pint of bitter in the dingiest south London pub he could find, or fly fishing on Hampshire's chalk-stream River Itchen. The off-duty activities were safety-valves, escapism, and fantasy. But, right now there was no escape. Horror was soaking into the fabric of the fantastical London he loved.

He entered the communal block and walked upstairs to his flat. His brain was so preoccupied with thoughts that he didn't notice that he poured two glasses of calvados and took both drinks to the armchairs. When he realised what he'd done, he smiled as he looked at the glass by Knutsen's seat. But he didn't remove the glass. He assembled and lit a fire and sat in his chair. He checked his phone. The last message on the WhatsApp group chat was from *Cyrano de Bergerac*. Lucas had written, *With my guy lights out, that's the last of them tucked up*. It meant, the runners were in their rooms and probably sleeping. He read an SMS from Knutsen saying that Lebrun was back at the hotel and all was well. He put his phone away, turned on the touchscreen computer, and opened the 'CHALICE' file. He drew lines and wrote notes between Lucas' team and the runners.

Prasad (Ravi Shankar) - Noah (Max von Sydow). Mercure King's Hotel, Darlington.

Baltzar (Screaming Harridan) - Parry (Nosferatu). The Steam Inn, Mallaig.

Bancroft (Baby Face Nelson) - Lucas (Cyrano de Bergerac). Crowne Plaza, Stratford Upon Avon.

Crease (Goth Chick) - Aadesh (Life Of Pi). Park Hotel, Barnstaple.

And he wrote *The Day Of The Jackal* next to his name. He wondered why Lucas had given him that nickname. Did the Frenchman think Sign dressed and deported himself like the actor Edward Fox who'd played The Jackal in the movie? Or was it because the fictional Jackal defied the odds to get close to his target but missed when he fired the shot?

He stared at the computer whiteboard.

At the phrase *The Library*.

Pick a name, he thought. He made a decision and in doing so established his job for tomorrow.

He looked at the phrase *The Thief*.

During the preceding hours, he'd had so many thoughts. Now, he distilled them down to three questions and one statement.

Are you a grandmaster?

Have you done nothing today?

Or, have you made a move?

Regardless of the answers, I'm ready.

CHAPTER 16

Baltzar paid cash for her room in the hotel and stepped out into Scottish rain that was heavy but thankfully vertical, meaning there was no wind and the nearby sea should be calm. She was wearing a four-thousand pound leather, *raspberry dream* coloured, Italian *Delray Biker Jacket* that she'd bought for fifty quid off eBay. Over the top of it was a see-through waterproof coat. Two rucksacks were slung over her shoulders. One of the bags was the one she'd worn when jogging into work. The other was a purchase in Glasgow and contained walking boots, hiking gear, and other clothes, all bought from the same shop. It also contained a hardy, fleece-lined and weather-proof mountaineering jacket. But, she wasn't in the complete wilds just yet. For now that meant wearing Delray.

She headed to the village's port. Though she was on time, turning up here was a gamble. The *MV Lochnevis* was the only ferry in winter that made the once-daily crossing to the Inner Hebrides archipelago of Small Isles of Rùm, Eigg, Muck, and Canna. In theory. Much depended upon the weather. But, the ferry was moored where it should be and activity around it suggested a sailing was imminent. She went to the office close to the embarkation jetty, purchased a ticket for Muck, and walked onto the ferry. The crossing to the island would take just over two hours. She took shelter in the seating area, waited for the ferry to commence sailing, and entered a toilet where she changed all outer garments and footwear and re-arranged her hair. When she emerged and sat down, she looked quite different from the woman who'd left The Steam Inn. But, she was easily recognisable to Parry who was seven seats behind her.

Thanks to the concierge of the Crowne Plaza who put him in touch with a rather brassy landlady from Huddersfield, Bancroft was now in a one-bedroom holiday-let flat in central Stratford Upon Avon. He'd secured the place for a week, though the landlady – Shirley, who looked at the young man like he was a tempting bar of full-fat chocolate – said he could have it for longer if he wished. The nearby Royal Shakespeare Theatre was 'between' plays, meaning actors weren't hanging around Stratford at the moment. This had a knock-on effect on local businesses. The flat was one of eight identical retreats, all surrounding a small communal courtyard adjacent to a side street, and only two hundred yards from where William Shakespeare was born, lived, and died. The residences were usually occupied by thespians that were in town for a month or two while rehearsing for and performing a play. They weren't here; commoners like Bancroft were; Shirley had to make a living.

Though the flat was furnished and had basic equipment and bedding, everything else he required for at least a week needed to be bought. He did this in stages – walking half a mile to the nearest supermarket to get groceries and toiletries; returning home and unpacking; heading into town to get clothes; returning and changing out of his suit and into more casual attire; going out again to buy washing detergent that he'd forgotten to purchase earlier; staying out for a while to walk around the town and admire the sixteenth century architecture that was in abundance; and returning back to the flat.

He sat on the sofa and wondered how he was going to occupy his time while in hiding. And he wondered what on Earth Sassoon was playing at making him do something like this.

Noah was right – Prasad was out of his comfort zone. The furthest north the GCHQ officer had previously been was on a school cricket team day-trip to the north London Home County of Essex. Now, he was so far north in England that he felt he might as well be on the other side of the planet. But, the Mercure King's Hotel in Darlington was nice and he had no intention of staying anywhere else while he was doing Faraday's bidding.

He'd chosen the large market town purely based on a study of a map of England and Internet research. Three things struck him about the place: first, it was a long way from anywhere he knew; second, he'd never heard of it; third, the town of approximately one hundred thousand people had absolutely nothing interesting to say about its present or past. It was anonymous; a 'grey man'; most likely utterly boring. That was good. He wanted to disappear and felt there was no better place to do so than in a large conurbation containing people who kept themselves to themselves and had no aspirations to show off. So, his decision to travel here made logical sense. However, that still left the thorny issue of what to do while he was here. Crosswords and other puzzles were a likely activity. Maybe he'd conduct a foray to nearby Durham where there'd be a lot more going on, or the coast twenty miles away, or the big and hip university city of Newcastle upon Tyne. The problem was he needed to lay low. He decided it was too risky to do any kind of tourist activity requiring travel. He'd stay in Darlington. Not for the first time he Googled on his phone "Darlington places of interest". He sighed and put the phone to one side. He rested on the bed while fully clothed, put his hands behind his head, and stared at his room's ceiling.

At ten AM Faraday arrived in London Paddington station, having briefly gone to GCHQ to send an Intranet message to his secretary saying he'd be gone for most of the day. After that, he'd jumped on a train, made a few calls, and here he was. He walked out of the station, hailed a taxi, and asked the driver to take him to The Athenaeum club in Pall Mall, St. James's. On arrival, he entered the salubrious building and signed in as a member. Founded in 1824, the institution was primarily used by esteemed academics and practitioners who'd attained acclaim in science, literature, engineering, or mathematics. During its history, members had included fifty one Nobel Laureates. Faraday's membership was embraced by others, given his award of The Fields Medal, the mathematics equivalent of the Nobel Prize. He used the club for meetings in The Drawing Room or one of the three libraries, events in The Picture Room, dining in The Coffee Room, and occasionally made use of its bedrooms if he was working late in London or arriving back to England at an uncivilised hour after an overseas work trip. But, today he went straight to The Morning Room and sat in a partial-enclosure containing five green armchairs facing each other in a circle and next to an open fireplace, golden lamps, and walls containing gilt-framed paintings of nineteenth century progressive thinkers. He waited.

Crease left the Park Hotel in Barnstaple and took a bus to the village of Hartland on the northwest coast of Devon. It took her nearly two hours. On arrival, she went into the local post office and introduced herself to a lovely elderly local lady called Emily who handed over house keys in exchange for eight hundred pounds cash. Emily told her that the holiday cottage was three miles away, accessible by car, motorbike, and bicycle providing there was no snow or ice, and was the perfect place to *get away from it all*. She also warned Crease that because the cottage was completely isolated, the nearest shop was in the village she was now in. Best you pick up your bread, bacon, tobacco, and rum from the village, she advised without a care in the world that her suggested shopping-list might sound old-fashioned. She further advised that there was a farm a mile away from the cottage where she might be able to get milk and eggs, if the farmer was in a good mood. Crease bought what she could from the only food shop, added the provisions to the holdall containing items she'd procured in Barnstaple, and walked south for three miles, along a thin country road, coastal footpath, and down a long track that led to a remote two-bedroom white stone cottage. The property was surrounded by rugged heath-covered hills and close to a cliff, beyond which was an uneven and boulder-strewn beach that overlooked the Bristol Channel and was accessible via a short path that weaved from the cottage through a lowland gap in the cliff. On the beach were wide and deep rock-pools. When the tide was out the pools typically contained fish, lobsters, crabs, conger eels, and sometimes they'd been known to hold huge man o' war jellyfish-like siphonophores, with their thirty-foot tentacles and agonising whip-like stings. Up to a hundred years ago, the fact that the nearest lighthouse was in Hartland was exploited by unscrupulous locals who used hurricane lamps to trick ships, wreck them, plunder their washed-ashore goods, and hide the swag in one of the many caves. Now, few but the most adventurous ramblers and nature-watchers came here. Perhaps that was a good thing because the area was quite truly a place of outstanding beauty.

She entered the cottage, read Emily's welcome pack literature, familiarised herself with the layout of the property and its immediate surroundings, turned on the heating and some lights, and decided that she'd take the bedroom that faced the sea. She looked out through the kitchen window while holding a mug of hot chocolate in one hand and the shotgun shell that Hare had given her in the other. She wondered if she should explore the beach after her drink. It would have to wait, she decided. She needed to take her next hit of crack. Walking over the rocky beach would be too risky when she was medicated. She looked at the cartridge. There was only enough left in there for today. After that it was time for cold turkey. She'd only used drugs when doing her undercover police work. Even then it had started off as just for show. But then it became no longer for show. Still, she hoped she wouldn't suffer withdrawal symptoms for more than a day or so. But, what did she know? However, even though she'd never taken drugs before, some of her school peers had. One of them was only sixteen when he split his skull, broke one arm, dislocated the other, cut an eyeball, and snapped three toes and two fingers when trying not to take crack by locking himself in his bedroom while his parents were away. She and a friend had found him on the floor. He was dead. His vomit had choked him. The expression on his face and state of his body was unlike anything she'd seen before. Now, as she stared at the beach, her grip around the cartridge tightening, she wondered if he would have preferred to have swum through a man o' war's tentacles than go through cold turkey.

The ferry berthed alongside a small jetty. Baltzar disembarked, walked along the pier, and set foot on the tiny Scottish island of Muck. She was in Port Mòr, the place where most of the island's population of thirty eight lived. She walked from east to west for one and a half miles on the island's only road, passing tree-less wild lowland containing free-grazing Luing cows and Lleyn sheep, and hills including Beinn Airein - the highest of only four hundred and fifty feet. This was a truly exposed and untamed place and she was glad she'd changed into her hiking gear. She didn't see anyone on her walk. Nor any vehicles, and that wasn't particularly surprising because vehicles from the mainland were for the most part not permitted on the two and a half miles wide by three quarters long dot of land. She reached a farmstead that managed the cattle she'd seen, processed fish from the port, made wool for rugs, and produced cheese. Alongside Mòr, it was the only place that suggested civilisation existed on the island. Even so, the island didn't contain shops, pubs, or a post office. She entered Gallanach Lodge hotel, spoke to the owner, and exchanged cash for keys to one of the two separate holiday-lets managed by the lodge. She walked for another thirty minutes, the weight of her two rucksacks causing her back to ache and parts of her skin to feel sore. It wasn't surprising that she felt tired when she reached the cottage that would be her home for however long she needed to stay out of London. She'd slept badly last night and was running on fumes. All she wanted to do was lay on a bed and sleep. She wouldn't be disturbed. There was nothing here but more windswept rugged landscape and the adjacent North Atlantic Ocean. She entered the lodge, dumped her bag, skim-read a house-operating document and also glanced at a thin tourist pamphlet. She could barely keep her eyes open as she learned that the name 'Muck' was disputed and could mean sea pig, swine, or sow, and might refer to the local whales or abundance of porpoises that lived here alongside otters, seals, eagles, and puffins. She went into one of the two bedrooms, pulled the curtains, laid on the bed, and slept. Four hundred yards away, Parry got upright, put away his binoculars, and walked to the other holiday-let cottage that was tucked out of sight and a five minute sprint away from Baltzar's place. He'd been lucky to get it, having thought that he'd need to watch her without shelter. He notified the group WhatsApp chat of Baltzar's status, read that his colleagues were also ensconced in their respective 'observation points', and decided that he was exhausted.

It was a given that it was impossible for him and his colleagues to watch their cares day and night. All Sign could hope from them was that they stuck close to the runners in case of need. Parry made himself a cup of tea, sat in an armchair, and fell asleep without touching the drink.

Detective Chief Superintendent Rex Hare exited the Metropolitan Police Service headquarters in New Scotland Yard. On the other side of the Victoria Embankment road, on the pedestrian walkway next to the river, Sign watched him. Since approximately eight AM, he'd followed Hare when the cop had left his home in the affluent area of Putney, southwest London. The Library member had taken a tube to Westminster and walked the remaining short distance to work. He'd been here ever since. It was now 1110hrs. It was obvious that Hare was waiting for a taxi. Sign unzipped the large backpack by his feet and snapped into place the lightweight metal contents. Hare flagged down a taxi, entered the vehicle, and drove off. Sign mounted Knutsen's folding *Brompton* bicycle, and followed. There were other ways he could have established Hare's destination, such as slapping a tiny beacon on the side of the cab or loitering close to the cop as he entered the taxi and told the driver where he wanted to go, but they were unreliable techniques. In any case, in central London only tubes reached places quicker than bikes, plus he fancied the exercise and could collapse the bike, slot it into the rucksack, and follow Hare onto a train if need be. He peddled as fast as the small-wheeled bicycle would go, weaving in and out of traffic, and never losing sight of the taxi. Ten minutes later he was on Pall Mall in St. James's. Fifty yards away, the taxi was stationary. Hare got out and entered The Athenaeum club, using the same entrance that had graced Charles Dickins, Benjamin Disraeli, Arthur Conan Doyle, Robert Louis Stevenson, Charles Darwin, Alfred Lord Tennyson, and other notable male alumni. If she'd so wished, Karin Lebrun wouldn't have been allowed to become a member of the club until 2002. Sign stayed at the top of the Duke of York steps, using the adjacent one hundred and thirty seven feet tall monument to the duke as a partial barrier between him and the front door to the club. But he still had sufficient sight of the entrance. Standing next to his bike, he leaned against a wall, munched on a sandwich, and watched.

Hare was the last member to enter The Morning Room section. Sassoon and Duggan had arrived five minutes' earlier and were sitting next to Faraday. The detective sat in the only vacant leather armchair and asked, "What's this about?"

Duggan and Sassoon looked expectantly at Faraday. It was clear they too were in the dark as to why they'd been assembled, without Raine being present and in a place that didn't belong to Mrs. Carmichael.

Faraday wasted no time. "Why did Raine pick us to form our club? Last night I found out. We're all fluent Norwegian-speakers, Peter included."

Hare frowned. "That's odd."

Duggan's expression was quizzical. "Norwegian? What the hell's that got to do with the price of fish?" He shrugged. "I do speak Norwegian. Learnt it many years ago, before a deep-cover operation involving a bunch of Scandinavian thugs."

Hare said, "My mother's Norwegian. When she raised us, she spoke to me and my brother in her language; my Dad spoke to us in English."

Faraday said, "I had to learn it for a joint intercept op with the Norwegians, attacking Russia. It was time sensitive once launched. Understanding my Norwegian friends made for quicker decision-making." He looked at Sassoon.

The MI6 officer said, "Peter's first overseas posting was as second secretary political in Oslo. He'll have had a year's one-to-one language training for that, given to him by a native speaker. As for me, I mastered the language for fun and in my own time. I had an interest in the works of the nineteenth century writer Christian Martin Monsen, in particular his 1846 poetry collection *Alpeblomster* and…"

"Yes, alright." Faraday wondered about ordering tea, but decided he didn't want to be here any longer than he had to. "So, what's the Norwegian angle?"

Duggan and Hare shook their heads.

Sassoon placed the tips of his fingers together and against his bottom lip. "We don't know, but that ignorance must be corrected."

He knew what he was about to say was obvious, but Duggan said it anyway. "There is a direct link between The Thief and the language of Norway. We don't know what it is but…"

"Raine does." Faraday looked nervously around. Like all GCHQ officers, he hated discussing secret matters in public, even though the four of them couldn't be overheard in the enclave. He looked back at his colleagues and said quietly, "I have thoughts."

"As do I." Hare leaned closer to the others. "The Thief speaks Norwegian. Either Raine thinks one of us is The Thief; or, he's The Thief and has let something slip that might identify him. That slip being use of the Norwegian tongue. He wants to keep an eye on us in case we discover the Norwegian angle."

"The Norwegian angle becomes an incriminating audit trail that leads back to The Thief." Sassoon was deep in thought. "It *could* be that one of us is The Thief, and Raine is trying to work out who that person is. *Or,* Raine is The Thief. He assembled the only CHALICE Norwegian-speakers so he could check up on what we might know about him. Perhaps he's doing a *keep your friends close and your enemies closer* routine."

Duggan asked, "Edward – what's your gut instinct on this?"

Sassoon waved a hand. "All of us, Raine included, have the wherewithal to be The Thief. And, we could all sit here and plead our innocence. It would serve no purpose. We need more data."

"Ay, that's true." Duggan addressed Faraday. "Why don't we have a little listen-in on Mr. Raine? Can you sort that out?"

The GCHQ officer looked nonchalant when he said, "I can get under Peter's skin, but we need to decide how far I go. With just a few taps on my work keyboard, I can listen in on his mobile and landline phone calls, even those from the FCO building, and monitor his personal and work credit and debit cards. But if you want other stuff – transmitters in situ; postal intercepts; tech attacks on mobile and pedestrian movements; video and camera footage; and the like – then I'd need a team of expert technical operatives. I can get access to a team like that, but questions would be asked as to why the target is a senior British diplomat. Without such a team, I'd be reliant upon you lot to help me out. And with the greatest respect to your no-doubt superb cloak and dagger skills, my suspicion is that I'd be holding my head in my hands if I had to endure watching the three of you trying to install a transmitter into Raine's car."

Sassoon smiled. "Quite so, dear chap. But, there'll be no need for a comedy of errors. Raine doesn't know we're onto the Norwegian angle and that we're having this discussion. For now we need to give ourselves a starting point – namely, is Peter a good fellow or a bad fellow? His phone usage and expenditure will give us an excellent insight into which way the wind is blowing."

Faraday looked at Duggan and Hare. They nodded in agreement. He was relieved. "I'll be back in Cheltenham in about three hours' time. I'll get straight onto it. I'll have coverage of Raine from no later than," he checked the time on his phone, "four PM this afternoon."

"Excellent." Hare shook his head. "This Norwegian thing has come as quite a shock. We should have checked from the outset as to why Raine approached us."

Duggan muttered, "We had no reason to. But, things changed. Seven days ago, Wick was murdered. Now, MAYFLY's live, and we've got our runners out there."

Hare nodded and stood. He said nothing for a moment as he looked at the others. Then, "If Raine is The Thief, by God he's a cold-hearted bastard. What he did to Wick was despicable."

Sassoon also stood and gathered up his coat. "It was perfect." He smiled and walked out of the room.

Sign watched Sassoon leave the club, pause and look at the sky as he put his coat on, and walk off. Hare was next. He grabbed a taxi that had just pulled up outside the Athenaeum and was dropping off passengers. As he drove away, Duggan came out and walked in the opposite direction from Sign, with no use for an umbrella despite the fact that rain was pounding his body. Finally, Faraday left the building and walked to nearby Regent Street, where he'd easily get a cab to take him back to Paddington station.

Sign grabbed his bike, walked past the Duke of York column, down the long flight of steps, and got on the bike when he was on The Mall. It took him twenty minutes to get to Southwark and home. He entered the flat, took off his wet coat, bagged Knutsen's *Brompton* and left it in the hall, and entered the lounge.

Knutsen was in his armchair, fully dressed but sleeping. The poor man looked exhausted. Sign decided not to make a mug of coffee, for fear the noisy kettle would wake his friend. He poured a glass of grapefruit juice and sat at the dining room table, while staring at nothing in particular and contemplating recent events.

Knutsen must have sensed his presence because he stirred, opened his eyes, yawned, and looked at his colleague. "What time is it?"

"Nearly one o'clock."

The former cop sat upright, stretched, and said, "Shit. I only got here thirty minutes ago. You might as well put the kettle on."

Sign did so and called out from the kitchen, "How is Peter?"

"At work. Karin and I followed him there from Hertford. She's hanging about in Whitehall. I'm taking over from her later this afternoon and am pulling an all night shift. Was hoping to get a couple of hours' kip under my belt before going out there again."

Sign brought him a coffee. "I'm so sorry if I disturbed you."

"You didn't." Knutsen wrapped his hands around the mug and sipped the drink. "I should've gone to bed and set the alarm." He smiled. "Haven't really slept since you put us on Raine-watch."

"I can do the night shift, if you wish." Sign sat in his armchair, gripping his drink in one hand.

"Don't be daft. I've only been awake for thirty or so hours. That's a walk in the park compared to other stuff we've done. Anyway, you need to be where you're at. Centre of the web et cetera." He put his mug on the hearth and vigorously rubbed his face. "Last time I was here, you said that your plan was to see if The Thief's plan was the plan that you predicted he'd conduct. Any good?"

Any good, thought Sign. That was indeed a question. "The Thief's going after Raine."

Knutsen said nothing.

Sign's tone was clipped and neutral as he said, "This morning The Library met without Raine. They know something is amiss. Without doubt they have ascertained they all speak Norwegian. One of them – The Thief – has the objective to make Peter look like The Thief. In doing so he will create a blood-lust within The Library. When they get hold of Peter there will be no due process of law. I will let them get close enough to Peter, with the hope that in doing so I spot The Thief. It's a huge risk."

"It is." Knutsen huffed. "Bloody *massive* risk." He gulped down the rest of his coffee and thought for a moment before saying, "You said aposematism needs fear, repulsion, and deterrence; that it's a contract between predator and prey. But, you also told me about your theory, the one that hasn't been written in the context of aposematism."

Sign nodded. "The use of camouflage to attract, yet misdirect. The Thief wishes to attract The Library to Peter. In doing so, he protects himself. The prey is the predator that fools another predator. The Thief is making Peter into a fake Thief. Going forward, we should refer to Raine as the 'Fake Thief'.

Knutsen stood, walked to the window, and looked at the rain-lashed square below. "Your analogy – a seafaring explorer and a neurologist. What do they see when they set foot on a desert island or cast their eyes on brain-matter?" He turned. "What do you see? Why is The Thief doing all this? Just money?"

Sign bowed his head. "Thus far I've failed to establish his aspirations. I need more information. And I need to be smarter." He looked up. "But, a heist for money just doesn't wash. We are seeing a performance of science, logic, brutality, and artistry. Nothing personifies that collaboration more than the nature of young Alex Wick's death."

"What next?"

Sign's voice was stronger when he said, "The Thief's made his move – somehow getting the others in The Library to realise they are all bonded by a second language. I've made my move – ascertaining that four members of The Library have isolated Raine. It is to my advantage that The Thief doesn't know he's playing me. Still, the next move must be his and I must wait. That said, things will happen quickly. Very soon The Library's long-knives will be drawn. Be ready."

Courtesy of a business-class seat on Scandinavian Airlines, The Thief arrived in Oslo, Norway. It was mid-afternoon. He'd travelled from London Heathrow on an authentic Danish passport in the name of Rasmus Østergaard. If questioned, he lived in the Nordhavn neighbourhood of Copenhagen, was a freelance medical consultant specialising in therapeutic human gene editing, was in London for a private client appraisal, and was in Norway to gain sight of some confidential and non-transmittable papers on the latest cutting-edge technique of clustered regularly interspaced short palindromic repeats. Like all of his guises, being Østergaard was something he could do in his sleep. But, he wasn't questioned and navigated the airport to take a connecting flight to Bergen, the "city of seven mountains" on the west coast of the country. If he'd had more time he wouldn't have used such a quasi-conventional means of travel into the country. He'd have entered Sweden from Finland, Latvia, Lithuania, Poland, or Denmark, and then crossed the border into Norway in a car. But, it wasn't only time that was against him. It was winter and that meant road and even rail travel was fraught. So, flights were the only option. Upon landing in Norway's second largest city, he took a taxi to *Pygmalion* bistro on Nedre Korskirkeallmenningen, close to Byfjorden, "the city fjord", He'd no intention of eating at the restaurant, but it was close to where he wanted to be. He continued the rest of his journey on foot; carrying a briefcase and wearing the same suit he'd worn earlier in the day, over which was a smart woollen coat. His expensive brogues crunched on shallow pools of ice that were dotted over parts of his route in the historic city that was in equal measures curious, industrious, and bohemian. His breath steamed in the crystal clear and still cold air as he passed the area where the outdoor fish market was open during the day. It was now early evening and dark, though tasteful artificial light abounded from waterfront cafes, bars, and eateries, casting glittering colour over the vast fjord. Inland, old lamps offered a subdued and subtle golden glow to discreet side-streets and alleys containing eighteenth century houses, tucked-away shops, and bistros for locals and famished travellers. He went into one of the side-streets. He was the only person here. Though it was on a slight hill, the route reminded him of the street leading to Mrs. Carmichael's antique bookstore.

Using a key he'd had cut in China's oldest city of Xi'an, he entered a terraced house that had been built in 1798. It belonged to Torbjørn Lystad. Ignoring the two downstairs bedrooms and sunroom that connected to a small grapevine-strewn courtyard, he walked upstairs to the open-plan lounge and kitchen area. The wooden-floored area was as he remembered it when he'd last been here thirteen months ago and was reflective of the cultured, uncluttered, and exacting professional facade that Lystad presented to clients. As well as minimalist but tasteful furniture, in one corner was an upright piano with the Norwegian composer Edward Grieg's Piano Sonata in E minor sheet music mounted above the open keyboard. There were only two paintings in the room – one an original portrait by Dina Aschehoug; the other by Lystad, depicting a mountain graveyard with caribou antler markers. The small dining table was permanently laid for one, with a place mat and adjacent polished silver cutlery and a crystal wine glass. There was only one artefact in the lounge area – a six-foot figurine that Lystad told his few guests was an original by renowned sculptor Gustav Vigeland, whereas in truth it was a fake that had been knocked up by a talented but unemployed artist in Bergen's Møhlenpris district. The kitchen area was functional, immaculate, but had its quirks including a ten-inch knife that was vertical and had its tip rammed into a wooden chopping board, and a set of pharmaceutical containers of herbs and spices. Overall, this part of the house was, The Thief believed, a place that was reflective of a man who didn't like to reveal his hand.

He went upstairs, into the converted loft. This place was different. It was not only Lystad's place of work and play but also his private space. No one else was allowed in here. There were easels with unfinished works, a work-stool, leather-covered walnut mahogany writing desk with inbuilt drawers and adjacent cabinets, office chair, armchair and mismatching side-table, modern and old books piled on the floor, sticky notes and arty posters haphazardly stuck to the inwardly sloping walls, record player next to which was a stack of vinyl, straw-lined wooden crate with an assortment of bottled berry wines, and a plethora of hanging plant-pot baskets containing paints and brushes.

The Thief opened his briefcase and withdrew items. Wearing surgical gloves and using tweezers, he put papers in the writing desk drawers. On the desk he placed a see-through plastic bag containing a mobile phone he'd purchased in Belarus. Next to the bag he put a plain A4 sheet of paper. He slid the phone out of the bag and onto the paper. Using the blunt end of the tweezers, he accessed the phone's draft messages, clicked on the only one in the pending box, entered a number, and pressed send. Cradling the phone in one palm under the paper, he slid the mobile into one of the drawers, scrunched up the paper and put the ball in his pocket, closed the drawer and his briefcase, and left the building.

He returned to Oslo on an Air Shuttle plane and took a Scandinavian Airlines flight back to London Heathrow.

CHAPTER 17

At six ten AM, Sign received a text message from Raine to his burner phone.

Can we meet at Versailles at 0700hrs? Urgent.

'Versailles' was the codename for the Westminster safe house. He texted the diplomat back in the affirmative and called Knutsen to learn Raine's whereabouts. His colleague said that Raine was on the London-bound train from Hertford and he was keeping an eye on him from one carriage away.

He showered, dressed in rugged clothing, walked to the Westminster flat, and buzzed the door. Having ascertained it was him at the entrance, Lebrun opened the door and continued towel-drying her hair with one hand while holding her powerful handgun in the other.

"Good morning." Sign beamed. "May I come in?"

It was obvious Lebrun hadn't been awake long. She gestured for him to enter, stepped aside, and muttered, "You know where the coffee is. Make me one, while you're at it. I'm taking over in an hour, once Raine's in town. Fucking babysitting job. You could have got someone for twenty Euros an hour to keep an eye on Raine. Instead you got a polizeirat."

Sign strode into the kitchen-area and flicked on the kettle. He spun around as Lebrun closed the door, his expression now earnest and devoid of sympathy. "You're significantly overqualified for the job in hand. I need you here, though. Your current task won't remain your current task, of that I'm sure. Thus, I need your cop training. In equal measure there's something else important. From the outset I told Peter that we might pick up one or two allies along the way. You think you're here as a rule-breaker. That's good as it gives you edge. But, in reality you're here as an official representative of your country." He smiled, but continued to stare at her intently. "Along the way, I've picked up Germany as an unwitting ally."

She slowly lowered her towel-holding hand. "If I shoot someone here or elsewhere, it no longer becomes a private British matter."

"Bravo, superintendent." He turned and spooned coffee granules into two mugs. "Things will escalate. The issue could absorb arch international political flavours. A high-ranking German detective hunting a British traitor. That'll grab the headlines. There'll be no room for mealy-mouthed Whitehall utterances."

She made no effort to hide her anger as she walked past him and tossed the towel onto the sofa. But, she still held her gun by her side. "You're using me."

"Yes, although it was Peter that spotted your value. Nevertheless, we're all using each other. And I'm using myself. Correct allocation of correct resources."

"You're playing with fire."

"Always." He softened his tone when he said, "But, there's more to your presence than a passport and curriculum vitae. I deal with people. I'm not interested in letters before or after a name. I'm interested in the person." He poured hot water into the mugs. "You said to me that if I had The Thief in my sights I mustn't hesitate; that I wasn't looking at me." He picked up both cups. "Your comment made me happy."

"Why?"

"Because it meant you were task-oriented and yet had one hundred and eighty degree vision of those by your side. Ultimately, it meant that, like me, you study the human condition." He handed her a coffee and sat at the dining table. "Take a seat, Karin. Peter Raine is joining us at any moment."

She sat at the table and placed the gun in front of her. "What's happened?"

He told her about the text and yesterday's Library meeting at the Athenaeum. "They're onto the Norwegian angle. But, I suspect they're confused and are investigating matters. They'll only confront Raine when they have more information. But, Peter's text message worries me. It could mean The Library now has the data it needs to make a move."

Lebrun thought fast. "The Thief's just dealt another card."

"That's my fear." He sipped his drink. "If so, things might change. You may no longer be on a twenty-Euro-an-hour gig."

Her face relaxed. "You're not even paying me that."

"No. The Deutsche Bundesbank is very kindly picking up my tab for my gross exploitation of one of Germany's most prized resources." He briefly smiled. "If I get through this unscathed, both Britain and Germany will have some questions for me."

Raine entered the flat without buzzing the door first. As ever, he had the appearance and grandiose aura of a 1940s silver-screen gentleman or knight of the realm. He was wearing a Saville Row *Davies & Son* bespoke two-piece royal navy woollen suit, double-cuff silk shirt, tie, and black *Church's* brogues. He looked the part, but was uncharacteristically unsettled. He tossed his overcoat onto the back of the sofa, next to Lebrun's towel, whipped out his non-covert mobile phone, and put the device on the table, in front of Sign. "Yesterday tea-time I received the gobbledygook message you're looking at. Obviously code. I tried to get hold of Rockstar Games; same bunch that cracked the code that got me onto the Lystad meeting in Bergen. Trouble was, Rockstar was out doing," he waved his hand in a dismissive way, "gamey things, or whatever. Couldn't get hold of my contact there until later in the evening. But, he was on point when I spoke to him. He worked through the night with a couple of his guys and got back to me five minutes before I texted you this morning." He pulled out a slip of paper. "This is what the coded text says."

Sign took the paper and read.

Problem? Clients lined up. Time pressing. TL.

He handed the paper to Lebrun and said, "TL - Torbjørn Lystad." He looked at Raine. "The message was sent from a Belarusian-registered number. Did Rockstar Games give you any insight into the device itself? Where the message was sent from? The phone's current location?"

Raine shook his head. "They just focused on cracking the code. Anyway, I'm not sure they can go all GCHQ on me. Plus, I'm on good terms with them. They've done me a favour. I don't want to press them too far."

Sign weighed the phone in his hand. "It would make sense for the phone to be pay-as-you-go and purchased in the same location as the SIM. As to its current location, I have an idea where that might be." He put the phone down, withdrew his own phone, and called Knutsen. "Mr. Knutsen – you can stop loitering outside the building Peter's in, and come up. There've been developments." He ended the call and addressed a somewhat confused Raine. "Tom and Karin have been keeping an eye on you. I told them to do that. If you have any notion of being affronted, I'll be forced to remind you of what you did to the Italian prime minister when he was at the G7 summit in Tokyo."

Raine looked uncomfortable.

"So, we move on." Sign clasped his hands. "We have a problem, but I want my muse here before we proceed."

One minute later Knutsen was in the flat. He glanced at Raine, then at Sign, uncertainty in his expression.

"It's okay, Tom. Mr. Raine is *cool* with you snooping on him. His backstory contains enough skeletons to make an undertaker blush with envy. I know where they're all buried. To save embarrassment, best I don't dig them all up." Sign told him about the coded text message. "This is The Thief's next move to turn Peter into the Fake Thief. The message is a twelve inch nail in his coffin. And it's The Thief's hope that there will be a coffin. Having convinced the rest of The Library that Peter is The Thief, our real thief will kill Peter." He looked at Raine. "Before you get to open your mouth and tell your side of the story."

Raine took an involuntary step back but said nothing.

Sign raised his eyebrows. "It will be a perfect murder, committed by a member of The Library on behalf of The Library. The innocent, expert, and deniable members of The Library won't begrudge The Thief his execution. They'll think they've got their man. They'll dispose of Peter's body and vanish. The real thief will have won."

Knutsen asked, "Where's the fucking Belarusian phone?"

Raine replied, "We don't know. I can't..."

Knutsen looked directly at Sign and repeated, "Where's the fucking phone?! If the innocent Library find it, I'm betting they'll find other stuff. If that happens, I might as well shoot Peter myself. At least it will be a clean kill."

Sign's lips reverberated as he slowly exhaled. "If it was me..."

"Yes, yes. If it was bloody you. Get on with it!"

Sign smiled. "The phone's in Lystad's house in Bergen. The Thief must make the Fake Thief as clever as he is. After all, for the benefit of everyone else, the Fake Thief *is* The Thief. That means Peter wouldn't be sloppy. His tradecraft and cognitive behaviour would be impeccable. Peter wouldn't leave any tell-tale signs that he was the culprit. But, Lystad might just make the tiniest slip-up, maybe out of desperation. The problem is that Lystad's dead. But, wait a minute. In the mix of those people that matter, only Peter, his cutthroats, and The Thief know that Lystad's dead. So, The Thief does a Lazarus-manoeuvre on Lystad. He's alive and kicking but getting ants in his pants because he hasn't heard from his co-conspirator for, say, a couple of weeks. This requires desperate measures and an emergency breach of standard operating procedures. As a last resort, dead Lystad sends The Thief, aka Peter, a coded message to his personal mobile phone. The real thief does this knowing that Peter's phone's been intercepted by the rest of The Library. Result – Peter's a dead man walking."

Raine was very unsettled. His voice was shaky as he said, "Maybe The Library will think I'm being framed. They're not stupid."

Sign sighed as he looked at Raine. "It's a matter of aggradation and escalation. The geological term 'aggradation' refers to the unhelpful increase in elevation of a river due to the deposition of sediment. The Thief is depositing sediment, namely evidence, and as a result is changing your course. Your redirection becomes an unstoppable reality in the eyes of the innocent Library. Matters therefore escalate to the point that the river must be dealt with. You've assembled the only fluent Norwegian-speakers in CHALICE; one obvious motive for doing so is that you're The Thief and something's happened that could lead back to you; therefore, you need to be very close to them. So, they bug your phones. The Thief pretends to be Lystad and sends you a message; The Library intercepts; this leads them onto Lystad because the Belarusian phone's been left in his house and Gordon Faraday *is* GCHQ and can trace one volt of electricity from one million miles away. But," He pointed at Knutsen and said quietly, "Tom's right. The Library will follow the bullet's path, go to Lystad's house, and find other evidence that will incriminate the eminent Peter Raine of Her Majesty's Foreign and Commonwealth Office. It's too late for clever men to consider the possibility that you might have been framed. The sediment trail's been deposited. You're royally shafted."

"Only if they get to Lystad's house!" Knutsen checked the time. "I'll get there first. And, if I can't gain entry, I'll burn the house down if I need to."

Sign shook his head. "Burning evidence will make matters worse. Anyway, you'd be able to gain entry. But, I don't want you to go."

"What?!"

Sign looked at Knutsen. "I told you, Tom. I will let them get close to Peter, with the hope that in doing so I spot The Thief."

Raine exclaimed, "Hang on! I don't recall having a say in this!"

"It must have slipped my mind to mention it to you." Sign kept his eyes on Knutsen. "You may or may not beat The Library to Lystad's house. Or, you may get there at the same time, which would be a problem because a fight would ensue. The results of that fight may not serve Peter's best interests."

"Or you interests." Lebrun waited.

Sign looked at her.

She continued. "Have you considered that now might be a very good time to kill Hare, Duggan, Sassoon, and Faraday?"

"Yeah," said Knutsen.

Sign looked at the ceiling and said quietly, "I considered it from the outset. And, forgive me Peter, that included..."

"It's alright, Ben." Raine had regained his composure. "It was an option. All concepts had to be considered."

Sign looked at Raine and smiled with warmth and appreciation. "Thank you, Peter." He breathed in deeply and spoke to Knutsen and Lebrun. "My position is as follows: I want The Thief to be incarcerated for the rest of his life or exterminated. Nothing else will do. But, I will not countenance the execution of three honourable men, even if it is now a logical and expedient solution and means to protect Peter. However, and under the circumstances, I believe the only person in this room who can make a decision on this is Peter. It's his life."

All eyes were on Raine.

The diplomat bowed his head for several seconds.

No one spoke.

Raine looked up and at each person. Then, "Let them come for me. I'll protect myself as I see fit and I hope you'll do what's necessary to keep me safe for as long as possible. But, beyond that I won't become a hanging judge. There'll be no black cap on my head as I pass sentence on innocents. We don't kill The Library."

Knutsen pulled a face, shrugged, and said, "Okay. It's your shout."

Lebrun spun her Smith and Wesson .45 ACP pistol, and waited until it stopped. "Sure. Whatever."

Sign nodded. His tone was business-like as he addressed Raine. "From a pay phone, call your family and tell them to go someplace discrete, while you're away overseas for a couple of days or so on FCO business. Don't tell them where you'll be. Make sure they go somewhere that has no connection to family, friends, or work. But, you don't want to know where that is. Tell your wife she must assume all calls are being monitored. She shouldn't be flustered by that, given she's spent decades by your side while being bugged to the wazoo by foreign countries. No locations are to be imparted in any telephone calls. You're on a high-priority HMG job. You can't be contacted until you're back. You'll tell her all when it's over. Assume everything you say to your wife is being listened to by The Library. But that's okay. You're The Thief. You're mightily aggrieved that Lystad sent an encrypted message to your personal phone. You have work to do."

Raine pointed at his personal phone. "It's easy to find me."

"With your phone close by, yes. When you leave here, Tom will go with you. Outside of the FCO building, you'll send a message to Duggan, Sassoon, and Faraday. It will state the following: "Let's convene very shortly. I'm about to leave for Europe, to pursue some thoughts on what happened to AW. I'll keep you posted. Problem with this phone. New one forthcoming.". Message sent, you'll turn the mobile off and give it to Tom. He'll destroy it. Going forward, the only phone you must keep is the burner phone I gave you. And that is only for emergency communications with me, Karin, and Tom."

"You don't think they'll get suspicious about me no longer using my personal phone?"

Sign shook his head. "You're The Thief. As far as you're concerned, The Library isn't onto you. But, you're also arch Whitehall mandarin Peter Raine. In our respective lines of work we frequently change phone numbers. Something's happened, but you don't need to give chapter and verse as to what that could be. Perhaps you're worried your phone's been compromised by the North Koreans. Or, maybe you're getting inundated with hate-texts from the prime minister of Tonga. You're applying good housekeeping and changing phones. Regardless, you'll have told them this morning that you'll shortly be in touch. They just have to wait for you to call the meeting with them. That's when your life ends." He smiled. "But, it won't happen that way. Not if I have anything to do with it. Also, there must be no use of your bank cards. Zero digital footprint whatsoever. Do what you told Alex Wick to do."

Raine recalled what he'd said to Wick in Room 79b. *"The Going Dark Bit."* He raised his eyebrows. "Young Alex never got to experience that segment of his deployment. Perhaps I should have done the Munich job."

"You know that if you'd done so we'd be no closer to identifying The Thief."

"Are we any closer, though?"

Sign ignored the question. "As of today, you'll stay at my flat."

"Your flat?"

"Yes. We've got a blow-up mattress you can sleep on. It needs repairing but we'll try to sort it. It was insecure for you to visit my place while you were out and about in London. But you'll be laying low in West Square and we'll be keeping you on a leash until this is over. It's the safest place for you now." Sign addressed Knutsen and Lebrun. "I have a notion, and you'll be pleased to hear that it doesn't involve you trawling between Hertford and London, or hanging around Whitehall. Tom – I want you back at our place; Karin, you should continue to sleep here. Our base of operations will be interchangeable between both residences." He placed his hands flat on the table and said with a slow and solemn voice, "Peter - The Thief has always known you're on to one of four Library members. He doesn't care that he's telling you he's framing you by sending you the code. But we don't know who's innocent in The Library and who's not. No matter how tempting it may be to do so, don't tell The Library what's really happening."

At 0900hrs, Faraday, Sassoon, Hare, and Duggan met close to the Round Pond in Kensington Gardens. The expansive central-London park was perfect for a winter landscape painting, with only a thin layer of predominantly unsullied snow covering expanses of open ground, clusters of trees, and ice on the pond. There was only a handful of other people in the park, braving the sub-zero temperature, one of them wearing a red overcoat and thereby adding to the artistic impression. An artist would have also picked out The Library members, because they looked striking and intriguing against the serene white backdrop – four men, in dark suits and overcoats, umbrellas open above their heads, facing each other in a small circle, the effect of the cold air on their breath making them look like they were a bunch of huddled smokers, no one else anywhere near them.

Faraday said, "At seventeen fifty-seven GMT last night, Raine received a coded text message to his personal mobile phone. The message was sent from a Belarusian pay-as-you-go mobile. I cracked the code. It said, 'Problem. *Question mark*. Clients lined up. Time pressing. *Dash. Uppercase* T *uppercase* L. *Full stop*'." Having already spoken to Hare prior to the meeting, he looked at Sassoon and Duggan. "The encryption was a bitch and a strong touch. Still, the sender's been careless. The phone's static, in a house on the outskirts of Bergen belonging to a man called Torbjørn Lystad."

"Never heard of him," said Duggan.

"Nor I," said Sassoon.

Faraday was motionless. "I solved the code just after eight PM. I'd have been quicker but got side-tracked by emergency burst transmissions from the sunken Russian submarine in the Beaufort Sea. I called Rex to see if he had any European law enforcement contacts he could talk to about Lystad. And while he set to work, I did my own digging."

Hare said, "I spoke to a French detective I know in Interpol. She got back to me within the hour and told me what she'd found out. Torbjørn Lystad is Norwegian and was a senior private banker for the Swiss wealth management firm Union Bancaire Privée, based in Geneva. He left the bank when he was fifty eight; he's now sixty four. My detective friend couldn't say what he's been up to since retirement, though his financial accreditations are annually renewed, suggesting his still active in some guise in the world of finance. No criminal convictions. Suspect he's still well connected. That's it from me."

"But not me." Faraday briefly glanced at the frozen pond and wondered if the ice could hold the weight of an adult. "I looked at his travel during the last twelve months; least ways, what was visible. There were many interesting journeys. Some were *particularly* interesting. Notably: a flight to Damascus two days before a Syrian spy, who MI5 was hoping to grab, was rescued from London by the Syrians; flight to Moscow one day before our Russian diplomat walk-in friend was assassinated by Moscow operatives in Hong Kong; arrival in Mexico City nine hours before a cartel turned its UK-bound drug smuggling ships around; and arrival into Rarotonga in the Cook Islands on the day my lot stopped getting juicy intercept gossip from an arms dealer, based on the island, and started hearing him and his cronies start blathering shit about his holier-than-thou aspirations to establish a string of charity schools in central Africa. There's other stuff that I strongly suspect is linked to the CHALICE breaches, unless his travel itinerary is the mother of all coincidences, but I've just given you the headlines."

They were silent for a few seconds.

Sassoon spoke. "Gentlemen. We have our broker; our Thief's intermediary. Torbjørn Lystad is The Fence."

"And he's in panic-mode and communicating with our Peter Raine," added Duggan.

"The Thief," said Faraday.

Sassoon was thinking fast. "We need more before we proceed against Raine. I want to see the inside of Lystad's home." He looked at Hare. "Fancy tagging along?"

Hare nodded.

"Why you two?" asked Duggan.

Sassoon smiled. "I fancy a spy and a cop might be an adroit combination for a spot of burglary. I'm a spy. Mr. Hare's a cop. Any objections to us popping over to Norway?"

Duggan shrugged. "Fine by me."

Faraday said, "If Raine's The Thief, he won't be pleased that Lystad's messaged him to his personal phone. He'll go to Bergen and deal with Lystad."

"Indeed." Sassoon looked at his watch. "I presume you all got the same text message I received this morning from Raine?"

They nodded.

Hare said, "Off to Europe. Doing a bit of private investigation on Wick. Do we read anything into the change of phone?"

"No." Faraday had lost all trace of Raine's phone at 0738hrs this morning. "Raine has to assume his phone's constantly attacked by any number of countries. The last thing he needed was a coded message popping into his inbox, not that the message would mean anything to anyone but him, Lystad, and us. So, he's ditched his phone and will get the FCO to get him a security-cleared new one. In the meantime, he'll go old-school and use other ways to make contact. All that matters now is that he's going to contact us to schedule another Library meeting. Before that happens, we need to move fast."

Sassoon looked at Hare. "Chop chop. No time like the present. We'll take a cab to your place in Putney, grab passport and some of your grubby back-hander dough, onto my pad in Chelsea, ditto passport and in my case some naughty slush-fund notes that previously belonged to dead scallywags, plus a nifty set of bones, then onto Heathrow and thereafter winter wonderland."

Sassoon and Hare peeled off from the group.

After breakfast in his hotel, Prasad spent an hour wandering aimlessly in the centre of Darlington. It was raining hard and dark clouds covered the town. He, and other pedestrians, persevered, though he had no idea why he was bothering venturing out in the miserable weather beyond he needed to escape the confines of his accommodation. His brief perambulation took in High Row's shopping district, sight of Imperial Quarter's independent cafes and restaurants, the indoor market of the Grade II listed Victorian Hall, and The Yards where one could buy artisan cheeses and fresh ground coffee. He didn't buy anything aside from a coffee, when a particularly harsh downpour forced him to seek quick refuge in a café. When the rain returned to a steady but bearable rate, he continued walking. He stopped when he saw a solitary vivid-green telephone booth at the end of an old, narrow brown-stone alley in Mechanics Yard. As rain struck his uncovered face, he stared at the empty booth and remembered what Faraday had said to him at the Cheltenham races – no contact with anyone he knew, don't touch public phones, nor private phones, use the burner phone in an emergency and only to call Faraday, no electronic payments, avoid talking to anyone, no hotel pay TV, make meal-times brief, do nothing to draw attention to himself, and ultimately imagine spending a week or two drifting through purgatory. The instructions were easy to follow, but Faraday and his well-meaning Pinkerton agent didn't know that Prasad's recently-rescued sister was eating all of the food her mother prepared for her and showing full signs of recovering from her ordeal while at the same time secretly vomiting every ingested morsel down the loo. She felt violated, foolish, and contemptuous of her being. And she'd confided in her brother before he'd left Cheltenham. Oh, how he wanted to call her and see how she was doing. They'd always been close when growing up. But now it felt like they were on different planets. He walked to the booth and looked at the phone inside. Was it really plausible that just one call, from a public phone, could make any difference? It could, he decided, if his parents' home was subject to an eavesdropping attack. A call would be traced to Darlington. He'd paid for his hotel in cash and hadn't used his name since being here. But he didn't know. Maybe a call could trigger someone who had skills he didn't have to find an unnamed person in a place containing approximately one hundred thousand people. And if that happened he'd have failed Faraday, GCHQ, and the broader picture of whatever was going on.

But, then there was his unwavering desire to be a non-judgemental support for his sister who, at the moment, only had their parents and other immediate family, and all of their loving yet forthright opinions. He placed a hand against the clear-plastic booth surround. He didn't know anything about payphones; had never used one. Maybe they only took bank cards, in which case it would be impossible for him to call. Due to the rain hitting the plastic, he couldn't discern if the machine inside was card-only. He didn't know if a tear was running down his face. He certainly felt wretched as he turned around and walked back down the empty and oppressive alley.

Baltzar felt energised after a day of rest. Earlier this morning she had notions of going out and exploring the island of Muck on foot. Maybe she'd still do that later, but right now sea-wind was hurling spray over the beach and close to the cottage, rain was near-horizontal and had the force of a sandblaster, and thunder came and went too frequently for the likes of a solitary walker who didn't want to be struck by lightning. She was by no means averse to inclement weather and rough terrain, but outside the isolated property it was borderline ridiculous. Even the hardy sheep and cows were nowhere to be seen, and that was saying something given Muck's cattle could ordinarily withstand most weather chucked at them. She lit a fire in the lounge, made a mug of black coffee, and considered her options. There were very few. But, there was one thing she'd been considering for some weeks and had been putting off. Maybe now was the time to get it done. And she'd come prepared, in case she decided to grasp the nettle and put thoughts into action while on what seemed like the edge of Earth. She withdrew stationery from a bag, sat in an armchair with a book of Muck's history on her lap, and began writing a letter to Duggan's ex-wife. She hadn't met the woman, but knew enough about her and where she lived. She described the way Hamish Duggan had cared for Baltzar, his hewn-rock persona that hid an enormous heart, dry sense of humour, piercing intellect, and unwavering reliability to always be there when it really fucking mattered. And she took the bull by the horns and described his feelings towards his wife; his recollections of them walking hand-in-hand through the parts of London she loved; that he felt so awkward singing in the Civil Service choir, but had joined to impress her baritone Welsh father; was convinced that she was the world's most beautiful and accomplished baker of fruit cakes; felt lost without her; and got stroppy if other women were described as pretty, always concluding with solemnity and a growl, "Aye, but she's not my Gwen". She finished the letter by saying that it might be a good idea for Gwen and Hamish to meet up at their favourite restaurant and talk about the time that Hamish punched a guy for looking at her the wrong way and then had to carry the poor bloke a mile down the Welsh mountain of Snowdon to the nearest medical centre. She wrote her name, knowing it would be familiar to Gwen, and held her pen over the paper while thinking. Then added, "P.S. Stop being a self-centred bitch". She smiled, inserted the letter into an envelope, wrote the address and stuck on a stamp, and put the letter on the mantelpiece. She'd post it when back in London. But for now it made her feel good to know it was ready. She looked out of the window, put on her boots and coat, and headed out while thinking, "Fuck you, lightening".

Bancroft loathed William Shakespeare. Well, his works at least. He'd been forced to study The Bard for GCSE and A levels. And in his first year at Oxford there'd been a compulsory semester on Hamlet. Had the sycophantic scholastic forced march not happened, Shakespeare might have avoided Bancroft's disgust at the mere mention of his name. Probably, Bancroft would have pigeonholed him as a reasonably okay writer and moderate storyteller, who just needed a really good editor and a lot more competition from other writers. Instead, Macbeth, Hamlet, Othello, et bloody al, were force-fed down his throat by teachers who seemed to him to be more like fanatical disciples of Shakespeare rather than academically rigorous intellectuals. And, there were so many better books out there to read. The problem he now faced was that Stratford Upon Avon lived and breathed Shakespeare. One couldn't turn without seeing a shop or café or museum that had some reference to its most famous resident. The town had so many other good things – a great look, history, civility, cool independent retailers and pubs, artistic vibe, and friendly, cultured people. The latter was particularly important. Thus far, Bancroft hadn't seen any oiks in Stratford. He didn't like oiks. But the hand of Shakespeare was all pervasive over the town and Bancroft could feel it as he walked down to the river, with a carton of tea in one hand and a paper bag of breadcrumbs in the other so that he could feed the swans on this crisp, sunny day. He sat on a bench by the River Avon and started tossing food at the birds that looked anything but graceful as they dashed to fill their serrated beaks. They were the oiks of Stratford, he decided. His thoughts drifted. Ten percent of his mind was pre-occupied with the memory of standing in front of his school class and reciting a soliloquy that blathered on about slings and arrows, conscience making cowards of us all, and the dread of something after death. Ninety percent of his brain was focused on going to prison for being in possession of stolen goods. It was his friend Timothy who was to blame. He'd been at school with him at Eton and they'd stayed in touch ever since. Tim, as he was known, was always a bit of a chancer who worked the angles – cheating in his final exams so that he didn't have to bother revising and instead could devote time to hosting lavish parties on one of his parents' estates, pretending he was tenth in line for the British throne so that he could bed a gorgeous Arab princess, and dropping out of Cambridge University to devote his energies to a City-based company that sold overseas land that didn't belong to them. Bancroft wasn't stupid. He kind of knew something was amiss when Tim asked him to look after a painting that Tim was convinced was a newly discovered *John Everett Millais*. But, Tim had a knack of getting others to overcome their misgivings and embrace his naughty charm while jumping on board his figurative pleasure cruiser. Bancroft had taken the painting. Two days later, the police knocked on his door. He'd tried calling Tim, but his friend was nowhere to be found. Tim did that sometimes. So, Bancroft had to go to the police station and was later released on bail and told to report back in three weeks. That was twelve days from now. On the *Twelfth Night*. Shut up Bancroft, he told himself. Focus. In less than two weeks he had to be at Kennington Police Station, London. His solicitor had advised him that if he turned up, at worst he'd be let off with a caution and at best he'd be released without any action taken. That was good. Sassoon and the rest of the British Intelligence community need never know about his unfortunate dalliance in the art-theft industry. But, if he failed to turn up he'd be tracked down and sent to crown court. Even if he got off jail-time, he wouldn't be able to keep his job. MI6 didn't give a damn about criminal activities. But, it cared enormously if someone was dumb enough to get caught. So, the Sassoon gig had to wrap up before the twelve days were over. Otherwise he'd be in a world of pain. He looked at a nearby bronze statue of a somewhat maudlin Hamlet holding the court jester Yorick's skull. He muttered, "I know how you feel, pal. My Tim is also a fellow of infinite jest and of most excellent fancy. Bastard." He smiled and wandered back to his flat. When he arrived, his landlady Shirley was waiting by the door, because she'd forgotten to give him her mobile number in case of emergencies. After taking the slip of paper from her and opening the door, for some inexplicable reason he found himself pausing, turning to her, and saying, "Get thee to a nunnery." Idiot. He apologised, said something about just watching a dress rehearsal of a play, entered the flat, shut the door, and leant against it while thinking that it wasn't Tim who was the fool. It was him.

Crease hadn't smoked crack cocaine for fifteen hours. She was now well and truly into the period when withdrawal symptoms were typical. She didn't need a Google search to tell her that. It was happening to her in real time. She felt wretched. She'd vomited in the night, and twice this morning. Her muscles ached more than when she'd done a twenty kilometre police charity run, without doing much training for the event. Vision was blurred; couldn't sleep, despite feeling exhausted and utterly lethargic; and to hell with Hare's description of having a 'monkey on her back' – as she tried to shuffle around the cottage she felt like she was strapped to a five hundred pound male silverback gorilla. And her mood – God, it was all over the place. She had a 'shit smoothie', she thought; a blend of paranoia, depression, irritability, dysphoria, and a constant nagging thought that it would be a good idea to die.

She kept telling herself that it was all a trick; that there was someone else inside her; someone bad and ill. What she was feeling wasn't her. She was feeling the bad person. But, what to do about the bad person? It was doing a very good job of feasting on her from the inside. It was a parasitic protest. Give me drugs or I'll keep eating you. Still, knowing that it wasn't her was half the battle. Didn't mean she'd win, though.

Of course, the craving for crack was constant. Just one hit to end all this. But there was no crack nearby; only a farmer a mile away who may or may not sell her milk and eggs.

What to do about the bad person? With what little remained of her lucid, rational brain power, she tried to think. It was a gargantuan effort. Hardest thing she'd ever done. Like trying to recite the nine times table while suffocating to death. Most ill people want to sleep. But, the bad person didn't like sleep. Distraction was no good because matters were way beyond diversionary tactics. She could be plonked into a room full of naked studs and all she'd think about was agony. Food and drink were a hit and miss affair. Sometimes she was famished; other moments ingesting anything aside from drugs was the last thing she wanted. Irrespective, whether she ate and drank or not, she wretched and puked. So far that had happened over bed sheets, the floor, and down her sweat-sodden vest while walking. Whether bile or something more substantial, what came out was her. The bad person was spewing and shitting the good stuff. As she stood in the kitchen, painfully gripping a work surface, she believed the only thing that would stop the bad person was to kill the parasite before it killed her. Starving it of the drug was the obvious solution. She'd stick at that. Had no choice. But, she was so scared. Unlike her to be that way. Unlike her to be in this condition, full stop. Would the bad person kill her when it knew all was lost? Be like a six foot tapeworm that strangles its host's organs in the throes of its death? She didn't know. Nothing she'd previously read about cold turkey had drawn comparisons between crack cocaine withdrawal and tapeworms. So, she had to deal with this on her own and come up with her own solution. The bad person didn't sleep; that much she knew. But, she could exhaust it. Make it hibernate. Make it wither away. Until it was nothing.

Exercise was the answer. Lots of it. Keep going. Defeat it that way, even if she had to drag the gorilla with her. That meant getting properly dressed. It took her a long time to do so; she didn't know how long; time was for normal people.

She exited the cottage. Thank goodness she'd remembered to bring sunglasses. It was freezing cold, though she thought it was hotter than a greenhouse, but there was no mistaking the bright light. Even through the glasses, it seared her eyeballs. She stumbled, wobbled, thought she might collapse, lifted her leaden feet, plodded onwards, down the footpath, and for the first time stepped onto the craggy beach. Was this a good idea? She wasn't sure. But, she had to believe that the bad person would hate what she was doing.

Mobility had been awful on the one hundred yard stretch between the cottage and the beach. Now, it was exponentially worse. There were boulders, smaller rocks, shingle, damp sand that sunk underfoot, the big and deep rock pools, and wind that came and went in gusts. But, she kept going, with no idea how she'd get back. Didn't matter. Killing the bad person was all she cared about.

After nearly three hundred yards, she thought she might pass out. She steadied herself against a boulder, breathing fast, perspiration stinging her eyes, mouth tasting of iron, throat and lungs caustic, muscles and skeletal structure feeling like they were on a medieval rack. Next to the boulder was a pool that was thirty feet wide and fifteen feet deep. The water in it was dark and still. She pushed herself away from the boulder and tentatively stood on the edge of the pool. She couldn't see the bottom, and had no knowledge as to what aquatic life might be in there in winter. But, she stayed there anyway, just staring at the water.

End this, a voice in her head stated.

Was it her voice?

Or the bad person's voice?

It was her voice, she decided. The bad person didn't want to die. It wanted crack. It wanted everything to be back to how things were.

But, she didn't want to die either. She wanted the gorilla, puke, giddiness, and rack to bugger off. Or did she want to die? Her police file conjectured that she might have a death wish, irrespective of her current condition. She didn't think it was true. Rather, she'd been angry – growing up with a mother who was no use; rough school; dinner money spent by her mother on booze; her and her brother having to choose to put on uniforms to get out; her doing so without the slightest interest in the police. Bunch of uneducated bullies, she thought of cops. That view was reinforced by seeing three burly police officers with stab-resistant vests taking it in turns to kick her seventeen year old defenceless female friend in the head. But one year later she joined up and came top of her class at Hendon because she wanted to prove to the Met that she was better than them. Anger had been her fuel of choice. Now she was trying to expunge an altogether different fuel. And in the process maybe now she did have a death wish, because if anger and crack were the only things she had in her life then it wasn't a life worth having.

It wasn't a conscious decision. It just happened. She fell forward, slowly it felt, no resistance or panic from her, just peace and a sense of control. When her body entered the icy water she let her arms and legs drift outwards, her face looking towards the bottom of the pool. She imagined that the salty water was good for her, cleansing and purging her clammy skin of impurities. She floated for a few moments, and then thought she might be sinking. It didn't matter. No doubt the bad person loathed being in here. And that meant she had to embrace what was happening. But it was no longer just about the parasite. It was about who she truly was.

She thought that maybe she should reach the bottom, look up, and see beauty above the water's surface. Or she'd see strange and wonderful creatures moving around her. Then she'd swim back to the surface, get out, and hope that the swim and her wet clothes would have stunned the bad person into submission. She was kidding herself. She doubted she could move her limbs to reach the top and she certainly didn't think she could haul herself out of the pool. So here she was, just drifting and waiting to die.

Something very strong gripped her around the chest. Maybe a conger eel? Man o' war's tentacles? Or perhaps the tape worm had escaped her body. Whatever it was it wanted something from her because it was holding tight and pulling. She didn't know which direction she was being taken. Nor did she care. Let the eel or whatever it was devour her. She'd had over sixteen hours of being eaten alive. Hopefully, what had her now wasn't a parasite and instead was a predator that would kill her quickly. Then everything would be over. She'd have lost; but so too would the bad person.

The thing kept pulling her. She was conscious of water moving over her face; but nothing else, aside from the grip on her. Trapped and moving, that was all that was happening.

Then air. And excruciating light. Her sunglasses must have fallen off. That mattered because her head was out of water. She started gasping. Good. It meant she wanted to live. Least ways, her body did.

She was pulled to the side of the pool and quickly lifted out of the sea water. God, whatever had hold of her must have been very strong. Perhaps she was just an insignificant ragdoll in its grasp. That's how she felt. A ragdoll.

She was placed on the beach, several feet away from the pool. As she lay there, she raised a hand over her eyes and squinted. There was a shape in front of her. Maybe human. Possibly alien. So difficult to tell given the sun was flecking her eyeballs with beads of its fire. She imagined it could be the bad person. Finally out of her. But way more angry than she'd been when she'd learnt her army brother would have survived the IED were it not for Ministry of Defence cutbacks on procurement spending. What did it want to do to her?

Aadesh said, "Bad day for a swim." The sturdy Gurkha tossed her over his shoulder and walked.

In the West Square kitchen, Knutsen handed Raine a mug of coffee and said, "Years ago Ben had to decline a place in the Great Britain Rifle Team to compete in the Olympics; once took on a bet and knocked out a former heavyweight champion boxer in round one; stripped and rebuilt a knackered jeep while me and him were stuck in forty degree heat in Chad, with lions watching us and while we were trying to track a lunatic; and set in train a series of deductions that led to the prevention of the assassination of a Spanish duchess, the starting point being that he spotted her eating figs for breakfast." He sipped his coffee. "And yet the buffoon can't repair and blow up an airbed."

Out of sight and from the hallway came the sounds of Sign cursing while trying to use a foot pump. "Mr. Knutsen!" he called out. "Do we happen to have any more sticky tape? Never mind. I think it's okay. Oh, for the love of God!"

Raine looked in the direction of Sign and said quietly, "His brain doesn't have room for blow-up bed repairs."

"Nah. He keeps plenty of space in there for more stuff. Trouble is, he's bloody selective. If he can't see a way that it might come in handy one day, he doesn't let it in."

"Do you think you should go and help him?"

Knutsen huffed. "Do *you* want to help him?"

Raine shook his head. "I prefer things the way they are."

"Me too. He'll work it out. And when the job's done he'll deliberately jettison knowledge of how he did it." He looked at the wall clock. "Karin will be here in a minute. You shouldn't have got her to go shopping for lunch."

"Why not?"

"It'll wind her up."

"She needs to learn our British ways."

"What? That we keep our women in the kitchen?"

"No. That we persevere with a stereotypical notion until the person either gets the joke, or doesn't and is therefore unworthy of our attention."

"Good luck with that."

Raine recalled Lebrun serving him Sign's food. "In any case. There is more to Karin than meets the eye. She enjoys being a woman."

"Err, right." Knutsen tried to ignore more shouting from the hallway. "Mind you – have you considered the possibility that she might bring us German food?"

Raine frowned. "And?"

"German food might be your last supper. Before you get butchered, and all that. Just sayin'."

"Ah. I hadn't thought of that."

"Seems you hadn't." Knutsen was getting irritated with Sign's kerfuffle with the bed. Referring to Sign, he said, "Bloody nincompoop. I suppose I'd better help him. After all, the airbed might be the last thing you sleep on." He walked towards the hall while calling out, "Just leave it, Ben. I'll do it. Just…" He reached the hall. "Oh, for fuck's sake, mate. What have you done?"

In the lounge of the Devon cottage, Aadesh put a pint of water on the table in front of Crease. "Drink. I don't know anything about cocaine withdrawal but I do know a lot about malaria. I'm guessing it's a similar shit storm. Hydration might not help, but it sure as hell won't *not* help."

Her hand was shaking as she reached for the glass. "You look like a hiker. But, you're not. Who are you?"

"Hired help. Your guardian angel, maybe. Call me what you want. My job is to keep you safe."

One hand wasn't to be trusted with the glass. She used both. "Then, you know everything."

"I very much doubt that. Doesn't matter. Keeping you alive does. Including stopping you going all *Kurt Cobain* on me."

The forty year old's reference was lost on her. "You obviously know I'm detoxing. What else?"

He shrugged. "That you're a fucked-up twenty year old cop who's been told to keep her head down while others hunt a nasty piece of work. There's a couple of other things I know about what's going on, but I don't know if you know what they are so I reckon we leave it at that."

She couldn't work out his accent. Maybe Indian or Pakistani or something else South Asian, tinged with a London or Home Counties lilt. She didn't want to ask. "Thank you for... getting me out. I don't know what happened. It just happened."

"Don't worry about it." Aadesh sat opposite her. "I once dived off an oil rig into the North Atlantic, around about this time of year. Did it for a dare. Dumb really. We do shit."

It had taken Hare and Sassoon four hours and ten minutes to fly from Heathrow to Bergen, via Amsterdam and courtesy of KLM Royal Dutch Airlines. They'd not sat together on the airplanes and nor were they together as they walked though Arrivals in the airport, looking like businessmen and wearing the same overcoats and suits they'd worn earlier. They met outside of the airport building.

Hare inhaled deeply and said, "I wonder if Raine's breathing in the same air."

Sassoon nodded while putting on his gloves and looking at the taxi rank. "Time to break some Norwegian laws."

They didn't speak as their taxi took them into the heart of the small city. They were dropped adjacent to Byfjorden, in the oldest part of Bergen around the bay of Vågen, close to the restaurant where The Thief exited his cab the night before. Snow covered the neighbourhoods and adjacent mountains, large flakes falling slowly in the half-light and captured by the port, street, and building illuminations. Yachts were moored nearby. Further out in the fjord was an anchored large cruise ship, its white exterior glittering with electric-blue cabin and deck lights. Probably, some of the vessel's passengers were dining ashore in the historical quarter that was bathed in rich bronze colour. Others must have stayed on board because laughter could be heard, travelling from the ship across the still water and to the harbour side. Restaurants and bars were buzzing and full, but few people were out on foot and there were barely any vehicles. Sassoon and Hare didn't blame the locals and tourists for staying indoors. As beautiful as the city was, it was bloody freezing.

Before leaving London and while in his Chelsea flat, Sassoon had retrieved from his study a 1940 map of Bergen that had been made by a German *Brandenburger* commando who was previously a cartographer in pre-war civilian life. He'd laid the map out in front of Hare and suggested they commit to memory certain detail. Hare had told him they didn't have time and in any case there were other sources of information available to them. Now, the detective used Google Maps on his phone to follow the route to Lystad's house. He couldn't decide if the MI6 officer by his side was genuinely unhappy with Hare's use of his expedient and technologically-advanced device, or whether he was playacting a caricature of himself. One never knew with Sassoon.

They reached the house in the quiet, cobbled side street. The property was in darkness. Hare expected Sassoon to be furtive, watchful, almost timid in his behaviour. It's how he imagined spies acted when overseas, though this experience was a first for him. Instead, the MI6 officer strode up to the door and pressed its buzzer three times. He waited twenty seconds and buzzed again. Satisfied there was no one in the house, he tried the door handle. It was locked. From his coat pocket he withdrew a small leather wallet. He opened its clasp and removed three thin whalebone utensils from a selection of more bones that were allegedly for restoring and repairing clocks. One by one, and at different angles, he inserted the bones into the lock. After nearly one minute of concentration, he gripped all three implements between the fingers of one hand and twisted. The lock opened. As head of the Metropolitan Police's SO15 Counter Terrorist Command, Hare knew specialists in his branch who could open most household locks in seconds using an electronic device the size of a disposable lighter. Then again, their devices would be detected if they tried to take them through airport security. The police technicians weren't spies. Sassoon secreted the tools and walked into the house. Hare followed, closing the door behind him.

Unlike The Thief, they spent time in the downstairs two bedrooms, sunroom, and the courtyard. They never spoke; just used eye contact, head and hand gestures to communicate tasks. Hare was now in his element. Searching places was his bread and butter. Sassoon was just as thorough, but Hare noticed there was something else about the way he was going about his work. Occasionally the spy would stop, motionless, his head at an angle. It was almost as if he was feeling the house.

They went upstairs, into the lounge cum dining cum kitchen area. They saw what the traitor saw - wooden-floor, upright piano, two paintings in the room, small dining table with silver cutlery and a crystal wine glass, fake six-foot statue, kitchen knife stuck in a wooden chopping board, and pharmaceutical containers of herbs and spices. It took them nearly thirty minutes to thoroughly search the area, all of the time listening for any indications that Lystad might be arriving home; worse, that Raine might be forcing entry into the property.

Having found nothing of interest, they moved into the top floor attic. This was going to be a job, thought Hare. Though it wasn't messy, it was cluttered and without any semblance of order. He made ready to start at one end of the room, but Sassoon put his hand on Hare's chest and looked around. Silently, he moved to an easel, lifted the first near-completed painting and rifled through the blank underlying sheets. He did the same with the other easels. Nothing. But he wasn't deterred. Without looking where he was going, he swung around so that he was in front of the writing desk. The way he'd moved there suggested it was his inevitable ultimate destination. He opened the first drawer; then the second; and the last. He gestured for Hare to join him. The detective did so. Sassoon pointed. In the first drawer was nothing, except a phone. Using his gloved hand, the MI6 officer removed the mobile and placed it on the desk. For someone who liked World War Two maps by mountain warfare experts, it appeared Sassoon also knew a thing or two about the twenty first century. He accessed Sent Messages, used his phone to take a photo of the coded text to Raine, and also photographed detail in Settings that showed the model type of the phone, its payment plan, serial number, and call history which displayed zero incoming or outgoing data. If this was a crime scene, Hare would have had the device analysed for skin prints and DNA. But, he wasn't carrying the technology to do such tests and in any case they didn't need fingerprints et cetera. They wanted photographic evidence.

Sassoon placed the phone back into the drawer, closed it, and withdrew papers from the second draw. He laid them out on the desk, studied them, looked at Hare, and nodded. There were seven copied CHALICE reports, written on a cheap typewriter, all from the last twelve months.

Sassoon took photos of the desk, put the papers back into the drawers and in the order he'd found them, and withdrew from the bottom drawer a thin file, which he opened. The file was a dossier on Raine. It contained a handwritten sheet of the diplomat's mobile and work landline telephone numbers, FCO address, personal bank account details, and email address. Another sheet was a photocopy of the pages in his British diplomatic passport showing his photo and adjacent data, the sheet bearing the logo and authority of The United States Department of Homeland Security, and stating that Raine's tenure as ambassador in the country was approved. Goodness knows how Lystad had gotten hold of the document. There was a *Le Monde* newspaper clipping showing Raine in Paris, shaking the hand of the Président de la République française, with the newspaper suggesting that Raine was a wolf in sheep's clothing. And finally there was a sheet containing the diplomat's home address, landline telephone number, and immediate family's email addresses and mobile numbers. Paper-clipped to the sheets were three photos: one of Raine's wife, and two of his teenage daughters.

Sassoon photographed all of the file's contents, returned the file, nodded at Hare, and tapped his wrist.

It was time to go.

They had more than enough to crucify Raine.

For the first time since they'd arrived in Norway, they spoke when standing outside Bergen Airport. Sassoon said, "The file on Mr. R is L's insurance. Something to pop into the post to the Brits if his colleague tries to cut him out."

"Yep. That's what it is."

"Bear with me." Sassoon pressed buttons on his mobile phone. He looked at the cop. "All photos are off my phone. Sent to another device in London. Saves me having to fool this lot," he waved his hand, "if I get pulled over and have to explain what's in my phone. I like Norwegians. But God, they do go on a bit."

The fact that Sassoon knew how to send the photos as an encrypted burst transmission to a covert MI6 receiver further reinforced to Hare that there was more to Sassoon's knowledge of data communication than antique cartography. "I'll make the call to the others when we arrive back in London. We'll get our heads together sometime tomorrow."

Sassoon replied, "A face to face tomorrow might be a bit tricky for me. But for sure, let's speak in some guise."

Hare frowned, then asked, "How do you feel?"

The MI6 officer considered the question. "Disappointed."

Both men were back in London Heathrow by eleven PM.

Hare was on his own when he rang Faraday. "We found a pot of gold at the end of the rainbow. The man who owns the house we went to see is the intermediary. One hundred percent. And it's now certain. Our friend in our society is the man for the job. Absolutely no doubt. Tell Mr. D. For now, do nothing. Let's get our heads together tomorrow." He ended the call.

One hour later, The Thief was on a train. Everything was going according to plan.

CHAPTER 18
SEVEN DAYS AFTER THE MURDER OF ALEX WICK

It was Saturday.

Aadesh woke up and rubbed his stiff neck. He'd spent the night grabbing slithers of sleep on the sofa in Crease's Devon cottage. Mostly, he'd been listening out for her, in case there were any problems. She'd visited the bathroom once, but aside from that had been quiet. During waking moments, he'd researched drug withdrawal. The results were too varied to be meaningful. As a result, he decided that he had to rely on his soldier training and deal with the problem in the same way he'd have to deal with a stricken comrade in a combat zone. That meant making her comfortable and stable and ensuring she didn't freak out and compromise their current situation.

It was seven AM. He checked his phone. Aadesh had updated Lucas yesterday, telling him that he had to make an emergency intervention, and was now staying with Crease. Lucas had taken the development in his stride and instructed his colleague to fight his battlefield as he saw fit. As per protocol at this time of day, he sent the group-chat another message to say that there was nothing untoward occurring at his post this morning, save having to babysit a drug-addled girl with issues. His colleagues also reported in. The other runners were fine and keeping a low profile. It was only Crease who was problematic.

He wondered if she was hungry. He wandered into the kitchen and had a look in the fridge. There was nothing in there of note. He remembered something she told him the night before, put his boots and coat on, and left the property. He reached the farm, one mile away, and rang the doorbell.

The farmer answered, wearing muddy chest-high waders, a woollen hat, and holding a mug of something hot in his hand. Seven AM was clearly not the beginning of his working day. "Yeah?" was all he said.

Aadesh gave a variation of the truth, saying that he and his girlfriend were in the coastal cottage, and that his girlfriend was ill meaning he couldn't risk leaving her for too long to buy food from Hartland. He wondered if the farmer would sell him something.

The farmer, a sullen fellow who was clearly in a grumpy mood, said he couldn't help.

Aadesh smiled and said he was sure he could.

The farmer was steadfast and told him that he could get to Hartland and back in thirty minutes if the roads were clear.

Seeing how this conversation was headed, Aadesh told him that he'd very happily snap the spine of any country bumpkin who was unwilling to supply sustenance to a stricken woman in need.

Maybe it was the way the former Gurkha said it, the look in his eyes, the unflinching grin on his face, or the fact that his short stature looked like it would stand firm if hit by a speeding truck. Either way, the farmer muttered something inaudible, disappeared, returned with a full carrier bag, handed it to him, said no payment was required, and told him to get off his land.

Twenty minutes later, Aadesh was back in the kitchen, cooking bacon and eggs. He made coffee and hoped the collective aromas would lure Crease out of her room. While he stood by the stove and frying pan, he reflected on his morning walk and the other reason he'd ventured out.

He'd seen no threats.

"Morning, guv'nor." Knutsen was holding a mug of coffee and standing over Raine.

The distinguished senior diplomat winced as he opened his eyes and twisted on the airbed. He tried to work out which part of his body didn't hurt. He forced himself to sit, yawned, stretched and regretted doing so, and said, "I'm guessing this isn't a bad dream."

"Could be. If so, appears I'm in it." He gave the mug to Raine. "Bathroom's free. Ben's out and about getting offal or something for brekkie. Karin's over in an hour. Best you get your ass in gear. You look like shit."

The Thief was close to his destination. But, he was patient. For now he just wanted to watch, get the lay of the land, and consider his options before making a move. It felt good to be in a new location, away from work and his role in pretending to catch himself. Here he could breathe and focus on a purer objective, one that would allow free reign of his creativity. And thank goodness, he could perform his art in peaceful solitude. He checked the time, sat down, and admired everything before him.

Ten minutes after Lebrun had entered West Square, Sign arrived bearing a wooden box and a paper grocery bag. "You are in for a treat, Mrs. Lebrun!" He gestured for her to come over to the dining table, where he'd laid his items. "Open the box."

She was bemused as she untied and unwrapped twine around the tiny crate, and lifted the lid. Inside were fish, resting on a bed of sea salt. "Fish," was all she could say.

Sign beamed. "This morning I met the driver of the *Flying Scotsman* locomotive. He'd brought the train into Kings Cross from Edinburgh, at near record time for the old beauty I might add. And he carried with him a precious cargo, marked for my attention. Not just any fish. The finest Scottish herring, smoked over fires of whisky cask oak shavings in a wind-powered brick kiln. I'm going to feed you the most traditional of British breakfasts – kippers and eggs on rye bread. Please think of the gesture as my way of saying thank you for temporarily giving me the use of Germany." He grabbed the box and bag, entered the kitchen, and called out, "Mr. Knutsen! Catch and help!"

Knowing what was about to happen, Knutsen urgently moved to Lebrun's side, just as Sign threw him a wooden chopping board. Next he was tossed a loaf of bread. And finally he managed to catch the handle of a razor sharp kitchen knife that wasn't designed to cut bread but sliced through it as if it was melting butter. Knutsen sighed, and started cutting the bread. Sign fried the fish, scrambled eggs, served, and brought four plates to the table.

Raine, who'd been watching the burst of energy from the far side of the lounge, sauntered over and said, "You forgot to brew English breakfast tea."

"Indeed I did, sir." Sign dashed back into the kitchen. "Two ticks. Somebody please get cutlery from the side cabinet." A moment later he returned with a pot of tea in one hand, four mugs held in the other, sugar sachets hanging from his mouth, and a plastic bottle of milk under one arm. He plonked everything down, sat, smiled, and said, "While we eat, the world temporarily takes a moment to reflect on its irascible tendencies."

The four of them began eating.

Knutsen glanced at Raine, who was looking at him. Because both men knew Sign, albeit from different perspectives and times, they could tell something was amiss. They realised their friend's breakfast frivolity was a pantomime; masquerade; smokescreen.

Raine gave the tiniest nods to Knutsen and looked at the former MI6 officer. "We dine and wait as they run their blades against strips of looted hide."

Sign frowned, shook his head fast, and asked, "Tennyson?"

"No. Me. Just to see if you were paying attention. You can cook breakfast in your sleep. You know Tennyson upside down and backwards. You're not with us, Ben."

Sign put his fork down on his half-eaten food. "I concede my thoughts are elsewhere. And nowhere meaningful."

"There's nothing more you can do right now. You've taken me, the king, off the chessboard. You've spoilt the game."

Sign huffed. "You're still on the board. It's just that The Thief can't see you right now. He'll find you. Or his pawns will."

"You have me here. You have the upper hand."

Sign raised his eyebrows. "And you have in me a friend who would dangle you like a carcass on a meat-hook, while waiting for a man eater."

"Stop being so melodramatic." Raine let the riposte hang for a moment, then laughed.

Sign looked at him and couldn't help joining in the laughter.

Raine was relieved his comment had worked. "Mind you – I suppose it's not melodramatic." A gentle smile was now on his face. "Be kind to yourself. When you know exactly what you're doing and are completely in control, you're the most patient man. Be that man."

Sign exhaled slowly. "Do I know what I'm doing? My thoughts are elsewhere and nowhere because my antennae are twitching. And for the life of me I can't work out why. I hate that. But, it's happening. And in this case I suspect it's not happening for a good reason."

Crease entered the kitchen, held her hand to her mouth, swallowed hard, thought for a moment, nodded, and said, "I can do this." She stood next to Aadesh and looked at the bacon and eggs in the pan. Recalling her meeting with Hare in *The Artful Dodger* café, she said, "Everyone's always trying to feed me up."

Aadesh handed her a plate and put food on it. "I don't care if you don't eat. But, I'm giving you a test. See if you can carry that to the lounge without dropping it." He piled the rest of the food onto his plate and followed her into the adjacent room. When they were both sitting at the small table, he said, "My name's Aadesh. I'm from Nepal. Unmarried, but you might be too young for me. No kids or other ties. I was a Gurkha. One time got the Victoria Cross. Can't remember where I put it. I left the British army in a hurry after I killed my commanding officer. Now I protect and kill people for money. I cook very good goat curry." He ate.

The Thief watched what was happening behind the cottage window. He was one hundred yards away, on a mound of gorse and behind a small bush. He was wearing green waterproofs, walking boots, had his hood up, and was holding a powerful but compact pair of binoculars. By his side was a military daysack. If anyone walked by, he might have looked like a bird-watcher, using the colours of his attire and kit to blend in to the rugged landscape. But, the only other discernible outdoor living things were free-grazing cattle belonging to the far-away farmer and gulls. The clear sky enabled good visibility, though tranquillity was amiss because the high winds and sound of the sea made the elements sound busy. And it was cold. Further inland and earlier in the morning, The Thief had seen frost and ice. Here, the salt-laden squalls ensured nothing settled.

Aadesh smiled when he saw Crease finish her food.

She leaned back, exhaled loudly, and said, "I'm not saying that was easy, and I might throw up anytime soon, but it's a start."

"You're a fighter. I had you down as a loser."

She huffed but was smiling. "Thanks. I think. Do you have a gun?"

"Of course."

"On you now?"

"Didn't they teach you anything in police training?"

"Nothing worth a damn. Anyway, I can't see a gun."

"You're not looking at the small of my back." He stood and gathered up the plates. "When I was in Gurkha training, I asked a lady out on a date. I was young and single and held the rank of private. She too was unattached and was pretty and English and an officer. I wasn't naïve. These things were frowned upon. But I had devil-may-care spirit. So, I asked her. She was kind, but one of her friends was less so. She'd overhead us talking and reported the advance to my training officer. My punishment was a ten mile run over the Brecon Beacons while cradling an unslung GPMG. Heavy bit of kit. The female officer saw me when I returned to camp, looking a mess. Maybe it was because I'd proved my worth, or perhaps because I smiled at her when I put the machine gun down on the parade square, but either way she took a huge gamble on her career. We snuck out of the base one night and had a drink. It's a shame our paths never crossed again. That's army postings for you. I heard she's out of the military now and has a guy and children. Still, we had that drink. I imagine that I would have needed to be a dull man not to have seized that possibility." His eyes glistened as he looked at her. "This morning, would you care to join me on a date that carries a similar degree of adventure?"

Crease didn't know what to say. Was this happening? Were the effects of the drug still messing with her head?

"There's a flask in the kitchen. I'll fill it with hot tea. Perhaps we could go for a walk. We could aim for five hundred yards in a direction of your choosing. We stop; rest; have tea; admire the view. Then we return back here. Little steps with great gains. What do you say?"

"I... err." She found herself lapsing into the undercover persona she so loathed. "A rehab date? You know how to show a girl a good time, *maan*." She regretted the flippancy. It wasn't reflective of who she truly was. "Little steps?" she said quietly and in her tone. "Yes. Alright."

Aadesh held her gaze for a moment, nodded, and said, "Then today is a devil-may-care day. I'll wash up while you get ready. Test number two is to see if you can manage a shower without requiring the assistance of a male stranger."

The Thief stood, put away his binoculars, and withdrew two items from his bag. With his rucksack slung over one shoulder, he walked towards the cottage. In one hand he held a SIG Sauer P365 with suppressor. In the other he was gripping a mallet like the one he'd used to strike the head of a knitting needle.

The man was an unexpected issue. The Thief would deal with him first.

As he finished the washing up, Aadesh could hear running water in the bathroom. He momentarily fantasised about going on the walk with Crease while not carrying a gun and being on total alert for any indication of a nearby hostile. It was a foolish fantasy and would have to wait. Wait? Why did that word pop into his head? He finished his chores, pulled out his Browning Hi-Power handgun from under his belt, placed the gun on the counter, and removed its magazine to check the seating of the bullets. Satisfied all was in order, he started sliding the magazine back into the weapon.

The Thief was silent as he entered the cottage, his gun at the ready. In the kitchen, the man had his back to him. He saw his left arm jerk in front of him and the unmistakeable sound of a magazine being slammed into position.

Parry half-turned.

The Thief shot him twice in the head.

He walked out of the cottage, continued walking for fifteen minutes, entered Baltzar's cottage, surprised her in the lounge, and hit her in the face with the hammer.

Over six hundred miles away, Aadesh and Crease left the cottage in Devon's Hartland peninsula. After a few paces, Crease linked her arm with his. At first, the Gurkha didn't like that; he wanted freedom of mobility in case of need. But, then he thought 'sod it', and let her hold him. After all, today was a devil-may-care day.

The Thief checked Baltzar. She was still alive, but unconscious. He lifted her into an armchair, withdrew items from his rucksack, and set to work.

Ninety minutes later, he left the cottage and walked to the cottage containing Parry's body. He looked at the Russian's phone. It was ID protected, but it was easy to get through that. He noted the updates on the other runners and decided they were protected by Raine's men. He'd tell the rest of The Library that Raine followed Baltzar to this location. But, he knew the other bodyguards would tell Raine that the dead man at his feet had gone quiet. As a result, Raine would know what happened here. That didn't matter. What did was disposing of the body. It was vital that the other members of The Library didn't find out that Baltzar had a protector. If they did, they'd assume that meant the other runners were also being guarded. And they'd wonder who'd tasked the guardians. Raine was an obvious candidate, because the other Library members would deny they'd commissioned such tasking. And if Raine had issued orders for the runners to be covertly protected, that cast significant doubt on the possibility that he was The Thief. So, the body had to go. Wearing gloves and with his backpack on, he picked up the former special operative and carried him out of the building and along the harsh coastline. The weather was different now. Clouds were darkening and flecks of rain were the precursor for an imminent downpour. With Parry on his shoulder, he reached the southwestern part of the island. It was the furthest point from civilisation. He wasn't overly bothered about completely getting rid of the body. He didn't have the time and resources to make it vanish. But this was a wild place and no one would be looking for the corpse on the sparsely populated island. Certainly there'd be no police swoop, with thermal imagery, X-ray technology, probes, DNA testing-kits, scent hounds, and good old fashioned shovels and elbow grease. All he needed to do was get the body out of sight in the short-term. Still, he was confident the island would take care of the rest and ensure there was no trace of the murder.

He walked onto a sandy beach and laid the body onto rocks. From his bag, he withdrew a knife and a hacksaw. Rain was now heavy, wind gusting, as he worked solidly for one hour, applying the same level of skill as a master butcher to transform the body into cuts of meat. But, not everything could be jointed with clinical precision. The bones, and in particular the cranium and mandible, had to be disfigured. He used his hammer against the knife's hilt to deconstruct the ribcage, take apart the skeletal structure of the feet and hands, put the skull into quarters, and smash any other obvious signs that human remains were here. It was hard work but had to be done. He scattered the body parts along the beach and beyond large outcrops of rock in the sea. He didn't care that bits might escape the trappings of the rocks and wash ashore. What mattered were decay, erosion, and the hunger of ravenous otters, seals, eagles, fish, porpoises, seagulls, dolphins, and crabs. Blood was aplenty along the strip of beach where he'd worked. But rain and waves would take care of that. He stood ankle-deep in the sea, splashed cold water over his splattered garments, and threw Parry's phone and gun over the crest of a wave. The job complete, he walked back to Baltzar's cottage.

Inside her lounge, he used her burner phone to lure The Library to the scene. Duggan was key to this. After all, he was Baltzar's handler. He sent a text message to the MI5 officer.

Muck Island. Suðreyjar Cottage. Man coming. Can't speak. Urgent.

He turned off the phone and put it in his pocket. He'd toss it into the sea when off the island. He walked to the mantelpiece and looked at the letter that was sealed and addressed to Duggan's wife. He smiled. The letter could stay there, untouched by him. It would further infuriate Duggan. That was good. Duggan would show no mercy to Raine.

He looked at Baltzar.

She was dead.

And arranged by him.

A special display.

Just for The Library.

He'd long ago decided that death could be turned into art. His was of a particular style, one that combined depiction with the mechanics of science and mathematics. He believed an image could only be true if it passed the stress-tests of human senses. It had to be passionate, thoughtful, yet logical. There could be no room for creative whimsy. And it had to be precise. Nothing grated more than a poorly mounted painting or a misplaced brushstroke. Symmetry was essential.

It didn't serve his purpose to kill more runners. Baltzar was all he needed to get Raine. But, he now had to ensure that Raine was quickly killed and before he opened his mouth to the rest of The Library.

He looked at Baltzar. She was such a pretty model. So young. So much life ahead of her. Just like Wick. The Thief was proud of his work.

He left the cottage and the isle of Muck.

CHAPTER 19

At 1317hrs that day, Sign was in West Square when he received a call from Lucas.

The former French Foreign Legion officer said, "Nosferatu's missed his check-up appointment. I'm wondering if a home visit might be in order."

Sign's response was immediate. "Keep the surgery running as normal. You have patients to attend to. I'll deal with this." The meaning was obvious. Lucas, Noah, and Aadesh had to stay put, watching their runners.

Raine, Lebrun, and Knutsen were looking at him.

Sign ignored them, made a call, and concluded, "Yes. Right now. We're on our way." He ended the call, walked fast across the lounge, grabbed his handgun and spare magazines, and stopped in the centre of the room. Addressing his colleagues he said, "Baltzar's in trouble. Karin – you're with me. Make sure you're armed. Thankfully, you and I are already dressed for a rugged outing. Tom – stay here with Peter."

While Lebrun was in the hallway, Knutsen came up to Sign and said quietly, "I should be the one coming with you."

Sign could see that his friend's feelings were hurt. He moved closer to him and said in a muted yet commanding tone that was only audible to Knutsen, "I know you. Understand? I know you. And that's why you must stay with Peter. Trust and track-record are paramount. Peter must be kept alive. You won't let anyone or anything get through you. So, I choose you. Got it?"

Knutsen's demeanour changed. "Got it."

"Good man." He put on his windcheater mountaineering jacket, walked fast into the hallway, and opened the door while saying in a strident voice, "Come detective polizeirat. We have a light airplane to catch."

Lebrun frowned. "Airplane?"

"Yes, yes. The pilot's a miscreant buddy of mine who I keep on my books and out of prison." He walked down the stairs. "We need to be in a field in Surrey in precisely sixty minutes. Then we take off and head north."

Faraday was on the Cheltenham to London train, travelling in a suit because he was heading for an afternoon meeting with Duggan and Hare and knew they would be similarly attired due to earlier work reasons. Sassoon couldn't make the meeting because of other commitments, but was free later on in the day to hear updates via telephone. The topic of conversation was to be Norway and what to do about Raine.

The GCHQ expert couldn't stop thinking about Raine after receiving the call from Hare the night before. His phone rang. It was Duggan.

The MI5 Library member wasted no time on pleasantries. "Thank God you answered. Can't get hold of Edward. Where the hell is he?! My runner's in trouble. Got a strange text from her. Only just picked it up. Was stuck in bloody morning meetings."

"What kind of text?"

"Trouble text. Something's happened. I've tried calling her but no answer."

"Where are you?"

Duggan sounded out of breath. "Euston. About to get on a train to Glasgow. Then I'm going to leg it west. You need to divert and get up there as well. And get Rex. Tell him to meet us up there. He'll need to bring a precaution." A gun. "I'll keep trying to get hold of Edward. I'll text you the exact address of my runner. Only just found out myself where she is. This is bad, Gordon. I reckon our man's north of the border."

Faraday's mind was racing. He could about-face and head to Birmingham and from there get a Scotland-bound train. If he was lucky he could hook up with Duggan not long after the MI5 officer arrived in the country. Hare was a different matter. If he travelled by train he'd be at least an hour behind Duggan; maybe much longer. Then again, the chief superintendent did have police modes of transport at his disposal. "Forget Edward. He warned me his phone would be off until tea-time. But, Rex and I will be there. Keep your mobile charged up. We'll swap notes as we travel." He ended the call, got off the train at Swindon, and took the next train to Birmingham.

Knutsen checked that the front door of the flat was locked and bolted, went into the lounge, told Raine to sit at the dining table at the far end, and removed items from a cabinet. He placed the items on the table and sat next to the diplomat, facing the entrance to the hallway. He pulled out his SIG Sauer P226 and put it in front of him and next to another pistol. "We can't keep this up all day and night but I want you to get used to the view from the only safe place in the flat. You'll hear if there's a front-door breach. Stun grenades might be used. If so," he pointed at two objects, "we've got a couple of our own." He told him how to use them. "Ear defenders are self-explanatory; ditto gas mask. And the gun's yours. Shit hits the fan - get here, don the kit, toss the grenades, and shoot anything that comes into the room."

Raine looked at the pistol. "A Webley Mark Six Top-Break revolver. In service in the British Empire and Commonwealth between nineteen fifteen and nineteen seventy. It's an excellent weapon and quite collectible. When I was in Jakarta in ninety…"

"Shut up. You're starting to sound like Ben."

Raine shrugged. "I was merely going to recall the time when I was offered a Webley in a street market and declined on the grounds that I'd thus far managed to avoid handling weapons and didn't want to change the habit. In fact, to this day I've not touched a weapon."

"Have you ever had this big a target on your forehead before?"

"I… Err…"

"Thought not. Given your circumstances, you might want to reconsider your noble *no-guns* thing."

The diplomat's hand hovered over the pistol, while he recalled some of the most dangerous places and situations he'd been in. "I suppose you have a point." He picked up the weapon and moved it mid-air while looking at it with a curious expression. "I've never touched one of these before and yet I know so much about them. What a strange life."

"You said it."

Raine placed the gun down. "If we're attacked, what happens if they don't breach? They could try to burn us out, using the same modus operandi deployed against the poor American ambassador in the US Benghazi consulate."

Knutsen looked at him. "I don't think anyone's coming here. They don't know you're holed up in the flat. But, if they do try to burn us out, fuck what Ben says about not trusting the cavalry. I'm straight on the blower to…"

"The fire brigade and an armed police tactical unit."

"Yep."

Raine blew out steam from his vaporiser. "But, Ben's right. I don't relish the prospect of being kept in police protective custody. It would open up a can of worms."

"It wouldn't happen. After they rescue us from here, we'd sit outside with blankets around us while the high-vis guys run around doing their thing; and then we leg it."

"I see." Raine looked at the tank on his device while trying to decide if he viewed it as half-empty or half-full. "We must consider the possibility that Rex Hare would get involved. He's a major player in the Metropolitan Police. He has sway. You might find that we get shot by tactical officers as we try to run."

"Then we fucking shoot back." Knutsen stood, picked up his gun, and nodded at the dining table. "Right. That's our *Rorke's Drift* garrison sorted. Now we have to kill time. Let's play chess by the fire. Bring your Webley."

Relieved that he no longer had to sit behind gas masks and explosives, Raine followed him to the armchairs. He took Sign's seat; Knutsen sat in his chair. Knutsen turned on the touchscreen computer on the coffee table between them, loaded a chess game, and said, "Use your finger to move the pieces. Imagine you're anointing someone, or whatever it is you diplomats do with your fingers in your free time." He made the first move.

"High priests use their digits to anoint with oil. I suppose one could draw parallels between the calling of a priest and the vocation of a diplomat. Then again, Kuna Indians anoint the tips of their arrows with poison." Raine moved a piece. "You've lost the game already."

"No I haven't."

"Ah, you *think* you haven't. Therein is your weakness."

"Your Machiavellian mind-shit won't work with me."

"Because words are not your preferred form of communication?"

"Because I'm smarter than you."

"So sayeth the witless."

"Well, this *witless* superior being's just anointed your bishop." He moved a knight.

The diplomat frowned. "Oops." He smiled and moved the threatened piece. "It rather looks like the clergy would like to have a private consultation with your queen,"

"Yeah, well she's not in the mood and wants to powder her nose in the restroom." He moved the piece out of harm's way, sighed, and said, "Going to be a long day."

Raine also sighed. "It most certainly is."

From the inside of the small Cessna 172 airplane, Lebrun leaned across from one of the four cramped passenger seats and called out over the noise, "Where are we going to land?"

They were approaching Muck, the flight having taken just over four hours. Light was beginning to fade but the island's features were still easily visible as they decreased altitude over the sea.

Sign cupped a hand around his mouth and said loudly, "Regrettably there's no runway. We'll use the road. It's more than adequate in distance, and it's straight and rarely used."

Rarely used, thought Lebrun. Oh great.

"But hold on tight," continued Sign. "The pilot's done a few hairy take-offs and landings in his time, but last time we did something like this the plane hit rough ground and flipped a few times. We were very lucky. Just cuts, bruises, and whiplash. By contrast, the plane was a mangled ball of scrap. You would have thought that anyone in the crash would have been dismembered and squashed." He leaned back and watched land grow closer, swaying as the plane was struck by gusts of wind.

The noise grew louder as they further descended, to a level that made it look like they were going to land on the sea. The direct route to line up with the road meant flying over the tiny Port Mòr. But that was too risky. If just one of the thirty eight inhabitants spotted a plane that was obviously looking to land on the island, panic would ensue. Helicopters were the only mechanical airborne objects that landed here. And they only came for medical emergencies. As a result, the pilot avoided the port, flew over wild land, and banked forty five degrees left to ensure the makeshift runway was below him. The sharp manoeuvre didn't aid Lebrun's temperament.

But, the landing was fine, if shaky and abrupt. Engines off, Sign briefly spoke to the captain, opened the door, climbed out, and extended his hand to assist Lebrun with her exit. She thought about dismissing his chivalrous gesture, but decided to do so would be silly. She grabbed his hand and jumped onto the road.

"Come on." Sign pointed in the direction they needed to go. He didn't need Google Maps or a compass. Using grid references, and referring to hard-copy maps and images, he'd memorised the exact location of every runner as soon as he'd been given their location by the cutthroats.

They walked across heathland, carefully examining the ground in front of them so that they didn't twist an ankle. Behind them, they could hear the Cessna's engine start up and its propeller splutter into action.

Lebrun asked, "Is he going to hide the plane?"

"No. He's heading back to Surrey, via a refuelling stop at a lorry depot in Cumbria. The topography here's too exposed to risk staying put. Whatever happens here, we'll be going home by other means." He raised his hand and forefinger upwards. "Radio silence for now."

As they silently continued onwards, Sign setting a fierce pace, Lebrun couldn't help but feel that she was as far removed as possible from the urban environment of her regular police work. Even in the rural surroundings of Munich, it was nothing like this. She felt that the island was untamed, cold, dark, wet, beautiful, and disconcerting. It wasn't, she decided, a place for humans to live. And yet, Sign seemed completely unfazed by his surroundings. He was at home here as he was in his tactician's armchair. And my goodness, he was fit. She was anything but a layabout and had stamina to rival the best of them in her police division. But right now she had to resist the temptation to break into a jog to keep up with him. And she was breathing fast; he wasn't. Maybe his height gave him an advantage – longer strides, less effort. Perhaps that was it. No, it wasn't, she reluctantly told herself.

He stopped, crouched down, and used his outstretched flat hand to point. Ahead of them was Baltzar's cottage. No lights were on inside. But, its structure and exposed surroundings were partially illuminated by the death throes of the sun and its reflection on the intermittently visible moon. She crouched next to him.

He whispered in her ear, "We wait fifteen minutes. Watch. Then move in."

Hare had moved fast since receiving the earlier call from Faraday. He'd requisitioned a National Police Air Service H145 helicopter to Glasgow and a Police Scotland Airbus T3 chopper to get him to Mallaig. The western Highlands port was as far as he dared go using the goodwill of the Scottish police chief constable. He thought Hare had been bounced with an urgent meeting with an extremely valuable PIRA source. He had no idea that the English chief superintendent was off duty, hunting a venerable British diplomat, and was going onwards to see what might be amiss on the island of Muck.

Hare met Faraday and Duggan at the quayside. Duggan had got here seventy minutes ago, but Faraday had only been thirty minutes behind him. The *MV Lochnevis* ferry to Muck had never been an option for them, given it only sailed once per day and in the morning. That didn't matter. GCHQ had secret onshore and offshore instillations in Scotland. Some of them were typically accessed by boats that looked like trawlers. Thanks to Faraday, one such boat was waiting for them in the harbour.

Duggan was pacing on the harbour wall, away from the others.

Hare asked Faraday, "How is he?"

Faraday shrugged. "Since I got here it's felt like I've been in the company of a father who's been told to wait outside the hospital room containing his daughter, surgeons, nurses, and a plethora of life-support equipment. Not good." He checked his watch. "Let's get on board. The vessel's fast and should make the crossing in about seventy minutes. Then, we've got a walk. Close to an hour by my calculations, which should be fun given we're all dressed for a civilised gentlemen's winter stroll in Green Park. Did you bring a gun?"

The cop nodded.

"I didn't dare ask him, but I bet Hamish has got one as well." He tried to smile. "Or an axe." He called out, "Let's go."

Duggan joined them, his face red. They clambered on-board the adjacent trawler. Five minutes later they were heading out to sea.

Sign tapped twice on Lebrun's arm, pointed at the cottage, and moved forward, keeping low, his handgun out. The German cop followed him, her powerful pistol held in both hands, eyes flicking left and right. Sign was silent. All she could hear was the sound of sea water running over shingle. The air smelled of peat and the North Atlantic Ocean.

The former MI6 officer reached the only entrance to the property. He moved to one side of the front door, and squatted; Lebrun went to the other side. Slowly, he placed one hand on the handle, turned it, and pushed. The door opened a few inches. He was still, listening. From his pocket, he withdrew a tiny torch and turned it on. He stood and used a foot to push the door fully open. His gun held in front of his chest, he entered the cottage. Lebrun was behind him.

Were it not for the torchlight, everything inside would have been black. The entrance area led into the kitchen. No one was in here. Sign moved right and into the bedroom. Baltzar's bedroom. It was unoccupied, though it was obvious the bed had been recently used. Lebrun turned and took point. She moved back into the kitchen, Sign behind her, and into the lounge.

That's where they saw the horror.

The torch picking up glimpses of the image.

And my God, what an image.

But, they had to move on, check the second bedroom and the exterior of the rest of the house. They did so and returned to the lounge.

Sign said, "Turning light on. Brace yourself." He switched on the room light.

They said nothing for a period of time that might have been seconds or could have been minutes.

All of the furniture in the room had been moved to the walls. In the centre of the space was Kazia Baltzar. She was fully erect but leaning forwards, her broken and battered arms dangling downwards, her legs locked straight and standing on carpet that was covered with her blood. Her hair was cut shorter; face bloody, indented, and almost unrecognisable; trousers transformed into shorts; rest of her legs and feet bare and severely damaged; and the only other visible garment on her was a white T-shirt that was crimson on the front and sliced open at the back. Protruding out of her back were two seven feet lengths of her intestines, the ends of which were tied at head-height to the handles of a wall-mounted cabinet. Her intestines, travelling mid-air across half of the room, were holding her weight.

Finally, Lebrun muttered, "Damn!"

Sign put away his gun and torch, and walked up to Baltzar. "Damnation is an apt word. But, the killer hasn't condemned Miss Baltzar to eternal punishment in hell. He's condemned the person who lays eyes on his work."

Lebrun was still holding her gun in the ready position. She didn't know why. "Are you sure it's Baltzar?"

Sign looked at Kazia's eyes. Such a striking Roma, he thought. The killer didn't hurt her eyes. Didn't want to. Leaving them untouched was essential to the image. "It's Baltzar." With his back fully to Lebrun, he said, "Karin – I mean you no disrespect when I ask the following: are you able to remain in this room without enduring undue distress? Or would you prefer to get some air? I will fully understand if you would prefer to step outside. You've got me this far, and for that I'm very grateful."

She forced her gun-arm down. Sign had got them here. She'd tagged along. He knew that. He knew that she knew that. "I'm fine."

"Then you'll be robust enough to withstand my forthcoming exacting terminology and actions." He placed his face close to the body, examining it head to toe, and lifted her shirt. "Her breasts have been cut off. They'll have been tossed away somewhere outside. They have no place here. But nor do they have any relevance to the killer as mementos." He touched her lower garment. "The killer used strong scissors, most likely meat shears, to cut the trousers around her upper thighs and make them look like shorts. The rest of the trousers and anything else the killer didn't need will be with the breasts. A pile of rubbish." He pulled forward the waist of her trousers and knickers. "Her pubic hair has been shaved off." He released the waistband and ran his bare hands over her body. "Her legs, torso, arms, neck, and head have been repeatedly hit with a heavy object, probably a big hammer. As a result, there are broken bones. The damage I can detect is as follows. Left leg – fibula clean break in two places; femur and tibia in one place. Right leg – fibula broken halfway along; patella is partially dislodged." He put his hands down the side of her shorts. "Hip bones are more difficult to assess in this crude way, but I can feel a ragged piece of wing sticking out of her skin on the left side." While smoothing his hand around her torso, underneath her shirt, he said, "The spine seems intact but I can't be sure. Four ribs on the left side are broken in at least seven places; no superficial indication that any ribs are broken on the right." He removed his hands. "In the left arm, the humerus is broken; so too the ulna and the radius. In the right, only the humerus is broken. In the left wrist, I suspect there's damage to the carpal bones, and three fingers are snapped. On the right hand and wrist, there's no obvious damage save she's received a big impact on her palm." He looked up. "In her neck, three, possibly four, cervical vertebrae are broken. And in the head – well, aside from the obvious disfigurement to her nose, it's hard to tell. But, there's no doubt she's received massive damage to the cranial and facial bones." He took two steps back while continuing to look at her. "The intestines are the longer small intestines. The killer used a very sharp knife to access them, from her back. It would have taken time and careful mastery of a blade. Inside, the intestines remain attached to her. He pulled out all the rest to use as ropes and tied the ends to the wall. They are an intrinsic part of the show. So too is the higher level of bone damage on her left side." Keeping them close to each other, he swept both of his arms through air, from right to left, as if he was striking a baseball. "The killer wanted to make it look like she received a massive impact on her left side, fell to her right, and received damage on her right side from the fall. In reality, he laid her on the floor and repeatedly hammered her in the places where he wanted to inflict evocative damage. After that, he got her upright and created what we now see." He looked at Lebrun, and said with measured anger in his tone, "When I have my gun trained on The Thief, I won't hesitate. I will not be looking at me." He breathed out slowly, went back to Baltzar, and put his face close to hers. Quietly, and in Romani, he said to her, "Sunt un prieten. O să-i găsesc. El va muri. Vei fi liber."

I am a friend. I will find him. He will die. You will be free.
She asked, "Estimated time of death?"
"Between seven eighteen AM and one sixteen PM today."
"That's specific! Ah – Parry's last check in and a minute before Lucas called you to say that Parry had gone quiet."
He walked to Lebrun and stood by her side, while looking at Baltzar. "What do you see?"
She thought of Alex Wick in the Hotel Opéra. "Prokofiev in a test tube."
Sign nodded. "Wick was made to look like a foetus that had been subject to a backstreet abortion. The purpose of the imagery was precise – make Wick look like an innocent child who can be murdered in a place that feels safe. The Thief was telling the rest of The Library that their children cannot be protected by them. So, what do we have here?"
Lebrun momentarily closed her eyes. "Another child. Made to look like a child. Older than Wick was made to look. Probably a toddler."
"Correct. The intestines are representative of controlled freedom. The runners are let loose, but not too far. They are given rules as to what they can and can't do. And they are secretly protected. They have, their parents believe, some liberty and absolute safety. Kazia Baltzar is put on extendable toddler reins. All is going well. But, the reins don't protect her when her parent briefly looks away, she steps onto the road, and a heavy goods vehicle smashes her tiny body."

"A tiny kid wiped out by a truck." Lebrun couldn't help but think of her own young children. She didn't want to. Now was not the time. But, the thought wouldn't go away. She had to do something. "We should properly search the place. Maybe she left something, identifying The Thief."

"She didn't have time. She was caught unawares and the assault was swift and brutal. Every second we stay here increases risk. The Thief wants The Library to see this. It was never for our eyes. He'll have used Baltzar's phone to message Duggan. With the MI5 man hooked, The Library will be on its way here. That's all that matters to us – knowing they're on their way."

"The phone?"

"In the sea or buried in bits." He walked up to the mantelpiece, and looked at the letter he'd spotted earlier. It didn't look like a man's writing. Almost certainly it was written by Baltzar. And the name above the address belonged to Duggan's ex-wife. It was a personal matter. Sign knew Duggan was separated from his wife and had not been the one to petition for divorce. The letter smacked of an attempt to get them back together. Due to its prominent location, The Thief would have noticed the letter. It wasn't part of his plan, but it was a bonus. So, he left it in situ. The letter would deepen Duggan's sorrow and resolve. And yet Sign also had to leave it unopened. One of The Library members coming here could be The Thief. Nothing could be touched, let alone removed, for fear of telling The Thief that someone else came here after the murder. He spun around. "We must go."

"Shouldn't we hide and watch the cottage from distance? Wait for them to arrive and see what happens?"

"Their arrival won't help us identify The Thief. Everything that's happening is designed by him. I know what will occur when they see this room. The innocent members of The Library will want to tear Raine apart. There's nothing to be gained by us watching that reaction."

"Parry?"

"Dead. His body will be somewhere on the island. But, it will be hard to find. It won't help us to look for him." He swept a hand through air. "We were never here. The Library will see this place as we saw it when we walked in. We leave now." He turned off the light.

They left, Sign leading the way. They walked fast across countryside, in a different direction from the way they'd come and keeping the coast close by. After forty minutes, they entered a cove. Sign made a call. When it was finished he said to Lebrun, "Our taxi's going to be here in twenty minutes. It's been waiting a mile out since we've been here."

It was nearer to fifteen minutes when they saw a motorized rubber dinghy driving fast to shore, the only source of light being a headlight on its bow. The driver pulled up the propeller as it hurtled into shallow water and then beached. Sign waded into the sea, grabbed the rope that was flung to him so that he could hold the vessel, and ushered Lebrun on board. When she was sitting down in the boat, he waded further out to waist height, pulling the dinghy around with him. He got into the craft and gave the thumbs up to the driver, an agent of his who he'd called before taking off in Surrey. The driver put the propeller back in the water, got the engine started, and gunned the boat out to sea. In deep water, they'd board a fishing vessel and head back to Mallaig. From there they'd get the next available train to take them back to London.

Hare, Duggan, and Faraday disembarked from the covert GCHQ ship in Port Mòr. A few house lights were the only signs that people might be awake in the settlement, but no one was to be seen. They walked out of Mòr and along the mile and a half long road that linked Muck's east and west coasts. It was night, but the earlier inclement weather had abated and stars and a slice of the moon could be seen between patches of cloud. There was no need for torches, even though there were no road lamps along the route. The men were in dark overcoats and suits, brogues, and carried rolled-up umbrellas. Depending on the perspective of an observer, if they'd been seen they'd have looked odd or frightening. Duggan was using his phone to guide them to *Suðreyjar Cottage*. Given they all spoke fluent Norwegian, The Library men knew that '*suðreyjar*' meant 'southern isles' in the Norse language. But they couldn't understand the connection to the Scottish island. Duggan had Googled it and advised the others that it dated back to the ninth century, when Muck and the other nearby islands belonged to the king of Norway. Faraday had lamely quipped that bloody Norway seemed to feature a lot in their lives right now. Duggan hadn't laughed. He had other things on his mind.

As they drew close to Gallanach Lodge hotel, Faraday pointed his umbrella to the left, signalling they needed to head in that direction and get off the road. Hare and Duggan followed him, their expensive shoes partially sinking in the heath that was still sodden from the earlier rain. They didn't care about that, or the fact that the wind-chill had taken the temperature to way below zero. All that mattered was getting to the house and finding out why Baltzar had sent her text message.

After five minutes of walking along the coast they spotted a house. Faraday looked at the others and shook his head, meaning it wasn't *Suðreyjar Cottage*. Hare pointed at his chest and the property. He wanted to check it out. He withdrew his handgun and walked to the place where The Thief had put two bullets into Parry's head. One minute later he returned, ran his hand back and forth over his throat. There was nothing to see in the cottage. He nodded in the direction Faraday was taking them. They continued. It took them twenty minutes to reach a point where they could easily observe the place where Baltzar had been holed up for two days.

Hare was still holding his gun as he said quietly, "Suggest I do the door; Hamish – you cover the back; Gordon – you stay here and give us visual and comms if anyone does a runner."

"No time for any of your police cordon nonsense." Duggan strode forward, his gun in his hand.

Hare and Faraday had no other choice than to follow him as he purposefully strode towards the cottage front door.

The MI5 officer made no attempt at stealth as he opened the door and entered. He turned on the kitchen light, looked around, and entered the first bedroom.

Hare and Faraday broke left, entering the lounge and turning on the light.

Duggan walked out of the bedroom and back into the kitchen.

Faraday intercepted him, his eyes wide. He placed his hands on Duggan's shoulders and implored, "Hamish – do not go in there. Don't!"

Duggan shrugged the smaller man off and walked into the lounge.

He froze.

Hare was looking at Baltzar, shaking his head. "I'm so very sorry, Hamish," was all he could say.

"No! No! No!" Duggan ran to his runner, hugged her, wept, and said, "What has he done? What has he done to you, my pickle?"

Faraday stood next to Hare, but said nothing. Neither man could think of anything to say. All they could do was watch Duggan's anguish.

Duggan stepped back, staggered, wiped his forearm against his eyes, and leant against the mantelpiece. He saw the letter, grabbed it, tore it open, and read. He stuffed the letter into his coat, and walked back and forth, beside himself, not knowing what to do, randomly pointing his gun at nothing, veins on his face and neck protruding. More tears ran down his face; his skin was flushed; eyes squinting; mouth open.

Hare went up to him. "We need to deal with this."

With one hand, Duggan grabbed him under the jaw, lifted him, and slammed him against the wall. "Deal with this?!" He put the muzzle of his pistol against the cop's throat. "Don't you worry, *PC Plod*. I'll be dealing with this." He released Hare.

The detective's jaw ached from Duggan's iron grip, but he didn't mind. He'd anticipated the MI5 officer would turn on him when he made the approach. He let it happen. "Hamish – I don't want to give you the *time-to-grieve-is-later* speech. Why don't you wait outside? Gordon and I will do what's necessary."

Duggan looked at the floor, his expression thunderous. "What's. Fucking. Necessary." He looked up. "I'll do to Raine what he did to my Kazia. And I'll keep him alive for as long as possible. Snap every bone in his body. Make him jelly. I'll leave his head until last."

"And we won't try to stop you," said Hare soothingly. "Meanwhile, let Gordon and I sort this out."

Duggan had contempt on his face as he looked at Faraday. "You expect help from *Numbers Man* over there? You'd better explain to him what to do, because I doubt he has any idea what he's looking at."

Faraday ignored the jibe. GCHQ officers were used to being labelled as a bunch of socially-inept computer nerds by the likes of MI5. It came with the territory. He was the opposite of inept and probably knew more about the nuances of human existence than anyone in MI5. And he'd seen dead bodies before. "We have to clean the place up. And like it or not, we must consider what to do with Kazia's body. We can't take her with us. She'll need to be laid to rest on the island. I can help Rex. I know what I'm looking at. And I know what needs to be done. I won't let you down, Hamish."

The last comment softened Duggan's demeanour. "Yeah. Well…" He looked at Baltzar. "But, you're wrong about what to do. She can't stay here. She's a free spirit. A wanderer. Muck's no place for her. Too lonely. Not enough…" his bottom lip trembled. "Not enough… *action* going on. She loved… loves… places. You know? Things to see and do. Ah, jeez. How do I get you off of here, my sweet girl?" He shook his head. "Think, think, think."

Hare's voice remained calm as he said, "We have to bury her here."

Duggan looked venomous again. "Don't bullshit me, Hare! Hadn't noticed you and Gordon turning up here with your buckets and spades. You've no intention of *burying* her. You'll drop her in some bog and hope the water deals with her. Or, you'll do worse. But you won't because whatever you try to do to her I'll do the same to you both. And I will, cos I don't bullshit." He rubbed his face and tried to get his brain working. "Your lot can't help, for obvious reasons. Bunch of fuckwits, in any case. And my lot have to be kept in the dark."

Faraday said, "Britain is MI5's patch. Surely you must have resources that could help you transport Kazia to a resting place of your choosing?"

Duggan huffed, his anger still evident. "Try working a patch that at best wants to kill you and at worst wants to post a video of you on the Net, on your knees and with a blunt penknife held against your throat. What do you want me to do? Ring up the Irish paramilitaries or jihadists and pull some favours?"

Faraday sighed. "I get it." He was thinking fast. "She's a wanderer. Would you consider burying her at sea?"

"What? Take her down to the beach and chuck her in? And watch her wash back onto land?"

"No. Deep sea?"

"Your trawler thingy that brought us here?"

"Yes. We'd have to smuggle her on board. Look, I know it's not ideal but, out of sight of the crew, you could lay her to rest overboard as we sail between Muck and Mallaig. Or not. It's just a thought." He looked at Hare, wondering how Duggan was going to react.

The MI5 operative walked to the wall, untied Baltzar's intestines, gripped them tight while taking Baltzar's weight, and commanded, "Mr. Hare. We're going to lower her to the floor."

Hare held her body as Duggan walked forward while holding the makeshift reins.

The MI5 man breathed in deeply several times, crouched, and pushed her intestines back into her body. He walked quickly into the kitchen, opened and closed drawers, and re-entered the lounge while holding a roll of gaffer tape. He wrapped tape several times around her torso, lifted her, cradled her in both arms, and said to Faraday, "Footloose and fancy-free is my Kazia. The sea will do her the world of good. Now, if you don't mind gentlemen. She and I are going to sit by the beach and have a giggle about some of our silly times. We'll leave you to clean up. You'll know where to find us when you're done. Just follow the laughter."

He walked out of the cottage.

It took Faraday and Hare over an hour to clean. Thankfully, the carpet had coarse fibres and the blood hadn't permeated. After moving the furniture back to where they thought it might belong, Faraday said, "Raine must have followed her here on the day she posted her MAYFLY report."

"Or, he got hired help to do that for him."

"Either, or." Many thoughts were racing through the GCHQ officer's mind. "In our third full Library meeting, Hamish said that it was easy to identify the names of our runners, but to do so would require a bit of snooping. He said that officers carrying suspicions about a *Snooping Tom* might go to Peter. And Raine replied that he'd set in place a mechanism whereby official or casual enquiries about the identities of the MAYFLY authors must come to his attention."

Hare shook his head in disbelief. "That put our minds at rest. If only we'd known that Raine was the *Snooping Tom*. Bastard took the job on to catch himself. And in doing so, keep us in the dark because we thought he was carrying the load and working with us. We didn't need to get involved. Meanwhile, he covers his tracks leading up here. He doesn't know we're on to him. As far as he's concerned, we're going to think someone else snooped, didn't get caught by Raine, and came up here to torture Duggan's runner to get the name of her MAYFLY source."

"And here we are." Faraday looked at the window. He couldn't see them, but somewhere nearby were Duggan and Baltzar. "I don't know if he'll ever get over this."

"Don't think about that right now. We'll gift him time to grieve and think about his future. Meanwhile our priority is to kill Raine, make his body vanish, and ensure the matter's closed and no one ever knows what we did. Agreed?"

"Oh yes. Most certainly, agreed."

"Good. Grab the tape. I'll find some blankets. We'll need to wrap the body before we leave."

They found Duggan, sitting on a cliff top, rocking while holding Baltzar and quietly singing her Finnish mother's favourite folk song, *Tuoll' on mun kultani*, a minor key love song about a man's yearning for his beloved.

They told him it was time to go.

They put Baltzar in her makeshift shroud and went back down the road, towards Port Mòr.

Duggan was carrying Kazia while walking in the centre of the road.

Faraday and Hare maintained a respectful two paces behind him.

They didn't speak.

But Duggan continued singing, his note-perfect voice carrying across the windless and maudlin landscape.

CHAPTER 20

Today was the sixth day of the one-week MAYFLY window of opportunity to catch The Thief. After that, providing The Thief was still at large, Raine would lobby the British prime minister to shut down CHALICE. Raine would probably get his way. But in the interim, The Library didn't want to tell the authorities what they believed they knew about Raine. They wanted to neutralise The Thief; not see the august Peter Raine cross-examined in a court of law.

Sign and Lebrun arrived back in London's Euston train station at eight AM. Neither of them had managed to sleep on the journey. They were jaded and raw. He suggested they have a coffee at the Westminster flat before he headed home to West Square.

In the flat, he took his drink onto the balcony overlooking the Thames. It was now nearly nine AM and the river was mostly devoid of activity. The sun had only just commenced rising, creating a thirty minute moment where – in Sign's view – London looked uncharacteristically benign.

Lebrun stood next to him and followed his gaze, her breath steaming in the icy air as she said, "There'll be a lot of secrets in the water."

"Many of them unconscionable. The river's name is derived from the Brittonic Celtic word *Tamesas*, meaning dark or darkness."

She looked at him. "You're tired."

"We both are."

"What would you like me to do today?"

"Keep Peter alive and capture The Thief."

She smiled. "I'll try my best."

"Exceed that aspiration." He turned and leaned against the balcony, the river to his back. "The British police and security services are of no use to me. Via you, the German police are a different matter. With your police hat on, tap your colleagues in Germany to request from our Met police a list of all credit and debit card payments for rail and air fares, during the last two days, to Scotland from London, Birmingham, Manchester, Leeds, Reading, Gatwick, Liverpool, Bristol, Cambridge, Sheffield, York, Southampton, Newcastle, and Cheltenham. I'll write those place names down for you. Say you're looking for a terrorist linked to a German plot, or similar excuse. Tell them it's urgent."

She raised her eyebrows. "You want the German police to do a British police job, because you can't work with the Brits? Cheeky. It's doable, but there's going to be a huge amount of data."

He sipped his coffee. "The Met will send your Kriminalfachdezernate, or whoever, an electronic file. Your people will send you the file. You're looking for the surnames Sassoon, Faraday, Duggan, or Hare. Even if there are tens of thousands of results, a word search will complete the job in the time it takes you to make a cup of tea. If you get a hit, there's a good chance we won't be able to pin down exact time and day of travel. As you know, electronic payments aren't always processed at the immediate time of card use. Still, I'm interested to see what might come out of the search."

"It's possible there will be zero hits."

"More likely, *probable*. It's a longshot. I'm looking for a forgivable mistake."

"Forgivable?"

"The Thief thinks he's playing The Library. In that context, he doesn't need to worry about the Scotland trip. On the contrary, it doesn't serve his purpose to do so. But, he doesn't know he's playing me. As a result, he has a blind spot." He rubbed his face. "You're right. I'm tired. I need to tell Knutsen and Raine about Baltzar and what it means for us." He thought about the six hundred mile distance between southern England and Muck. "And I need to re-fuel. After you've submitted your request to Germany, get some sleep. Let's reconvene when you've heard from Germany."

Five minutes later, he left and walked the one and a half mile route across the river and into Southwark and its West Square. He called Lucas and told him that Parry was missing and almost certainly dead. He gave him a cryptic account of what he'd seen the day before, without using names, given he was on an open line. Lucas hadn't given much away on the call, though said he'd alert Noah and Aadesh and tell them to maintain the highest levels of vigilance. After the call ended, Sign entered the flat, walked down the hallway, and stopped when he took one step into the lounge and felt the end of a gun barrel touch his temple. He smiled. "Stand down, Mr. Knutsen. 'Tis I."

Knutsen was flush against the wall, to the right of the entrance, fully upright, legs apart, gun-arm outstretched. He lowered his weapon and stepped away from the wall. "You were lucky. Last night I had a load of pots and pans stacked against the inside of the door. I put them away this morning, because I thought you might be back anytime soon. But there was a slim chance I might have deliberately forgotten, just so I could stun-grenade you when you walked in."

"That's a pity. A flash-bang might have been just the ticket to blow away the cobwebs." Sign took off his coat and hung it on the stand. "Where's Peter?"

"Shower."

"You haven't slept, I presume."

"Nah."

"Then we are both dead men walking, so to speak."

"Not as dead as Peter."

"True." Sign walked into the kitchen. "Coffee, coffee, coffee!" He made drinks, put them next to the fireplace, and sat in his armchair.

Knutsen picked up his mug and sat facing him. "All quiet here. Scotland?"

"A land of diabolical deeds."

"Ah."

"Kazia Baltzar's dead. I'll wait until Peter surfaces before I give you details." He sipped his drink. "It's a rum affair, my friend."

At eleven AM, Sassoon sat on a low wall, under an archway on London's South Bank. Despite being Sunday, he was in a bespoke suit and royal navy overcoat, highly-polished black shoes, white shirt, burgundy silk tie in a Windsor knot, and had his legs crossed and hands clasped. There was a watchful stillness about him. The attire was his nod to the formality of the occasion and the fact that Hare, Duggan, and Faraday were about to meet him in the same business clothes they'd been in yesterday. They were coming here immediately upon their return to London.

He was one hundred yards away from the Royal Festival Hall, and could have met the other members of The Library there, within its celebration of all matters art. But, he preferred to be here, with the street-legal graffiti on the walls, skateboarders pulling daring feats on the broad walkway in front of him, incongruous presence of the houses of parliament on the other side of the river, and the noise of grime music blaring out of the skaters' sound system. He'd chosen the spot because he'd mischievously decided that not everything needed to be formal. He believed there was always room for rebellious contrarianism.

He probably looked like a refined antique to the young bucks who were hurling themselves through air and thwacking back onto their boards in time to the beats of the music. But maybe a savvy photographer would have seen that there was an interesting image to be had by capturing him, the surrounding drab walls that had been splashed with colourful designs and messages, and the vibrant energy of the bouncing and flying youngsters. Perhaps it would have made a cool shot. Sassoon didn't know. He doubted he was ever cool; only different.

"What the hell are we doing here?" Hare sat next to the MI6 officer. "And where've you been?"

Sassoon wondered why Hare sometimes pretended he was from the rank and file when the reality was he was officer-class and nothing like a policeman. "To your first question: my desire for an agreeable dichotomy. We're looking at the same sundial, from a different angle. The joys of coexistence abound. And to your second question: I was working, safe in the knowledge that any new developments would be processed by you and our friends."

"Do neither again. You've heard what's happened?"

"Of course."

"Hamish is on the rampage."

"He will be."

Hare saw Faraday and Duggan approaching on foot. Quickly, he said to Sassoon, "Go easy on Hamish. Don't do your *Doctor Hannibal Lecter* thing."

Faraday and Duggan said nothing as they reached the low wall and perched next to Hare and Sassoon. None of The Library looked at each other; they just sat in a row, all in their finery, staring at the skaters, embankment, Thames, and epicentre of power.

Duggan said with sarcasm, "Nice of you to join us, Edward."

Sassoon made a tiny dismissive gesture with the back of his hand. "It was remiss of me to be off-air for a few hours. I had an intractable issue with one of my…"

"I don't care what you damn-well had. You should have been with us."

"Yes, yes," countered Sassoon with a deliberate tone of irritability. "I resolved the intractable and am here now, to sort out the mess that arose during my absence."

"Mess?!" Duggan stood.

Faraday grabbed his thick wrist. Though the GCHQ officer was only half the width of Duggan, the endurance athlete's grip was as unforgiving as the noose of a self-tightening snare. "Don't rise to it, Hamish." He pulled him back down and looked at Sassoon. "Choose your words less carefully."

The MI6 officer liked Faraday's chide and nodded appreciably.

Hare asked, "Why did Raine do this? He knows MAYFLY is bullshit."

Sassoon watched a black cormorant fly low along the river surface, looking for prey in the water. "Raine is acting like a non-Raine Thief and deliberately falling for the MAYFLY trap. He's doing what we originally hoped The Thief would do. But, we thought the runners were untouchable. The non-Raine Thief would have needed to torture Baltzar to get the name of her source. And when she told him it was all a pack of lies, he killed her in a way that sent a message to whoever was trying to trap him. That message was 'back off'. Just like Wick. But that was just window-dressing. Raine's real objective was to nullify our second tactic and continue to see what, if anything, we'll do next. He's also watching out for the Norwegian angle. Like the non-Raine Thief, he'll now put CHALICE theft on temporary hold. He'll come to our meetings until we just give up. Then he'll continue to work."

"In a new form of CHALICE. One that he'll set up and be privy to. And one that the likes of us can't access." Duggan leaned forward, put his elbows on his thighs, and cupped one hand around his fist. "But we know The Thief is Raine and he doesn't know we know that. We've got him."

Faraday said, "Maybe he'll go after the other runners."

"He might not know where they are." Sassoon wondered whether grief or fury were the stronger emotion in Duggan. "In any case, he has no need to go after the others. He's made his point with Baltzar."

"Her name's Kazia." Duggan could see parliament and the Met's Scotland Yard, but MI5's Thames House was just out of sight. Regardless, he looked in that direction. As a skater momentarily blocked his vision, he remembered Kazia approaching him on Millennium Bridge and joking about new meeting old, a reference to London's architecture but also to her and him. He wondered how different life would have been had he pursued a promising career in law after university graduation, rather than heading south. He supposed he'd traded the option of repeated punch-ups in the courtroom bear-pit for an insidious existence within the poisonous vipers' nest. He looked at the others. "Edward's right. Raine's not going to go after the other runners. He's made his point. My Kazia had to take the fall so the rest could live."

This time, Faraday touched his arm gently. "It wasn't her fall to take. It should never have come to this. I agree with you, though. And Edward. He's got no reason to hurt Bancroft, Prasad, and Crease."

Hare looked at Sassoon. "I don't see why we shouldn't tell the runners to come home. Their job's over."

Sassoon nodded and glanced at Faraday and Duggan.

Faraday also nodded and looked at Duggan.

The MI5 officer sighed. "Aye. Bring the whipper-snappers home. Tell them to keep their mouths shut. None of this happened." He stood, and this time Faraday let him. "We play dumb and wait for Raine to get back from wherever he's gallivanting." Addressing Faraday, he asked, "Is it worth you checking to see if Raine left any trace as to how he got to Muck? No point, I guess. He'll have paid cash, or used non-public transport, or another name."

The GCHQ officer's tone was firm but tactful when he replied, "We know he was there. We saw what he'd done. That's all we need to know. But, I'll do some digging if it helps you understand what's happened. I can't spend too much time on it, though."

Duggan nodded, and said quietly, "Thanks. I understand." His voice strengthened when he said, "I doesn't matter where he is right now. When he wants to meet us, we meet him. And I deal with him."

Between ten and thirty minutes later, Prasad, Bancroft, and Crease received calls from their handlers. They were told to pack their bags and leave their locations, without telling anyone. They were to return home today.

Half a mile north from The Royal Festival Hall, The Thief walked fast along central London's Northumberland Avenue, passing One Whitehall Place – once home to The National Liberal Club and luminaries such as Gladstone, Lloyd-George, Churchill, and the first chief of the Secret Intelligence Service. The route was quiet, save outside *The Sherlock Holmes* pub where people were gathering for lunchtime service. The Thief assumed that the hostelry's punters were drawn to the deerstalker-and-Calabash-pipe type of memorabilia contained in the place, unaware that the memorabilia was not derived from Conan Doyle but rather his excellent illustrator Sidney Paget and less-respectful Hollywood adaptations of the stories. Certainly, he doubted many who were about to sit down to a Sunday roast knew that the building they were in was once the Northumberland Hotel, as featured in Doyle's *The Hound of the Baskervilles* and *The Adventure of the Noble Bachelor*. Their ignorance is their bliss, he thought. For him, ignorance was anything but bliss. He needed to know where Raine was. It was a spanner in his works to learn on Friday that Raine's phone was no longer operable and couldn't be used to trace the diplomat. Later that day, Faraday had also listened to an earlier recording of Raine calling his wife from a payphone and telling her to take their kids and go into hiding. As of Friday, all of Faraday's phone and other communications' intercepts had become useless. During the subsequent fifty hours, The Thief had been busy with Norway and Muck and meanwhile none of The Library had heard from Raine. The Thief needed his Library associates to be in the same room as the man he'd framed. If he or his colleagues didn't kill Raine within eight days, he'd still be a free man. But he wouldn't be able to continue his thefts and finish his project. As a result, he was now anxious and had to be proactive.

He reached the southern part of Trafalgar Square, turned left, and stopped outside Canada House, the offices of the High Commission of Canada in the United Kingdom and formerly the base of the Royal College of Physicians. He had no interest in the near-two centuries' old Grade II listed building's current occupants, although had a passing interest in its Greek Revival architecture. But he was interested in the single fully-functioning old red telephone booth that was on the pavement outside. He entered, used a debit card that wasn't in his name, and called the Hotel Opéra.

When the hotel reception answered, he said in English and with a well-spoken accent, "Hello. Please would you connect me to Mr. Peter Raine."

The German receptionist asked who was calling.

He looked at Nelson's Column. "Horatio Woolward. I'm calling from London."

The receptionist told him that she was sorry but hotel policy forbade her from disclosing details about its guests, and that included connecting unscheduled calls.

"I understand. But this is an emergency. I'm a doctor."

The receptionist asked him to hold while she transferred him to the concierge.

When he answered, The Thief repeated his name and added, "I'm a physician at The Harley Street General Practice. I'm Mr. Raine's doctor. I understand that he might be staying at your hotel while on business. He warned me that his mobile phone would be off for periods of time. I need to speak to him."

The concierge repeated the hotel's stance on enquiries about guests.

The Thief feigned exasperation when he said, "It's a genuine emergency. In strictest confidence, Mr. Raine requires daily doses of aldosterone inhibiters and angiotensin receptor blockers. I've prescribed a new batch of ARBs, Eplerenone, and Spironolactone. He was supposed to pick them up before he travelled but hasn't done so. Either he's forgotten or had to fly earlier than planned. He needs them. He's run out of his previous prescription."

The concierge was sympathetic, but said that he'd have to think of other ways of getting hold of him. Perhaps a work colleague? Family member? Or maybe wait until he picked up his voice messages?

"I don't know his colleagues or his family. Look, I don't even know for sure if he's staying at your hotel. The reason I called is that he mentioned he'd stayed at your hotel before. He loves the Opéra's art works."

The concierge repeated his apologies and suggested that he call the German police or British consulate in Munich.

The Thief sighed. "That would involve too much time and bureaucracy. Mr. Raine needs to take his next medication by eleven PM this evening your time. If he doesn't, there is a strong possibility that he will become very ill. *Critically* ill. The pills are of a new design that I've handpicked for him. They're not available in Germany. But, via a courier and with full customs and medical authorisations, I can get them to your hotel before midnight. I'd need to pull out all the stops to do that. My question to you is should I bother?"

The concierge was silent for a moment. Then he said, "No."

The Thief momentarily closed his eyes. "Thank you. Are you able to make some calls to other five star hotels in your vicinity to see if Mr. Raine is staying at one of them? He'll only be in a five star hotel."

The concierge said that unfortunately such a service wasn't even available to paying guests.

The Thief thanked him again, said that he'd liaise with the consulate, bade him a good day, and ended the call. He breathed deeply, looked around, and amused himself with the notion of smashing up the retro booth.

He walked down Parliament Street, past Horse Guards building where two cavalrymen from the Queen's Life Guard were on horseback, and entered Westminster tube station.

Sign had managed to get a couple of hours sleep, before showering and dressing in smart slacks and shirt. Now, he was in his armchair. Raine was in the kitchen, making cups of tea and lunch. Knutsen was in Hertford, checking Raine's house was secure after his wife and daughter had vacated two days ago and gone to a location that even Raine didn't know about. Sign was looking at the 'CHALICE' whiteboard. He updated the schematic notes.

Next to Raine's name he added 'Fake Thief'.

In the 'Dead' box, and alongside Lystad and Wick, he added the names Baltzar and Parry.

He created a new box, titled 'Tactics'. In there he put brief data.

Library Tactic 1 – Dry up Thief's revenue stream. Result: Thwarted by Thief.

Library Tactic 2 – Use false MAYFLY intel to force Thief to panic. Result: Thwarted by Thief.

Thief Tactic 1: Frame Raine as The Thief. Result: Achieved.

Thief Tactic 2: Kill Raine. Result: Ongoing.

Raine brought mugs of tea and a plate of sandwiches, sat in the empty chair, and looked at the computer. "*Ongoing*? I suppose it is." Frustrated, he asked, "I understand his tactic against me, but why is he doing all this? Why attack CHALICE? Could it just be money?"

Sign looked at him and said nothing for a moment. Quietly and with solemnity he said, "What a dreadful state of affairs it is to gain enlightenment from an abhorrent act." He breathed in deeply. "The murder of Kazia Baltzar has clarified my thinking. I believe I know what all of this is about. But, understanding what is motivating The Thief doesn't help me identify who he is. If my theory is correct," he touched the centre of the screen where The Library names were written, "any of these four could fit the bill." His phone rang. Lucas. He listened to the team leader and said, "Stay with them for their journeys. Providing nothing bad happens, you and your men will then meet me in the capital. Call me when you're ready to convene." He ended the call and said, "The runners have been instructed to come home. The Library has decided that you have no logical reason to go after them."

"Are they right?"

"Yes, providing you're not a rabid maniac. And I don't believe that to be the case." He wondered how long it would take Lebrun to hear any news about the flight and rail manifests. In these days of European inter-state collaboration to combat terrorism, covert *Big Brother* data collection was as swift and incisive as a Facebook algorithm. "Your cutthroats will be coming here once they've tucked the remaining runners safely into bed."

Raine laughed, but the sound was hollow. "My *cutthroats*. Between us, we do have some names for Lucas and his team - cutthroats, buccaneers, marauders, lynch mob."

Sign smiled. "And thanks to our WhatsApp codenames - Cyrano de Bergerac, Max von Sydow, Life Of Pi, and Nosferatu." His smile faded. "But Nosferatu's had a wooden stake put through his heart. Or similar." He shook his head. "I underestimated The Thief. No dodging a bullet here. Baltzar's death is on my conscience."

"It shouldn't be."

"You're wrong." He leaned forward, studying his notes. "There are two objectives that are irresistible to The Thief. First, kill you, now that you're framed as The Thief. Your death will end matters. Second, make one last big heist. From the outset, we knew from the Syrian defector that The Thief wanted to cash in his chips. But he can't make his heist at the moment because of the MAYFLY tactic to get all immediate action CHALICE intel taken off the database for fourteen days, leave only long-game intelligence on there, put fabulous but fake intel in the pot while knowing The Thief knows it's a bad ingredient, and ensure there are no source IDs meaning there are no sales to be had of accurate or embellished data."

"And he couldn't make his big heist before I came along because he wasn't ready." Raine also leaned towards the board. "No source ID is not his only problem, because it's probable The Thief lacks the foreign connections to sell his CHALICE reports. After all, why else would he need Lystad? Short of hawking his wares around the foreign embassies or agencies of Russia, Iran, China, Syria, et al, it's going to take him time to manufacture access to potential clients."

"Yes."

Raine looked up. "You're thinking."

"I have been for some time."

The diplomat judged that whatever was going on in Sign's head was at an embryonic stage. He decided not to probe. "If The Library manages to kill me before I shut down CHALICE, what happens next?"

Sign smiled because he remained impressed by his friend's stoic objectivity. "You don't seem to fear death."

Raine huffed. "Oh, I fear death alright. I *greatly* fear my death, so don't misunderstand me on that matter. I have vivid dreams when I sleep. They're unpleasant. But then I wake up."

Sign looked at him. "I understand." He breathed deeply. "Providing you're killed before your deadline, one or more of The Library will somehow – perhaps anonymously, or not but with one hell of a spin attached - alert the Joint Intelligence Committee about the findings they've got on you. And those findings are damning. The Library will withhold a lot of detail about how those findings were obtained, in particular the nature and methods and probably even the existence of The Library. You'll have vanished. There'll be no declaration that you were executed. You'll be a wanted man. The mainstream counter-intelligence army will be hunting you, but they'll be relaxed in the knowledge that they know who The Thief is. Their eye will be off the ball. You won't have had the shutdown-CHALICE conversation with the prime minister. CHALICE will remain intact. The Thief will make his final heist and somehow try to sell his wares. Then, like you, he vanishes."

It was early afternoon when Bancroft got off a train at Marylebone, took tubes across London, and exited at Kennington Station in South London. As instructed, he'd left Stratford Upon Avon without telling anyone, including his landlady Shirley. She'd be disappointed. Still, he'd left her a tip in the holiday let, plus a thank you note.

He walked the remaining distance to his flat. It felt unusual to be back in London, even though he'd only been away since Wednesday. Maybe it was because the last few days had felt dream-like and surreal. He'd have to get used to the feeling, he told himself. The itinerant and at times unfulfilled nature of being an MI6 officer meant carrying a semi-permanent sensation similar to jetlag and disorientation. And he'd only been to the Midlands. How would he feel if in due course he was spending months in inter-continental transit and holed up in dives where no one knew him and spoke no English and some people wanted him dead? Stratford had been easy. Sassoon's job for him had been a doddle. Therefore, he shouldn't feel weird. But he did because he suspected he'd done something without the backing of Her Majesty's Government. He'd broken the law, and it was the biggest law to break – tampering with national security. He stopped outside Kennington Police Station. In ten days he'd need to report here to answer his bail. For certain, he'd be let off with a caution or more likely a police declaration of No Further Action. Inadvertently getting involved in Tim's art theft scam seemed so silly now, compared to what he'd done for Sassoon. Perhaps, in some way his MI6 controller had given him backbone. If, at some point in the future, Tim came knocking on his door again and tried to charm him into getting involved in his latest escapade, Bancroft would now have the strength of conviction to look him in the eye and say, "Whatever you're planning, I have done considerably worse. Best you fuck off."

He carried on walking, in his suit and overcoat, rain now heavy, his shoulders hunched, hands thrust through the handles of clothes-laden carrier bags and into his pockets. For some reason, he couldn't stop silently reciting the sentence Sassoon had imparted to him in Greenwich Park.

I knew a simple soldier boy.

Since Faraday had called him at 1131hrs to say that he had to leave Darlington, it had taken Prasad exactly four hours and fifty minutes to get from the Mercure King's Hotel to his home in Courtenay Street, Cheltenham. He entered the terraced house-share, without noticing that he was being observed by a Swedish former special reconnaissance operative called Noah. Given it was a Sunday, four of Prasad's other GCHQ housemates were off work; two of them in the basement playing an Xbox game because they'd been rained-off from a game of football; the other two sitting at the kitchen table containing wires, tools, a bottle of aftershave, modelling clay, 9-volt batteries, dismantled alarm clock, bag of flour, and a toy Claymore mine.

Prasad said hello to the guys in the kitchen. They asked where he'd been and said they were hoping to make a controlled explosion in the hallway that would hopefully cover their shady landlord in flower when he next made one of his usual unannounced visits. Prasad smiled, nodded approvingly, and went to his room.

He placed his bag down, withdrew from a drawer his personal mobile phone, sat on the bed, and activated the device.

He called his sister. "Hey. How ya doin'?"

She was silent for a couple of seconds. "Why didn't you call?"

"Ah, I was away at this stupid conference. We weren't allowed to switch on electronic devices. You know how it is."

She did. She knew who her brother worked for. "Are you coming down anytime soon?"

"Next weekend, if that's alright. This week's tough because I'm back to…"

She started crying.

"Sis. I'm here now. I…"

"It's just so bad, Rishi. So bad. They keep watching me. Think I'm going to do something. Mum caught me yesterday, in the bathroom. I made her swear not to tell Dad. He'd go crazy, yeah? Maybe I'm crazy. Fucked up, bro. Whole thing is fucked up. I think, what's the point? You know? All that, then this? Prisoner in Mumbai. Prisoner here. Least it's only my fingers I put down my throat here."

"Sis!"

"Whatever. I don't care. Not anymore."

Prasad had never heard his sister speak like this before. "I'll throw a sickie. I'll be there tomorrow. In the morning. Okay?"

She was still sobbing. "Don't throw a sickie. Your boss…"

"Don't worry about him." Faraday wasn't his boss, but right now he might as well have been. He wouldn't object if he took a few days off. He had him over a barrel on that. "I'll be there. That's my side of the bargain. Yours is to not do anything mental before I get there. Agreed?"

Her crying eased. "Sure, bro. Yeah. Will be good to see you. Can you take me out? Walk? Coffee? Anything?"

"We'll do loads of things. I'll tell my boss that I'm out for the count for the rest of the week. Sound good?"

Her voice was shaky, but she laughed. "Fucking right."

Her told her he loved her, in a kind of no-choice-in-the-matter way. And he asked that if she killed herself before he got there, could he have her percentage of their parents' trust fund.

When the call ended, he thought for a moment, breathed out slowly, felt relieved, stood, walked down the hallway, and said as he entered the kitchen, "Try a mixture of flower, treacle, and chilli powder."

Crease and Aadesh exited the tube on Old Kent Road and walked along the route. It was a rainy and dark early evening in South London. Traffic was heavy on the long thoroughfare, cars and lorries moving slowly, their headlights and wipers on. In other parts of Britain, people would have avoided going out in the gloomy and cold atmosphere. But here, life went on. Like every other day of the week, the place was bustling with kebab shops, burger joints, cafes, and pizzerias, serving tea-time snacks to multicultural locals. Despite the rain, old-school boozers were spilling out die-hard smokers onto the pavements. Brightly illuminated taxi cab booking centres had swarthy men loitering in and outside, the ambience being one of *ducking-and-diving* goings-on. Kids of various adolescent ages were hanging about in small groups containing some who were sitting on static pushbikes and scooters and others who were fooling about. Everyone was talking, some shouting to be heard, and there was laughter. Stories were told; information exchanged; comments made; banter aplenty. Anyone could come here and be accepted, providing they didn't mind the possibility of being stabbed. No one batted an eyelid as the former Gurkha and undercover cop walked by, carrying bags, her arm linked with his.

They reached the block containing Crease's flat. It was nondescript, dowdy, functional, but clean. She said to Aadesh, "Thanks for walking me here. I'd invite you in for a coffee, but my place is a mess."

He pointed at the block. "I grew up on the banks of the heavily polluted Bagmati river, in a slum in Kathmandu. Me, my parents, and my sisters and brother lived in a shanty home. Soil floor; no loo, heating, or lights. Six people in a box. Is your place better?"

She looked at him, a trace of a smile on her face, her eyes glistening. "Yes."

"Come on then. I'll put the kettle on."

They went into her one-bedroom place. It wasn't a mess, though was indicative of a single occupant who wasn't expecting guests and didn't have obsessive compulsive disorder. He made coffee – black, because the milk was on the turn. He handed her a drink and sat on a cheap sofa, sinking more than he liked.

She looked at him. His short, solid frame was crushing the tiny furnishing. Like a bar of gold on wet mud, she thought. God knows why that image had entered her head. "A shanty town? That's not what I expected."

"You imagined that in Nepal we spend all day running up and down pure white mountains, breathing the free air, living the life? Much like the Swiss? But in Switzerland and Nepal, normal things happen like everywhere else. It's just we have mountains. How long have you lived here?"

"Since I joined the service. *Service*?" She smiled and huffed. To herself, she said, "Should have stuck to 'Force'. More accurate."

He sipped his coffee. "How are you feeling?"

She considered the question. "It's strange to be back. I was starting to like it at the Devon place."

"You'll go back there. But I meant, how are you feeling physically?"

"I know what you meant." She breathed in deeply. "You know how you feel when pain suddenly stops? Like that. Got a buzzy feeling. Energy."

"You're better."

"Well, I…"

"You're better." He kept his eyes on her. "Go back to the cottage in the summer. This time take a swimming costume."

And will you come with me, she thought. Help pull me out of the pool again? This time she made no attempt to kid herself about why the thought had entered her head. "Maybe I will. What are you going to do now?"

He stood. "My job's not finished."

"Catch the traitor."

"Play some part in that, yes."

"And when that's done?"

He broke eye contact. "More work. Keep moving."

"What happens when you can no longer do either?"

He looked dismissive. "Sit on top of Everest, with my shirt off, I guess. Something like that."

"That's dumb." She smiled. "By then your tree-trunk legs won't be as supple. You won't make it up the mountain, remember?"

"I don't know, then."

"No. You don't know." She went to her handbag, withdrew a pen and old shopping receipt, and wrote on the blank side of the paper. She handed the slip to him. "My telephone number. Take it. Doesn't mean we're engaged or anything. Just a number."

He hesitated.

"Come on, Mr. Devil-May-Care. Don't hang about or I'll be posted somewhere else, will get lonely, hook up with whoever I can find, get up the duff, and then that'll be game-over." She smiled but her stomach was in knots.

He took the paper. "Maybe don't wait for summer. It's a long way off. Spring might be better."

"Bring some trunks."

"Gurkhas can't swim."

"Is that true?"

"I just made it up."

"Thought so." She stood close to him and ran her hand along his cheek. "Before then, call me. Take me out somewhere nice. Let's be naughty and jump over the wall. Yeah?"

He bowed his head.

Softly, she repeated, "Yeah?"

He looked up and caressed her hand. "Yes, Molly."

Faraday was alone in his pretend Nissen hut in the grounds of GCHQ. He was desperate to get home, grab an hour or two of sleep, and maybe later go for a long run. But for now he had to honour his agreement to give Duggan some kind of meaning by checking Raine's bank cards to see if he'd left an audit trail during his journey to Muck. It was a pointless exercise. Whether Raine did or didn't use his real name to get to Scotland was irrelevant. He was there. But, Faraday supposed that Duggan was starting to pull strands together so that he could muster data and one day gain some form of closure on Baltzar's death.

He tapped on his computer keyboard. It took him less than four minutes to ascertain that, during the last five days since MAYFLY had gone live, Raine hadn't used his cards to pay for any form of transport to Mallaig and beyond. He called Duggan and gave him the results. Duggan audibly sighed, thanked Faraday for looking, and said his findings were to be expected.

After the call ended, Faraday drummed his fingers while thinking about Duggan. He was worried about his state of mind and what kind of future lay ahead for the MI5 officer. Duggan was robust and a survivor. But there was a danger he might have been pushed to the brink. His marriage had started out joyous and ended catastrophically and sadly, all because his good-time wife couldn't work out what she wanted. And they'd never had kids. Baltzar was the nearest thing Duggan had to a child. His wife resented that. There were so many things she resented, while saying cruel things to him. Apparently she hadn't always been like that. Now, his wife was gone and Baltzar had been taken from him in the most horrific way imaginable. And then there was what happened to him in Ireland, when he was a young operational officer. Faraday didn't know much detail, aside from Duggan had been captured by the IRA and was rescued by the Brits. Apparently he wasn't in good shape. Among other events, electricity had been applied to his steel spine. To this day, Duggan didn't talk about the experience. He'd buried the chapter of his life. Or so he thought. Most senior intelligence officers have gut-wrenching memories. All of them are cancerous.

Faraday decided home would have to wait. He needed time to think and the hut was the perfect place to do that. Some of his thoughts remained focused on Duggan. For the next few days, he hoped the MI5 officer had the ability to keep emotion at bay. The rest of his thoughts were about Sassoon and Hare. Together, The Library had to remain professional and clinical. There was an execution to be had.

CHAPTER 21
THAT EVENING

At six ten PM, Lebrun pressed the downstairs communal door buzzer to the flats in West Square. She spoke to Knutsen on the intercom and he let her in. As she walked up the four flights of stairs, she could see Knutsen watching her from the top floor. Rather, he wasn't watching her – he was looking for what might be behind her, pointing a gun at her back. She said hello to Knutsen when she reached him. He gave one final glance down the stairs, and let her into the flat, locking and bolting the door behind them.

In the lounge, Raine was sitting at the dining table, using Sign's expensive stationery to write letters to his wife and daughters.

Sign was standing in the centre of the room. "Good evening, Mrs. Lebrun. I do hope you come laden with stout evidence of the excellent bonhomie between the Metropolitan Police Service and the Bundespolizei."

She reached into her coat pocket, walked right up to him, and placed her hand in front of his face. "I brought a memory stick."

He took it from her. "Memory stick?" He looked at it, quizzical. "The last time I saw one of these, two nearby men and one woman leapt to their deaths from a precipice in the Appalachian Mountains. It was curious because…"

"Ben!" Knutsen tucked his Sig SAUER into his waistband and walked to Lebrun's side.

Sign weighed the stick in his hand while looking expectantly at Lebrun.

Raine stopped writing, and looked up. He wanted to hear what she had to say.

She nodded at the stick and said, "There's a lot of stuff on there. God knows how any of you breathe in this country without your security agencies knowing. It's thorough. *Very* thorough. Load it up and have a look."

Sign smiled. "No need. I have you. Headlines please."

She wasn't used to being talked to like a subordinate, but swallowed her pride. "You warned me that dates and timings would be vague, and they are. But's it's clear that – give or take a day or two – The Library were active in Scotland around the time of Baltzar's death. Most of The Library, that is. Some of them."

Sign was silent, still watching her.

"Faraday bought a train ticket from Swindon to Mallaig. Duggan bought a ticket from London to Mallaig. Sassoon's journey is unusual – he bought a ticket from London to Newcastle, but your guys flagged it. Don't know why."

Knutsen said, "Most likely because Glasgow was the stop after Newcastle. He was on the Scotland train. Sassoon got as far as Newcastle and for some reason got off there. Probably took a hire car over the border and across the Highlands. Might have been quicker than trains, factoring in connections and the slower cross-country leg."

Sign nodded.

Lebrun continued. "And there's no mention of Rex Hare. I've checked and checked and checked. Nothing. If he got up there, he didn't want to leave a footprint saying so."

"Hare?" Raine put his pen down.

"Interesting." Sign handed the stick back to her. He walked to the mantelpiece above the fire and leaned against it, deep in thought. "We talk about 'The Thief'. The name almost becomes an abstract concept. Then, real names are entwined with the concept." He looked at them. "Let's join Peter at the table. Peter – gather up your last will and testament and make some space for others." He strode over to the table and sat down.

Lebrun and Knutsen joined him.

Sign looked at his colleagues. They were staring at him, expectant. He placed his hands flat on the table, and addressed them in a tone and demeanour that he rarely deployed, save in grave moments. "I remind you of the traitor's theft of British intelligence and the resultant catastrophic damage. No more secrets must be stolen. This must end once and for all." He waited, looking for the slightest hint of uncertainty in their eyes. He proceeded. "Tomorrow at nine PM there will be a meeting between Peter and The Library. After I finish this briefing, Peter will send The Library text messages from his burner phone." He glanced at Knutsen. "Immediately after the messages are sent, Peter's phone must be destroyed. Battery out; SIM card in microwave on full power; no time to take the phone outside and destroy it elsewhere." He returned his attention to all of them. "Peter will set the meeting up, saying that he has new information about the murder of his runner. He will also say that he knows who the traitor is. Obviously, both hooks are lies. He will have no knowledge of the death of Kazia Baltzar. Lucas, Noah, and Aadesh will escort Peter to the meeting, but will remain invisible to others. Peter will go into the meeting without them. But he won't be alone. I will be with him. When the meeting's over, Lucas and team will ensure Peter leaves safely. And safety is paramount because one of the four men he's invited is the traitor. He wants him dead. But, so do the three innocent parties. Peter will be walking into a very bad place. And yet, he has to do that without hired guns around him. My objective is to scare the traitor and prompt him not to attend the meeting. Then, we've got him. If, three turn up, I will explain to the innocent members of The Library what has happened. If four turn up, then we have a very different situation to deal with. It could become very messy."

"No shit," said Knutsen, quietly.

"Attending the meeting if four turn up is my last resort, because The Library's emotions are at their highest. There is a strong possibility that innocents could die. And there is also the possibility that nothing will come from such a blunt challenge. I prefer a more clinical, exact approach. I want to isolate the traitor. Thus, it's my hope that he doesn't turn up."

Knutsen asked, "Whether three or four turn up, why not go into the meeting with me and Lucas' team?"

"Because this is not a time for gun-barrel negotiations and confrontations. Guns can force people to clam up. If they cooperate, they do so unwilling and always with an eye on saving their skin. They become untrustworthy; and certainly not wholeheartedly on one's side. And there is always the possibility that a missing fourth man may not solve everything. What if he's missing for another reason? What if The Thief's one of the three?"

Lebrun asked, "Meeting location?"

Sign replied, "Mrs. Carmichael's bookshop."

Raine's brain was spinning with everything he was hearing. He drummed his fingers. "I don't know."

Sign looked at him. "Dear fellow. I'll be with you throughout."

"Not that." Raine rubbed his face. "Look. I'll go. Hairy stuff, but I'll do it. Makes sense. Yes. Makes sense. But… Mrs. Carmichael's shop? I wonder. It's familiar. Maybe too familiar. And it's London. The Library's patch. They'll have over twenty four hours to plan the meeting. It'll be easy for them. Why not wrong foot them? Somewhere else?"

Sign conceded it was a good thought. "I'm all ears."

Raine breathed deep to control his breathing. "Anywhere in the UK is a problem. Why not overseas? Why not…" he looked at Lebrun. "Yes. Why not Germany? We could meet there. We could meet at…" he angled his head, his eyes narrow. "That's it. At nine PM we could meet in a conference room in The Hotel Opéra in Munich."

"Your passport?"

"The diplomatic one's in my office. Easy to collect."

A trace of a smile emerged on Sign's face. His tone lightened, became enthused, and sped up when he said, "Yes. You're in Germany, chasing up leads on Wick's death. Why not meet there to provide The Library with hot-off-the-press updates? It'll make perfect sense to them. And it makes perfect sense to us. Travel, cross-border security checks, and a foreign location in general, all provide complications. And they kill chunks of time. Planning a hit becomes fraught. Planning an execution, getting away with it, and escaping the country, requires a whole different level of logistics. You'll control the ground. Your phrase is perfect. You'll be *wrong footing* them. And, it occurs to me that there might be another major advantage to Munich." He looked at Lebrun. "We could put our dear polizeirat to good use. And her colleagues."

Lebrun's eyes widened. "No, no, no. Don't you dare…"

Sign's smile widened. "Oh, come now, superintendent. Your name will be in lights. *German detective captures British spy.* You'll get the Iron Cross, or whatever your highest award is these days."

Lebrun shook her head and muttered, "I suspect you know what our highest medal is." She looked directly at him. "I'm not doing this for my career. I'm doing it for…" She looked at Knutsen. "What is it you told me?"

Knutsen said, "*Shits and giggles.*"

She looked back at Sign and said in her thick German accent. "Yes. I'm here for shits and giggles."

Sign nodded. "Meaning, *for the hell of it.* And a put-down of my vacuous suggestion that you might be swept off your feet by the prospect of clamouring journalists and their cameras and shattering lightbulbs."

Knutsen frowned.

Raine laughed, then remembered he was probably going to die tomorrow.

"Anyway." Sign leaned toward her, his smile gone. "I know why you're here. *Prokofiev in a test tube.* And then what you and I saw in Muck. I need you, Karin. We've got to finish this. But, I cannot let The Thief leave Munich. Your police can put one hell of a cordon around the Opéra. With you in command and control. And inside that cordon, me, Peter, Tom, Lucas, Aadesh, Noah, Hare, Sassoon, Duggan, and Faraday, get to have a little *kick about.* Please give my football playing field some white lines."

"A ring of fire," she said quietly.

"Yes. With you in charge. I really hope The Thief doesn't turn up tomorrow. But, if he does and I can force him to confess, the due process of law becomes paramount. And it will be German law, not British, that enacts justice. If he's still alive, you can make the arrest. The arrest will be for the murder of Alex Wick."

The men looked at her, waiting.

Slowly, she nodded her head while thinking and looking at the table. She looked at Sign. "Prokofiev in einem reagenzglas. Fuck it! Shits and giggles. Ich gebe dir deinen feuerring." The English translation of her last sentence was, I'll give you your ring of fire.

Sign momentarily closed his eyes. "Vielen dank, Frau Lebrun." He went to the corner drinks cabinet on the other side of the lounge and returned with a bottle and four glasses. He placed them in front of Lebrun and said, "German Schnapps. It's not expensive, but it's robust and I nearly lost my eye to a Prussian swordsman in order to win the bottle. Now, that's a story to tell one day, if Mr. Knutsen will ever let me recount the tale. Mrs. Lebrun – you'd be doing us an honour if you poured us a glass each. Just one glass. It'll be our last meaningful fortification until this business is done with us."

She poured the drinks and handed them around.

When they all had glasses in their hands, Sign said, "After we drink," he looked at Raine, "you send The Library the text message and then grab your things," he looked at Knutsen, "you destroy Peter's phone and help me with a little jaunt," and he looked at Lebrun and winked at her, "and you piss off to Germany this evening and mobilize *Munich's Finest*." He raised his glass. "Up and at 'em!"

"Up and at 'em!" they replied in unison, before downing their drinks.

Hare was in his lounge at his home in Putney when he received a text message from a number he didn't recognise. He read the message, and re-read it several times. Two minutes later his phone rang.

Duggan asked, "Have you just got what I just got?"

"Yep."

"I'm going to call Gordon now. See if he's on this." He hung up.

Hare called Sassoon.

The MI6 officer said, "So now we know where he's been. We need to swap notes via texts to ensure we're all on different flights tomorrow. I'll call Gordon to see if he can trace…"

"Duggan's calling him."

"Okay. Gordon was popping in to his office this afternoon to check on the other thing Hamish spoke about. If he's still there, he'll give us a result in seconds. Keep me posted."

One minute after the call ended, Duggan called again. The MI5 officer said, "Spoke to Gordon. Zilch. He reckons our man's hopping from one phone to another at the moment, all because of that Norway message he got. The phone he used for tonight's text can't be traced. It's been properly messed up, Gordon reckons. Doesn't matter. We've got to go along tomorrow." He didn't need to say why. Tomorrow was The Library's last day before Faraday had to re-upload all immediate-action intelligence onto CHALICE. And it was the last day before Raine spoke to the prime minister and advised him that the database must be closed and all personnel changed for a new database of his choosing. Duggan said, "We sort things out. Start looking at travel. Keep your phone by you all evening."

When the call ended, Hare made sure the volume on his phone was turned up to the maximum and put the device in his pocket. He went to the safe by his writing desk, entered the code, and opened the steel door. Inside were papers, on top of which was a Glock 19M handgun and spare magazines. He was going to bring it with him when Raine called a Library meeting. But, everything was now different. He couldn't take the weapon overseas. He hoped his spy colleagues had access to weapons in Germany. It was crucial that one of them had a gun, or knife, or length of wire, or anything else that could kill a man. And that person didn't have to be him. All that mattered was that somebody in The Library carried something that would end Raine's life.

At seven thirty three PM, Sign knocked on the door of room 226 in Portland Place's The Langham hotel, London. Aadesh let him in and didn't say a word as he led the way down the short hallway towards the large bedroom containing armchairs, desk, a tea and coffee making facility, widescreen TV, and Lucas and Noah. Aadesh grabbed the only empty chair and lit a cigarette. His colleagues were already smoking. They were wearing the same casual winter clothes they'd been in this morning in Stratford, Darlington, or the Hartland peninsula.

Sign had the choice of sitting on the bed or remain standing. He chose the latter. Addressing Lucas, he said, "You moved fast."

Lucas nodded. "Always. We've got three adjacent rooms."

"You could have stayed somewhere more discrete."

Lucas was unfazed. "The Langham's got three hundred and eighty *elegantly appointed* bedrooms. That's a big rabbit warren. Plus, there's something else." He blew out smoke, picked up a hotel welcome brochure, and turned to the first page. "Opened in 1865. Early on was run by an American former Confederate turned Union Army officer. Patrons include Mark Twain, Napoleon, Toscanini, Dvořák, Sibelius, King Edward VIII's Mrs. Simpson, Noël Coward, Emperor Haile Selassie of Ethiopia, and us." He tossed the brochure back onto a coffee table and looked at Sign. "It's iconic." He glanced at his colleagues. "We like iconic, don't we?"

Noah and Aadesh nodded.

Impatiently, Sign said, "Alright. Just don't draw attention to yourselves. With that in mind, you shouldn't be smoking in here."

Lucas pointed at the open windows and the smoke alarms that had been duct-taped by his team.

Sign sighed. But when he spoke his tone was authoritative. "Tomorrow you're on duty. Urban environment. Smart attire. Armed. I'm bringing matters to a head."

Lucas tapped ash into a saucer. "One runner dead on your watch; one runner dead on my watch. But, we're not equal in our failures are we Mr. Sign? I've also got to account for Torbjørn Lystad and Parry."

"The priority now is to keep Peter Raine alive and kill the traitor. We'll examine our consciences at a later date."

Lucas smiled, though his thousand-yard stare made his expression cold. "At the end, I very much doubt if men like us get the opportunity to reflect on our past misdemeanours and errors of judgement. Still, that's the *gig*, as the *Johnny Reb* turned *Federal* former general manager Captain James Sanderson of this place might have said." He stubbed his cigarette out. "We'll be ready tomorrow. Call me with details."

"Raine will give you your briefing. Lay low tonight."

"We're staying here. But, we have a busy evening."

Sign frowned.

Lucas explained. "At eight o'clock we've got room service dinner. I've ordered us a starter of langoustine grillée, followed by coquille St. Jacques, sablé aux algues et anguille fumée, accompanied by a bottle of Château Haut-Brion burgundy. Courtesy of the hotel and Raine's wallet, we've got people from Harrods – or somewhere like that - coming here at eight thirty. They're bringing suits and shirts and shoes and ties and other things befitting of a…" he paused for effect, though didn't need to because his English was perfect and knowledgeable, "discerning gentleman about town. While we continue dining in this room, we'll be swift in our decision-making with purchases, because at nine thirty sharp we've got an appointment in the hotel spa with a locally-sourced high-end barber for haircuts, manicures, and wet shaves. I anticipated that you'd want us well fed and fit for your inspection, *mon general*." The former Foreign Legion officer smiled, the look mischievous.

Sign knew that Lucas expected him to be shocked by the evening schedule. "You French have your ways." He pulled out his phone while saying to the former commandant, "You'll be having an extra guest for dinner." He called Knutsen and said, "Bring him up." He ended the call and said, "The guest will be sleeping in this room tonight. I've arranged for a pull-out single bed to be sent up later. He'll be sleeping on that. Or you can. I'll leave sleeping arrangements to you both."

Lucas withdrew another cigarette from his carton. "Raine." He shook his head. "How did you manage to tamper with my hotel booking?"

Sign smiled. "The current general manager isn't American and hasn't fought in a civil war, but she is a rebel and a friend of mine. Also, I told her that the Frenchman in room 226 has toilet problems and that it was best his English brother-in-law stayed the night in the same room as him to assist and avoid causing the hotel cleaners any undue embarrassment."

Lucas was about to speak, but there were three knocks on the door. Sign carried on talking to Lucas as he walked down the hallway to the area containing the bathroom, cloakroom, and entrance. "Peter doesn't like shellfish, so I've taken the liberty of ordering him an hors d'oeuvre of seared foie gras, rabbit, and pig's trotters on toast, and a main of hanger steak and baked bone marrow, courtesy of the hotel's *Roux At The Landau* restaurant. The restaurant doesn't normally do room service, but hey – my gal's a rebel." He opened the door, gestured to Raine and Knutsen to come in, and carried on calling out to the Legionnaire, "And I've thrown in a bottle of Château Lafite-Rothschild, to pair with his courses." He re-entered the bedroom with his friends by his side. Looking directly at Lucas, he beamed, pointed at the table where the meal would be served, and said, "Ce sera un bon repas pour les gourmets et les gourmands. Vous décidez qui est qui."

Lucas waved his hand, his expression suggestive that he didn't care, or at least wasn't going to accept he'd been outplayed.

Raine placed his suit-carrier and holdall onto the bed – the bags and spare clothes within purchased by Sign to help the diplomat with his stay at West Square. He went up to Lucas and extended his hand. "Good to see you Lucas. I won't ask how you've been."

Lucas shook his hand, but didn't get up, his eyes squinting as smoke drifted over his face from the cigarette dangling in his mouth. "One down and three to go."

"Let's hope not." Raine sat on the edge of the bed, crossed his legs, and said to Sign, "Ben – I shall take it from here."

Sign nodded. He and Knutsen left without saying anything.

Raine looked at the mercenaries, his eyes unblinking, his air one of absolute leadership. Calmly and with steely precision, he told them what was going to happen tomorrow. "Mr. Sign and I are in complete agreement as to what needs to be done. Everything I've told you must be carried out to the letter. As far as you're concerned, there has been an agreed transfer of power. You now answer to me again. No one else. Are we clear on that?"

They nodded.

Sign and Knutsen walked south, across central London and towards home. Their umbrellas were up; rain was steady but not torrential. The streets were relatively empty of pedestrians and traffic, creating a somewhat eerie atmosphere, although the reality was that London sometimes got like this when it was bad weather and people had caught their trains to go home.

Neither man spoke for most of the journey, but after they'd crossed the river Sign asked, "What's on your mind, my friend?"

"You."

"Ah. You have your work cut out."

Knutsen stopped on the embankment, next to one of the old-fashioned lamps that lined the route, and leaned against the wall that divided humanity and the Thames. He stared over the water at the Cleopatra's Needle obelisk on the northern bank. "I'm not sure if you're doing the right thing."

Sign followed his gaze. "She's three and a half thousand years old and weighs two hundred and twenty-four tons. In 1878, she was towed from Alexandria to London in a metal cigar-shaped container that was manned by sailors. The towing boat and needle-vessel were hit by a terrible storm in the Bay of Biscay. The ship sent a six-man rescue team to try to save the sailors on the needle. The rescuers drowned. But the sailors they were trying to get to made it onto the ship. Alas, the needle was by then adrift. However, it was spotted four days later and towed into Spain. There were so many other adventures on that journey. And here it is."

"With two adjacent sphinxes that are facing the wrong way, thanks to a contractor's mistake." Rain was drumming harder on Knutsen's umbrella. "For fuck's sake, Ben. I'm struggling to understand why you just gave me your mini history lesson. Was it because, like *Cleo*, you get there in the end? Or you get there, but your lion protectors ain't looking where they're supposed to be looking? So what then? The lions are like me and Karin? Or the cutthroats?" He shook his head. "Thing is though, I don't think it's any of that symbolism shit. I think it's distraction. When I was three, my parents didn't want me. They had to sit me down, with a social worker present, and tell me what was happening. I stayed in touch with the social worker throughout my subsequent childhood. You know – going through all that foster parents and youth centres stuff. She told me about that moment when my Mum told me she didn't want me. Apparently my Dad was in tears. He didn't want it to happen. And what broke his heart even more was that he and my shit-head mum had been instructed to tell a three year old that his whole world was about to end. Dad didn't want to be there. He didn't want me to be in that room. If he could, he'd have taken me by the hand, walked out, put us both on a coach, and we'd have gone somewhere nice. Away from the bad people. But he couldn't. His probation officer made sure of that. So apparently I sat there, Mum blathering on, saying the same thing over and over again and asking if I understood. Bitch. I was in shock. Devastated. But I wanted to be a little soldier. I didn't want to be weak. I wanted to be strong. Tough. But I wasn't. A kid. Shaking. Red faced. Couldn't stop crying. Care worker said I looked away. I wanted a distraction. Anything. There was a painting on the office wall. One of your mate Turner's ships, I think. I pointed at it, bottom lip was quivering. And I said, "Boat"." He closed his umbrella and let the rain wash over his face. "Your stories, your memories, your knowledge - as entrancing and interesting as they all are, well, they're all just your way of distracting yourself. Create a world of wonders. All real. But, all very carefully selected by you. Forget the horrors. And by God, you've seen horror. From what little you've told me, anyway." He pointed at the obelisk but kept his eyes on Sign. "Just a piece of rock. A symbol of something or other. Men died to get it here. What a waste. But, I'm looking at you, right? When I say that you're on my mind, I don't mean I'm thinking about the time you were a young officer and posed as an anti-Soviet busker outside the KGB's

Lubyanka headquarters in Moscow, just so you could get arrested and be temporarily held in the building while you worked out the angles of their internal security cameras. Stuff like that is fun, but it's selected by you. A real memory that distracts others from enquiring about how you felt when you couldn't save that poor kid from scum in Jeddah, or how it was when you cradled your dying wife's head and for once in your life had no idea what to do. So, so many other things that no one should have in their brain. "I'm an MI6 spy who steals secrets and changes landscapes". That's what you say and that's what you do. Sounds awesome. Full of gumption, verve, and bravado. But I know you. Sometimes the secrets aren't what you want or like, and the landscapes don't quite turn out the way you envisage them. But, you don't talk about that. You talk about poisonous pygmies in Peru, or something like that. Distractions because…"

"Beneath it all is a boy who wished he didn't need to point out the boat." Sign moved to the wall and looked at the river. He said nothing for a while. He looked at him. "People come and go."

"Not all of them."

Sign bowed his head. "You think my plan for tomorrow is wrong. Don't lose faith in me."

Knutsen sighed. "For God's sake, Ben. Hand The Library over to the British authorities. End this."

Sign looked up. "And then what? Listen to me wittering on about aposematism and some such? The only way to end this is to see this out. The authorities can't be trusted to get a confession. By contrast, we can be unconventional and rule-breakers. We've got a chance, maybe just one chance, to grab this."

Knutsen said nothing for a while, not caring that his hair was sodden. "You must have an idea who The Thief is."

Sign nodded. "I have four ideas. They're all plausible."

Sassoon was sitting at his writing desk in his pad within an Edwardian building in Oakley Street, Chelsea, London. Outside rain was striking the windows hard. Inside, only an old-fashioned green desk lamp and two tasteful wall lights illuminated the small but beguiling oak-panelled lounge that contained books, paintings, charts and antiquities, including a free-standing globe that had been manufactured by the Italian cartographer Giovanni Cassini in 1792, and a wall-mounted nineteenth century Inuit whale harpoon that had been a gift from an imprisoned and generous Canadian who'd sold out his country on behalf of Marxist ideology.

On his desk was a single sheet of paper containing his scant notes from earlier calls and messages with The Library. He read them over.

Raine: Suggests 9 PM meeting, conference room, Hotel Opéra, Munich.

Faraday: Says 1020hrs Air France flight from Birmingham to Munich.

Hare: Says 1040hrs British Airways flight from Heathrow to Munich via Hamburg.

Duggan: Says 1350hrs Lufthansa direct flight from Heathrow to Munich.

He'd told the others that his flight to Munich tomorrow was at 0855hrs and would arrive close to noon. He'd insisted that his flight was the first to Germany. given he had the most overseas operational experience and wanted to be in Germany ahead of the others so he could analyse the ground before they arrived.

He picked up his fountain pen, read the notes again, and wrote a question mark at the bottom of the sheet.

CHAPTER 22

MONDAY

It was the final day of the seven day MAYFLY window. Tomorrow, Faraday had to ensure that CHALICE was back to full operational status, meaning The Thief could once again easily steal saleable immediate-action intelligence. Tomorrow was also the day that Raine had said he'd commence proceedings to ensure that CHALICE was permanently shut down, all its staff removed, and a different database of his choosing was created and managed by new personnel.

It was eight forty five PM in Munich.

Karin Lebrun was wearing black fire-retardant overalls, tactical boots, radio and harness, and a padded life-saver vest that had the word *POLIZEI* emblazoned on the front and back. On her upper arm were flashes that showed she held the rank of polizeirat, and around her waist was a holster containing a Glock 17 handgun,. Over her head were small earphones that connected to a throat mic. She was on the third floor of a tastefully designed building that normally housed a German insurance company, but right now only contained police officers. The cops had taken over a rectangular meeting room that had large windows overlooking St Anna Strasse. Lebrun was in the centre of the room and could easily see the street, its surroundings, and, on the opposite side of the wide road, the front of the Hotel Opéra. And she was in charge of everything she saw. No more Detective Lebrun in civilian attire or skulking London-based covert operative. She was on her patch, on official German duty, a superintendent, in uniform, and right now answered to no one.

Between her and the windows was a desk that ran the length of the thin and broad room. Aside from office chairs, there was no other furniture. No lights were on in the room. The only illumination came from the multitude of electronic equipment on the long desk. To her immediate left and right, four uniformed officers were sitting in front of eight laptops that showed live images of the hotel exterior and street from different perspectives. More cops were standing close by, looking through night vision and thermal binoculars. In the far right and left corner were two snipers from the police *Spezialeinsatzkommando* – SEK – who were staring through the telescopes of their HK PSG1 rifles. Their SEK commander was near to them, connected by radio to other SEK operatives who were armed with Heckler & Koch G36 assault carbines or Remington 870 pump-action shotguns and in various positions around the hotel and further along St. Anna Strasse. There were three other commanders in the room. The senior chief inspector of the *Kriminalfachdezernate*, the Investigations Bureau, was Lebrun's number two in the detective unit and was obtaining radio updates from his colleagues who were loitering in plain clothes on foot or in unmarked vehicles in the street. The head of *Polizeipräsidium München*, the regular Munich Police, was issuing orders to her uniformed officers via radio while at the same time communicating updates via mobile phone to the chief of the *Bayerische Staatliche Polizei*. And there was a senior liaison representative of the *Bundespolizei*, the Federal Police, who was monitoring the situation and on the ground in case matters spilled outside of Munich and required the involvement of his officers. This evening, all of the commanders took their orders from Lebrun. Right now, every law enforcement officer in Munich was under her control.

The only non-German in the room was Ben Sign. To her colleagues, Lebrun had billed him as an observer and senior representative of Her Majesty's Foreign & Commonwealth Office. He looked the part, wearing a smart suit and exuding an aura that left no doubt that he was the go-to person for any questions pertaining to Great Britain.

His position was not the only lie that Lebrun had supplied to the German authorities. According to her, the reason why there needed to be a police ring of fire around the hotel was because tonight there was going to be a meeting in the Hotel Opéra between four international arms dealers. She'd been investigating the worst of them and wasn't interested in the other three. Though the intelligence supplied to her by her sources was good, there was uncertainty as to whether he'd turn up. If he did, he'd have protection. And any attempts at an arrest would be met by one hell of a firefight.

The distance from Lebrun's command post to the entrance of the hotel was ninety eight yards. The area around the Opéra was blanketed in snow. More snow was falling, buffeted by erratic bursts of wind. The external reception section of the hotel and the strasse itself were busy – people coming and going from the Opéra and walking up and down the street; cars moving slowly, their headlights on. Despite being night time, visibility would ordinarily be good at this time of evening. The route was lit up by ornate street lamps; some of the imposing and regal white coloured buildings that lined the street had internal lights on; a café further down the road shone blue light over snow; strings of brightly lit bulbs were draped over bare trees adjacent to the wide pavement; and there were amber lights on the hotel's ground floor and attached wing, and subtle white lights that picked out its façade. But the weather made visibility poor and confusing.

Lebrun was motionless, standing and slightly leaning forwards, her fingertips touching the desk, utterly focused as she looked at what was happening outside. But, as Sign had once recognised about her, she had complete awareness of what was happening in her immediate peripheral vision. Colleagues came to her and whispered in her ear; she nodded, but didn't speak or take her eyes off St. Anna Strasse.

Sign was on the other side of the room and close to one of the snipers. His phone rang. Knutsen. Sign knew his colleague was in civilian winter attire, had arrived in Germany six hours ago, and was somewhere nearby. The only police officer who was aware Knutsen was here was Lebrun. She'd given him a pistol.

Knutsen said, "Bloody unreliable mercenaries. They were supposed to be here two hours ago. But, they're not." He was referring to Lucas, Noah, and Aadesh.

Quietly, Sign replied, "They're not the only ones. Peter's also a no-show." Raine was supposed to be in the room with him. "I'll try Peter again. If he doesn't answer, look out for a flatmate who's decided to brave the cold and has no idea why." He ended the call and phoned Raine. For the fourth time in sixty minutes, there was no answer. No doubt, something was very wrong. It was now eight fifty one PM. He moved to Lebrun's side, looked out the window, and said, "No Peter. No cutthroats."

"What?" she muttered between clenched teeth. "I've done my part. This is on you," she added quietly and angrily.

"Everything's on me, Karin. I should have briefed you better. This is my fault."

"Why?"

"Travel manifests. Some matters are best discussed one-to-one. It may be pertinent."

She broke her gaze on the street and looked at him as she was about to say something.

But he had his back to her and was walking to the other side of the room, his mobile against his ear as he tried Raine again.

Knutsen raised his forearm as a blast of snow and ice struck his eyes. It might be picture-postcard pretty here, he thought, but it was colder than a meatpacker's refrigerator. The snow had lost its appeal hours ago, and the wind was a pain in the arse. He walked, slowly at first until the headwind stopped and he was marginally able to pick up pace. To the untrained eye, everything in the area looked normal. He was close to the hotel, in St. Anna Platz, a three-sided large neo-Renaissance-style square that contained the Romanesque parish church of St. Anna, houses that had been listed as historical buildings, café, school, and a Baroque Franciscan monastery. In the warmer months, no doubt the area would be a lovely place to visit. Now, the one hundred by eighty yard square contained six civilians and two detectives in the café, a stationary transit van with four hidden SEK commandos in the area where the square widened and joined St Anna Strasse, a few locals and other plain-clothed cops walking across the square but not stopping, and an SEK observation post with snipers on the roof of one of the historical buildings. During the preceding three hours, he'd done numerous discrete and varied laps within the zone containing the hotel. It was much the same in the nearby streets and buildings – more detectives milling around in ones or twos and stamping their feet to stay warm as they pretended to wait for a bus or tram, civilians legitimately doing similar, static vehicles with engines running and not looking out of place given the throughput of regular traffic, and locations where earlier today men and women had quickly disgorged from cars and entered buildings while wearing non-descript winter-wear and carrying heavy holdalls containing their equipment and SEK combat attire. The untrained eye wouldn't have seen what Knutsen had seen. Nor would it have thought it odd that there was absolutely no evidence of a law enforcement presence in the area. Locals and tourists in the zone were simply too busy going about their business to stop and wonder why there weren't patrols cruising by. Knutsen knew where the *Polizeipräsidium München* were – over one thousand yards away from the Opéra, parked-up in their uniform vehicles, all twenty seven of them, able to cut off or pursue any vehicle no matter what direction it tried to escape the hotel zone. It was an excellent and unobtrusive cordon, designed by Lebrun, but was only effective if The Thief escaped in a car. There were too many variables if he bolted on foot. And the circumference of the cordon was too vast to put uniforms in every possible nook and cranny. But that was okay. Inside the cordon were enough armed detectives and commandos to make a private army look to its laurels. Lebrun had opted for a sledgehammer approach, and she was right to do so. But none of it would amount to anything if Raine didn't turn up, The Thief wasn't identified, and Sign couldn't weave some kind of magic. And where were the cutthroats? The fact that both they and Raine weren't here was too coincidental. Something was afoot. He stopped in an area of the square that sometimes had a market that sold flowers, bread, and knick-knacks, but was now empty. The snow sank three inches under his boots. He checked the time on his mobile. It was now eight fifty nine PM. One minute left until The Library was due to start its meeting.

Sign looked over the shoulder of one of the cops and stared at the laptop screen that showed the entrance area of the Hotel Opéra. It was impossible to discern the faces of people entering the establishment. He looked at his watch. How did he feel about Raine not turning up? How did he feel about everything? Bloody awful, he suspected, but that feeling had to be buried right now because his mind was racing, trying to improvise, problem-solve, adapt, invent, and imagine so many potential outcomes of what could happen next. He went to Lebrun.

She was on her mobile and held one finger up as she saw him approach. She said, "Okay," to whoever she was speaking to, ended the call, and stood so close to him that her body was almost touching his. Quietly, she said, "That was the hotel concierge. I've had him on standby. Three of the men are in the conference room. We don't have their names. They simply said they're here to meet Raine. What are you going to do? It's time."

It was.

9pm.

Sign shook his head and muttered, "Damn you, Peter."

Lebrun's eyes were wide, expectant. "What are you going to do?" she repeated.

He glanced at the hotel, then back at Lebrun. "No fourth man is okay. No Peter skews everything."

"Then think, Ben!"

He tried to keep his frustration in check, but was failing. That was no good, he told himself. Cool as cucumber Karin Lebrun had stepped up to the plate with exemplary leadership. He was so proud of her, seeing her standing there, watching the hotel, everyone around her in no doubt she was the boss and knew what to do. It was rare for him to feel such pride, given he applied the same standards to others as he did to himself. But she'd done well. And here she was, looking at him, needing to know what to do, handing over the baton of leadership, silently telling him that she was now putting him in charge of her. She was right. He had to think. And he had seconds to do so.

She could see in his eyes that his brain was motoring at full pelt. Her overriding emotion was a desire to help him. But how? Get him focused on the basics, she decided. "Who do you think is The Thief?"

Goodness, Lebrun's voice sounded so distant. One tiny voice within a million pieces of data that were hurtling towards him. But her voice mattered. He pushed all other data aside. For now. He looked her in the eye. "If my theory is correct, I know who The Thief is. But, it's a theory. So much depends upon whether I've gauged The Thief correctly. I'm imagining what I'd do if I was The Thief."

For three seconds Lebrun said nothing, her expression intense. She broke silence. "Heaven help us all. Do what you have to do. And do it fast. I've got fingers on triggers." She turned away and resumed her focus on the hotel.

He walked out of the room, into an open-plan office space that normally would contain insurance professionals but now was empty. He called Raine again, expecting no answer.

But Raine did answer. There were no greetings or apologies or anything that suggested the diplomat was about to make amends for his absence. Instead, "You didn't have the stomach for what needed to be done. I did. German law be damned. I've dealt with The Thief. There's nothing for you in Munich. The matter's closed." He ended the call.

His heart pumping fast, Sign tried calling him back. No answer.

Anger coursed through him as he walked back into the police command centre and approached Lebrun. She was listening to one of the commanders, but ushered him away as she saw Sign walking towards her with an uncharacteristic expression that suggested he was about the deliver an almighty and terrifying dressing-down to someone.

When he was in front of her, he said, "The Thief is playing a straight back with The Library. He's always asking himself, what would an innocent man do? But, he's also telling himself that innocent people do things that make them look suspicious. The latter doesn't help him. He doesn't want there to be any room for misinterpretation. He's decided to hit The Library over the head with his innocence and garner zero suspicion. No misinterpretation. No room for misunderstandings. Whiter than white. As a result, he's made a mistake. But, so have I. When I asked you to check out the travel manifests, I wasn't interested in who went to Scotland in their own name. I was looking for who didn't. But, I didn't express that thought to you. Nor did I ask you to relay your findings to me privately. I've been stupid. So wrapped up in my thoughts. And now Peter's been a naughty boy. I'm going into the Opéra. If one of your cops shoots me on the street before I get there, Tom will hunt down that cop and kill him or her and anyone around the officer. Tell the concierge that he and his staff would do well to stay out of my way as I go to the conference room. Time for me to create a wholly believable illusion. Do nothing until you hear from me. Wait for my call."

He didn't give her a chance to respond. Instead he quickly exited the room, walked down stairs, and out of the building. Though the wind had temporarily vanished, the weather was so bad that he should have brought a coat to put over his suit. But he didn't care about the cold. As he stepped onto the strasse, his eyes were locked on the hotel on the other side of the route. He walked towards the Opéra.

Lebrun watched him from her position three stories up. Sign was walking over the road that was constantly being replenished with snowflakes the size of doilies. The strasse bore no visible evidence that traffic had been using the route. And right now people were gone. Probably hotel guests had completed their arrivals and departures, and non-hotel-related people had decided that the weather was too much. So, he was alone down there, watched by her, cops with binoculars and cameras, and police commandos with sniper rifles. It hadn't occurred to her to speak to Sign privately about the manifests results. The implication of doing otherwise was now partially clear to her. Hare's name had been notable in its absence on the manifests. Raine had overheard that detail. And somehow he'd acted on that information. Sign hadn't chastised her for her lapse of judgement. Instead he'd taken the blame. And shouldered all responsibility. She had one hundred and fifty eight guns under her control. At this precise moment, they were useless. Sign was on his own, unarmed, and she suspected he was about to provide an impromptu theatrical performance. While he was crossing the street, he was hurriedly learning his lines. As the English expression goes, he was about to *wing it*.

Sign entered the hotel's bustling lobby, ignored the concierge's gaze, and looked at his surroundings. He saw what Alex Wick saw ten days ago – Romanesque meets German Renaissance and Romanticism splendour, stone columns between the marble floor and high ceiling, and heavy sashes of rich coloured velvet and linen. He spotted the route he needed to take and walked past the same paintings that the dead diplomat had seen – reproductions of works by Dürer, Friedrich, Caravaggio, Bockhorst, and Raphael - and he passed the conservatory and garden that Wick had thought resembled an opulent Roman spa. The wall-mounted mirrors that had reflected the diplomat's image now reflected those of Sign. Unlike Wick, he ignored the way his reflection looked like it was lit up by the colours of blue, gold, white, and red jewels and metals. And he ignored the hotel's aromatic scent of wood apple, gingerbread, jasmine, hog plum, and cinnamon. All that mattered was the door at the end of the corridor. On it was a gold plaque with the German words 'Business Center: Der Sitzungssaal' and the English words 'Business Centre: Meeting Room'. He stopped outside and composed himself. This was a game, he told himself; a combination of Texas Hold 'Em poker and speed-chess, played out against masters who needed to be convinced that they'd won. He knew it was anything but a game. But now was not the time for him to be scared. He opened the door.

The room contained two booths with desks, telephones, and computers. And it had a boardroom table and chairs, with three men in suits sitting at one end.

Gordon Faraday.

Hamish Duggan.

Edward Sassoon.

Duggan and Faraday frowned as they looked at Sign, and watched him close the door behind him and stand against a chair at the head of the table.

Sassoon didn't frown. He was motionless; unflustered and intense; his expression icy. "Gentlemen," he said in his well-spoken tone. "This is Ben Sign, formerly of Her Majesty's Secret Intelligence Service. The fact he is here suggests an ill wind is blowing our way."

Sign looked at them at the other end of the long table. Hare wasn't here. And that meant Sign had to pull off the biggest improvised performance and bluff of his life. "I'm here representing Peter Raine. May I?" He nodded at the chair in front of him.

Sassoon nodded, though his expression remained cold and his eyes were unblinking as they stayed fixed on Sign.

Sign sat and felt, as he always did when he was in the most extreme of circumstances, physically and mentally detached from his self. He was another person. The sensation gave him utter peace; and it enabled him to be completely devoid of nerves. He loosely crossed his arms and rested them on his legs, and calmly looked at each man before gently yet firmly saying, "No doubt this is a somewhat *embarrassing* situation, but I'm sure we can work through it together."

"Work through what?" asked Duggan, with no attempt at hiding his hostility.

Sign was unperturbed. "You call yourselves *The Library*. Your assembly was the initiative of my client. And on that – I'm paid to be here; I have no other vested interests. The Library wishes to catch a traitor, codenamed by you as *The Thief*. Thus far you've tried two tactics. First, to dry-up The Thief's revenue stream by discrediting him to potential foreign customers. To do that you deployed a young diplomat called Alex Wick. He came to this hotel and was murdered here. The Library is convinced he was killed by The Thief. It was agreed by you that it was too risky to continue using tactic one. So, you moved to a second tactic, namely creating the *MAYFLY* file within CHALICE and to temporarily remove all other intelligence from the database that might have saleable value to The Thief. Your objective was to cause The Thief to panic and try to ascertain the identity of the source of the four MAYFLY reports." He paused. "Correct me if anything I've said thus far is incorrect."

They didn't say anything, just kept watching him.

He continued. "Mr. Raine's primary objective has been to identify and capture The Thief. When he returned from his Washington posting, he was frustrated to see that the counter-espionage effort to capture the CHALICE traitor was making zero progress. So, he recruited his *band of irregulars*, as he calls you. Creative thinkers; highly trained operatives; senior, meaning you have a wealth of experience and don't have bosses looking over your shoulders; and crucially, individuals who know that things don't get done if one always complies with the rulebook. He made the right decision. Tactics one and two were excellent initiatives. But, my client didn't get to his rank within the Diplomatic Corps without carrying a degree of, shall we say, applied caution. There are nine hundred and eighty two CHALICE staff. One of them is the traitor. And that person could be a member of The Library."

"He kept an open mind," said Faraday, "and did his own little *private eye* routine against me, Rex, Edward, and Hamish."

"Rather more, he kept a *weather eye*. He didn't suspect any of you anymore than the rest of CHALICE. That said, he came to the conclusion that the suspect was probably senior, so that narrowed possibilities down somewhat. So, private or otherwise, he kept an eye on you."

"And something came out of that." Sassoon was making a statement, not asking a question.

Sign nodded. "Rex Hare." Anticipating questions, he held up his hand. "I don't know the ins and outs of why Mr. Raine had suspicions about Hare. He didn't wish to go into that with me. But he told me straight that he had reasons to be suspicious about Hare and was pursuing those suspicions."

With deliberation, Sassoon asked, "Why and when were you brought in, Ben?"

"I was consulted by Mr. Raine two days ago. He told me everything I've just recounted to you, plus three other things that you won't be aware of. First, when you all declared the identities of your runners, as you call them, Mr. Raine decided to use some men to follow and watch over the runners. It was merely a precaution. He didn't know who to trust. Second, one of his men went quiet two days ago. It was ascertained that a certain Kazia Baltzar," Sign looked at Duggan, "was brutally murdered. No doubt this was the work of The Thief. The only way The Thief could get to Baltzar was if he had sufficient warning that she was a runner who soon was going to go into hiding. On the day she posted her MAYFLY report, he – or someone in his employment – followed Baltzar to the isle of Muck. Either then, or a day or two later, he slaughtered her. And third, my client then decided to check if anyone from The Library had been to Muck, or close to Muck, on or around the day she most likely died. He checked travel expenditure. It turns out you all travelled to Scotland," he looked at Sassoon, "or very close to Scotland, hours after she was found dead by Mr. Raine's men. But, when I say *"all"* I mean all of you excluding Hare. Chief Superintendent Hare either didn't go to Scotland with the rest of you, or he did go but didn't want to leave a record of doing so, or he was in Scotland already."

Duggan shook his head in disbelief. "Stupid, stupid man." His eyes were venomous as he looked at Sign. "And I don't mean Hare. I mean Raine. And you!"

Faraday looked equally incredulous and angry as he addressed Sign. "Hare was with us when we went to Muck. We all dashed up there by whatever means we could. Well, not Edward – turns out he was on other business in Newcastle, hence his proximity on the day to Scotland. But Hare? Jesus Christ, man! Hare got to Scotland on police helicopters. There'll be no bloody ticket stubs for his trip. He got up there on tax payers' money. Official travel. And I'll tell you one thing for sure – if Mr. *Bloody* Raine had bothered to check, he'd have found that there's a fully documented police record of Rex Hare's trip."

Sign deliberately frowned. His fake projected confusion was paramount now. After all, this was one big act. But, none of this was a surprise. Hare was innocent and therefore didn't think to leave an obvious record of his trip to Scotland. Someone in this room wasn't innocent and had gone out of his way to ensure that his journey was visible to investigators. That was the traitor's mistake that he'd referenced to Lebrun. The Thief had been too careful to appear innocent. And Sign's mistake had been to let Lebrun blurt Hare's name in front of Raine.

Sassoon said firmly, "You haven't given us an answer as to why you're here, Ben."

Sign kept the frown on his face and when he spoke he injected uncertainty into his tone. "It was a straightforward arrangement. These days I'm a businessman. Mr. Raine paid me fifty thousand pounds to come here and talk to you. The message is simple and as follows: Hare is The Thief; Mr. Raine will deal with matters in a way that the rest of The Library cannot be part of; Mr. Raine thanks the rest of The Library for its invaluable contribution in the investigation; he is sorry for the subterfuge in getting you to Germany, but wanted you out of the country while he dealt with matters; he hopes that, in sending me to convey this message, you realise that he admires your contribution to the effort and respects you fully." He breathed in deeply. "Finally, The Library must now disband and never talk about its prior existence. My client's had to move quickly against Hare. MAYFLY failed. Today was Mr. Raine's deadline to set in train steps to create a new CHALICE. But that third tactic is not guaranteed success. Even though he didn't want to admit as much to you, he could be overruled by the prime minister. Unconventional and rapid action needed to be taken against the man who was without doubt The Thief."

"You fool." Duggan withdrew his mobile phone and made a call. The MI5 officer said to the recipient of the call, "Detective chief superintendent Rex Hare of the Metropolitan Police Service. Head of SO15 Counter Terrorist Command. I want to know if he's had any agro in the last twenty four hours. Check with plod and get back to me ASAP." He listened. "No. I'll expect your call within sixty seconds." He ended the call and placed the phone in front of him.

A trace of a smile was on Sassoon's face. "What shall we talk about for sixty seconds? I know – shall we ask Mr. Sign where he buys his suits from? You're looking a bit *department store* these days, Ben."

Sign pretended to look affronted as he smoothed a hand against the sleeve of his bespoke Saville Row handmade suit. "Shut up, Edward."

Sassoon's smile broadened.

They sat in silence.

Until Duggan's phone rang. He listened to the caller, said, "Alright," and hung up. He looked at his colleagues before looking at Sign. "At seven thirty one hours this morning a British Airways limousine driver was supposed to collect Hare from his home in Putney and drive him to Heathrow so he could get a ten forty flight to Germany. The driver was snatched by armed men while he was waiting near Hare's home. The chauffeur was driven off in a van and dumped in a country layby thirty miles outside of London. His car has a company tracking system. The car was found torched somewhere in Hampshire."

Sassoon said, "Some of Raine's men grab the driver and drop him off somewhere nice and quiet. One stays behind to pretend he's the BA driver. Hare comes out of his house, bleary-eyed and oblivious to what happened further up his street. Fake driver takes Hare towards the airport. All's going well, thinks Hare. But then the other men pull their van alongside the fake driver. Hare is bundled into the van and driven off. The fake driver goes onwards, torches the car, and uses other transport to join his colleagues." He raised his hands. "So, Hare is dead."

"Jeez," said Faraday.

"I had no part in this," said Sign urgently. "Mr. Raine made it clear to me that my role was simply to convey his message. I was given no insight into my client's plans for Rex Hare."

"Yeah. *Messenger Boy* who doesn't know that he's been given a pile of shit to shovel." Duggan looked at Faraday and Sassoon. "If only we could tell him why this is one big cluster-fuck."

Sassoon raised a finger. "I think he can be told. Ben belongs to my world now. And what an unforgiving world that can be." His smile was gone when he said, "Ben – you've been duped. This is all a mistake." He glanced at the others. They nodded. He looked back at Sign. "Peter Raine is The Thief." He told him about the Norwegian angle – that four days ago they'd learnt that everyone in The Library spoke fluent Norwegian; that they thought Raine's motive for assembling a team with such a language in common was suspicious; that they'd bugged Raine's communications systems; had intercepted a coded message to his phone; went to Torbjørn Lystad's home in Bergen where they found incriminating evidence against Raine; and realised that at some point Raine, or more likely Lystad, had let slip something that showed The Thief was a fluent Norwegian speaker. "Raine assembled us because he wanted to keep his enemies nearby. He wanted to see if we were getting close to him. His men, if they exist and I doubt that, didn't find Baltzar. Raine knew she was dead. He killed her. He tricked you, Ben. He doesn't know we know he's The Thief. So, he had everything to gain by sending you here. He wanted you to unwittingly hoodwink us into thinking he'd rolled up his sleeves and done the unpalatable job of killing the man who he wanted us to believe was The Thief. He kills Hare; we think it's case closed; we go back to our day jobs; CHALICE stays open for business; and sometime soon Raine makes his final heist. All very neat and tidy. But, it's not *neat and tidy*. It's the mother of all lies."

Sign placed his hands on the table. He acted stunned, speechless; confused; embarrassed. "I… I… What to say? What to say?" he said with a distant voice. "This is…" He breathed out loudly. "Look. I took the money in good faith. No agenda, but I thought it was a good thing. Playing my part to catch a traitor." He looked at Sassoon. "You'll see. The old days go sooner than you think, my friend. Then it's just picking up scraps where you can. No more *queen and country* stuff. Crappy, most of it. Then this came along. I've known Peter a while. We go back. It was good he came to me. I thought. Good. Chance for me to do something again."

"Be the mighty Ben Sign again." Sassoon didn't say it in a sarcastic way. His tone and expression were wholly empathetic. "I'm sorry, Ben. So very sorry." He sighed and looked at the table. "But, my world is my world." He looked up, his expression again cold. "I'm going to help you. I'll turn your blood money into notes that are purer than the stuff that's been settling over Munich all day. You'll do a job for me. You'll go back to Peter Raine and tell him that you conveyed your message, that we're shocked to hear about Hare, that we appreciate his discretion and the way he ensured we didn't get involved in the dirty business, and we're relieved Hare's been identified as The Thief and covertly dealt with. Via Mr. Duggan's MI5 connection to the Metropolitan Police, we know what happened outside of Hare's home this morning. We take it this was Raine's work. This is good. The police suspect foul play, but they'll never know what really happened. Hare's disappearance will quickly come to the attention of the CHALICE counter-intelligence effort. They will soon put two and two together and realise that Hare's absence from CHALICE has complete relevance to their efforts. Conclusions will be reached. With no more CHALICE intel being stolen, it's obvious Hare's The Thief. He's come a cropper, the counter-intelligence effort will deduce, because he's been swimming in murky waters. The counter-intelligence bods will look for him, but their efforts will grow half-hearted. The Thief has been identified. No one can find him. CHALICE is safe. There'll be no blowback onto The Library. The Library is disbanded with immediate effect. None of us will ever breathe a word of what happened. Life goes on." Sassoon shrugged. "I'll leave it to you as to how you describe our reactions to the news that Hare was The Thief. We threw our hands up in horror; disbelief; disgust; that kind of thing; whatever you fancy, really." He pointed his finger at Sign. "But, that's the only thing I'll leave to your discretion. Everything else will be done exactly as I've told you. I, and the gentlemen by my side, represent the national security of Great Britain. You'll do as you're told."

Sign bowed his head. "Of course, dear chap. Of course. I'll tell him tomorrow."

"Where are you meeting him?"

Sign replied, "I'll call him when I'm in London. We'll meet at my place, or somewhere else, or his place."

Sassoon glanced at his colleagues then back at Sign. "Very well. Now. If perchance you've taken the liberty of ensuring there are precautions surrounding this meeting, us being twitchy and volatile blokes and all that, may I strongly suggest that you make a call or send a text and ensure that no ruffians hinder our passage out of this delightful city."

Sign stood. "Yes. Yes of course." He texted Lebrun and told her to stand down all police units and that The Library was not to be touched as it left Germany.

Her response was immediate and said, *Okay. And fuck you very much.*

Wondering when Knutsen had taught her such English phraseology, Sign said to the men, "That's done. You're good to go." He angled his head, conjuring a quizzical expression. "What are you going to do about Raine?"

Duggan laughed. "Don't worry about that, laddie. He thinks he's got away with this. He'll soon be swanning about Whitehall as usual. We'll get him."

They grabbed their coats.

After Faraday and Duggan left the room, Sassoon handed Sign a slip of paper. "This is the number to call me on tomorrow, once you've met Raine."

Sign took the paper. "I didn't see this coming."

Sassoon put his hand on his shoulder. "Times change. You were outplayed." He smiled. "I'm looking forward to the day I'm outplayed. It means I've finally retired." He put on his overcoat, took one step to the door, and hesitated. "Meeting at your place, somewhere else, or his place, you say. Word to the wise, dear fellow: best you avoid his place. Ta-ra." He left the room.

As the door closed behind The Library, Sign gave an involuntary sigh of relief and smiled. Everything had worked perfectly.

His smile vanished as a thought entered his head. He whipped his phone out of his pocket and used a shaking finger to bring up Raine's burner phone number. He pressed Call. No answer. With the same finger he started urgently writing a text message.

Raine exited the taxi in the quiet street adjacent to the long driveway leading to his home in Hertford. It was nine PM; ten PM in Western Europe. He paid the driver, watched the cab leave, breathed in the crisp night air, and took a moment to appreciate the quiet. All of the other houses on the road were like his – large, detached, big grounds, spread apart so as to afford maximum privacy, and set-back and only on one side of the road, the other being open countryside. Some of the houses had lights on, but there was no sound coming from the properties. For him, and others like him, it was the perfect place to be in England – close enough to London and far enough away from the capital. It was his retreat from madness. And my goodness, today he'd seen his fair share of madness, culminating in him standing outside a farmstead building in Norfolk and saying to Lucas, "I want him to suffer. Make sure he's a shadow of his former self. Keep him alive for seven days. Let him realise every day the consequences of what he's done. Then kill him and make sure there's no trace of him left on Planet Earth."

He walked down his drive. His house was in darkness. It would be good to have his wife and daughters back here. He'd call them when inside and give them the good news that they could come home. He'd smile if they told him to bugger off because they were having a good time and he'd have to wait until the weekend until they returned. All that mattered was that things were back to normal. The Thief had been captured and dealt with. Hare would never damage Raine's beloved country again. It was a distasteful business but needed to be done. When he'd first met Knutsen, he'd accused him of being one of Churchill's *rough men*. As he looked at his nearest neighbour's house, over two hundred yards away, he supposed he too had become one of those men. No longer the man who was reluctant to pick up a Webley pistol, or indeed any weapon. So be it, he thought. People in this street could sleep soundly in their beds because men like him were willing to do things to people who intended to harm everything he now saw.

He withdrew keys and heard his mobile phone ping. He glanced at the mobile's screen and saw he had a message from Sign. The screen showed the first word of the message.
     DON'T...

He smiled as he ignored the phone, entered his code into the house security keypad, and placed the key into the lock. Don't what, he thought? Don't do anything to Hare? If that's your message, Sign, then you're too late for that. He'd read the message in full when in the house. And he wouldn't reply. Sign could huff and puff as much as he liked but it would all go over Raine's head. He had the ears of some of the most powerful leaders in the world. All Sign had were his memories, skills, and friendship with Knutsen. That was true but so unfair, he told himself. Sign was the most decent and talented man he knew. Life had dealt him some severe blows, none of which he deserved, but through all of that he'd somehow managed to retain his dignity, honour, moral compass, sense of humour, loyalty, and mischievous twinkle in his eye. No doubt he was unusual. His intellect was weird. And God only knows how Knutsen put up with him. Then again, Knutsen wasn't a run-of-the-mill fellow. Somehow, the two oddballs got along together, despite being wholly different from each other. He wondered if that's all Sign had left – friendship with a former undercover cop who could recite the poems of Mikhail Lermontov while standing amongst the mob in the terraces of a football stadium. And Knutsen would do something like that while knowing that Sign was at home and writing a monograph on the predisposition of serial killers to enjoy repetitive and soporific hobbies; or standing waist-deep in slime in a sewer beneath Coventry while charting the city's hitherto unknown subterranean rivers. One day he hoped Sign would meet a woman and fall in love again. But, for now, maybe his lot wasn't such a bad one after all. He was occupied. And by God, Sign was someone who needed to be kept busy. He was irascible, to say the least, during unwanted lulls of activity. But that was the worst of him. In every other respect, the world was a better place for having Ben Sign in its midst. And Raine was privileged and glad to have gained a moment to have rekindled some kind of friendship with the man. He hoped the friendship would grow, though goodness knows what his wife would make of Sign if she met him. He felt better about himself for correcting his initial arrogant comparison between Sign's status and his. Sign was a good guy; he'd make sure he was looked after; he hoped to enjoy Sign's enigmatic company more often; and that's all there was to the matter. He turned the key.

The explosion from his house obliterated his body.

CHAPTER 23

TWO DAYS LATER

Mrs. Carmichael walked up the cobbled side street that contained her bookshop and entered the Strand. It was nearly eight in the morning, sunny yet cold, and London was fully awake, with vehicles and pedestrians filling the busy thoroughfare. The seventy-something, average height, slightly plump, lady was *turned-out-fit-for-purpose*, as she liked to describe her look when she had things to do. As usual, her silver hair had been immaculately sprayed in place; and she was wearing a pearl necklace resting over a starched high-collar white blouse, cardigan with leather elbow patches, her 1950s girls' school pleated knee-length charcoal grey skirt, and one pound and six shillings black shoes. And this morning she wore a purple duffle coat to *stop chilly willy winds*.

She turned down an alley that was not dissimilar in appearance to the street containing her property, though was closer to Shaftesbury Avenue and as a result got more attention from theatre goers, tourists, and locals who were in the West End entertainment trade. She entered Mr. and Mrs. Fingerhut's place. It had been in the family for two generations. Mr. Fingerhut's German-Jewish parents had been tailors, as had their forefathers, and indeed their Yiddish surname meant 'thimble' and denoted the bearer was a couturier, seamstress, or garment-maker in general. But, times change and now the small shop was a bakery that also had a couple of tables and some chairs for people to sit down and enjoy a hot drink and pastry.

Mrs. Fingerhut smiled as she saw her loyal customer approach the counter. Mrs. Carmichael always came here before she opened her bookstore, to buy biscuits and other provisions for her reading-room customers. Not that she had any customers.

"Good morning, my lovely." Mrs. Carmichael looked at food within the display cabinet. "Still nothing with bacon, I see."

Mrs. Fingerhut, of similar age to her counterpart, as ever held her ground. "One day you'll see the light." She gestured to the display. "Actually, I wouldn't mind. But, you know how Mr. Fingerhut is about these things. He tends to be a bit more…"

"Kosher? Nonsense. If he's so clean and pure, why's he partial to nice-bum-Sue's prawn and mayonnaise café sarnies?"

Mrs. Fingerhut laughed. "He plays the game."

"His orthodox father's investment in this place will do that." Mrs. Carmichael leaned forward. "Ooh. These are new. Ginger and apple. I'll have a dozen of them."

"Fresh out of the oven an hour ago." Mrs. Fingerhut bagged up the biscuits and handed them to her, together with today's folded-up mid-week edition of *The Telegraph* newspaper. Mrs. Carmichael bought the paper every morning. For some reason she called it *The Prodigal Son* and often said that she didn't trust it but liked to be close to it. "Busy day?"

Mrs. Carmichael waved her hand dismissively. "I'm expecting a delivery of a book about fifteenth century drawings of how aeronautical engineering could look in the future. But, I've been waiting for a few weeks so who knows?"

"Customers?"

Mrs. Carmichael smiled, her eyes twinkling. "You know that phrase, *if you build it they will come*? Well, that's a load of codswallop, isn't it?" She winked at her, turned, walked away while holding up her bag at head height, and called out, "Thank goodness for state pensions. Toodle-pip,"

She walked back to her shop. Inside, she entered the broom cupboard. She placed one of the biscuits onto a torn-off bit of kitchen roll paper, the rest into the vintage BBC film reel canister, put the kettle on, got a teabag out of the Dutch Indies cigar box, and dropped the tea into a mug. After the drink was ready, she went into the adjacent reading room. She always did this before opening hours. She placed her tea, biscuit, and newspaper on the Smithfield butcher's block coffee table, quickly looked around to check there were no new spiders' webs on the bookshelves and paintings, and sat in the chair that Raine had used in his Library meetings. She unfolded the paper and frowned when she saw the headline on the front page.

One senior British official murdered, one missing.

The first paragraph explained that a senior diplomat had been killed by a bomb at his home in Hertfordshire. Though there were no suspects, there was speculation that the atrocious act could be state-sponsored and somehow connected to the diplomat's prior involvement in complex negotiations with the likes of Russia and Iran. A security expert conjectured that it was more likely to be linked to the diplomat's brinkmanship approach while acting as an interlocutor between the United States and Central American drug cartels.

The second paragraph said that it was possible that a detective chief superintendent from the Metropolitan Police Service's elite counter-terrorism division had been snatched outside his home in Putney. It described what happened to the British Airways driver. A police spokesman had given a briefing to the press, stating that the three men responsible wore balaclavas, two of them were in jeans, boots, and hiking jackets, one of them was in a suit, and that they barely spoke but when they did the driver was sure they had Irish accents. The spokesman further explained that the BA car was driven out of London, most likely by the man in the suit, and torched in Essex. Almost certainly the detective was taken in that car, although there are no human remains in the wreckage. Thus far, no terrorist organisation had claimed responsibility for the abduction, though this was a rolling event and the police were hopeful that there may be more details in due course surrounding this tragic and grossly provocative event.

She reached for her tea as she started reading the third paragraph. But her hand froze before it touched the mug. The paragraph named the police officer – Rex Hare. She didn't know who he was. And it named the diplomat. She most certainly knew who he was.

She raised her hand to her mouth, her eyes watering, head slightly shaking. "Oh dear. Oh dear, oh dear, oh dear." She had to read the name over and over again, to make sure she was reading correctly. She was. "Not you, Peter," she said almost inaudibly. "Of all people, not you, my dear."

Sign had known about Raine's death before *The Telegraph* and other British and foreign newspapers had gone to print. Lebrun had called him yesterday morning with the news. She'd heard it from Mark Hogarth, the 1st secretary political and economic Berlin-based British diplomat who'd introduced her to Raine when she'd attended the Hotel Opéra to examine the Wick crime scene. As a result, when Sign called Sassoon later in the morning, he had to act ignorant and say he couldn't get hold of Raine. Sassoon had said there was a reason why he was unobtainable and that the home secretary was about to give a public televised statement, condemning the murder of Peter Raine. Sassoon had given him further details and, using careful language, had said that Hare had access to confiscated weapons and other lethal armaments, including explosives. He surmised that Hare planted the bomb, although he'd done so without the rest of The Library knowing. That was okay. The Library had an unspoken agreement that the death of The Thief would be the result of a *first past the post* system wherein his execution could be a team sport, or the job of a solo athlete. All that mattered was a win. And if it was a solo effort, then why burden the others with prior information about the event? Hare killed Raine, but not before Raine killed Hare. Regardless, The Thief was dead, The Library had disbanded.

Sign had learnt about Hare from Lucas who'd called him to say that he was in the awful position of being rudderless. He'd said that Raine had secretly tasked his team to deal with Hare, but he couldn't get hold of Raine to report that all subsequent actions had been enacted as requested. Sign had to explain that Raine was dead after being falsely accused of being The Thief. In return, Lucas told him where Hare was.

It was late morning in Norfolk, the eastern county in England. Sign stopped his hire car on a sandy track, in remote countryside close to the northern coast and one mile away from the nearest road. The only evidence of human life in the area was a cluster of three buildings close to the beach. Up until a few years ago, they'd been used as a base to catch the much-prized Cromer Crabs, a decapod crustacean of the brown variety whose flavoursome taste is enhanced by the sea's chalk shelf and nutrient-rich waters. But, there was concern by ecologists that the chalk shelf was in danger from the seabed potting technique of catching the abundant crabs. As a result, the fishermen went and the chalk bed and crabs stayed. The three buildings were now empty, unused, and a reminder of a once-thriving industry that believed its techniques were harmless.

Sign walked towards the buildings, over sand and small hillocks containing sun-bleached and windswept long grass. Beyond the buildings, the sand and shingle beach, dunes, and soft glacial cliffs were easily visible. The day was clear, though the North Atlantic sea air was forceful and cold. Behind him, and spreading for miles on all other points of the compass, was more countryside that was rolling or flat and held a plethora of wildlife. As a teenager, he'd spent many years exploring the region's salt and tidal marshes, drainage dykes, arable and woodland belts, flight ponds, and parkland. Sometimes he drew fen orchids and white waterlilies and hid in reeds while listening to birdsong and trying to spot marsh harriers, barn owls, booming bitterns, darting kingfishers, playful otters, cranes, and the rare and beautiful Swallowtail butterflies. Other times he'd stalk with a beagle by his side and a single-barrel shotgun in his hands as he tried to bag a brace of wildfowl, such as pheasant, partridge, geese, or wild duck. And when the sun rose or began setting, he'd often walk alone with a bamboo rod in his hand and a satchel over his back while hunting pike, and sea and brown trout. They were different days; so far removed from what followed.

Self-loathing didn't even begin to describe his inner feelings as he approached the small stone buildings. Noah was on the beach, his back to him, just standing and staring out to sea, his blonde hair buffeting in the wind, the colour of his blue hiking jacket a vivid contrast to the yellow ground and murky water. Nearer was Lucas, leaning against the middle hut, smoking a cigarette and watching the former MI6 officer as he got closer. Like Noah, the Frenchman was in outdoor gear. Tucked underneath his belt was a handgun.

Sign walked up to him. "Well?"

Lucas nodded at the door by his side. "He's in there."

Sign looked around. "Is Aadesh in there with him?"

"No. He's gone. He did what he had to do in London and then left. He didn't want to be part of this. And he said something about a cottage, new life, and taking a woman out for a drink. Women, eh?"

"There's still time to make amends. Hare isn't The Thief. I'm going to take him home."

Lucas scoffed. "It would have been good to know that Raine got the wrong guy. *Very* good to know." He flicked his cigarette onto the ground and stamped on it. "I think you'll change your mind about taking him anywhere."

Sign frowned.

"Raine ordered me to kill Hare seven days after capture. Five days left. What do you think? Are you now in charge, *mon general*? Or should I use my... discretion? It's easy to get rid of his body. All those delicious crabs in the sea here will take care of that. They don't leave any crumbs on the plate."

Quietly, he replied, "I'm in charge. Wait for your new orders."

Lucas held out his gun. "You might need this."

"No ropes? Cuffs? He's free to move in there?"

Lucas shrugged. "Raine told us to keep him comfortable."

Sign held the former legionnaire's gaze for a moment, took the gun, and entered the hut.

The room had nothing inside, save a metal bench that previously would have been used for cleaning crabs and gutting inadvertent but valuable catches of fish. The bench was in the centre. On it was Hare.

He was lying on his back, facing the ceiling, his eyes open, a compression pad and bandages around his mouth and jaw. Over his body and up to his throat was a white sheet. Over the sheet was a leather strap with buckle that was holding him firm against the bench. Next to him and tilted against the wall was a six-foot long piece of drift wood. At head-height and attached to the wood by a nail was a clear bag containing liquid. And from the bag to somewhere under the sheet was a plastic tube.

Sign said, "My name is Ben Sign. I'm a former government official who's been commissioned to identify and neutralise an individual who you call The Thief. You are detective chief superintendent Rex Hare. You too were trying to capture The Thief. You have been falsely identified as that person. I wish you no harm and had no part in bringing you here. Nor did I have any knowledge that you were going to be abducted. I am here to take you to safety. Nod or speak if you understand."

Hare nodded, his eyes now wide.

He unbuckled the strap. "If you are unable to walk because of drugs or injuries, I'll carry you to my car and take you to hospital. Discretion will be absolute. I have contacts in the medical profession who…" he pulled back the sheet. And stopped speaking.

Hare was naked.

And had no arms and legs.

Bloody bandages covered the stumps where his limbs had been cut off.

Sign's heart raced, but his hand was steady as he removed the bandages and padding on his face. The applications hadn't been there to muffle his speech. He didn't need to be muffled.

His tongue had been cut out.

Hare's eyes were fixed on him. His expression held terror. Tears rolled down the side of his face. He just stared at Sign.

Sign took a step back, gripping the gun, knowing why Lucas had given him the weapon. He tried to compose himself. But, how could one compose oneself when confronted by such horror? Something so unnecessary? An act that was so wrong? He moved forward and leaned close to Hare's face. "I arrived too late. Forgive me."

Hare tried to say something, but could only utter a strained hiss, his eyes wincing in pain.

Sign leaned back. "Blink three times if you want me to carry you out of here. Make each blink slow and obvious."

Hare's eyes remained open.

He tried his hardest to keep his voice measured as he said, "Close your eyes, count to five, and open them if you want me to kill you."

Hare started shaking, looking left and right.

"I regret to say that you must make a decision, one way or the other. Medical attention or death." He felt nauseous but swallowed hard to maintain control. "I'm so sorry that I don't have gentler words."

Hare stopped moving his head and looked at him. His expression changed – maybe calmer, possibly resigned, or perhaps enlightened. It was impossible to be sure, but there was no doubt the look of fear was gone.

Sign was very still. His feelings now were also different. He didn't like it when that happened. It meant there was a job to be done.

Hare hissed and gurgled again.

Sign wondered why. Was he trying to speak? Smile? Grimace? "You have my word that I'll ensure the honour of your name remains intact. You've done nothing wrong and everything right. You tried to protect our country. But, men like us sometimes face the very worst of unexpected situations. When that happens, we must be brave. Chief superintendent: give me your instruction."

Hare nodded.

Then closed his eyes for five seconds.

Sign said nothing as he raised his gun and shot Hare twice in the head.

He checked the body. Hare was dead. He walked out of the hut. Lucas was in the same place. He handed the ex-legionnaire the gun, said, "Sort it and vanish", and walked to his car.

It was early evening. Sign was alone in the West Square flat. Images and words seen and spoken during the preceding hours cascaded through his mind. He didn't want them to. They wouldn't stop. He did some essential work on his laptop and made a few calls. After those jobs were complete, he crouched in front of the fireplace and started assembling kindling. In the centre of coals, he put a twig upright and leaned others around the stick. He lit a firelighter at the base of the wooden cone and watched flames lick over the wood. It was a fire-accelerant technique that he'd been taught as a child by his father. The mind was a funny old thing, he thought. Right now it was putting a random childhood memory into his head, to act as a splint against his metaphorically injured brain tissue. He tried to busy himself with other tasks, though didn't really know what to do. After wiping clean the already-clean dining table and dusting the pristine mantelshelf, he gave up on distraction activities and slumped in his armchair.

Knutsen entered the lounge, holding a carrier bag. "Thought you might be back. I just nipped out to get some grub. You hungry?"

"I don't think I am."

"Oh come on." He smiled. "You've been gone all day. Where have you been, by the way?"

"Norfolk. The coast."

"Oh. Why?"

"To see Hare."

Knutsen sat in his chair. "Explain."

Sign did so.

Knutsen looked at the fire, nodding slowly. Then he said, "Fish and chips from *Captain Ahab's*." He reached into the bag, withdrew two paper parcels, and tossed one onto Sign's lap. ""I made sure you got extra salt and vinegar. They were out of haddock, so I got us cod."

Sign unwrapped his parcel, ignored the enclosed tiny wooden fork, and used his fingers to gingerly eat. "Thank you."

"Man's got to eat." He put a chip in his mouth and decided to take a gamble on his friendship with Sign. "Especially if he's a cop-killer."

Sign considered the phrase. "I hadn't thought of it that way. But, now that you mention it I suppose that's what I am." He looked at his friend, nodded, and presented a trace of a smile.

It's all Knutsen needed.

And it was what Sign wanted to give him.

It meant Knutsen's comment had worked; they were good; and if one couldn't eat fish and chips while spinning the absurd and diluting the abhorrent into a *movie-style* phrase then one wasn't Knutsen and Sign. And for Knutsen, it meant that Sign was still in the here and now.

Knutsen reached into the bag, took out two cold cans of beer, opened them, and handed one to Sign. "So - Hare killed our client; you killed Hare; a young British diplomat's been murdered; an MI5 officer's been killed; a Russian former Spetsnaz soldier's been vaporised; and The Thief slit the throat of his own broker. How do you think the case has gone so far?"

"Swimmingly, dear fellow," replied Sign with sarcasm. "But, Hare didn't kill Peter. That was the work of The Thief. It was his final chess move. He thinks he's won."

"He has won, hasn't he? Sassoon, Duggan, or Faraday - whoever's The Thief - will carry on as usual now. We're no closer to knowing which one of them is the traitor. Sorry my friend, but you're right – he made his move and took Raine. That was checkmate. Game over."

Sign fully pulled open the wrapping and peered at the contents. "Cod, you say. Not my favourite, but I don't object to its existence." He looked up. "Tomorrow evening you'll have the opportunity to eat pan-seared lionfish, cracked conch ceviche, and chilli and coconut sauce. Or similar."

Knutsen gulped beer. "What have you been up to then? Had a word with Ishmael and told him to pimp-up his chippy's menu? Or are you *treating* us to a nice end-of-case break somewhere tropical?"

"Not *us*. You. Tomorrow morning you're on a nine thirty five British Airways flight to Antigua, and then onto Providenciales in the Turks and Caicos islands."

Sternly, Knutsen asked, "Where are the islands and why am I going there?"

Sign examined a morsel of fish, nodded, and popped it into his mouth. "The archipelago's in the Atlantic Ocean, close to Cuba, the Bahamas, Dominican Republic, and Florida. Providenciales is the most populated island. I've booked you in for two nights at the Ritz-Carlton. After that you'll fly to Geneva where I've booked you in for one night at the InterContinental. You'll be busy; which is a shame because Providenciales has beaches that are ranked as the best in the world, and a walk through Geneva's medieval old town is to be highly recommended at this time of year, given it's decorated with beautiful night lights."

Knutsen didn't move. "Busy doing what?"

"Making crucial preparations for *my* last chess move." Sign sipped his beer, thought the can made the liquid taste metallic, and immediately pictured Hare's mouth. He put the drink to one side. "I've purchased you an off-the-shelf three year old dormant company from Companies House. The company's listed activities come under 'non-financial services advisory'. I've given the company a new name - *Flinders Chart*. You are its director and specialise in human connections. You put unusual and creative entrepreneurs together. If those connections bear fruit, then you take a bite. At ten AM the day after tomorrow you will be meeting Mr. Simon Putt of the Turks and Caicos islands' Financial Services Commission. He's expecting you at his office in Caribbean Place Plaza and will hand you papers to sign. You'll do so. As a result Flinders Chart will have a fully registered and regulated license in the offshore financial centre – under the category of 'designated non-financial businesses and professions'. You'll then go to a serviced office provider in Grace Bay and use your new license to secure a complete company office footprint on the islands, should anyone check. On Saturday you'll be in Switzerland and on Monday you'll be meeting Monsieur Julien Nicoud at eleven AM at the Union Bancaire Privée headquarters on rue du Rhône, Geneva." He paused, frowned, and muttered, "I need a glass." He stood. "Do you want a glass for your beer?"

Knutsen shook his head while squinting in disbelief that he was being asked. "No. No... Just... Get a glass. Whatever."

"Jolly good." Sign walked to the corner cabinet and continued talking as he retrieved a tumbler. "Nicoud is the director of human resources for the private bank. Your appointment with him has been established on the premise that you wish to make a discrete enquiry about a former UBP employee who one of your clients wishes to do business with. Your client, who must remain anonymous, is an ultra-high-net-worth individual with capital located in the Turks and Caicos financial district. He wishes to engage the services of a Torbjørn Lystad." He sat back down. "But your client needs to know that Lystad has no financial conflicts of interest. He is aware that Lystad previously worked for UBP and needs to be reassured that Lystad has fully severed all connections with the bank. To that extent, it would be most gracious of Monsieur Nicoud if he could furnish you with Lystad's handwritten letter of resignation from the bank. A photocopy will do."

Knutsen said, "You want Lystad's handwriting. All of this for that." He nodded slowly. "Nice. But, Nicoud might not give me the letter."

"He will. The letter can be obtained through other official channels. It's a public document that even the most secretive of Swiss banks cannot withhold. The reason why you're in the bank is that you want to reassure your client that you obtained a copy of the document from the bank itself, rather than from, say, The Swiss Financial Market Supervisory Authority."

"Okay."

"And then next Monday you fly back to London, document in hand." Sign smiled. "Four and a half days to do that. Regrettably, a chunk of it will be occupied sitting on twelve hour flights."

"Yeah thanks." Knutsen wondered if Sign didn't want to do the trip because he'd be trapped on a plane and have too much time to think. "I'm guessing you want me to copy Lystad's writing."

Sign nodded. "You are rather good on all-matters calligraphy. You'll write two letters. The first will be in a woman's handwriting. The woman will be Argentinian and will be a broker, much like Lystad but with even better connections. She wants to buy as much of CHALICE as possible, and she's willing to pay a one off substantial seven dollar figure for the intelligence. She wants to meet The Thief and make an exchange. The second letter will be from Lystad and will be his verification of the woman's credentials and trustworthiness. The letter is his introduction of her to The Thief. He says that The Thief has his letter and the woman's letter because something has happened to Lystad. He gave his letter to the woman in case he was unable to meet The Thief again. He goes onto say that The Thief could probably get a bit more money if he sold the last CHALICE heist piecemeal to different clients. But, time isn't on their side and his strong recommendation is that The Thief accepts her terms, given the sum she is willing to pay. She will pay on delivery of the intelligence. The Thief and Lystad will not be involved in the sales to foreign clients. It is a simple, linear, expedient, and exceptionally lucrative transaction. But, if The Thief has reservations, or doesn't want to do this full stop, then that is fully understood. In the woman's letter she will suggest a time and place to meet. You will deliver the letters to the person who I think is The Thief. Of course, the fictitious Argentinian woman will not be at the meeting location. You me, and Karin Lebrun will be there."

Knutsen spent a moment to digest the information. "When and where?"

"You get back on Monday. Hopefully we get face to face with The Thief on the following Friday. Meeting location: Norway."

The former undercover operative rubbed his face. "I don't know. Will he meet?"

Sign tossed his food wrapper into the fire and watched it burn. "The Thief's first objective was to frame Peter and kill him. He achieved that. I'm using The Thief's second irresistible objective against him. He must make one last heist of CHALICE intel. He can't risk stealing in the way he did before, for fear of getting the counter-intelligence effort back up and running. At the moment, or certainly very soon, they think The Thief is Hare and the innocent Library is convinced it was Raine. Both conclusions would change if more CHALICE intel was slowly but surely stolen and sold with definable repercussions. Thus, The Thief's desperate. He killed his broker. If he falls for my trap, he's going to think Lystad deposited the letter with the Argentinian before the Norway incident. I'm hoping The Thief sees this as his only hope to cash in his chips. The Argentinian woman is his solution."

"He'll want to call the Argentinian woman before they meet."

"There'll be a number in the letter. If he calls it, Karin will answer."

"In a German accent!"

"Her mother's Spanish. Karin's bilingual."

"How do you know that?"

Sign shrugged. "I know the strangest of things."

Knutsen sighed. "Will he meet?"

Sign smiled with resignation. "I think so."

"You'd think twice about turning up."

Sign shook his head. "I'd meet".

"Why?"

"Because I'd be brave enough to confront my opponent and tell him I'd lost. It would be the end of the matter. I'd have nowhere else to go. If I ran, I'd be found." He repeated, "I'd meet." He lowered his head and quietly said, "And then there is the other thing."

"What?"

Sign raised his head. "At every step of the way, as unpalatable as the technique is, I have to think what I would do if I was The Thief. Unbridled logic is paramount in that thought process. If I'm right, The Thief and I are exactly where we should be at this precise point in time. But, at the final stage of this grand opus, our thought processes diverge. I have no wish for recognition. By contrast, though The Thief finds adulation a petty construct, it's vital to his plan that his actions are remembered and thus have meaning. I would ride off into the sunset, satisfied in the knowledge that my correction is complete and yet my hand remains unseen. But, The Thief wants his hand to be seen. His message must be loud and clear. That's why he wants to make one large heist of CHALICE. He doesn't care about the money. What matters to him is that people understand. He descends with a huge broadsword and causes carnage. But, then he lingers so survivors can behold his image as they tremble in astonishment and drop to their knees. If he falls for my trap, he will come, because even at the end I become his pawn; a messenger boy to run back to others and explain what's happened."

"Well, you can start here and now by explaining to this *man-on-the-street* what's happening. Why's he doing all this?"

Sign sighed. "It's just a theory, Tom."

"In your hands, I doubt that. Talk."

The former MI6 officer placed his palms on his thighs, straightened his back, held Knutsen's gaze, and nodded. "Alright." When he spoke, his voice was clear, measured, and firm. "The Thief is a showman. And deliberately so. His performances must be dramatic and wholly impactive. He didn't care about Wick and Baltzar per se. But, he very much cared that they were the perfect material to create fear. He spent time on Wick and Baltzar. He sculpted them to create masterpieces. The other runners were irrelevant to him. But, as I said to Karin, in re-creating Wick and Baltzar, he's condemned the person who lays eyes on his work. He condemned The Library to eternal damnation in hell. And not just them. The Library represents the most powerful and untouchable components of the British establishment. The establishment is his target. He is displeased with them. He must enact a terrifying correction. He has done so."

"A punishment?"

"Not a punishment. He has no use for that. He wishes to correct matters. And though he doesn't have all-pervasive power, he does have sufficient power to apply his correction in a clinical precise, and brutal manner. He is superior in every respect to those around him. But, the powerful members of the establishment are necessary. Without them, he is like a general without an army However, insurrection and incompetence must be dealt with Corrected. His soldiers have let him down. He has taken away their weapon – CHALICE – and he has given them imagery that will haunt them forever. He is cruel and merciless, but he is right to be so. The state of Great Britain has displeased him. That cannot be left unaddressed."

Knutsen digested his friend's words. In a near-whisper, he said, "He is God."

"As we imagine God to be, yes. But, he doesn't wish to be a deity or indeed have any form of complex. He is who he is: a superior being who sees the world for what it is and with eyes that see things we cannot see. We would label him insane. In response he would smile and say that we are ignorant fools. He believes he is sound of mind. He knows what he sees. And he knows what needs to be done. He must take control."

"And make one huge fucking *correction*." Knutsen shook his head.

"That's what he's done. And, he's had fun along the way. He has immense talent. Why waste that gift? The great artists invoke awe amid their audiences. But, such awe can manifest itself in different ways. Always ask yourself – what is the intention of the artist: what does he or she want to do to us? The Thief wishes to destroy minds and souls with his art. He has done so."

"Why? What have we done to piss him off?"

Sign clicked his tongue and raised his eyebrows. "I strongly suspect that it won't be one specific event that has caused his displeasure in the British power-elite. It will be a long, slow series of events. A gradual decline. Over years. Maybe centuries. And then like nature does on occasion, he steps in and corrects. Britain, he believes, has not being properly stewarded. People in power had the ability to do something about that. They didn't. They must be removed. And that message must be relayed to the establishment. He will ask me to do so at the end. The elite must understand what has happened. Then, his work is complete."

Both men were quiet for a moment.

Knutsen asked, "What will you do while I'm away?"

"I need to go back to Germany and brief Karin. She doesn't know about my plan. She might take a bit of... persuading. But, all will be well. And I need to make preparations for Norway. I'll be back here by Monday. Then, as Edward Sassoon might say, we cast the perfect fly."

"Perfect?"

"As close an approximation to perfection as I'm able to muster."

"Which might mean your artificial fly is the crappiest excuse for an attempt to mimic a dipteran insect."

Sign laughed, glad of the blithe and astute put-down. His expression switched to earnest and urgent, as he leaned forward and grabbed Knutsen's forearms. The action was a rarity. "Listen very carefully to me, Tom. This is my last move. I have nothing else if this fails. No back-up plan. Nothing. We live or die by this final tactic. Do you understand?"

Knutsen momentarily closed his eyes. "Yeah." He opened his eyes. "Yes. I understand."

Sign kept hold of him. "Even if he turns up, he may do so with official Norwegian or British armed forces. If he does that, he's either The Thief and is calling my bluff; or, I've got the wrong man. Tactically, I can't see him calling my bluff. It would be too risky for him to do so. But, there is every possibility I may have asked you to post the letters to the wrong person. Sight of armed men means I've failed."

"Then let's hope he does turn up and does so alone. Then, we've got him."

Sign nodded.

So did Knutsen. "Let's do this my friend."

Sign leaned back and felt relieved. He trusted Knutsen's judgement so much; more than he let on. "Splendid."

Knutsen watched him, a ready smile now on his face, lit up by the orange glow from the fire. "There is one thing, though."

"Yes, dear chap?"

Knutsen's smile broadened. "I need to deliver the letters to someone. So do me a favour and tell me who that person is."

CHAPTER 24

NORWAY

Friday.

Four days after Knutsen had returned from Geneva and Turks and Caicos.

Three days after he'd posted an envelope through the letterbox of the house belonging to the person who Sign believed was The Thief.

Nine days after Sign had put Hare out of his misery.

Eleven days after Sign had confronted three members of The Library in Munich and Raine had been destroyed by a bomb.

Thirteen days after Kazia Baltzar had been made to look like a toddler on extendable reins who'd been hit by a truck; and bits of Parry's body had been tossed into the sea around the isle of Muck.

Sixteen days after the fake MAYFLY intelligence reports had been posted by the runners.

Twenty days after Alex Wick had been glued to a wall in the Hotel Opéra and made to look like the result of a backstreet abortion.

Twenty five days after Raine had eaten homemade curry snacks and sipped Cobra beer while presenting the CHALICE case to Sign and Knutsen.

And twenty seven days after Raine had been sitting in a transit van while looking at a computer screen showing night vision and thermal imagery of the exterior and interior of a Norwegian farmhouse.

It was one PM; two hours before the intended meeting with The Thief.

Believing he was calling a woman called Emilia Cortez, a man had telephoned Lebrun on Wednesday. Posing as the fictitious Argentinian broker, she'd suggested the time and location of the meeting. Norway was her idea, because she was hoping to separately meet Lystad while she was on the European side of the Atlantic, though she still couldn't get hold of him. As per Lystad's request, she'd arranged for the letters of introductions to be hand-delivered to the caller's address in England, after she'd not heard from Lystad for several weeks. The man had said that he agreed with the arrangements and would be there. She said that she always travelled with a bodyguard - just one - and that she'd understood if he did the same. But, she'd added, no more than one apiece. He said he'd be alone.

It was impossible for her to know who'd called. Obviously, she knew Raine's voice, but she'd never heard the other members of The Library speak. And the caller had adopted a neutral English accent. The accents of the remaining suspects were distinctive – Faraday's Mid-Atlantic; Duggan's a circumstance-driven seesaw between Scottish Highlands and posh English army officer; and Sassoon's a pitch-perfect classical movement whose delivery range included pianissimo, accelerando, allegro, to the slower andante, and upwards to crescendo, and fortissimo if required. Whoever had called had disguised his tone. That was to be expected.

Today, Lebrun had decided she'd look how she imagined Emilia Cortez would be – wealthy, independent in every respect, confident, and with absolutely no desire to blend in. She was wearing a new purchase of skin-tight thick cream leggings, designer purple snow-boots, three-quarter length black and white chequered wool jacket, and flamboyant lilac scarf, all from Berlin's prestigious *Andreas Murkudis* fashion store. Today was not a day for tactical police attire, including bullet-proof gear. She was in the house where the meeting was to take place. It was a four-bedroom stone property with adjoining stables, next to a track that was gritted but now was covered with two inches of snow. Everywhere in the area was covered in snow. Over one hundred years ago, the remote and isolated house was a place where horse-drawn carriages could stop. Travellers were supplied with a meal and bed if required; horses could be fed and allowed to rest; repairs to equipment could be made in the rear smithy; and when ready, travellers could continue their arduous journey in the mountainous region. Now, it was a holiday let. Families and other groups came here to hike and bike-ride in the warmer months; and snuggle up in the colder climes and admire the stunning views over the nearby glacial lake. It was peaceful; over twenty miles from Bergen; and six miles from the nearest house. In front of the building and beyond the track that ran across the property's front, were two hundred yards of open flat ground that led to the lake and its surrounding mountains. Close to the sides and back of the house was a vast forest that gradually, then sharply, increased in elevation as it reached the foothills of more mountains and their high-level pools and rivers. It was a stunning location.

In the kitchen, she put bread, cheese, and cold meats onto a plate and walked with the dish out of the back of the house and into the enclosed rear garden containing the now-disused blacksmith's workshop. Inside was Sign, sitting on a stool that would have previously been used while shoeing horses. He was in a suit and overcoat, looking completely out of place because around him were reminders of days gone by – tools, empty furnace, raw metal, and manufactured iron objects that were dangling from the ceiling. The owners of the house had kept the smithy as some kind of novelty museum. Maybe Sign wasn't out of place, she thought. Perhaps he too was a novelty reminder of days gone by. It was a flippant thought. She was stressed up to the eyeballs and was grasping for anything to lighten her mood. "Eat." She handed him the plate.

"Bless you, my dear." He looked at the rudimentary meal. "An honest plate for a dishonest man."

"Or, food for the fool."

He smiled. "You've been loitering in the company of Mr. Knutsen too long, methinks."

"I like his words."

"They *cut through the mud*."

"He doesn't use the word 'mud'."

"I'm sure he doesn't." The only things on the rectangular wooden work bench next to him were a gun-metal flask of tea, radio, and a Heckler & Koch USP handgun. The gun was chambered with twelve .45 ACP cartridges that were so powerful they could knock a tree over from one hundred yards away. He needed the projectile's power and unwavering flight path, because he might only get the chance for one shot. He poured tea into the flask's unscrewed cup. "How's Tom?"

She shrugged. "Walking around. *Freezing his tits off.* Pretending to be my security detail and checking out the grounds."

"Jolly good. And your *Waffen-SS Skull Unit?*"

"Don't call them that." She sighed and smiled. "I'm going to check on them in a minute." She nodded towards the radio. "Communications between all of us are fine. Don't move far from your comms."

He sipped his tea and adopted a naughty schoolboy expression. "I shall be sitting here like a guilt-ridden child, waiting to be summoned by the disgruntled headmaster."

"Erm... okay." She left the smithy, donned wraparound green-lenses reflective sunglasses, and walked down the track; the forest and mountains on one side, the open ground and lake visible on her left. She passed Knutsen, who was walking towards the house and looked like a VIP bodyguard in his expensive suit, overcoat, and smart shoes that had plastic covers. She said, "I'm going for a walk."

Keeping his eyes on the track and house ahead, he muttered, "Don't be long."

She carried on walking, her boots crunching in the snow. The air was crisp and still; there was no snow falling, and the sky was blue and cloudless. Save for the sound of a distant woodpecker, all was quiet. The air smelled fresh and carried the scent of pine. Ordinarily, the walk would have been invigorating and atmospheric. But, today there was no time to admire beauty and embrace pleasant feelings. And it wasn't helping matters that her Glock pistol was rubbing against the base of her spine.

Six hundred yards away from the house, she reached a part of the track where there was a small clearing in the adjacent forest. In the clearing was a stationary white van that had chains on its tyres and a white mesh camouflage sheet draped over its exterior. The van was facing the track, ready to reach the house in nineteen seconds.

After seeing her through the windscreen mesh, the driver stepped out of the vehicle, bringing his Heckler & Koch MK416 tactical carbine. Head-to-toe he was wearing white arctic-warfare clothes and kit, with a Glock 17 handgun strapped to his thigh and radio earpiece underneath his balaclava. Over his eyes he wore anti-glare goggles.

She went up to him and said in a quiet voice, "This is the last time I'm here. After this, it's radio stuff only. All good?"

The man was Karl, a team leader in Germany's elite GSG9 – a unit comparable to Britain's Special Air Service and Special Boat Service, France's GIGN and DGSE Action Division, and America's Delta Force and DEVGRU SEALs. In the rear of the van were seven more GSG9 men. They were here covertly and in doing so were breaking Norwegian law. Under other circumstances, Lebrun would have asked the Norwegian authorities for direct action capability in the guise of Norway's secretive Forsvarets Spesialkommando. These were not other circumstances. Plus, no unit was better than GSG9. Karl didn't say anything. Just nodded and got back into the driver's seat.

She walked back to the house.

Knutsen reached the house and waited outside the front, parked close to which was a silver Mercedes S-Class Saloon – a hire car that Knutsen thought would be befitting for Emilia Cortez. Like his colleagues, aside from Sign, he had a discrete earpiece linked to a throat mic and radio transmitter-receiver that was fixed to his belt. Even close up, it would be difficult to tell that he was wearing communications equipment. And his devastatingly powerful SIG Sauer P226 handgun was hidden under his coat. But, even if someone ascertained he was carrying that equipment, it would seem normal, given his job was to protect the shady goings-on of his client. He wasn't too cold, but stamped his feet, rubbed his gloved hands, and folded and unfolded his arms, to make him look like he was suffering more than he was. He checked the time on his phone. Nearly sixty minutes until The Thief was supposed to turn up. He stared at the ground ahead of him and the lake. He imagined that he was a bored hired-gun, who was sick of looking at bloody mountains, and was wearing clothes that were better suited to the cocktail bar in the Palacio Duhau hotel in Buenos Aires.

Though he was playacting a role, he was alert and watchful. He looked, listened, and even smelled for anything that could suggest someone, other than Lebrun and Sign, was nearby – footprints, drag marks in the snow, other markings, disturbed foliage, an odd scent in the air, sounds that didn't belong here, movement of any kind, frightened creatures, flashes of light or colour. Anything. But there was nothing out of the ordinary. Least ways, nothing obvious. It would be easy for someone who'd never set foot in countryside to watch the house without being seen. The area around him was too vast, the topography too varied, and there were too many natural hiding places. But, he looked anyway - not hoping to find a watcher; but rather in case he spotted a man suddenly break cover and rush towards him while brandishing a gun.

His breath steamed in the air as he slowly exhaled and maintained his vigil.

Sign screwed the cap back onto the flask and tried to clear his brain. There was nothing more he could do other than wait. Everything that could be done had been done. That's what he kept telling himself. But there was doubt. And as a result he couldn't stop thinking. Was he doing the right thing now? He'd been wrong in the past. He thought his idea to dry up The Thief's revenue stream by deploying Wick had been a canny move. He'd been wrong. His initiative to combine the CHALICE Norwegian speakers into a unit called The Library had resulted in two of its members dying. The MAYFLY idea had come from Sassoon, but Sign had warned Raine that, once the Library was assembled, the trick was to adapt to forthcoming ideas that didn't come from Sign or the diplomat. He'd adhered to that principal and ensured the MAYFLY runners were protected. That didn't work out so well for Baltzar. And here he was, sitting on an obsolete blacksmith's stool, close to a distinguished police officer who was once again jeopardising her career and life, a band of German operatives down the road who'd prompt the mother of all political fallouts if they got caught, and a loyal friend who was standing between him and death. Knutsen would say that what he was feeling wasn't self-pity. Instead the ex-cop would rightly observe that he was giving himself a walloping pre-emptive bollocking. There were so many reasons he liked Knutsen. As Lebrun had observed, his friend's ability to cut through the crap was one of his many strengths. And that strength was infectious.

Time to snap out of analysis, he decided. He cleared his head of anything to do with The Thief and the CHALICE case and spent the remaining waiting time dwelling on memories that he hoped would calm his mind and body. The memories were of times when he really smiled, including catching his first trout when he was a kid, staying on a kibbutz in Israel and meeting his future wife, proposing to her on the roof of Balliol College, Oxford, and walking out of MI6 headquarters for the last time. There were numerous other recollections that passed through his mind. He didn't dwell too long on any of them because some were also tinged with sadness. Instead he flicked through the memories, much like one would do with a photo album, picking out the good stuff and skipping the less good.

Lebrun entered the smithy. "Two minutes to three. Time for you to come through."

Sign picked up his radio and handgun and followed her into the house.

In the lounge, there were four large windows facing the open ground and lake. She said, "Stay away from the windows."

She was right to remind him to do so. Sign wanted The Thief in the house, so that he could confront him face to face. Before that happened, he couldn't be seen. Faraday, Sassoon, and Duggan didn't know what Lebrun and Knutsen looked like. It was fine for them to be noticed while they continued their roles of being Cortez and her bodyguard. Sign was a different matter. If he was seen, the trap would be blown and everyone would have to attempt to take down The Thief before he escaped. And all of this meant that, for the remaining few minutes, Lebrun was still in charge and Sign was redundant.

She went to the window.

And heard Knutsen's voice in her earpiece. "I've got someone on foot approaching. Approximately two hundred yards away. Close to the lake. Possibly male. Can't be sure."

She turned and walked to the centre of the room where Sign was sitting at a dining table. She didn't say anything; didn't need to. He'd also heard Knutsen on his handheld radio.

Knutsen was in the same spot he'd been standing for the last hour – directly outside the house, close to the front door. Whoever was by the lake would easily be able to see him. All he could do was remain where he was and act like this was a run-of-the-mill occurrence in his line of work.

The person stopped on the shoreline, half-turned, and was now facing the property. The distance between the person and the house remained two hundred yards. The individual was wearing dark clothes, but it was impossible to discern any other details without using binoculars. It wouldn't be catastrophic if Knutsen was seen to take out binos from his overcoat and hold them to his face, but he'd decided that such a move would make him look amateurish and more importantly a man in his position had no need to know what Ms Cortez's client looked like. So, he held his nerve and watched.

He didn't move his lips as he said, "Person's moving. Walking towards me."

Karl said to everyone, "Heard."

Lebrun said the same.

Come on, come on, thought Knutsen as he kept his eyes fixed on the individual. At the same time, he tried to remain aware of any potential movement either side of the encroaching walker.

The person was now one hundred and sixty yards away, moving slowly. Knutsen was an expert shot with a handgun. On a range, this distance was extremely difficult, but doable. Providing he didn't have to whip-out his firearm from underneath a cumbersome coat; was wearing light and stretchy clothing; had solid ground beneath his feet; didn't have a racing heart and hands that were sweating underneath gloves; and the target was static. And then there was the possibility that, if he did manage to get a shot on target before obtaining facial recognition, his P226 round might have decimated the head of a Norwegian rambler.

"Hold. Person's stopped. Think person's reaching into a pocket. Person's now got arm up, hand close to head."

Lebrun's mobile phone rang. The phone had been given to her by Sign. She glanced at the former MI6 officer and then looked away as she accepted the call and spoke. "Si?" She listened and then said in English and with a Spanish accent that she hoped would pass for Argentinian, "Yes, yes. Just come to the house." She listened some more. "No. Just me. And Colin. He's out the front. Can you see him?" She waited. "Yes, just us two. Of course he's armed. But, he's okay. He's here for both of us. Just come in. Colin's had a look around. He's confident we're good. I trust Colin." She ended the call and looked at Sign. But, she didn't say anything. Nor did he.

Knutsen's voice was heard by the team. "Person's moving again. One forty yards to me…one twenty…one hundred. Still, can't see face. Hand's in pocket again… eighty yards…seventy…sixty…"

Lebrun pulled out her gun and moved to the hallway.

Sign remained motionless, his weapon on the table in front of him.

Karl placed his hand on the ignition key, ready to start the engine and race with his GSG9 team to the house when he was given the green light.

In a near-whisper, Knutsen said, "Fifty yards and stop. Head bowed. No hat on. Should be able to see him. Can't because his bloody face's down. Looks like a man, though. City clothes. Bloke ain't out for a spot of mountain fresh air." All he could imagine now was moving his left hand to pull open his coat, his right hand to pull out his gun, dropping to one knee while gripping the pistol in both hands, and shooting if it looked like the man was going to fire back. He didn't want that to happen. Sign most certainly hoped that didn't happen. He wanted The Thief to walk up to Knutsen and tell him that Emilia Cortez was expecting him, Knutsen to stand aside and let him pass, and The Thief to enter the house.

The man's hand was still in his pocket.

Slowly, he raised his head.

Until his head was fully up.

The Thief was looking straight at Knutsen.

A smile was on his face.

As Sign had predicted, The Thief was Hamish Duggan.

The sound of an explosion further down the track was unmistakeable. For a split second only, Knutsen's eyes darted in the direction of the loud noise. That split second was enough. Duggan's bullet struck him in the centre of the chest. Such was the power of the bullet, he flipped backwards and into the air, crashing onto the ground. He was in agony and felt like he'd been hit by a sledgehammer. But that was the worst of it; underneath his coat he was wearing a bulletproof vest. But he stayed on his back, in the snow, for two seconds, desperately trying to overcome disorientation and pain while trying to reach his gun.

Lebrun rushed out of the house, screaming, "Karl, Karl. Go! Go! Go!" She stood by Knutsen, her weapon held at eye-level, scanning her surroundings. "Where the fuck is he?" Duggan had vanished. "Karl! Speak! Karl?! Anyone in the team. Speak!" She heard nothing from the GSG9 unit. Keeping her gun in one hand and eyes ahead of her, she reached down with her free hand, grabbed Knutsen's arm, and started pulling.

Wincing, he said, "It's okay, okay," as he brushed her hand away, got to his feet, staggered, gained stability, and pulled out his gun.

"Protect Sign," she said. "I need to get to the team. Something's wrong."

Knutsen was breathing fast, but was alright. "No! The explosion. Sign can look after himself. We need to find Duggan. He'll be in the woods."

"Stay! Sign told me The Thief will come for him. You staying here is our best chance of getting Duggan."

"No, Karin…"

"Do it!" She jogged down the track, towards Karl's location. Over the area of tall trees where she was headed, a large black plume of smoke was drifting skywards.

"Shit!" muttered Knutsen. He held his gun with both hands as he entered the house and went into the lounge. Sign was supposed to be here. He wasn't. "Ben! Ben! Where the hell are you?!" He moved from one room to the other on ground level, and repeated the same drill on the upper floor. He went outside, checked the smithy and rear garden, ran around the full perimeter of the house, and stopped in the same place where he'd been knocked *ass over tit*. Breathing fast he muttered, "Fuck, fuck, fuck." He looked around. "Where have you gone, Ben?" He ran into the woods.

Sign was running as fast as he could over uneven ground, his gun held with both hands, smart shoes wholly unsuited to the terrain and sometimes sinking to ankle-level in the snow. He darted between trees, keeping his eyes on the nearby track where he'd seen Lebrun take off after checking on Knutsen. He knew where she was going – the GSG9 van – and his priority was to get to her before Duggan did. The moment The Thief had shot his friend, Sign realised what was happening. Duggan wanted to meet Sign on his terms. In order for that to happen, he needed to get rid of unwanted inconveniences. Sign had to do everything he could to re-dress the balance. But, he couldn't see Lebrun. Probably, she too was using tree-cover alongside the track. He didn't know. Everything that was happening right now was unscripted and chaotic. He clambered up an escarpment, close to the base of a mountain, and nearly tumbled as he went down the other side. But, he was able to pick up pace again. Until he reached the clearing containing the van. It was no longer white. The vehicle was on its side, black, crumpled, bits of it turned into jagged shards, smouldering, noxious smoke drifting out of windows that no longer had glass, and had flames licking over parts of its bodywork. Lebrun was nowhere to be seen. He took a step towards the carnage, but the heat was too unbearable. Cautiously, he circled the van until he could look at its rear. The back doors were open. Inside were the remains of seven men. It was hard to tell which bits of body belonged to whom. All the flesh was black and some of it melted. He walked further around so that he could see into the cab. Karl was in there; or a version of Karl. He'd met the same fate as the rest of his colleagues. The GSG9 team was no more. Duggan's bomb had seen to that. He'd either somehow attached it to the vehicle – most likely the undercarriage, given the result of the explosion – or he'd predicted the team would park here and had placed the bomb in the clearing before they'd arrived. There was no time to wonder how The Thief had managed to do this to one of the most highly trained eight-man special operations teams the world could produce. What mattered was finding Lebrun. More slowly and using a different route, he headed back towards the house, hoping to see Lebrun running towards him.

Lebrun felt she must only be a hundred or so yards from the GSG9 clearing, but she couldn't be exact because she'd been zigzagging through the forest, always conscious that Duggan could be close. She had to get to Karl and his men. If they were alive and had simply been suffering a radio malfunction, then she could marshal them and get them to go into hunter-killer mode. Everything would change then. Duggan wouldn't stand a chance. She knew she was kidding herself. There was no doubt there'd been an explosion. The target was obvious. She continued anyway. She just had to be sure. And if they were hurt but alive, she had to help them, even if it meant blowing the whistle on everything and calling in the Norwegians to evacuate casualties and swamp the area with man-hunters.

It felt odd at first – like someone had clapped two empty coconut shells and with the power of that noise had caused her right leg to lose all sensation and strength. But, then she fell to the ground, the numbness in her limb now replaced with a searing sensation that went from her knee to her gut. As her face smacked the trunk of a tree, she knew that she'd been shot. Her gun was out of her hands. Somewhere. Didn't know. Vision was blurred and ears were ringing. Unable to do anything else, she crawled in the direction she'd been travelling. This was all she could do right now. Just crawl. What else could or should she do? She saw the smoke again. Then the van. Then she knew. There was no mistaking what had happened to Karl and his men. "Bastard!" she muttered, blood from her mouth flecking over the snow in front of her. She continued. Could anyone be still alive in that god-awful wreckage? Not a chance. Was she going to stop crawling towards the van? Not on her watch.

The second bullet entered the side of her ribcage. This time there was no initial numbness. Instead, she felt like her insides had been utterly violated. Like Wick must have felt when the knitting needle was struck down his throat. Turns out she had to stop. She couldn't move. Sorry Karl, she thought. A smart brogue shoe touched her right shoulder. Sign's shoe, she wondered? He had similar shoes, though she seemed to recall he laced them differently. She was pushed onto her back. Of course, not Sign. Duggan. He stood over her, his gun pointing at her. He didn't say anything. She wanted to spit her blood at him. But couldn't. Couldn't even move her lips. What a shame. She hoped her husband would look after their kids. Duggan shot her twice in the head.

Sign heard the two shots, but it was near-impossible to know from which direction they came. The noise echoed and could have originated from anywhere around him. All he could do was keep heading towards the house, hoping that Lebrun was somewhere between him and the property. In a straight line, the route could be covered in under a minute. But he had to cover so much more ground, running back and forth over the track to search woodland on one side and patches of open ground on the other. There was no way of knowing if the gunshots he'd heard had come from Lebrun's weapon or Duggan's or Knutsen's. What worried him was that there were no more gunshots, and nor were Karin or Tom calling out that The Thief had been shot. He crossed the track again. And then saw her. Lebrun was on her back. Her face was unrecognisable. A bloody trail covered snow from her feet to the base of a nearby tree. He was about to run to her. Movement ahead stopped him from doing so. It belonged to a dark shape; about forty yards ahead; a man; moving in and out of trees; his back to Sign; going in the direction of the house. The man sidestepped past a tree and for a moment was more visible. It was Duggan. Sign stopped and took aim.

Knutsen saw Duggan coming towards him. And Duggan saw him. They were eighty yards apart. Both men fired. Duggan's bullet sliced alongside Knutsen's hip, forcing him to involuntarily drop to one knee. His bullet hit the centre of Duggan's shin, causing The Thief to drop forwards.

Just as Sign squeezed his trigger. His bullet travelled through air where a nanosecond ago Duggan had been standing.

Duggan rolled onto his back, knowing that someone had shot at him from behind. He saw Sign, raised his gun, and fired at him.

Sign threw himself behind a tree, checked his gun, quickly looked around the tree, saw Duggan was on his feet and limping away, and readied himself. He fully broke cover, ready to shoot.

But Duggan was now mostly obscured behind more trees, dragging his useless leg as, inch by inch, he walked to the area where he'd last seen Knutsen.

Sign knew Duggan was going for Knutsen. To his left was the track. Because of the toughened ground underneath the snow, the track was the fastest route to use on foot. He needed to get ahead of Duggan and find Knutsen before The Thief dispatched him. But the track was exposed and therefore one almighty risk. He ran onto the track and kept running.

Knutsen gritted his teeth as he limped through the forest. He had no idea where he was going but wanted to find higher ground where he could wait for Duggan and kill him when he got close. Duggan would find him if he wanted to. Knutsen was bleeding down one trouser leg and leaving spots of blood on the snow. The blood was okay. It looked more than it was and in any case the bullet had only carved a groove through the thin layer of fat and muscle on his hip. The problem was he was also certain that the projectile had also taken out a small chunk of bone. Attached bone that was left in the injury would be serrated and causing as much damage as the bullet itself. It would be lacerating more flesh with every step he took. And that's why it felt like he was walking on a bed of syringes. He saw an incline, leading to a plateau that was about twenty feet high. That would be a perfect place to wait. He just had to get up the incline. He took one step forwards with his bad leg and figuratively felt his heart go into his mouth as his foot sank quickly into snow that reached his knee. Beneath the snow must have been some kind of hollow. Didn't matter. What did was that the thick snow had encased half his leg and he had no idea how he was going to release it without passing out from pain. He was stuck. Trapped. And somewhere behind him was Duggan.

The Thief saw Knutsen's spots of blood and followed them. His breathing was fast and the pain in his shin was awful. But he kept going. Had to. The job was not yet complete. He'd achieved so much and wasn't about to let a splintered tibia and mangled calf flesh hold him back. The man he was looking for was the last of them. He'd deal with him and then have his tête-à-tête with Ben Sign. Everything now was about Sign. He was the only person who deserved to have an audience with Duggan. Everyone else was insignificant. He'd selected Sign to be his representative. Only he could understand what was happening. After the meeting with him, nothing mattered. He limped onwards, noticing that the distance between each spot of blood was getting shorter. The man he was hunting was slowing down, he decided. He was close.

Sign didn't think – couldn't think – about his safety as he jogged along the track, looking left and right, desperate to find Knutsen or spot Duggan and end this. There was something ahead on the track, a discolouration maybe, but he couldn't see what it was because it was too far away and perspiration was getting into his eyes. He wiped his brow with his forearm as he carried on running. Now he knew what was on the track. Blood. Whose blood he didn't know. He followed the trail off the track and back into the woods, trying to move quickly while at the same time maintaining effective control of his pistol. And right now he hated every bit of snow that was currently in Norway. He worked hard to move onwards as snow deepened and the elevation rose. Ahead of him was the base of one of the mountains. He was certain that's where Knutsen was headed. His friend was searching for a vantage point on higher ground. He was setting himself as bait, hoping Duggan would come close enough so that he could drop him. It was an exceptionally brave and selfless thing to do.

Knutsen tried to turn to see what was behind him but even the slightest twist caused him to get giddy. It was no use. Duggan could easily saunter up to him and shoot him in the back of the head. So, this was it, he thought. Injured, trapped, and unable to go down fighting. This wasn't how he wanted it to be. And he thought he had so much more to give. Then again, if Sign got Duggan then maybe this wouldn't be a bad end. Without doubt, this had been the hardest case he'd worked with his friend. So complex; so many variables; too many casualties. But they were here, with The Thief. To his knowledge, Sign wasn't hurt. There was still hope. He heard movement behind him. Breathing. Snow crunching. Clothes rustling. Maybe he'd have liked to have had his life flash before his eyes. For some reason, that wasn't happening. All he could think about was how annoying it was that Sign had got away with not paying the tenner he owed him for the last dry cleaning bill. The sound of movement was so close now. It was time.

Sign crouched by his side. He faced the way he'd come, his expression focused, eyes scanning everything before him, pistol in one hand. "Karin's dead. The GSG9 team is dead. You've put a hole in Duggan, but he's still got the bit between his teeth and is looking for you. Got to get you out, old boy. Going to hurt, to say the least. Not much I can do about that. Are you ready?"

"Karin's dead?" The news hit Knutsen far harder than anything else that was happening.

"Are you ready?!"

Knutsen didn't really know what to say, aside from, "Fuck, yes."

"Good man." He used his free hand to dig around Knutsen's leg. He got as far as the trickier area around his ankle and decided he could dig no further. To do so, he'd have to get prone. If he did that, he'd no longer be able to keep a look out for Duggan. "Time to pull you out. Keep your tongue away from your teeth." He wrapped his free arm around Knutsen's chest, pointed his gun down the escarpment containing his friend's trail of blood, gripped tight, and stood upright while maintaining hold of Knutsen.

The pain was indescribable. Knutsen wanted to die.

Sign took two steps forward and lowered his friend to the ground. Knutsen's leg was clear of the snow-hole. He glanced at his friend then returned his attention to the area ahead of him. "Say something. Anything."

Knutsen was palpitating, his eyes screwed shut, his expression a grimace.

"Anything will do, Tom. I'm here. I'm not leaving you. You won't have to go through anything like that again. I'm here. Say anything."

"You..." He swallowed hard. His brain felt like it had been turned into molten lava. "You… you…"

Sign had to get him talking. If Knutsen lost consciousness, other complications could arise. Sign didn't have time to watch over his friend. Not right now. "Fill in the gaps. You what? Call me anything. Use your most robust Anglo-Saxon language. Make the most of it. I'm giving you a *free pass*, as I believe the Americans say. Why waste the opportunity?"

Knutsen focused solely on slowing his breathing down. Even getting rid of the pain was now a secondary objective. He knew why Sign was encouraging him to speak. Staying awake was the priority. And to do that he needed to sort his frickin' diaphragm out. "You… dry cleaning bill. Tenner. Fucking pay up, tight arse."

Sign smiled as his eyes darted left and right. "Well said, sir. Actually it's nine pounds seventy five pence. But, under the circumstances, I'll round it up to a tenner."

"About time."

Sign tensed and placed his hand on Knutsen's shoulder. "Duggan."

Knutsen couldn't see anything apart from the blue sky. "Distance?"

"Probably about one eighty yards."

"Out of range, pal."

"Almost certainly."

"Shame if he saw you and about-turned though."

"Quite so, dear fellow."

"Still, you could easily track him down."

Sign huffed. "That would mean leaving you. Remember – last time I left you unattended you started doing Portuguese language lessons."

"Oh yeah. Well, you'll have to give it your best shot then." He smiled and wished he hadn't as he started coughing.

"I'll miss."

He breathed in deeply. "Time for you to… remember something. You had a place, yes? Great Britain Rifle Team. Never competed in the Olympics. Turned the team down, didn't you. Shy boy, and all that. Time for you to see how you might have done."

"Hmm. Yes." He stood fully upright, adopted the correct stance, and held the gun with both hands.

"Factor in arc of bullet; air's density's moderate to thin; no cross-winds."

"Yes, yes. All of that."

"You going for a head shot?"

"I don't think that will be necessary. Hush now." He breathed in deeply and exhaled slowly. On the third time of doing so, he half-exhaled and stopped. Two seconds later, he fired.

His bullet struck Duggan in his good leg. It was exactly where Sign had wanted the bullet to go. The Thief was now on the ground.

Sign said, "I have to go down there now. I won't be too long. While I'm away, I want you to remember the names of every girl you've kissed or wanted to kiss. You can award yourself extra points if you make those recollections in order of first to last. Up for the challenge?"

"Yeah, but you might need to take your time."

"Splendid." He walked down the route, his gun trained on Duggan who was immobile and on his side. As he got closer, he said in a loud voice, "It would be a shame if you tried to shoot me. I'd be forced to shoot you first. I doubt you'll get a shot off. I will. And I won't miss."

Duggan watched him get closer. "I'm not going to shoot you, laddie." He tossed his gun away.

"Of course you're not." Sign kept his gun pointing at him as he got alongside him and used his foot to push him onto his back. He smiled. "Hello again."

Duggan looked at him and smiled back. "Mr. Sign. The man who controls smoke and mirrors."

Sign's smile was gone and replaced with a cold expression. His voice was measured when he said, "I could say the same about you. But, then there's the other bit. You're also a cold-blooded, murdering, bastard."

Duggan raised his eyebrows. "Come now, Mr. Sign. I'd hoped your analysis would've been a tad more erudite. And I'd hoped that you of all people would have understood what was going on."

Sign was motionless. "Thanks to you, my friend is in trouble. I don't have time to stand here grooming your ego. I need to be with him. You believe you had the power and self-given authority to apply a correction to the British elite. I could wax lyrical on the subject but won't, for the aforementioned reason."

Despite his injuries, Duggan's eyes twinkled and he looked genuinely pleased. "Clever, clever, Mr. Sign."

"Yes. Well that's all *lovely-jubbly*, as my friend might say, but it gives me no joy whatsoever to hear your assessment of my cerebral capabilities. If there's one thing I've learnt from my good friend up top, it's that men like you and I have a habit of *talking daft and praising each other for doing so*. Now, I suspect you want me to take your message of displeasure back to the British establishment. I need to understand what you believe they've done wrong."

Duggan placed his hand on the upper-leg injury. "Tell them… Tell them this. It's said that power corrupts. That's not true. Corruption is a human condition. Power in its own right is a good thing." He was now breathing faster. "I'd hoped that the Age of Enlightenment would not only have laid a firm foundation of reason, but also fostered an evolutionary leap forward of humankind. A move away from base emotions such as greed, lust, manipulation, and lies. But it never happened. Today, most people are more knowledgeable than people during the Enlightenment, but we are still victim to the same follies." Blood was starting to cover the snow beneath him. "It's not just that the wrong people are getting into power. Rather more, it's that we're not producing the *right* people. No evolution. No step-change." He winced. "I think you shot me through my femoral artery. That's not ideal." He chuckled then coughed. "Name me one British politician, senior civil servant, military commander, or senior cleric in the last two hundred years who hasn't in some way been corrupt. Yes, a correction needed to be made. Tell them. Tell the idiots that it took me to see that enough was enough."

"And so you stole their toys."

Duggan huffed. "They didn't deserve CHALICE or anything else that gave them power. I can yield power. Maybe you can. They can't. I watched them. I gave them a chance to improve. They didn't. I corrected matters. Leave me to die here. But, tell them. I'll be gone and someone like me won't come along again for another couple of hundred years, maybe more. Meanwhile, they have to realise their limitations. Tell them that this is a reminder that they are still underdeveloped."

"You want me to leave you here?"

"Might as well. Reckon I won't last the hour. Doesn't matter. My project's complete."

"And you want me to go back to London and speak to the prime minister, his cabinet, other senior members of the establishment?"

Duggan nodded. "All of them. And their bloody overseas allies. This is a wake-up call. You tell them what you know. And you remind them that this can happen again."

Sign sighed. "And if I do that, you'll be at peace?"

Duggan grunted. "Yes." He shook his head. "No doubt you think I was heavy handed. I took no pleasure in being that way. But, it had to be done. Yes - if you tell them, I'll be at peace."

"That's good to know." He looked up, and for a moment thought he could feel the sun on his skin. It was the first time in a while that he'd experienced the sensation. Maybe it was the first sign that the season was changing. He looked back down. "When Kazia Baltzar was sixteen, you walked into her Roma camp near Birmingham. To all intents and purposes you rescued her and raised her as your own daughter. She loved you. And look what you did to her. It was clever. No one would suspect you could do such a thing. But, it was also abhorrent. I'm not going to tell anyone why you did all this. You're a monster. You failed. I won."

The smile on Duggan's face vanished. His eyes were wide. "No. No. You have to tell them. You must tell them."

"No. I don't have to do anything. I'd like to say it's been nice knowing you, but it hasn't."

Sign shot him in the head, half-turned to leave, stopped, turned back, shot Duggan two more times in the head, and walked back up the hill.

He told Knutsen that they'd use the hire car to get to the hospital in Bergen. The remnants of everything else that had happened in the area would have to remain in situ. And Sign and Knutsen were never here.

He asked Knutsen if he'd like to be carried back to the house.

Knutsen said he'd rather stick his leg back into the snow-hole.

Holding onto Sign, Knutsen managed to get to the track. There, he put his arm around the top of Sign's back and over his shoulder. Sign gripped his waist. The two men walked slowly along the track. Both men were sweating; Knutsen's breathing was heavy.

As they neared the property, Knutsen said, "Don't let them keep me long in hospital. No over-night stuff."

Sign held him firm as they continued their slow walk. "You'll be in there for only one hour. The doctors will want to monitor you after the operation. That won't happen. I'll get you back to London tonight. You'll be in pain during the flight, but that'll be sorted by a nice glass of calvados at West Square."

"Sounds… Sounds good." Knutsen tried not to show the pain he was feeling. "How did it feel? Shooting Duggan? I expect you'll say it was like putting down a rabid dog. Something like that."

"I didn't feel anything."

"Kinda… Kinda expected you to say something like that as well. You're a bad liar."

"Am I?"

"Maybe. Maybe not." Knutsen kept his eyes fixed on the car door, fifty yards away. "Calvados, and - if you're up for it - that deep-fried chicken goujons recipe you do with paprika and your homemade relish dip."

Sign smiled. "Of course, dear fellow."

Knutsen couldn't help wincing as a fresh jolt of pain ran up one side of his body. His fingertips dug into Sign and he stopped walking, while breathing fast. After catching his breath, he looked at him and asked earnestly, "We did alright, didn't we?"

Sign's smile faded as he looked at his friend. He didn't reply straight away. Then he quietly said, "Yes, my friend. We did alright."

THE END

Printed in Great Britain
by Amazon

64960371R00219